FORBID
THEM NOT

FORBID
THEM NOT

A NOVEL

MICHAEL
FARRIS

BROADMAN
& HOLMAN
PUBLISHERS

NASHVILLE, TENNESSEE

0-8054-2433-4

Published by Broadman & Holman Publishers,
Nashville, Tennessee

Dewey Decimal Classification: 813
Subject Heading: FICTION
Library of Congress Card Catalog Number: 2001043674

Unless otherwise noted, Scripture quotations are from the Holy Bible, New International Version, © 1973, 1978, 1984 by International Bible Society.

Library of Congress Cataloging-in-Publication Data
Farris, Michael P., 1951–
    Forbid them not : a novel / Michael Farris.
        p. cm.
    ISBN 0-8054-2433-4
    1. Parent and child—Fiction. 2. Sex education—Fiction.
3. Public schools—Fiction. 4. Women teachers—Fiction. [1. Children's
rights—Fiction.] I. Title.

PS3556.A7774 F67   2002
813'.54—dc21

                                                      2001043674

1 2 3 4 5 6 7 8 9 10 06 05 04 03 02

Although the law in this book is completely accurate,
this story is fiction—
for now.

WASHINGTON, D.C. After a landslide election, which swept a Democratic majority into both houses of Congress, Senate Democrats, joined by a cadre of moderate GOP senators, voted 69-31 to ratify the United Nations Convention on the Rights of the Child.

LEESBURG, VIRGINIA.
Sunday, March 20, 2005.

"All right, kids," Laura Frasier called out in her perkiest voice, "it's about time for our lesson to begin."

Getting ready to pay attention to the Bible story, seven nine-year-olds, all girls, began to whisper in a much quieter voice. Unfortunately, five nine-year-old boys were still standing in the doorway locked in a blazing battle with their "finger guns."

"Justin, would you and the other boys please get in here right now," Laura said firmly, but without hope that things would truly quiet down on only the second try. To her delight, the boys suddenly fell into a complete hush and moved with quick motions away from the doorway toward their seats.

The cause for their unusual response was soon apparent. A woman in her early forties stood in the doorway smiling. "Miss Frasier?" the stranger asked.

"Yes, may I help you, ma'am?" the twenty-five-year-old Sunday school teacher asked. Laura stepped out into the hall and smiled blankly at the older woman.

"I was told that you were the third grade teacher and that I might be able to sit in on your class today."

"Uh, uh, I guess so," Laura stammered, shrugging her shoulders. "Can I ask why you want to attend my class? We have several adult classes here at First Baptist that you might be interested in."

The woman laughed briefly and extended her right hand in greeting. "Let me introduce myself. I'm Nora Stoddard. I'm from the National Commission on Children in Washington. I'm just here doing a survey on opportunities for children in our area. We are trying to get a comprehensive sampling of the lives of children in ten communities in our nation. Leesburg was chosen as one of these ten. And I have been assigned to lead the survey here."

"The National Commission on Children? Is that a federal agency or something?"

"Yes, Laura—may I call you Laura?" Seeing an affirmative nod, Stoddard continued. "Yes, it is a new agency—just created after our historic vote on the treaty that protects children. And we believe it is very important to look beyond our government programs and take a comprehensive look at the way children live. No reasonable person would doubt that spirituality is important for children. I assure you my visit is just routine. I promise to sit quietly in the corner and not make a sound."

"Well, I guess it's OK," Laura replied. Even though Laura was a public school teacher herself, she didn't know what to make of a government worker interested in "spirituality."

Stoddard moved a child-sized chair and sat in the corner. The skirt of her dark gray business suit scraped the floor. She pulled a small leather-bound writing tablet out of a navy blue canvas briefcase and settled in expectantly.

The kids had been deathly quiet the entire time the two women had been talking. They had strained to hear every word but had only a vague notion that something was up.

Laura rifled through her Bible looking for her class notes, which suddenly seemed to have disappeared. Thirty seconds later she found them right on top of her teacher's manual sitting on the music stand—the same place she put them every week.

"Kids, we have a visitor today, as you have obviously noticed," Laura began, smoothing her shoulder-length black hair with an unconscious stroke of her left hand. She remembered to smile halfway through the sentence. Normally she smiled as she taught, without having to think. "This is Nora Stoddard. She is from a government program in Washington that is taking a survey on the lives of children. Ms. Stoddard wanted to visit a Sunday school class and she happened to pick ours."

In some parts of the country a sudden appearance by a government worker from Washington would create a huge reaction, even among nine-year-olds. But to these kids used to living in the shadow of the Beltway, it was not that big a deal. In fact, two of the kids in the class had fathers who worked for the government in Washington. Another two dozen adults in the church worked for the various agencies located in the D.C. area.

Laura looked carefully around the room and saw that the kids were starting to fidget a bit more normally. It calmed her down a bit. "OK, kids, take your lesson books out. We are on the topic of missions once again. Any of you remember why we believe that missions are important?"

One boy's hand shot up.

"Yes, Layton," Laura said.

Layton Thomas was the one who knew nearly every answer. And his behavior was exemplary, at least once the class got started and he was away from the other boys. "Because people who don't know Jesus Christ as their Savior die and go to hell," he answered.

"Right," his teacher responded. "And we don't want that to happen, right?"

All of the kids—except two boys who were watching a spider cross the corner of the room—nodded affirmatively.

"What's another reason we should go out as missionaries?" Laura asked.

"Because Jesus told us to," Emily Garvis, a little redheaded fireball, answered.

"And where did he do that?" the teacher asked. "Anyone know the Bible verse?"

Five hands shot up—the kids who attended the church's Wednesday evening Awana Club knew most of the verses she asked for. At Awana, there was a big emphasis on memorization.

"All right, Seth. Why don't you tell us the verse?"

Seth stood, then rattled it off without breathing. "Matthew 28:19–20: 'Therefore go and make disciples of all nations, baptizing them in the name of the Father and of the Son and of the Holy Spirit, and teaching them to obey everything I have commanded you. And surely I am with you always, to the very end of the age.'"

"Very good, Seth," Laura said, smiling. She noticed that Stoddard was rapidly writing notes on her pad. "One last review question. What about people who believe in other religions? If they sincerely believe, won't they go to heaven too? Anyone know a verse to answer that one?"

Only Emily and Layton had their hands up this time.

"All right, Emily, you help us with this one."

"It's found in John 14:6," she said. "Jesus said, 'I am the way and the truth and the life. No one comes to the Father except through me.'"

"So people who believe in Islam, Buddhism, and any other way to God except Jesus, will be lost forever, right?"

"Right," three voices called out.

"OK, let's open your lesson books. This is the story of Adoniram Judson, an early American missionary to the Karen people in Burma."

Nora Stoddard kept taking notes throughout the class. She occasionally stopped, looked up at Laura or one of the children, and smiled—a smile Laura could not bring herself to like—and then she would get busy with her writing once again.

Laura asked Layton Thomas to close the class in prayer. When he finished, the children rushed out of the class—with slightly less than the customary amount of noise.

Stoddard stood and walked forward to the front of the classroom clutching her notepad in one hand and the canvas briefcase in the other. "Thank you so much. That was a very enlightening class."

Laura mumbled a soft thank-you.

"A couple of the children seemed especially bright. I was noticing Layton and Emily. Where do they go to school?"

Laura wasn't sure whether to answer, but she did anyway. "Well, Layton is home schooled by his mother, and, actually, I'm Emily's third grade teacher at Paeonian Springs Elementary."

"Oh, is that so?" Stoddard replied. "How many of the children in here don't attend the local schools—public schools, I mean?"

"It's about half and half—and the half that don't go to public schools are split about evenly between home schooling and attending one of our local Christian schools," the teacher replied.

"That's very interesting. Do you think that Layton's parents might talk with me? I would be very interested in seeing a home school in operation as a part of my survey."

"They might. You could ask them yourself. They are here this morning."

"Where would I find them?"

"They lead a class for young married couples just down the hall. I could take you to them."

Stoddard smiled with obvious pleasure. "OK, that would be great."

Laura stuffed her notes and notebooks inside her large white bag, pulled the tan leather straps up over her shoulder, and said, "OK, this way."

Two couples were locked in an intense conversation in the doorway of a classroom. Laura stopped about twenty feet away. "They seem busy right now," she whispered to Stoddard.

A couple in their midthirties—a husky man about six-feet-two and a pretty woman of average height—had their backs to the classroom. A younger couple, looking barely twenty years old each, stood facing them.

"That's great, Bill, see you next week," the husky man called out loudly as he patted the younger man on the back, ending the whispered conversation.

The older couple turned and took a couple of steps toward Laura and the stranger. "Morning, Laura," the pretty woman said, smiling brightly.

"Hi, Deanna. We have a visitor who wanted to meet you. This is Nora, um . . . I'm sorry," she said, turning toward the guest. "I've forgotten your last name."

"Stoddard—Nora Stoddard," she replied cheerfully, extending her hand.

"I'm Rick Thomas, and this is my wife, Deanna," the man replied shaking hands.

"I'm with the National Commission on Children, and I just attended Ms. Frasier's class, which was delightful. I'm doing a survey for the commission on the lives and services available to children. Ms. Frasier was kind enough to let me observe her class today, and I noticed that your son, Layton, is especially bright."

"Thank you," Deanna said, nodding, doing her best to suppress a proud little smile that was trying to emerge.

"Ms. Frasier tells me that you home school Layton. And I was very much wanting to include an observation of a home school as a part of my survey. I was wondering if you would be willing to let me come to your home and just let me sit in a corner and watch for an hour or two sometime soon?"

"What is this survey?" Deanna asked.

"Oh, it is purely an academic exercise. We are trying to catalog a variety of situations that children have available to them. We want a firsthand look at the lives of children so that we can guide government policies more appropriately. I fear that many times the government makes decisions by just sitting in our office buildings downtown, without interacting with real children. And the directives we have received from the secretary of HHS has been to be inclusive of all programs for children—not just government programs that we typically study."

Deanna looked up at Rick. He shrugged and raised his eyebrows in a move that she knew to mean, "Do what you want."

"I guess that would be OK," Deanna said.

"Is Layton your only child?" Stoddard asked.

"He's the only one who is home schooled. We have two others—Nikki, who just turned four, and Trent, who is two."

Stoddard pulled out her pad and took down the directions to the Thomas home. She said good-bye, adding that she could hardly wait for the visit on Friday.

GENEVA, SWITZERLAND.
March 31, 2005.

The Noga Hilton International Geneva may have been a five-star hotel, but the carpet in Nora Stoddard's room was still garishly orange. Between the effects of the carpet and the jet lag, a massive headache loomed somewhere in the hours ahead. A couple of extra-strength painkillers might help. And maybe just a short little nap.

Two hours later, after struggling to awaken herself, Nora headed through the revolving doors out into the brisk air. A bellman dressed in silver gray with a top hat greeted her with a flourish. *"Bonjour, madame. Avez-vous besoin d`un taxi?"* he asked.

"Yes, sir," she replied. At least she recognized the word *taxi.*

Two taxis were waiting in line—a newer Mercedes and a ten-year-old full-size American-made Chevrolet. Nora got the Chevy, which was first in line.

After a series of lefts and rights through back streets, the taxi headed along Lake Geneva—Lac Leman, in French—for a few blocks. The top of Mont Blanc was obscured in the distance by some high thin clouds, but the view was spectacular nonetheless.

As the taxi pulled up to Nora's destination—an eight-story silver and glass office building—the UN Palais des Nations sign could be seen a few blocks further up the hill. Nora started to ask the driver if he had brought her to the right building, but then she saw the UN symbol presiding over a massive atrium, which doubled as the building's lobby.

A fiftyish male security officer greeted her from behind a checkpoint at the entry. After a brief attempt to speak with her in French, he made a quick transition to English. "Seventh floor conference room," he said after securing her identification.

Stoddard nodded and headed for the bank of elevators.

Three minutes later she paused at the open door of the receiving room. A display of breakfast pastries and a selection of rich, dark breads, together with three kinds of cheese, were arrayed on a table against the right wall. Another table with coffee and tea was immediately adjacent. Three women holding china cups and saucers were chatting quietly in what sounded like a Slavic language. They nodded at Nora, but she did not recognize any of them.

She hesitated in the outer doorway for a moment. Finally, she marched ahead into the conference room through a door on the left side of the entry area. She glanced nervously around the large conference table. The view of Lac Leman a few blocks away was beautiful, but a familiar face was what Nora wanted to see more than anything. There were clumps of two or three people engaged in conversations, mostly women, scattered around the room. Finally a short woman in her midfifties, who had been facing the bank of windows, paused in her conversation to survey the room quickly over her left shoulder. "Erzabet Kadar," Nora said to herself. She recognized the chair of the UN Committee on the Rights of the Child even though they had never met.

Kadar moved to the side, revealing the first truly familiar face. The long brown tresses and flawless skin of Jody Easler were as unusual in this room as her light tan, formfitting suit. Nearly everyone else in the room was dressed in black or charcoal. And it seemed that everyone else was at least ten or twenty years older than Nora's striking fellow American. They were the longtime veterans of the international children's rights movement. Nora herself had been involved in the movement, albeit on the state and national level, for a lot longer than Dr. Easler. But appointments to the U.S. delegation to the UN in Geneva demanded a level of electoral participation that had never been Nora's forte. She had been a faithful in children's rights politics for nearly two decades, but she was not a person to be noticed by elected officials.

Nora was grateful to have day-to-day charge of the U.S. agency that had been created to enforce the UN Convention on the Rights of the Child. Even though she ultimately reported to this younger, less experienced woman, Nora could question neither the competence nor commitment of this Ph.D. who looked more like a local news anchor than an expert on the sociology of children's rights.

"Good morning, Nora," Easler called out. "Come on over, I'd like for you to meet the chair of our committee of experts."

Stoddard walked quickly around the mahogany table.

"Dr. Kadar, this is Nora Stoddard, our director of the National Commission on Children. She just arrived yesterday from

Washington. And, of course, Nora, this is Dr. Erzabet Kadar, the chair of the committee here in Geneva."

"Welcome to the United Nations," Kadar said in a thick accent that Nora took to be Hungarian.

"Nora is a longtime advocate for children who has worked her way up from local activism to, now, an important national position."

"International position," the other woman corrected.

Jody smiled broadly and perfectly, revealing the skilled work of an orthodontist from Minneapolis. "Of course, international. Our movement toward ratification of the Convention has lived with frustration so long that even our terminology began to adopt nuances of hopelessness. We have known for some time that the treaty was our only hope for true advancement of children's rights, but we . . ." She shook her head as if to wipe away the cobwebs of a bad memory. "But those days are now gone. We are here not just to consult but as full partners, finally."

"Perhaps we should get started then," Kadar said. She nodded at a young woman with black hair tinted with a dark violet rinse who was standing against a wall some few feet away.

Her aide slipped quietly around the room, whispering a word or two to each of the small caucuses. The groups made their way with reasonable promptness to the table, although five or six people first made their way to the back wall to grab an ashtray from the stack on a table.

Moments later, the six women and four men who were voting members of the committee were happily seated around the table. Paper nameplates indicated the places for the official participants.

Their skin colors covered the entire range of humanity, but nearly all those at the table had gray hair, with the notable exception of the lead American.

Ten people sat directly at the table, signifying their official membership on the Committee on the Rights of the Child. Nora, like the other dozen or so staffers in the room, sat in another ring of chairs about two feet behind the line of chairs reserved for the voting members.

Erzabet Kadar leaned forward in her chair. She sat, as always, in the center of the table, with her back to the wall. She apparently didn't want people staring out the windows at the view when they should be listening to her.

She looked around the room solemnly, but Kadar said nothing as she stared down each person in turn, fixing an unblinking gaze until the other person averted his or her eyes. She finally spoke.

"My friends, this is a momentous morning in the history of our movement. For nearly thirty years we have awaited this day. The long spell of frustration, not just for our American friends but for all of us, has finally come to an end."

White legal pads lay unused in front of each person as they listened with focused attention.

"We are gathered here to plan the next stage of our international strategy for the well-being of children. The ratification of the Convention by the United States has brought us to the threshold of a new world of possibilities—a world where children can be liberated from the superstitions and prejudices that have enslaved and abused both their bodies and minds. We must make decisions this morning that will have worldwide implications for decades to come. We need no longer believe that our vision should be achieved gradually. The day for bold action is upon us."

Nora's body tingled somewhere deep inside. Kadar might have the look of a run-of-the-mill bureaucrat, but her voice communicated the passion of a highly effective political advocate.

"As the newest member of our committee, we have requested Dr. Jody Easler, the director of the National Commission on Children in the United States, to prepare an analysis of the alternative scenarios for immediate implementation. Nora Stoddard, who is seated next to Dr. Easler, personally led the field team for the investigation that led up to this report. Dr. Easler holds the title of deputy secretary of state as well as the rank of ambassador here in Geneva, a position of considerable prestige that demonstrates the commitment of the new administration to the Convention. Dr. Easler, please brief our friends on your findings."

"Good morning. On behalf of the United States, let me say how satisfying it is to bring you this report today. We appreciate the long-suffering spirit that has been shown to us by your respective nations as we have labored through this period of regressive thinking." Easler's bright eyes and contagious smile warmed something deep inside of each of the hardened bureaucrats, but on the surface they were taken aback because her manner differed so radically from the norm.

"As requested, we have researched four possible implementation plans for the Convention in the courts of the United States. And we have ranked these potential cases in terms of their political volatility."

Easler nodded to Nora, who pulled the reports out of her bag and sent two stacks in opposite directions around the table.

"On the first page, you will see the case of Kesala Jones. She is a seventeen-year-old girl on trial for capital murder in Bakersfield, California. She is being tried as an adult under California law, accused of beating a seventy-year-old man to death in a robbery. We rank this action as the least volatile.

"While the American people still cling to the archaic notion that the death penalty is just, our survey data indicates that the notion of putting a seventeen-year-old female to death is highly controversial. We would gain great favor among significant portions of the American public if we would employ this treaty to override California law."

A hand shot up from a man sitting at the far end of the table. He wore an identification tag that indicated he was from Belgium. "Can you please tell us," he began in a pleasant French accent, "what provision of American law allows this legal implication from the treaty? How does the treaty have the ability to override local law? I know there is something, but it would help me follow your report if I could be refreshed on this point."

"Certainly," Easler replied, smiling. "Our Constitution has a provision in Article VII called the Supremacy Clause. It says that the Constitution, laws passed under the authority of the Constitution, and treaties which have been ratified are the highest law of the land. Treaties always override the laws of our fifty states."

The questioner nodded and wrote quickly.

"Page 2, if you please. Our second potential case would arise in Charlotte, North Carolina. Under state law, parents are required to consent to an abortion for their minor daughters. Now, of course, there is a provision that allows for the prospect of a judicial override.

But under the treaty, even this possibility of an override is still an interference with the girl's rights under the treaty. A minor's right to reproductive freedom is absolute—as you know.

"We view this as somewhat controversial. But we believe that the fault lines of public opinion will divide along traditional pro-choice and pro-life—as the antiabortion forces like to call themselves—lines. Of course, based on our recent elections, the pro-choice forces are in ascendancy, so the controversy is not likely to shake the confidence of our allies in the Senate.

"Any questions?" she asked.

A woman sitting behind a nameplate that read "Hua Zhuan, People's Republic of China" raised her hand.

Easler smiled and nodded. "Yes?"

"Would not your Supreme Court reach the same conclusion under your own law and under the treaty? It seems that they have been entirely on the right side on this issue," the Chinese woman asked.

"The Court has been very good," Easler said agreeably. "But there have been a few aberrations. And even though we expect more pro-choice justices under the new administration, we cannot estimate how long it will be until the vacancies occur. So for now, it is only the Children's Treaty that will guarantee the result we would want.

"Any more questions?" the American asked. Seeing no hands, she turned her page.

"All right, if you will look at the third scenario. We have a core issue of importance to our treaty, the spanking of children. Unfortunately, our nation still clings to this archaic theory of brutalizing children. And while we could file this case anywhere in the country, because so-called moderate spanking is allowed in all states, we are recommending that a case on this point be filed in Iowa. A decision of the state's supreme court in the mid-1990s held that even if the spanking leaves temporary redness such actions do not constitute child abuse. Taking on this precedent under the authority of the Convention would bring much satisfaction."

"Indeed," harrumphed the British delegate, a man in his late sixties.

Easler smiled warmly at the Brit. "And though the whole issue of corporal punishment has its political supporters, the entire ratification debate in the Senate seemed to focus primarily on this issue. No one can claim that they are surprised to learn that spanking has been banned nationally as a result of ratification. So while this will be hotly controversial in some places, it will be viewed as a foregone conclusion by our friends in the Senate."

Turning the page slowly, Easler surveyed the room, waiting for questions. When none came she resumed. "Finally, we come to our most controversial scenario—one that Nora Stoddard personally investigated. We have found a church in Leesburg, Virginia, that clearly teaches children that world government is inspired by Satan."

Disdainful snickering swept through the room.

"Moreover, they teach that their particular brand of Christianity—so-called born-again Christianity—is the only road to God. We could not touch them if they were just teaching adults. Our American Constitution would certainly protect their rights in that regard. But since the Constitution is silent on the subject of children and parental rights, the better legal opinion is that children who are taught such things have suffered a violation of their rights under the UN Convention. In fact, our friends at the American Bar Association put this legal opinion in writing in the 1980s in a book supporting ratification of the treaty. So, we believe that we can show that this reading of the treaty falls within the intent of the Senate. After all, they had the representatives of the ABA testify in favor of the Convention in the hearings.

"But there is a bonus in this particular scenario. A number of children from this church are also home schooled. This means that their parents remove them from both public and private schooling and do all of their own academic instruction. The vast majority of home schoolers in the United States are among these Christians who call themselves 'born-again.'" The phrase seemed to drop off her lips with just a hint of elegant disdain.

"We would pursue this case—if this group chooses it as the test case—in the state courts of Virginia. We would bring an action in the juvenile courts arguing for supervisory custody over children who are being subjected to both this intolerant religious instruction and the isolationism of home schooling."

A Russian woman, Raisa Kreshnikov, raised her hand and began talking immediately. "Would this mean that the children would be removed from the home?"

"No—at least not initially," Easler answered, shaking her head. "Nora, can you explain how the process would work?"

"Certainly," Stoddard replied nervously. "At the beginning we would simply be asking for the court to appoint a supervisory guardian who would have the ability to protect the child from these aspects of their parents' indoctrination. We would ask the court to protect the best interests of the child. Only if the parents refused to cooperate with the court orders would the prospect of removal of the children become an issue."

Kreshnikov continued. "How many children would be the subject of this action?"

"We would recommend two children," Stoddard continued. "One child who is home schooled and one child who is a member of this church but also attends the public school. But, this is only if this particular alternative is chosen. This is by far the most controversial of our alternatives. It leaves no room for gradualism."

"Which alternative do you suggest, Dr. Easler?" Hua Zhuan asked.

"My staff, led by Nora here, unanimously recommends that we pursue the Iowa case which concerns corporal punishment," Easler replied, nodding at Stoddard. "We think the American sensibilities would tolerate this case within acceptable levels, perhaps even with a sense of resignation. But the religion and education case would potentially touch off a firestorm of reaction."

Kreshnikov spoke again. "From my study of American religions, it would seem to me that people who pursued the sort of fanaticism you have described are normally the same kind of people who practice corporal punishment. Could you not consolidate the corporal punishment case with the one involving religious fanaticism?"

"I suppose we *could*," Easler replied, her voice revealing a slightly irritated edge even though her practiced smile continued unabated. "But our own staff strongly recommends the Iowa case.

And I have to say that I agree. The Virginia case is simply too fast for American sensibilities."

Kreshnikov started to speak again but saw Kadar stirring to speak and quickly decided to remain silent.

"American sensibilities are no longer the issue, Dr. Easler. I thought you understood that," Kadar said, pronouncing her words with a slow, deliberate cadence. "I thought that is why you worked so hard for the ratification of our Rights of the Child Convention," the Chair said in a voice with icy coolness.

"Yes," Easler responded hesitantly, "but, well, I guess you are right."

"Think it through, my friend," the Hungarian leader said a bit more warmly. "Will you lose the case?"

Easler shook her head as she said, "No, not likely."

"Can the ratification be reversed?"

"Not without a vote of sixty-seven senators going the other way," the American replied in the singsong fashion of a school girl giving a recitation to her history teacher.

"Is there any danger that you will see more than thirty senators change their minds so quickly?"

Easler again shook her head, while starting to smile as she began to see the point.

Nora, however, felt more and more ill at ease. It was one thing to override the wishes of obstinate Americans, but for enlightened Americans like herself, she expected better consideration.

"You have to remember that the rest of the world has waited a long time for the American ratification. We will just keep on making our reports and having them collect dust on a shelf until the

American courts begin enforcing our decisions. That is the leverage we need to turn moral obligations in other nations into binding legal obligations. America may be the last to ratify, but it is clearly the one nation we have been waiting for. However, there is one thing I can do for you," Kadar said in a louder voice as if she was making magnanimous concession, "we can give you plausible deniability."

"What do you mean?" Easler added.

"As you know, the treaty gives non-governmental organizations enforcement authority under the treaty. We can have the case brought by the Children's Defense Fund and the National Education Association. Both groups are properly certified NGOs. Your Commission can remain relatively quiet in the public."

"That's perfect!" Easler intoned, with measured brightness. "Our Senators can say things like, 'We'll just have to wait and see what happens in the court. It's a matter of concern, but I think reason will prevail.' It is just the kind of dodge they love."

"Is it unanimous then?" Kadar asked. She knew that it was because she had made her own position quite clear. "We have decided on Virginia."

PURCELLVILLE, VIRGINIA.
April 19, 2005.

Deanna Thomas heard the crunch of the car's wheels on the gravel road leading to the house before she actually saw it turn into the driveway.

It was a beautiful spring day, and Deanna couldn't teach one more hour of lessons inside. Trent was down for his nap, the portable monitor was at her side, and the schoolroom was temporarily relocated to the picnic table in the backyard.

Nikki happily carted her dolls and tea set outside. The regular site for her imaginary home under the swingset beckoned to her.

Layton was the first to notice the car. "I wonder who's coming, Mama."

"Beats me," Deanna said, getting up from the table as she headed toward the driveway. "Maybe the UPS man."

Drop-by visitors to their rural home were rare. Friends normally called first. As Deanna turned the corner, she was indeed curious why a brown Loudoun County Sheriff's cruiser was headed down her five-hundred-foot-long driveway. He was a good driver, she thought, having noticed the skill with which he dodged all the potholes that needed to be fixed.

The cruiser pulled to a stop directly behind her Ford Windstar. The deputy inside appeared to be gathering some paperwork before opening the door about fifteen seconds later.

"Yes, sir. Can I help you?" Deanna asked.

"You Mrs. Thomas?" the trim officer in his midthirties asked.

Her heart ran a little fast. *Rick has been in an accident.* "Yes, sir. Is there a problem?"

"Oh, I've just got some legal papers for you, that's all. Don't ask me what they're about. I don't know. Don't ever know. I don't read 'em. I don't write 'em. I just deliver 'em," he replied. It was his standard incantation.

"I have no idea, either," Deanna replied, relieved that her husband wasn't dead.

"Just sign here, ma'am," the deputy said, "and I'll leave you to read these papers for yourself."

Deanna signed and began tearing open the manila envelope before he was back in the car. As the brown car headed down the driveway, Deanna stared at the documents as if she had been delivered radioactive moon rocks. She was afraid to keep holding them, but she was compelled to keep reading.

"In the Juvenile Court for Loudoun County," the heading read, across the top of the front page. She scanned the document, clueless as to the full meaning of the document, but it appeared that there was some kind of hearing scheduled on April 29, and she and Rick had to be there.

The second sheet informed her that a guardian ad litem—an attorney named Rachel Hennessey—had been appointed to represent Layton. The bottom dropped out of her stomach as she read those words.

The third sheet appeared to be the beginning of a long document. "Petition for Dependency," read the caption. She was baffled. She was beginning to understand that someone wanted to supervise Layton's activities, but she wasn't exactly sure who or why.

She kept reading. Details were starting to become clearer to her. Home schooling, spanking, and religious instruction all were mentioned. And something very strange about a treaty obligation of the United States.

As she read deeper into the seven-page petition, the edges of her ears gradually changed from pink to fiery crimson. The Irish temper of her Boston-bred father began to well up inside her. But it was her very Southern mother from Richmond who chose the somewhat dated words she spoke. "That wanton hussy!" Deanna exclaimed out loud.

She threw her head back with her eyes closed and forcibly exhaled all the air in her lungs. "I can't believe I was so stupid as to let that woman into my house. Government survey, indeed!"

"Layton, honey! Come here," she cried out.

Layton rounded the corner at a full run. He stopped immediately upon seeing his mother's beet-red face. He did a quick mental review of his recent actions to see if he had done anything to deserve her anger. His conscience tentatively acquitted him.

"Mama, what's wrong?" he asked, with a frightened tone in his voice.

"Oh, it's probably nothing," she said, as her motherly instincts took over. "It's just some papers that say we have to go to court about something—I don't get it. Will you just go get me the portable phone? I need to call your dad. I'm a little upset with these papers, and I just don't feel like going inside right now."

"Yes, Mama." He was off with a bound and returned quickly with the phone.

After sending Layton off to play with Nikki in the backyard, Deanna called Rick's private number at work. She got voice mail. Her full-blown anger was just slightly infected with a tinge of fear. She wanted to spill out her emotional words to her husband *right now,* and she needed his reassuring voice. She hung up and called his cell phone.

As soon as he answered, Deanna knew that she was going to be more frustrated than ever. Rick actually said, "Hi, this is Rick, can I help you?" But he sounded like a scuba diver gasping for air. Washington Cellular might have great ads, but the cell service around Leesburg was pathetic.

The only thing Rick heard clearly was Deanna's cry, "Come home!" He had been on his way to a sales call in Tyson's Corner, but he took the first exit off the Dulles Greenway and doubled back over the road, heading toward Purcellville.

Deanna marched up and down the asphalt driveway with the papers clutched tightly in one hand and the phone in the other. She wanted to plot revenge. She wanted to find a way to get back at this woman for invading her home and her life and her family. But, she knew too little to do this effectively, so she just fumed.

About three minutes later, the phone rang. "Hello," she said, trying to sound calm.

"I'm on my way—that was the only thing I understood in the first call. What is going on? Are the kids OK?"

"You've got to come home right now! The kids are physically fine, but a deputy sheriff was out here and gave me some legal papers about Layton. I just can't understand it all, but someone wants to take us to court about the way we are raising him. It has to be that government woman who came out here to do that so-called survey who's behind this whole thing."

"Oh, there's got to be a mistake. Are you sure about all this?"

"All I know for sure is that we have a court hearing on April 29, and that a woman lawyer named Rachel Hennessey has been appointed as a guardian of some Latin name or something for Layton."

"I'll be right home. Don't do anything."

Deanna wasn't always a submissive wife, but on this occasion she had no problem obeying her husband's command. She had no idea what to do anyway.

❧ ❧ ❧

Rick was in a five-mile stretch of good cellular reception, just over the rise at Clark's Gap on his way toward Purcellville. He hit the number of his racquetball partner and then the send button.

"Jameson and Stone," came the reply.

"Hi, Nancy. Cooper, please—Rick Thomas calling."

"He's meeting with clients all afternoon, Mr. Thomas, but I think he'll want me to schedule something for you two at the health club in the next couple of days. What do you have in mind?"

"Nancy, thanks for that, but we have some sort of legal emergency on our hands. Deanna just called me and told me that a sheriff served her with papers this afternoon, and someone is apparently trying to take custody of our oldest son, Layton. Or something like that. There's some mention about a guardian being appointed. Can we get in to see Cooper right away?"

"Sure," Nancy replied. "I'll squeeze you in. Or let me see. Never mind the squeezing part. I see that his four o'clock appointment is Lynn Whitman—she is always at least twenty minutes late. Come around 3:45."

"We'll be there. Thanks, Nancy."

❧ ❧ ❧

Beyond the designated historic district, Leesburg, Virginia, had exploded in the past fifteen years. First there was the Kmart on the edge of town, then the Wal-Mart to the north, then the outlet mall, then the onslaught of the chain restaurants. Leesburg was now the county seat for well over two hundred thousand people—a population that had doubled in the last decade. Yet, the legal community had not experienced a similar spurt of growth. Most of the big law firms were in Fairfax or Washington, thirty minutes to an hour away. The lawyers of Loudoun County still felt part of a tight-knit, small-town community, and they were suspicious of outsiders until they had proved themselves to be true Virginia gentlemen. Oh yes, or Virginia ladies. There had been that pesky challenge to tradition. Population growth wasn't the only thing that had changed since Warren Jameson had opened his law practice.

Thirty years earlier, Jameson had converted an old Victorian home on King Street into a law office. The core of the downtown had changed little in that span of time, with the exception of the new palatial county government center and the even newer courthouse expansion. But most of the balance of the six-block downtown still bore the imprint of a very old and elegant Virginia town. Jameson still liked to walk to the courthouse although he was doing that less and less as he moved toward semiretirement.

Cooper Stone should have been accepted a little more quickly into the local legal fraternity. After all, he was born in Loudoun, and he was Warren Jameson's nephew. But Cooper's Yankee father, after marrying Jameson's sister, moved to Spokane, Washington, when Cooper was not quite three years old, and so the boy was not educated in Virginia at all, not even law school.

Cooper had practiced law in Spokane for two years in the small firm of Peter Barron & Associates. But in his spare time, Cooper had volunteered for a Washington candidate for the U.S. Senate, who had ended up winning. Cooper took a job with Senator Matthew Parker for six years. But the incredible sweep of the Democrats in the 2004 election had left both the senator and Cooper without jobs. The senator landed with a lobbying firm that kept offices in Seattle and Washington. Cooper had found refuge by joining his uncle. He had moved a mere forty miles, from Capitol Hill to downtown Leesburg.

Rick and Deanna made the ten-mile drive from their home just south of Purcellville into Leesburg without speaking a word. They had talked, though some of Deanna's talking sounded more like crying mixed with yelling, for more than an hour after Rick arrived home. Rick had put his arms around his wife and his children and had prayed. Then there was a lot of heavy silence, especially after their fifteen-year-old neighbor girl showed up to watch the kids. There was simply nothing more to say until they could get Cooper to untangle this legal puzzle for them.

Rick pulled into a parking space behind the law office, shifted into park, and with his hands still on the wheel and the shift lever, smiled warmly at Deanna. He knew better than to make a long speech to his volatile wife. "God will be our protector," he said simply.

"I hope so," she replied, her voice choking.

Rick rounded the car and helped her down from the front seat of his Chevy Suburban, a courtesy that had been drilled into him by the refusal of this Southern belle to get out of a car unless he opened the door for her. He gave her an extra squeeze and kept his arm around her as they walked together into the front door of the old Victorian home. With Rick at her side, Deanna's sense of vulnerability waned just enough for her fierce maternal instinct to rise to the surface of her conscious mind.

"Hi, Nancy," Rick said, as they entered the former living room turned reception area.

"Well, look at you two love birds," she drawled. "With all the people wandering in here wanting divorces, it is nice to see you arm in arm."

"Thanks, Nancy," Rick said, still holding on to his wife. He could feel her body slightly quiver every minute or so. He had seen her angry many times, but this felt different. The only other times he had felt her tremble like this were in the early stages of her three labors. "Please tell Cooper we're here," he requested.

Five minutes later, Cooper Stone came bounding around the corner, "Hey, Rick, what in the world . . ." He suddenly stopped his loud racquetball-buddy banter when he saw Deanna perched on the edge of waiting room chair, biting her lower lip. "You two need to see me, I understand," he said much more softly. "Come on down to my office."

They followed Cooper down the hardwood-floored hallway into the first office on the right-hand side. The young lawyer motioned them to the two upholstered chairs situated squarely in front of his desk.

"Nancy says you have been served some legal papers. May I see them?" Cooper began. "Do you know what they're about?" he asked, as he pulled the stack of papers out of the manila envelope.

"Sir, some lying government bureaucrat is trying to take my child—that's all," Deanna drawled bitterly.

Her choice of words made Cooper want to grin so badly that the corners of his mouth began to ache, but he managed to demonstrate a suitably somber impression as he looked up from the papers he was quickly scanning. "Yes?" he replied. "Go on."

Deanna nodded at Rick to tell the story. She was just too angry.

"A few weeks ago, this woman from some government agency showed up at our church. She ended up in Layton's class. I don't know how that came about. Anyhow, Layton's Sunday school teacher brought her down the hall to us after class and told us that the woman wanted to meet a home schooling family. She was all nice and everything and just wanted to come by and meet us for this survey she was doing. We said yes—what could it hurt? Or, so we thought. But we are pretty sure that's where this came from, even though we can't find the name of any government agency or her name on it anywhere."

"Do you know this woman's name or the name of her agency?" Cooper asked.

"That . . . that . . ." Deanna was about to describe the woman's lack of adherence to the norms of civilized behavior in more colorful language.

Cooper looked up from the papers with raised eyebrows and a suppressed smile. "Yes?"

"A 'wanton hussy' is what my Southern wife calls her," Rick said, forcing a smile. "But her name is here on her business card. I found it in a desk drawer."

"Hmm," Cooper grunted, as he examined it closely. "Nora Stoddard, Director of the National Commission on Children. You didn't get just some random bureaucrat in your house. It appears that she is the top dog."

"'Dog' is ever so fitting," Deanna muttered.

Rick put his hand firmly on his wife's knee as a signal to go no further.

Cooper thumbed quickly through the stack of papers one by one. "Yeah, that's the thing that has me puzzled as well. I have never heard of a dependency petition being filed by a private party,"

Cooper replied. "If it wasn't signed by one of the Beltway's biggest firms, I would have thought this was a joke."

He stopped suddenly and reached to his right to activate the buttons for his speakerphone. "I want to check something out," he said. "I know the clerk of the juvenile court, and I want to ask her about this."

A few minutes and two call transfers later he said, "Patty, this is Cooper Stone, and I have a couple here in my office with some very unusual papers that have been filed in your court. Have you ever seen a dependency petition filed by a private party before?"

"Are you talking about one of those two treaty cases?" she replied.

"Two cases?" the surprised lawyer answered.

"Yeah, two lawyers from some big D.C. firm showed up here the other day to get Judge Holman to sign an order appointing a guardian ad litem in two different cases. He asked them the same question—how can a private party bring a case like this?"

"I take it that they had an answer because he signed the order," Cooper replied.

"Yeah, they showed him some provision in this treaty that gives certain organizations standing to enforce the treaty. In thirty-five years I have never heard of such a thing," Patty said contemptuously. "Judge Holman told them that he would sign the guardian order, but that if he got the case for hearing, he was going to look more closely at their standing to file these cases."

"So who is the other family?"

"I don't know which family you are representing, Cooper, and besides that's confidential—juvenile case, remember?"

"Good point," Cooper replied.

"But you'll probably find out soon enough. The judge told me that he is thinking about consolidating the cases for trial."

"Good enough," Cooper responded. "In any event, Rick and Deanna Thomas are my clients. Their son, Layton, has been named in the petition. If the other family contacts you and wants information, you have our permission to tell them that I am representing the second family."

"That'll work," Patty replied. "I'd like to see you get cracking and beat these hotshots from Washington who came in here like they owned the place. I will be only too happy to tell the other family or their lawyer about you since you've given me permission. I may have to file their fancy D.C. legal paper, but I don't have to like them."

With a few pleasantries, the conversation ended.

"Well, that's interesting," Cooper mused, shaking his head.

"Is that 'good' interesting or 'bad' interesting?" Rick asked.

"It's hard to say. All we know for sure is that you won't be going through this alone. And, yeah . . ." Cooper suddenly shifted in his chair and grabbed his pen and began writing. "Judge Holman is clearly interested in the question of standing. How in the world do these private groups get the power to file these kinds of cases?" He scribbled furiously for about ten seconds. "I wanted to get that down, just to make sure I don't forget."

"So what do we do next?" Deanna asked in a remarkably matter-of-fact tone. The fact that another family shared their predicament had an inexplicable soothing effect on her emotions.

Cooper leaned back in his chair, chasing several trains of thought in his mind. "I guess you two don't have to do much of anything," he replied. "Everything is on my shoulders for now. I certainly have a ton of legal research to do. We are dealing with issues that are not only new to me, but I'm pretty sure have never been dealt with by any lawyer in the country. Treaties. Third party plaintiffs in dependency cases. Constitutional rights."

"Sounds intimidating to me," Rick said, and he meant it.

"Yeah, I can see why you would say that," Cooper replied. "But from a lawyer's perspective, these are the kind of cases most of us dreamed about in law school."

A hot, angry tear slid down Deanna's cheek. "From a mother's perspective, I can tell you this is no dream—it's my worst nightmare."

Rick slipped his arm back around his wife and held on. He looked up at Cooper. The young lawyer's head was leaning on his left hand. The phrase "ton of research" suddenly acquired a new meaning for Rick.

"Cooper," Rick began. "How much is this going to cost us?"

Cooper wanted to say, "Nothing, buddy, I'll do it for free." But he knew he couldn't. He could see right away that this case might take several months, and he knew he couldn't give away that much of his time.

"I really don't know, Rick," Cooper said, shaking his head. "It could be a lot." Cooper paused, rubbing his neck and shaking his head. "I'll tell you what. Let me put in about ten hours for free. I can do that much for you as a friend. After that, I'm going to have to be paid, but we can figure something out. And at least I can have a better idea of what's going to be involved. OK?"

"Sure," Rick replied. "And thanks."

After a few more words, the couple exited the building as they had come in, arm in arm. They drove home in relative silence. As they crossed over the short range of hills between Leesburg and Purcellville, Rick remembered that when they passed this spot on the way to Cooper's he had felt an extraordinary burden for his wife and his son. That sense of burden was still strongly present. But there was a new load on his mind as well. *How am I going to pay for all this?* was the question that kept replaying in his mind. He didn't dare say a word to Deanna. Her load was too much already. He shrugged and kept on driving, lost in his circle of thoughts.

CHAPTER 4

LEESBURG, VIRGINIA.
April 19, 2005. Evening.

Cooper had his briefcase open on his desk, ready for a final few documents before he left for the evening. Tonight would be all work, including study of some previous cases he had quickly printed off LexisNexis as resources for his ten volunteer hours on the Thomas case.

"All work" described most of his evenings ever since he had left Capitol Hill. There had been long hours there, as well. But on the Hill there were always social opportunities mixed with the work, for invitations to receptions and dinners were routine for any well-connected Hill staffer. Cooper had seemed to get more than his fair share. Young single women familiar with the Hill usually had a hand in finalizing the guest list, and Cooper was a popular target. They couldn't understand why Cooper was not married or at least "taken." They kept him on the "A" list in a collective effort to solve his bachelorhood problem.

A few of these invitations followed him to Loudoun County but not for long. His good looks were no longer enough for the Hill crowd; access to power was essential as well, and he was no longer well connected. In most situations, former staffers were considered prime candidates for access brokerage, but Cooper's situation was doubly different. Not only did his boss lose his bid for reelection, but the majority party had changed as well. Cooper's relationships were soon worth about as much as a day-old newspaper.

He closed his briefcase and began his normal routine of searching for his car keys. His hands lightly slapped the piles on his desk to see if they were hiding under a stack of papers, as usual. He found a telltale lump on the far right-hand side of his desk just as the phone rang.

"This is Cooper Stone," he said.

"Cooper, it's Rick."

"What's up, buddy?"

"We've found the other family."

"Other family?" Cooper asked in confusion, then he suddenly got it. "Oh, you found the second family who's being sued in this treaty deal."

"Yeah, they go to our church. The parents are Doug and Jeanne Garvis. Their daughter, Emily, is in Layton's Sunday school class."

"Do they home school also?" Cooper asked.

"No, Emily attends Paeonian Springs Elementary."

"Hmm. Public school kid. I thought this was all about home schooling. So much for that theory."

"Yeah, I guess the Sunday school class is the common thread," Rick replied.

"How'd you find out?" Cooper asked, perching on the edge of his chair.

"Layton's Sunday school teacher called us and asked us if we had heard anything from the court. The Garvises had called her right after they got their papers. They also think that the Stoddard woman with the so-called government survey was behind this. So Laura called us right away because she remembered that the woman had been especially interested in our family."

"I take it that Laura is the Sunday school teacher," Cooper said, pulling his notepad back out of his briefcase.

"Yeah, Laura Frasier. It just so happens that she's also Emily Garvis's third grade teacher at Paeonian Springs."

"That's interesting. Quite a coincidence, don't you think?"

"Might be in Washington," Rick replied. "This is West Loudoun. Not much of a coincidence in our part of the county."

"Yeah, I guess," Cooper replied. "So do they have a lawyer?"

"No, I just got off the phone with Doug. They are hoping that you would take this on for them as well."

"I don't see why not," Cooper replied. "Can you have them call me and make an appointment first thing in the morning?"

"I could," Rick replied, "but we were all hoping that we might get together tonight and talk. You got plans for dinner?"

"I was really looking forward to putting a box of Lean Cuisine in the microwave, but I guess I can be flexible," he quipped. "What time do you want me there?"

"Seven fifteen," Rick replied.

Cooper glanced at his watch. Six thirty. "Sure, I'll be there. Will the Garvises be there?"

"Yeah, and Laura Frasier as well."

"Great," Cooper replied. "I'll just sit here until then and read a few cases that I was taking home to begin my research. And then we all can talk."

Rick sighed heavily. "Thanks, Cooper. I really appreciate it."

"No problem, Rick. But all I did was agree to come to dinner."

"Yeah, but I mean for everything. And even coming to dinner is a bigger deal than you might imagine."

"What do you mean?"

"This whole thing is really hard for Deanna. She is so used to trying to solve whatever problems she faces. And until this dinner idea came up, she was more upset than I can ever remember. But since we hatched this plan for the evening, she's been bustling around the kitchen as if her efforts to make a really good meal will make this whole case disappear."

"Wow," Cooper replied softly. "I have a lot to learn about clients—and women."

"Especially women," Rick replied with a soft laugh. "See you soon."

∽ ∽ ∽

Cooper drove his car slowly over the rise at Clark's Gap, and then a half-mile later, Route 7 rose and fell a hundred feet or so. As he descended, there was a gorgeous vista ahead of a ten-mile-wide valley with the Blue Ridge Mountains at its western edge. Washington State had views that were more spectacular, but the subtle beauty of Virginia somehow seemed richer. The flowering trees, which would turn to blazing reds and yellows and oranges in the fall, certainly added to the enchantment he felt as he drove on.

He had visited his relatives in Loudoun County often during his childhood, but upon returning here to live he felt like he was in a different place altogether. The Purcellville exit came up quickly and he turned south toward town.

Ten minutes later, he turned right onto the Thomases' narrow gravel road and headed up a steep hill. Dust from the red Honda just in front of him caused him to slow down a little so he could see clearly. A few seconds later a flashing blinker told him that the Honda was headed to the same dinner invitation.

Both cars dodged the holes in the Thomases' driveway, but each had to drive at a slower pace than the sheriff's deputy had managed earlier that day.

Cooper pulled his old Buick Park Avenue off to the side of the driveway, right next to the neighbor's garden area. A raven-haired woman in her late twenties parked the Honda behind Rick's Suburban. One look at her face and Cooper wished his car would transform itself into a Mitsubishi Eclipse or a BMW or anything but the twelve-year-old big Buick his aunt had given him. He was saving for a big down payment on a home, with a decent car as a distant future goal. He was often embarrassed by his old "grandpa" car but not enough to go into debt. Listening to some Larry Burkett tapes about staying debt-free had drilled that conviction deep.

The woman stood behind her car, obviously waiting for Cooper.

"Hi," she said, with a friendly smile.

"Good evening. You must be Laura," he replied.

"Right. And you are Rick's friend, the lawyer?"

"Yeah, I'm the lawyer. Cooper Stone is my name."

"Oh, Deanna told me your name, but I thought Cooper Stone was the name of the whole law firm, not just the name of one guy."

Cooper paused, not knowing what to say. Laura could see she had taken him aback and was immediately embarrassed.

"Don't worry about it, Laura. If I had a dollar for every time someone has called me Mr. Cooper, I wouldn't be driving that old Buick over there."

They both laughed and then smiled, and then self-consciously turned and walked in silence to the front door.

Rick welcomed them both at the door and then ushered them into the family room immediately to the left of the center hall entryway. A thirtyish couple with grim smiles were waiting on the blue love seat which sat against the front wall of the room. Doug Garvis, a man of average height and a husky build, was clutching a manila envelope and his wife Jeanne, a trim dark-haired woman with a wholesome kind of prettiness, was tightly clutching their daughter, who sat on her right.

"Cooper, this is Doug and Jeanne Garvis and their daughter, Emily. And I see you already met Laura Frasier outside."

"It's nice to meet all of you," Cooper replied, as he stood politely in the entryway.

Rick motioned for Cooper and Laura to sit on the large couch, which was at a right angle to the love seat along the adjacent wall. Cooper sat at the end closest to the Garvises. Deanna could be seen scurrying about in the kitchen behind them, apparently carrying food into a dining room that was just out of sight.

"I see you have a packet of papers like the one the Thomases gave me earlier today," Cooper said. It was awkward in the informality of a home to begin an attorney-client relationship, but it had to be done.

"Yeah, all the papers are here, not that we understand why any of this is supposed to make sense," said Mr. Garvis, in a gravelly bass voice.

"Mind if I look at them?" Cooper asked.

"Not at all. I figured that's what might come first," Doug replied.

It was obvious that Jeanne was not a Virginian as soon as she opened her mouth. Cooper took her accent to be one from New Jersey, though he would soon be corrected. "Long Island is not New Jersey," she informed him. "So do you have any idea why they picked our two families for this case?"

"Not really. At least not yet," Cooper replied, skimming over the papers to try to discern if there were material differences from the set of pleadings he had read that afternoon. "Actually, Laura," he said, turning and facing the Sunday school teacher seated four feet to his right, "I was hoping to ask you that question. Did Nora Stoddard give you any explanation of how she picked your church and your Sunday school class?"

"I have continually asked myself that question, Cooper," she replied, shaking her head. "There is nothing that comes to mind at all. All I can remember is that she said that her commission was interested in all areas of children's lives. And she mentioned that she thought spiritual life was important. I got the impression she was something like a government pollster, only wanting general information."

"Did she say anything about being the director of the National Commission on Children?"

"No, I am hearing that for the first time right now. She said that she worked there, but nothing came out about her being the director."

"So she didn't give you a business card?"

Laura shook her head. "I guess I should have asked for that, shouldn't I?" she said in an embarrassed tone.

"I really don't know what difference it would have made if you had," he replied. "It just adds to the air of sneakiness. She sauntered into your class like she was a low-level government servant, when in reality she is very high up."

Cooper slowly turned to face the Garvises. "When she came to your home, did she give you a business card?"

"Yeah, I think she did," Jeanne replied, "but we couldn't find it this afternoon. I think I've got it somewhere."

"Did she tell you that she had been to visit the Thomases when she called to set up her appointment?"

Jeanne shook her head. "All she said was that she had visited another family in our church, and I didn't think to ask her who it was."

"Do we have any reason to believe that she may have visited anybody else in your church?" Cooper looked around the room at everyone.

Rick shook his head, as did the Garvises.

Laura spoke. "I have called every parent with a child in my class within the last couple of hours. No one else got a visit or a phone call. We don't know how she found the Garvises. I introduced her to Rick and Deanna. But I don't know the connection to Doug and Jeanne."

"Well, from what I can see in your papers—and this is just on a quick read-through—there are only a few minor differences in the allegations between the two families. Rick and Deanna are being cited for violating the UN Convention on the Rights of the Child by engaging in home schooling, which the Convention claims is contrary to the child's best interest. Doug and Jeanne are being cited for removing Emily from the family life education program in her public school classroom—your classroom, Laura," he said turning toward her again.

"Both families are being cited for violating the treaty by using corporal punishment," he continued. "There's one other thing. It's a little vague, and I am not sure what they are getting at. There is an allegation in both sets of papers that the children's religious freedom is being hampered by instruction in religious intolerance. Does anybody know specifically what that is all about?"

Everyone said "No!" in unison.

"Did she ask either of you what you taught your kids about religion when she made her home visits?"

Again a chorus of no's was the reply.

Cooper shook his head. "Why would they make a similar allegation against both families? You school differently from each other, and you didn't talk with her about any teaching content. Any ideas?"

As he looked around the room, Cooper suddenly had an idea himself. He addressed Laura. "It's you. Your Sunday school class. That's the instruction the two kids have in common."

"I . . . I guess so," she admitted.

"Do you remember what you taught that week?"

"We were studying missions. I can't remember the details without looking at my notes."

"You still have your notes?"

"Yeah, I have a file at my house. I'd be happy to give them to you."

"Where do you live?" he asked. His stomach fluttered at the thought of getting her address and phone number so easily.

"In the townhomes just off Sycolin Road near the Route 7 bypass in Leesburg."

"Got it. I know exactly where you mean." He wrote down her address and phone number.

"Do you think I could stop and get your notes on my way home from work tomorrow—around five-thirty or six o'clock?"

"Sure, that would be fine," she replied, with a bit of a nervous smile.

Deanna called them to dinner a moment later, and the rest of the evening was spent getting to know one another, with only casual mention of the details of the lawsuit from time to time. Both couples were relieved to hear of Cooper's six years' experience as a lawyer assigned to be his boss's representative to the Senate Foreign Relations Committee. No other lawyer in Leesburg would have gotten that close to treaties.

Laura sat quietly in her assigned seat by Cooper. She had to admit to herself that she was impressed. But not so much with his experience as with the mixture of zeal and confidence she saw in his eyes as he explained the unexplored field that they were all entering. She was sure that if she ever needed a lawyer, Cooper Stone would be the first man she would call.

5

LEESBURG, VIRGINIA.
April 20, 2005.

The following day Cooper was in the Loudoun County Law Library from nine to five, though he was not very focused. He opened a law book—*United States v. Missouri* (1950)—to find out how treaties affect a state's rights, but he was constantly looking at his watch, waiting for 5:30 to arrive. He had had his fair share of dates since coming east, but it was the first time in a very long time that he had thought ahead to an evening with a young lady with a sense of excitement instead of anxiety.

At 5:25, he pulled his car out of the courthouse lot and negotiated his way through the tight turns in the historic district before easing out into the four-lane section of Market Street. He found himself smiling as he glanced once again in the mirror. "Yeah, the hair's still there," he said to himself.

And then he was there. His footsteps echoed loudly as his heels tapped against the brick walkway. No doorbell. Three crisp knocks. Wait. Wait. A little noise. Smile. Clicking sounds. The knob turned.

"Oh, hi, Cooper," Laura said in a quiet voice. She stepped quickly out of the door to meet him on the front step. "That's right, you did say you would come by today. Let me go get my notes. I'll be right back." And like that, she was gone.

"Hi, Laura, nice to see you. Pretty good, and you?" he whispered to no one in particular after she was well inside. His mind began to reel, spinning rapidly into his old pattern of anxiety.

Less than a minute later she was back and resumed her place on the front step. "Well, here they are." She handed him the papers and immediately clasped her hands behind her back, rocking gently toe to heel.

"Thanks, Laura. Umm," he stammered, "I was hoping to look them over a little and maybe ask you a few questions if that's OK."

"Well, it's really not the best time for me," she replied.

He waited for further explanation, but when it was apparent that none was coming, he spoke again. "Well, I guess that's fine. We can do it some other time. In fact, I was hoping to ask you about getting together some evening. Not about the case, but just to get to know you a little better." He looked uncomfortably at his feet.

Laura stopped rocking and smiled. "I was afraid you were going to ask that," she said. Seeing the hurt in Cooper's eyes, she quickly continued. "Not that I don't think you seem like a really great guy. It's just that I am in a serious relationship and have been for several years. In fact, he's our pastor's son—Terry Pipkin. I thought Rick might have told you about him."

"Oh, I am so sorry," Cooper said, trying to conceal a sigh of disappointment. "Rick said nothing and I had no idea."

"Of course you didn't, and I am not upset with you for asking. In fact, I'm flattered. If only . . ." She bit her lip and then shook her head. "Well, anyway, I think you understand."

"Again, please forgive my presumption," he replied, with a brave smile. "I'll just look your notes over and give you a call if I have any questions—if that's OK."

"Sure, Cooper. That would be fine."

"Bye," he said, turning to walk away.

Laura started to speak but, instead, stood silently in the doorway as he walked back to his car.

"Who was that?" Terry asked, looking up from the newspaper as he leaned back in her kitchen chair.

"That was the lawyer who is helping the Thomas and Garvis families. He needed my Sunday school lesson notes from the day that the government worker came to the class," she replied, as she returned to her recipe, trying to remember where she had left off.

"You mean that deal with the treaty that you mentioned last night?"

"Yeah, that's right," she replied.

"I don't get what that's all about—treaties and Sunday school lessons and spanking. It seems bizarre."

"Yeah," Laura said, nodding. "It's hard to figure out."

Terry shrugged and resumed his perusal of the *Washington Times,* and Laura busied herself with dinner. For several minutes no one said anything.

Terry looked up from the paper and studied Laura's face for a few seconds. "It just hit me. Why would a lawyer come here to get your notes?"

"He just wanted them right away, I guess. When we met at the Thomases' home, he said he would like to get them today if possible, and coming here tonight just seemed like the easiest thing," she replied, blushing.

"So who is this lawyer anyway? Do I know him?"

"His name is Cooper Stone. He's fairly new in town. I guess Rick Thomas met him in some Christian men's group, and now they play racquetball together."

"Oh, I think I heard my dad say that there was a new young Christian lawyer in Leesburg. Hmm." As Terry watched Laura's body language and facial expressions, he sensed that something was making her uneasy. "So how young is he?" he asked.

"He's about your age, I would guess," she answered, as she hid her face behind the open refrigerator door.

Terry shook his head, stood, and walked slowly up behind his girlfriend. Grasping her gently by the shoulders, he smiled as he spoke with a teasing voice. "So what's going on? Are you embarrassed about something?"

Laura tried being evasive, but nothing occurred to her quickly. "OK," she said, with a sigh of relief. "He asked me out on a date when I handed him the papers. I felt uncomfortable just walking back in here with you right after that."

"What did you say?"

"What do you mean? I said no, of course," she quickly responded, with just an edge of heat in her voice.

"Oh, OK. Just checking. Still my girlfriend?" he asked.

"Yeah, I'm your girlfriend . . . still." There was a hint of bitterness in the last word.

❧ ❧ ❧

The office was the last place Cooper wanted to be, but there was nowhere else to go. His basement apartment at his aunt and uncle's was empty. All the restaurants would be full of couples. Movie theaters were out of the question. The files on his desk seemed to need him, and being needed was a feeling he craved at the moment.

His mind told him that he had no right to be upset. It was not as if his girlfriend had dumped him. He had met a girl. She seemed very nice. Maybe very, very nice. But she was taken. He knew that. But the loneliness was harder to bear than any emotion he could remember feeling in a long time.

Uprooted from his most recent home near Capitol Hill, Cooper felt more displaced than he had since moving to Leesburg. He was from Spokane. He had worked for a senator from Spokane. He had gone back to western Washington frequently and had welcomed visitors from home just as often. His professional life had been a constant whir, leaving little time for introspection. But tonight, even though he had moved only forty miles from Capitol Hill, he suddenly felt twenty-five hundred miles away from his home.

He pulled the Thomas and Garvis files from his briefcase and flipped open the first of the many photocopied cases he needed to read. They captured his mind for awhile. He concentrated on them enthusiastically for well over half an hour.

Gradually, a little thought he had been trying to suppress leapt fully into his consciousness. He really should read Laura's notes from her Sunday school class, one side of his brain argued. He tried to look only for things that might raise relevant legal issues, but he kept evaluating her personality and spiritual maturity instead. Only once did he allow himself to think, *She is even better than I thought.* He then said it out loud.

Slowly he began to talk himself into focusing. This treaty case was the biggest challenge he had ever had as a lawyer. Perhaps it would be the hardest of his career. The last thing he truly needed right now was a new romantic distraction. He would work on this case. He would concentrate. He would win this case. He would make his mark. He would do a good thing for these families. He would do a great thing for America.

It became a mantra of sorts. Hard work. Concentrate. Make my mark. Do good for America. He played it back to himself over and over. It was working. He read and read some more.

Around 9:30, his stomach finally announced that it had had it— supper could be postponed no longer. Cooper picked up his cell phone and car keys and stuffed his sunglasses back into his jacket pocket.

He shoved his old Buick into drive and headed to Wendy's, on the other side of the courthouse. He flipped on the radio and hit the button squarely in the middle of the dial. WBIG, the oldies station. It was the only button that he hadn't changed after getting the car from his aunt. Only rarely did he listen to his "aunt's station," as he called it. But at the moment he thought he needed something a little lighthearted, something easy and fun, though not elevator music.

A seven-chord introduction signaled that the Everly Brothers were about to sing. The song caught the edge of his consciousness.

I want you to tell me why you walked out on me.
I'm so lonesome everyday.
I want you to know that since you walked out on me
Nothing seems to be the same old way.
Think about the love that burns within my heart for you
The good times we had before you went away, O me
Walk right back to me this minute
Bring your love to me don't send it
I'm so lonesome everyday.

His mind told him that they hadn't had any good times. Quite simply, Laura hadn't walked out on him. There never was anything between them. But his emotions didn't get it. He had conjured up love and laughter and life together. His "Work hard—concentrate—do good" mantra failed him. At the moment, the Everly Brothers seemed to understand him far better than he did.

He listened to his emotions and sang.

LEESBURG, VIRGINIA.
April 25, 2005.

"Cooper, it's a reporter on line 3," Nancy's voice announced.

"Got it," he replied. *Reporter?* he thought. He picked up the receiver. "Cooper Stone here."

"Mr. Stone, my name is Greg Kachadourian—I'm with the *New York Times'* Washington office."

"Yes, Mr. Kachadourian," he replied smoothly, "how can I help you?"

"I am calling to ask you some questions about your hearing this Friday in the matter involving the UN Convention on the Rights of the Child. I believe you represent the Thomas and Garvis families. Is that right?"

"Well," he answered slowly. "I don't know if I should answer that. Juvenile cases are confidential, and I am not supposed to talk with the press about any cases I might be handling. How did you find out about a case in Leesburg anyway?"

"Mr. Stone, you may be aware that we don't reveal sources, but I can tell you what I know because it is nothing. I got a call from our correspondent in Geneva who asked me to help her with a story she is working on. I am not the lead on this one."

"Geneva? You mean Switzerland?"

"Yeah, right," the reporter answered.

"Oh, well, I guess it figures. UN Convention, Geneva headquarters. It makes sense, but I have to tell you I am totally surprised."

"I figured you might be surprised, Mr. Stone," he replied sardonically. "Anyway, are you willing to talk with me or not?"

"You know I can't talk with you about the children, but what else do you want to know?"

"Not much else. I am trying to get background on these families. I understand one boy is Layton Thomas, and the other is a girl, Emily Garvis. I know that much. I have their parents' names and addresses. No phone numbers, though. I was hoping you would give them to me. But I guess I can get them through directory assistance."

Cooper shook his head in amazement. "You do have good sources," he said. "Tell you what. Let me call the judge and see what he directs me to do. I don't think there is anything truly confidential about this case. No sensible person would think that there is any allegation that either the children or parents have done anything wrong. That's the purpose of the confidentiality rules. Can I call you right back?"

"Sure," Kachadourian replied, giving him the number.

Cooper pulled out his legal directory, looked up the judge's office, and hit the buttons.

"Judge Holman's chambers," an older woman's voice intoned.

"Good morning, ma'am, this is Cooper Stone with Jameson and Stone," he began.

"Yes, Mr. Stone, I know who you are. How can I help you?"

"I just got a call from the *New York Times* about the juvenile matter we have scheduled in front of Judge Holman on Friday. The reporter knows the names of the kids, the names of the parents, and the basics of the case. He seems to have gotten the information from another reporter in Geneva. I was hoping to talk to the judge to see whether I am shielded from talking to the press because it is pretty obvious that someone from the other side has leaked a lot out already."

"Oh, my," she said. "Let me check to see if the judge is available."

Cooper silently held the phone for more than a minute. "Cooper, this is Judge Holman," came a voice. "You've discovered a little leak in the confidentiality of juvenile court proceedings, I hear." The judge spoke pleasantly, in a bemused tone.

"Yes, and it appears that it sprang in Geneva, Judge," Cooper replied.

"That's what my secretary was saying." The judge cleared his throat. "Cooper, I don't know what to tell you to do. There is certainly no reason that I can see why the rules of confidentiality would apply, under the circumstances. But, I don't think I can just absolve you, especially in a phone call. It's always hard when only one side plays by the rules."

"Should I let the reporter talk to the parents?"

"On the whole, I don't see a reason why that would be a problem. Newspapers are not bound by our own rules of legal ethics, so there is no review board sitting in Richmond like there is for you and me. The only problem your clients could have is if I got angry at you for talking—and I can guarantee you that I won't, given what has already happened."

"That'll probably solve the problem, Judge," Cooper replied, ready to hang up.

"And, Cooper," the judge added, "I don't think there is an ethics panel in the world that would blink an eyelash if you simply talked about the legal issues with this treaty and so on, carefully avoiding anything about the children or their factual circumstances."

"That's more room than I really need, Your Honor. Thanks a lot."

"We Loudoun boys have got to stick together a little," Holman said warmly. "Can't help you with any rulings on the substance; you'll be just another lawyer on that level. But when our own boys start getting hit sidewise by the *New York Times* and the big out-of-town firms, we can at least get a couple licks in for ourselves."

"I appreciate it a lot, Judge."

"No problem, Cooper. See you on Friday."

We Loudoun boys. Cooper liked the sound of that when he rolled it over in his mind a time or two. He punched the number for the reporter.

WASHINGTON, D.C. April 26, 2005.

The coffee was steaming in the Yale Law School mug. The chilled cream was in its customary spot. His $58,000-a-year assistant had tended to the details immediately after receiving the call from the front desk that Randolph Suskins was on his way.

He pulled a pair of gold reading glasses out of a leather holder on the left-hand side of his massive mahogany desk. He placed the holder back into his center drawer and carefully picked up the coffee mug. The sixty-year-old lawyer started to pick up the *Washington Star* from his stack of three morning papers, but he noticed that Brenda had clipped a photocopy of an article to the *New York Times.* "From page 3," she had written on a yellow note stuck to the article. He opened the paper, preferring to read it from the original source.

"Children's rights showdown in Virginia," the headline screamed across the entire width of the page. "Test case on UN Convention brewing," the secondary header called from the left upper corner.

He stood sipping his coffee slowly as he scanned the article. He smiled with satisfaction in a moment. In the first sentence, in paragraph 2, appeared his name and affiliation: "Randolph Suskins, former White House counsel and a partner in the K Street firm of Baxter, Connolly, and Suskins, said yesterday . . ." The quote was a good one. The half-hour he had spent with the reporter honing the words for the quotation had paid off.

He continued to scan quickly until he found the first mention of his opposing counsel. "The parents' lawyer, Cooper Stone, of the Leesburg firm of Jameson and Stone said, 'The unprecedented application of a treaty to domestic family law is a dangerous invasion of both our families' rights and our right to self-government. Parents, not the UN, should be the ones who determine how children are disciplined, what they are taught about God, and where they attend school.'" *Not bad for a small-town, small-firm lawyer,* Suskins thought.

The article was far too long to complete while standing, so he sat his mug down, walked to the right side of his office opposite the bank of windows looking down on K Street's busiest intersection, and placed his custom-tailored suit jacket on the cherry wood hanger. As he did so, he noticed movement in his peripheral vision.

"Good morning, Randolph," a fortyish woman dressed in a black pantsuit announced.

He was taken aback for a moment. *Ah, that's right, she did make partner last month,* he thought. Partners and only partners were allowed to call him by his first name.

"Good morning, Melissa," he said with a smile. He walked deliberately back to his desk, dumped an additional dab of cream into his mug, and stirred it quickly with the spoon. Melissa VanLandingham sat quietly as the silver-haired leader of the firm prepared himself.

"Well, I assume you read about our case," he said, as he picked the coffee mug up once more.

"Yes, sir," she replied, falling back quickly into the patterns of speech she had learned in the seven years she had been an associate assigned to his cases. "Did you notice our opposing counsel?"

"Yes, he acquitted himself better than I expected, for one of those small-town lawyers. Stone, wasn't that the name, Melissa?" He peered back down at the article. "Cooper Stone. That's it."

"Yes," she replied. "I've checked him out."

"Law school?" Suskins asked peered over his reading glasses.

"Gonzaga University in Spokane." She pronounced it "Spoh-cain," like the lifelong East Coaster she was. "After law school he went to work for a small Spokane firm, Barron & Associates. The firm's name means nothing although the lead partner does have one U.S. Supreme Court victory to his credit."

"What was the issue?"

"Parents' rights," she replied, with a raise of her eyebrows that indicated just a hint of respect.

"How did Stone land in Virginia?"

"For six years he was deputy counsel for the Senate Foreign Relations Committee. He worked for Matt Parker, the one-term senator from Washington State."

"Yeah, Parker. What an arch-conservative. Glad he's gone. His politics were quite a nuisance," the former president's lawyer mused.

"It appears that Cooper Stone might be more experienced than we might have guessed a Leesburg lawyer to be," Melissa remarked.

"A little more, perhaps. But don't we have four former ambassadors right here?"

"Six, actually," VanLandingham replied. "And the chief counsel for the State Department during your party's administration."

"Yes, and we have all those law professors standing by for the amicus briefs. I think we can take on a small-time firm from Leesburg, even if the junior partner was once a junior counsel for a Senate committee." He was smiling, almost smirking as he spoke. "So is everything ready for Friday?"

"Yes, sir, we think we have it. Certified copies of the rulings of the committee in Geneva and the briefs have been filed with the judge. Our courier is instructed to serve Stone the briefs at the end of business tomorrow—complying with the rules, but only giving him a day to reply. And we have issued a subpoena duces tecum for the children's Sunday school teacher. She is to bring with her the lesson that Nora Stoddard heard."

"Fine, fine," he said, picking up the *Wall Street Journal*. "I will be ready to prepare for the hearing in about an hour. Have the briefs on my desk at eleven."

"They are on your credenza in their usual spot, right now," she replied as she stood to leave.

He swiveled in his chair to look at the stack next to his computer. "Oh, so they are," he said. He turned back to his desk and opened the *Journal* to the stock listings. "Very well," he said without looking up, "I'll let you know if I need anything."

LEESBURG, VIRGINIA. *April 28, 2005. 3:00 P.M.*

"Cooper, it's someone named Laura Frasier on line 1. She says it's important," Nancy's voice said over the intercom. "Do you want to take the call, or shall I take a message?"

He had told Nancy to hold all his calls for the day, after he was buried by a stack of paper from Baxter, Connolly, and Suskins at 4:45 the previous afternoon. Cooper had done computer research until after midnight on Wednesday, and the prospects for tonight looked much the same.

He had done well in driving any thoughts of Laura out of his mind. He was just lonely, that's all. It seemed like a very objective verdict and had nothing in particular to do with her. Now what? He asked himself.

"Put her through," Cooper replied.

He swiveled in his chair away from his computer. He breathed deeply, pushed his half-eaten lunch aside, and picked up the phone.

"Hi Laura, this is Cooper." He rocked back in his chair and closed his eyes.

"Oh, thank you for talking to me, Cooper. Your secretary told me that you were not taking calls today because you were preparing for court. But that's why I'm calling you."

"Oh, really?" he replied, leaning forward quickly. "What's happened?"

"I just got served with a subpoena to appear at the hearing tomorrow. Is it normal to get such short notice?" she asked.

"I sure wouldn't treat a witness that way, but this D.C. firm has been doing everything it can to manipulate the local rules to its advantage."

"You would think it was just common courtesy..." she said bitterly.

Cooper laughed softly. "You don't know too many lawyers, do you? Common courtesy isn't our profession's stock in trade."

"Well, what do I do about this?"

"You're going to have to come to court tomorrow. And I am going to have to prepare you for that. It should only take about an hour. Can you come to my office? I have to stay here and finish the brief and exhibits. There's no way I can get away."

"Sure, I can do that. I certainly don't want to go into the courtroom knowing as little as I do now about what to expect. When should I come?"

"Whenever you want. This is all I am working on, and I am going to be here until very late."

"Well, if it is OK with you, I would like to come around seven. I have plans before then."

"That'd be fine," Cooper replied. "See you at seven."

PURCELLVILLE, VIRGINIA. *April 28, 2005. 5:00 P.M.*

"Don't stir so hard, dear, you'll turn the potato salad into mashed puree," Deanna's mother directed in her soft refined drawl. Anyone else listening would have believed that the words were a quiet suggestion. Deanna grew up with her and knew better—these polite sounding words were a command.

"Leave the poor girl, alone, Beth. She's just upset about the hearing tomorrow."

Deanna breathed deeply and exhaled slowly. She appreciated her dad more than usual just then. He could be full of fire on occasion, but then again he could be extraordinarily calm in the middle of a fracas. When it came time to defend his only daughter, he was resolute steel, not an uncontrollable hothead.

"Oh, Daddy, thank you," she whispered in his ear as she went by the kitchen table where he was seated.

"When is Richard going to be home?" her mother asked, trying to change the subject.

Deanna knew that a simple answer wouldn't do because she had not been asked a simple question. "Why isn't Rick home already?" was what her mother was really asking. "He said he would be home around six. That's his usual time. Rick is going to take off all day tomorrow for the hearing. He has to finish up a few things at the office."

Beth McGranahan wasn't silenced that easily. "But shouldn't he . . ."

Her husband cleared his throat loudly and glared at his wife. She stopped midsentence and went back to chopping the ingredients for the tossed salad.

In her own way, her mother's disposition toward control and criticism actually helped Deanna gain some mental relief from her worry about the case. She was so focused on defending herself from her mother's comments that she had little time to worry about the law firm of Baxter, Connolly, and Suskins.

About ten minutes later, Deanna heard Layton and Nikki making noise in the basement. "Daddy, do you think you could go and tell the kids to get washed up for dinner? I think that by the time they get done, Rick will be home and we'll be ready to eat."

"Sure, honey," he replied. The retired banker was still in superb condition. He had walked three miles nearly every day for the past three and a half decades. He walked quickly down the steps. Deanna could hear him talking to the kids in the basement.

Her mother wasted no time speaking up. Something had been on her mind for several minutes, and she knew this was her opportunity. "You know, Deanna dear, that there are marvelous private schools in Richmond. I can understand why you wouldn't want your children attending the public schools, especially in Northern Virginia." The word *northern* sounded like a sophisticated curse word when it rolled off her lips. "But our schools in Richmond are excellent. Why can't the children attend Briarcrest like you did? You turned out just fine. And then wouldn't this whole case just go away?"

"Why don't you just go away?" Deanna almost retorted. But even at the flashpoint of annoyance, Deanna restrained herself. She knew that her mother loved her and the children, and Deanna loved her mother in return. But there were moments . . . "Mother, there are three issues in this lawsuit. Two of them have nothing to do with home schooling. You don't think we should give away our authority to spank Layton and our ability to teach him that Jesus is the only way to God, do you?"

"Of course not, dear. I just can't imagine a Virginia judge putting a stop to traditional things like that. But home schooling is different. I think that's the only thing that really puts you at risk."

Deanna stared at the orange glazed pork chops just removed from the oven. "I don't know, Mother, sometimes I just don't know." She walked away from the island and gazed out her back window toward the swing set as she washed her hands. Suddenly Rick came into view and waved at her. Deanna smiled warmly at her husband, relieved that his arrival would curtail the conversation that had gone awry.

Dinner conversation was light. Beth knew better than to take up any of the recent topics in front of the children with both Rick and her husband present. Deanna, though, began to feel a growing sense of panic as she watched her children eat and laugh and talk to their grandparents. She felt open and exposed, even with her dad and her husband right with her. It was an unfamiliar and unsettling feeling.

LEESBURG, VIRGINIA. *April 28, 2005. 7:00 P.M.*

The brief was already at forty-two pages on his word processor and there were two issues to go. *Thank heaven for computers,* Cooper thought.

He had just signed on to LexisNexis for the tenth time that day when a voice suddenly startled him.

"Hello, anybody here?" the female voice called. It came from the waiting area.

Cooper bounded from his chair and rounded the corner into the waiting area. Laura was dressed in jeans and a light blue oxford shirt with her sleeves rolled up a turn or two. Her hair was pulled back into a loose ponytail with a pale yellow ribbon. *She is really stunning,* he thought.

Immediately he was angry with himself. There were many reasons he wanted to stay off that path, not the least of which was his realization that he was facing a brawl with a major national law firm, and he needed to keep his concentration focused. "Hi, Laura. Glad you found your way in."

She nodded and smiled as the two stood and looked at each other a little uncomfortably. Cooper noticed that she was carrying a shopping bag in her left hand.

"What's in the bag?" he asked.

"I brought some dinner," she replied. "You said you had been here late last night and would be working again tonight, so I figured a home-cooked meal might be appropriate. After all, you are working to defend two of the kids in my Sunday school class."

"Wow!" he said, with a big smile. "This is a first for me. A witness comes for trial preparation with dinner! I think I might make this mandatory in the future."

Laura laughed and looked at Cooper expectantly, waiting for direction for a place to set up the meal. Shortly she spoke. "So where would you like me to set up dinner for us?"

Cooper's heart skipped. He had assumed she had just brought some dinner for him to be eaten later. "Oh, sure," he answered enthusiastically. "We can go in the conference room. It's right down the hall."

He led Laura to the vacant room, holding the door open for her. She sat the bag down on the table and pulled out an envelope.

"This is the subpoena I received at school today," she said, handing it to him.

Cooper scanned the document quickly. "This is a subpoena duces tecum, which is Latin for 'come to court and bring some stuff with you.' Not a word-for-word translation, of course. They want your Sunday school lesson notes and all other materials used in preparation for this class. I assume that these are the same notes you gave me the other night."

"Well, there are two other things I used. I also used the teacher's manual of my Sunday school curriculum and my Bible."

"Do you have your manual with you? I think your Bible is probably the same as mine."

Laura smiled and pulled the teacher's manual out of the shopping bag. "This is it. Pretty normal material. I don't know what it has to do with a lawsuit."

Laura began putting dinner on the table as Cooper flipped open the book to the place she had marked with a yellow Post-it note.

"This is truly a bizarre case, Laura. What they are claiming is that these parents—and you, by implication—are violating these children's rights to freedom of religion, which is guaranteed by the UN Convention on the Rights of the Child."

"How can teaching them about Jesus be a violation of their rights of religious freedom?" she asked incredulously.

"Good question, and one I'd like to ask too. But here is their theory. They are arguing that children have the right to believe any religion they want to. If their parents systematically indoctrinate them in one religion and tell them that all other religions are false, then this violates their rights to form their own beliefs. They think it is fine to teach about Jesus, as long as we just say that he is one way to God. Or, perhaps they would think it OK if we just left the other religions alone. Do you remember reading about how some members of the Clinton administration criticized the Southern Baptist Convention for trying to evangelize Buddhists? They claimed that this was unacceptable intolerance. It's the same assertion that we are facing in this case. We are being called intolerant and are being accused of forcing this intolerance on little children."

"I get cold chills when I hear you say that. And I feel a little guilty, too," she replied.

"Guilty?" he asked. "Why?"

"I forgot to vote in the last election. Just got too busy. And look what has happened."

Cooper wanted to say something comforting to her, but nothing occurred to him quickly. "Well, that dinner sure looks good," he said, changing the subject.

Laura had arranged two plates of oven-baked chicken, wild rice, and a tossed salad attractively with silverware and napkins. "I forgot to bring anything to drink," she said sheepishly.

"Drinks we have," Cooper replied, with a flourish. "We have bottled water or pop—I mean sodas, as people call them around here. There's Coke and Diet Coke, I think."

"I guess I would like a Diet Coke," she replied.

"Two Diet Cokes coming right up." He left the room and headed down the hall to his left.

Less than a minute later he was back with two cans and two tall plastic glasses full of ice.

"All right, I guess we can begin," he said, sitting down across from where Laura had seated herself while he was out of the room. "Can I pray for us?"

She nodded and smiled. Cooper prayed for the dinner and then for the case. Laura saw that he was deeply concerned about the upcoming hearing, and she felt a spiritual depth in his prayer that she hadn't yet seen in him.

After he prayed, they engaged in light personal conversation for a few minutes. Laura asked him how he had come to move to Virginia from way out west, where they call Cokes "pop." They told each other about their college backgrounds and then began to exchange stories of how they had each come to accept Christ as Savior. Laura told Cooper that she had become a Christian at the age of seven, while Cooper had become a Christian during his junior year in high school.

Cooper was enjoying the personal conversation immensely, but he had a growing sense of urgency about needing to get back to his trial preparation. He gently guided the conversation to the subject of the hearing and told her what to expect, and how to handle the examination that was likely to come from the other side.

As it became obvious that they were done with that subject, Laura asked Cooper how late he expected to be working on the case.

"I guess until midnight," he replied. "I have to finish my brief and then make copies of it along with several exhibits I have already prepared."

"There's nothing I can do to help you with the brief, but I do know how to run a copy machine. Is there anything I can do now for you to save you some work later on?" she asked.

Laura's helpfulness was a little too much for Cooper to understand. There hadn't been a hint of flirtation in her demeanor, but she was so warm and friendly. "That would be great," he replied. "You don't have to do it, but if you want to, it really would be helpful."

"I'd like to help," she said, lowering her eyes. "Maybe it would relieve a little of my guilt for not voting last time. Like I'm trying to help set things right."

Cooper laughed softly. "Come on," he said, beckoning her in the direction of his office. "Let me get you started."

She was there running the copying machine and collating until nearly ten. She handed Cooper the stack of papers, and he thanked her for dinner and the help. She slipped out into the warm spring night with a quick good-bye and no fanfare.

Cooper turned to his computer, resolving to interpret the events of the evening later, after the hearing tomorrow.

PURCELLVILLE, VIRGINIA. *April 29, 2005. 2:00 A.M.*

The Thomas-McGranahan family shared an extended time of prayer before the children were put to bed, and it seemed to calm everyone, even Deanna. But around two in the morning, Rick noticed that the place beside him in the bed was empty. Groggy with sleepiness, he lumbered down the big oak staircase to find his wife sitting sideways on the love seat just off the hallway in the family room. The room was dark. Deanna, dressed in the long

T-shirt she wore for a nightgown, sat stiffly with her arms wrapped around her bent knees.

Rick leaned over and picked her up in one swoop, and sat back down with her in his lap. Deanna's ball-like position had not changed. Her hands were still clutched tightly over her knees.

"I'm sorry you have to go through this, sweetie," He squeezed her and moved her around a bit, hoping to cause her to let go of her knees. "Is there anything I can do for you right now?"

She said nothing but shrugged her shoulders almost imperceptibly. They sat in that position for nearly twenty minutes, without speaking or moving. Finally, Rick noticed his wife's head bobbing softly. He stood with her still in his arms. Her hands had finally released from her knees and snuggled against him quietly as he carried her upstairs. He placed her gently back into the bed and covered her with the quilt and comforter.

Finally he heard her breathing in a slow rhythm, and that gave him the emotional go-ahead to roll onto his side and try to go back to sleep.

CHAPTER 7

LEESBURG, VIRGINIA.
April 29, 2005.

A uniformed deputy sheriff scoured the courtroom once more with his eyes. There were just too many people for a closed-door juvenile matter. He had quizzed both lead attorneys closely, and everyone was accounted for. But with all the media crawling around the plaza in front of the historic Loudoun County Courthouse, he was deeply suspicious that an infiltrator had somehow slipped through.

Reluctantly, he gave a nod to the judge's secretary. He could see her down the short hall to the rear of the courtroom. She nodded back. Those who knew to listen heard a short rap on the door that led from the courtroom into the judge's chambers.

"All rise!" the deputy cried, just a little louder than normal. "The Circuit Court for the Commonwealth of Virginia in and for Loudoun County is now in session. All having business before this honorable court, please draw near. The court is now in session!"

"Be seated," the balding judge announced. He paused and looked around the courtroom, taking his own survey of the nearly twenty people arrayed around the room.

"All right, Counsel," the judge said. "Let's have your appearances for the record."

Cooper, seated at the table to the judge's right, stood first. "Cooper Stone of Jameson and Stone appearing for the parents, Your Honor."

"I assume that the fine looking couples seated with you are the . . ." the judge began. He fumbled through some papers for a moment and then continued, "are the Thomases and the Garvises."

"That's right, Judge," Cooper replied. "The Thomases are closest to me, and the Garvises are to their right."

"Thank you," he replied, making some notes. Judge Holman looked up over his reading glasses at the man and woman standing patiently at the counsel table on his left. "And Miss Hennessey, why don't you go next?"

"Good morning, Your Honor," the young Leesburg attorney announced. "Rachel Hennessey, appearing as guardian ad litem for Layton Thomas and Emily Garvis."

"Thank you, Miss Hennessey."

The judge shifted his gaze from the young woman who appeared regularly in his court. Holman nodded and smiled politely at the man about his own age who stood silently next to her. "And you, sir, we have not had the privilege of meeting previously."

"Good morning, Your Honor," the lawyer brushed back some disobedient strands of his brilliant silver hair, which was a bit on the long side. His deep blue suit hung perfectly on his trim physique in a manner that strongly suggested a custom tailor. "If it pleases the court, I am Randolph Suskins of Baxter, Connolly and Suskins, appearing for the petitioners, Children's Defense Fund and the National Education Association."

"Welcome to Loudoun County, Mr. Suskins," the judge replied. "Please be seated."

Holman quizzed each of the lawyers about the unusual number of people in attendance for a juvenile case. Suskins had brought two other lawyers, a paralegal, three representatives from the Children's Defense Fund, and two from the National Education Association. Nora Stoddard was also present as a potential witness. Apparently satisfied, the judge paused, looking down at his notes.

Suskins stood after a few seconds of silence. "Your Honor, it would be our intention to call—"

"Mr. Suskins, why don't you take your seat for a moment?" the judge interrupted. "I have some preliminary matters to cover that may change the order of things that you had in mind for this hearing in *my* courtroom." His tone was pleasant, but Holman stared at Suskins with raised eyebrows and an ever-so-slight-smile that gave a clear message as to who was in charge.

Suskins nodded deferentially. His silent return to his seat assured the judge that the two had reached a quick meeting of the minds.

"All right, there are several things to cover initially. First, we have written requests from several media organizations, some of whom are represented by counsel, to be admitted to these proceedings. Now as you know, juvenile matters are normally closed to the press and public. But I certainly can understand why the press is interested in this most unusual juvenile proceeding. There is no doubt that this case has national implications. Can I have the thoughts of counsel on this issue? Mr. Stone, why don't you go first?"

Cooper fastened the middle button of his gray suit jacket as he rose to his feet. "Your Honor, my clients have no objection to the admission of the media. As you know, certain representatives from the government and these petitioning organizations began talking to the press about this case some time ago. And it is our view that this kind of leakage is not likely to end. We would rather have the media see the case firsthand than hear about it only through leaks and press releases."

Holman nodded slowly. "Mr. Stone, can you tell me whether or not you predict any sensitive material about these children being released in the course of these proceedings? They are my first duty, and I intend to prohibit the release of any information about these children that may embarrass them or harm them in any way."

"No, Your Honor," Cooper said, turning to look at Layton and Emily. "We know of nothing embarrassing at all that has been alleged. In fact, we don't even know any wrongdoing or harm that has been alleged, much less that will be proven. The only allegations that exist in this case are that these families have taught their children traditional Christian doctrine, that they have disciplined their children in a manner that has been not only legally accepted for all of our nation's history, but has been deemed good parenting ever since the Book of Proverbs was written, and that the Thomas family has chosen to teach their son in the same manner as chosen by the first governor of this Commonwealth, Patrick Henry. The only embarrassing thing is that our national government thinks that there is something wrong with this kind of parenting."

Judge Holman smiled wryly at Cooper. "Well, Mr. Stone, you have managed to argue your case pretty thoroughly on an introductory manner. I see that your uncle's proclivities have been passed down to you. Tell him that you did a little better today than he has done in the past few years. In any event, Mr. Stone, I will accept that as a 'no objection' to the request for admission by the media."

"Mr. Suskins?" the judge asked, swiveling his chair to his left to face the silver-haired attorney.

"Let me say first, Your Honor, that we strongly disagree with Mr. Stone's characterizations of this case as failing to allege any wrongdoing. We believe that the treaty in question has caused our nation to become committed to what is best for children and any deviation from that standard in fact causes—"

"Mr. Suskins," Holman interrupted. "You don't need to argue the merits just because our young Mr. Stone has done so. You and I have been around the block a couple of times, it would appear, and so I will just assume that you are a very competent lawyer and that you can give a good substantive answer for little speeches like the one Mr. Stone just gave—although I will say as a speech it wasn't that bad."

The deputy buried his mouth in his hand to keep from laughing aloud as he watched from his bailiff's perch.

"Why don't you just tell me your position on the media being admitted?" the judge continued.

"All right, Your Honor," Suskins replied, with a nod. "We support the request to open the door to the media. We are, of course, sensitive to the needs of the children in this matter—after all that is the essence of our petition—but we believe that there is a distinction between the facts and issues in this case and the normal juvenile matters. The allegations here are not viewed as the kind that our society looks at as moral failures. We are not alleging sexual abuse or starvation or some other act that our society views as heinous behavior. And we are not suggesting that these parents have done anything that deserves a loss of custody of their children. The failures that we allege are in a sense a failure of our society. We have no reason to believe that these parents will fail to comply with our new national standards once this court makes it clear that they must do so. In fact, we believe it would serve the public interest to open up this case so that all families would learn what their responsibility is under the treaty."

The judge took off his small, gold wire-rim glasses and cleaned them with a cloth he pulled from a side drawer. "Miss Hennessey, what do you have to say on this point?"

The young redhead stood as tall as her five-foot-three frame permitted. "Judge Holman, I have to disagree with both counsel for the parties. As the children's representative, I have only one interest, and it is these two children. However fascinating this case may be to the public at large, officially I am only allowed to care about them. Therefore, no matter how much this case will focus on legal issues, there will be some facts presented about the lives of Emily and Layton. And there is some potential that some of these facts will be embarrassing in some context. For example, one of the issues in this case is about spanking. If we get into details of how and why these two children are spanked, and they come out in the press, then their friends could read such reports. And I think we all know how children treat each other about such things. I can just imagine Emily on the playground hearing a group of boys teasing her about being spanked and maybe even threatening to do the same thing to her. So, Judge, I would have to oppose the motion."

"Thank you, Miss Hennessey," Holman said, resting his forearms on the edge of the bench while dangling his gold pen loosely in his right hand. "Well, Counsel, despite my strong instincts as a judge to keep juvenile matters closed, I am going to grant the request. But Miss Hennessey has convinced me to add one proviso. Any media outlet that chooses to come into my courtroom will do so with the understanding that the entire news organization is barred from approaching or interviewing these two children. Moreover, they will be barred from discussing any matter that I find to be embarrassing. If I thought that there was any likelihood that very much of that sort of testimony would be coming out during the hearings of this matter, I would keep them out altogether. But I will liberally grant any request to embargo any factual answer that reveals some potentially harmful or personal information about the children. Miss Hennessey, I will depend on you to help me keep track of this and to advise the media of matters off limits.

"I think the sheer barrage of questioning that is likely to come from the media could cause harm to even the best kids in the world—and these two may well be such kids. So no press questions of Emily and Layton. Those press organizations that agree to abide by this proviso will be admitted. This is probably the only juvenile case in my life where I will admit the media."

Judge Holman surveyed the counsel table for signs of objection. Seeing none, he nodded. "All right, we will be in recess for ten minutes while the herd that's outside pours inside." The deputy sprang to his feet and directed all present to rise, as the judge quickly disappeared through the door behind him.

It took less than five minutes for the steps, sidewalks, and grassy areas outside the venerable brick and columned structure to be free of all reporters, save the television cameramen who remained barred from the courtroom. The courtroom was not quite full. The capacity of the high-ceilinged chamber was about one hundred in the spectator rows; perhaps fifteen more could have crammed into the vacant spaces. The print journalists got quickly busy scribbling phrases like "brown hardwood benches grooved with the marks of more than a century of justice-seekers," "arched colonial windows rising for two full stories," and other descriptions of the courtroom to give their articles that extra verbal edge.

Whenever the undercurrent of conversation began to grow a little loud, the deputy rose from his position on the left-hand side of the courtroom and walked slowly, hand on his gun, to the court reporter and whispered only a word or two as he glared at the audience. If he could have ruled instead of the judge, there wouldn't be any reporters in *his* courtroom, that's for sure, he told the stenographer.

The judge gave his short rap on the door, and the deputy called the room back to order as Holman briskly climbed the two steps to his bench. "You may be seated," the judge said, as he picked his reading glasses up and put them on.

"Now I know that while you were still outside my bailiff advised all of you from the media of the rules for admission, but I want to make sure that I have done so on the record. You are advised that you are to leave these children alone. No requests for interviews. No shouted questions as they are coming or going from the courthouse. No questions in writing. Period. Leave them alone. And if the parents or other parties tell you they don't want to talk, you are to take them at their word. I am holding each of you individually responsible to ensure that your paper or radio station or whatever outlet you represent follows this understanding. My bailiff has the business cards you gave him as you entered. We *will* contact you immediately if we are informed of any violation of these understandings."

Judge Holman searched the room with his eyes. "OK, your continued presence from this point is an indication that you agree to these conditions. All right, Counsel, we need to move to the second preliminary matter on my agenda this morning. Mr. Suskins, let me speak with you for a second."

A bit bewildered, Suskins rose, flicking back the longish strands of silver hair that continually bedeviled his forehead. "Yes, Your Honor," he replied, as if he had fully anticipated this exchange.

"Mr. Suskins," Holman said, holding up a three-inch stack of legal papers, "when did you file this document that is euphemistically called a brief?"

"I believe we filed them on the day indicated by the local rules, Your Honor. That would have been earlier this week."

"Mr. Suskins, the local rules of this juvenile court indicate a *deadline* for filing," Holman said, rocking back while lacing his fingers together and placing his hands behind his head. "There is no rule that prohibits you from filing these papers at the last possible minute. However, there is a bit of difference between your submission and the typical brief we get in this court in a juvenile case. We may get five pages on some issue of criminal law. And, sometimes we get six or seven pages on some issue of juvenile procedure. But most of the contested cases in this division are a dispute on the facts, not about the law, and there is little need for lengthy briefing.

"Now, Mr. Stone has responded in record time with his brief. I am not about to try to digest three inches of text from you and an inch and a half from Mr. Stone in the time that your late filing necessitates. I am simply not prepared to take testimony, nor am I prepared to make any ruling today because I need more time to digest these briefs. And if you ever, and I mean ever, make another last minute filing of this magnitude in this case or any other, I will hold you in contempt of court!"

He stopped. His face was starting to turn red. "Do I make myself clear, Mr. Suskins?"

"Yes, Your Honor, and we apologize for any inconvenience."

"Save your apology, Counsel. I am entering an order today that adds ten days to any submission that is longer than seven pages. So if the normal rule would require you to file five days ahead, then you will file it and serve it on opposing counsel fifteen days ahead, instead. And this cuts both ways. Mr. Stone, you understand that?"

"Yes, Your Honor," Cooper replied, managing to rise a couple inches out of his chair before sitting right back down.

Suskins stood silently while the judge just glared at him for a moment or two longer. Finally, he, too, sat back down.

Judge Holman leaned back in his chair and closed his eyes as if he were gathering his concentration. With eyes still closed, he spoke again. "All right," he said, rocking back and forth in his chair. "OK, Mr. Suskins, I think I know where I want to go next."

Suskins slowly resumed his position on his feet. "Yes, Your Honor."

"I want you to outline for me your theory of the case. There is so much for me to read, I frankly haven't been able to focus on the papers enough yet to have a succinct list of issues. And I have to tell you that I think that this case raises extraordinarily dangerous legal theories. But I understand my responsibilities to both the plaintiff and defense. I will follow the law even if I don't like the law.

"So, in order for me to get a grasp on the nature and scope of the issues," the judge continued, "I have three questions I want to ask you, one at a time. First, why do you think that the National Education Association and the Children's Defense Fund have legal standing to bring this lawsuit?"

Suskins bounced on his toes ever so slightly as the judge was speaking. Finally they were getting to matters for which he had prepared. He brushed back his hair off his forehead once again as he began to answer.

"Your Honor, if I can direct your attention to tab A in the appendix to our brief. It is the text of the UN Convention on the Rights of the Child that our Senate ratified just this past January. The provision that answers your question about standing for these two organizations is found in Article 45, on page 21 of the appendix." He paused, waiting for the judge to finish flipping pages.

"As you can see from this section, NGOs—that is non-governmental organizations that have been officially sanctioned by the United Nations—are given the authority to assist the UN in the implementation of this treaty. This provision is, of course, part of the document that has been ratified by our nation, and thus, under the U.S. Constitution's Supremacy Clause, the UN Convention on the Rights of the Child is now part of the highest law of the land. We recognize that this is a change from the standard procedures in our nation's courts, but that is what a treaty does—it changes and overrides the prior law of our nation.

"I know that normally only the government has the authority to enforce laws such as this. And we do not mean to suggest that the treaty allows purely private people to ignore the rules of standing and to file lawsuits against parents they don't like. But, the essence of our standing is that the Children's Defense Fund and the National Education Association stand cloaked with the authority of the United Nations itself and, in fact, are limited international government agencies for the purpose of enforcing this treaty."

Suskins waited silently for a reaction from Holman, but the judge just continued to read the text of the treaty.

Finally the judge spoke. "Where is the documentation—I'm sure it is here somewhere—that your two groups are in fact UN-sanctioned NGOs?"

The young woman on his right, Melissa VanLandingham, opened the appendix to the correct page and handed it to Suskins.

"That would be on page 3 of tab D, Your Honor," Suskins replied.

Holman flipped to the page, leaned forward in his chair, and wrote a stream of notes on the yellow pad in front of him. He leaned back in his chair when he finished and then rocked for a couple of moments. "I don't mind telling you, Mr. Suskins," he said, "that your whole theory troubles me. I am not saying that I am going to find against you on this or any point, but it troubles me deeply that the treaty seems to give this kind of authority to private organizations."

Suskins unconsciously flipped his strands of hair back once again. "Well, Your Honor, that was one of the issues debated before the Senate. It is a policy decision that had to be made, and it was settled in our favor by the ratification vote."

Cooper rose to his feet and waited to be recognized by the judge, who was looking at the text of the treaty once again. Realizing that Judge Holman did not see him, he spoke without being recognized. "Your Honor, we strongly dispute their standing to bring this lawsuit. Our argument on this issue is covered in section 2 of our brief, beginning on page 12. I am prepared to address this matter if the court desires."

"No, Mr. Stone, that won't be necessary. I am not planning to rule on the matter today, and I guarantee you that I will carefully read everything that all parties have filed in this case." He paused and pulled his glasses off his face, and began to wipe the lenses with the edge of his robe. "For now, I am just trying to get a sense of whether this claim is even plausible. Under all existing statutes, I would be prepared to throw this case out right now, with no need for any more inquiry. Private parties simply cannot file cases of this kind. End of discussion. But from the information Mr. Suskins has given me, it appears that he has a plausible argument that I need to review carefully. And I guess that is really as far as I need to go today."

"Fine, Your Honor," Cooper replied, sitting down.

Deanna clutched her husband's hand tightly as the judge concluded his remarks. Any chance for an easy out was apparently gone. Rick heard a muffled sigh from Jeanne Garvis to his right.

The judge's comments were not lost on the contingent of reporters who scribbled furiously to recapture the last exchange in writing.

"OK, Mr. Suskins, let's continue our little colloquy," Holman said, focusing his gaze on the silver-haired lawyer once again.

"Fine, Your Honor." From his inflection, it was clear that Suskins was regaining his confidence from the earlier tongue-lashing.

"Tell me very briefly how these families have violated their children's rights under this UN treaty."

"Yes, Your Honor, there are three basic ways we have alleged in our complaint and have supported in our brief and exhibits. First, both families practice corporal punishment. Spanking, if you will, Your Honor. This practice is unquestionably banned by Article 19 of the Convention. Second, the Thomas family home schools their son, Layton. In the same vein, the Garvises have removed their daughter, Emily, from the school's Family Life Education program. Taking a child out of official government-mandated educational programs can be done but not until the child's rights and wishes have been appropriately reviewed to see if such decisions are in the best interest of the child."

"Reviewed by whom?"

"Ultimately, by the courts. Initially, however, such review can take place by any party who has standing under the treaty. The National Commission on Children, a state department of social services, the public schools, or an NGO authorized to help with the enforcement of this treaty."

"So who did the review in this case?"

Suskins turned and gestured toward the first row behind the bar. "Nora Stoddard, the director of the National Commission on Children, personally conducted the review in this case by doing a home visit with the Thomas family."

"And I take it that she found the instruction to be inadequate?" Holman asked.

"Yes, Your Honor, we have filed an affidavit from Ms. Stoddard giving you the details. But the sum of it is this: While these people are well-intentioned, they are depriving their son, Layton, with the opportunity to receive instruction in a fashion that promotes both his social and academic well-being. The isolation of home schooling denies him proper socialization."

"Does that mean that the National Commission views all home schooling as contrary to the treaty?"

"Not necessarily, Your Honor. At least not in 100 percent of the cases. But, it would be a fair summary of our position to state that there is a strong presumption that home schooling is lacking at least in appropriate socialization. It may often also lack proper academic breadth. Here, for example, there is no evidence that the family is providing anything that comes close to matching the family life education program that is required by the state for public schools."

"But parents have the right to remove their children from the family life education program as a matter of state law. This is exactly what the Garvises have done with Emily," the judge countered.

"While that is true, Your Honor, the UN treaty now trumps all state laws. It trumps both state law and home schooling laws. It overrides opt out laws like the one for the sex education courses in Virginia. The treaty is just like the U.S. Constitution. It is supreme over all state law," Suskins replied.

"All right, Mr. Suskins, I think I understand your claim. You can move on to your third and final area of claimed violation."

"The third issue, Your Honor, comes from the religious instruction given by these parents to their children through their church."

Holman leaned so far forward in his chair it looked like he was going to leap over the bench and grab Suskins. "What is wrong with what they teach at church?" His voice was hot.

"I appreciate the concern that is apparent, Your Honor. Let me make what we believe is a very important distinction. Churches and parents can teach their children anything they want about their own religion. We have no quarrel with that at all. The problem is what they teach about other religions. Miss Stoddard attended the children's Sunday school class and found it is teaching these children to despise other religions and to deny them equal standing in the minds of these children. Children who are trained to hate other religions are denied their right to develop the kind of tolerance that is essential if we are going to live in peace throughout the world."

"So they teach kids to *hate* other religions? How so?" Holman asked.

"They teach the children that the other religions are false and the people who follow them are condemned to hell if they do not convert to their brand of Christianity. These are words of hate, even though they are cloaked in other motives. It is very likely that the Sunday school teacher has what she believes are good motives, but the words have the effect of teaching intolerance, nonetheless."

"I just can't believe it," Holman replied.

"Your Honor, we have an affidavit setting this out very properly, and I think if you review the affidavit filed by Mr. Stone from the Sunday school teacher, you will see that there isn't any real denial of our factual recitation on these items. I think you will find the proof in the record to back up everything I have said."

"You misunderstand me, Mr. Suskins." Holman spoke quietly and with an expression of grim determination. "I am not questioning your factual recitation. You strike me as a careful lawyer who would not exaggerate beyond the record. What I meant is that I can't believe that the U.S. Senate would ratify a treaty that puts such an issue before my court. You are asking for judicial review of a Sunday school lesson in a court of the Commonwealth of Virginia—the state of Patrick Henry and Thomas Jefferson and James Madison. These men were champions of religious liberty, as I am sure you know, Mr. Suskins."

"Yes, Your Honor, and we see no inconsistency with children's rights, the review we ask for in this case, and true religious liberty. We want all religions to be equally tolerated by all. What greater principle of religious liberty is there than that, Your Honor?"

"Oh, Mr. Suskins, if I were a senator and you were my colleague on the Senate floor I would answer your question with gladness. But I am a judge who has taken an oath to follow the law, even the parts I do not like. And I do not like being asked to review a Sunday school lesson. But if the law of this nation requires me to do it, I will do my duty. You can rest easy on that account."

"I see, Your Honor," Suskins replied quietly.

"Well, Counsel, here is my intention. We will reconvene this hearing in thirty days. I will allow each side to take up to four depositions of not more than a half-day each in the next three weeks. You should expect to come here for a full evidentiary hearing on that date. If I think any portions can be resolved on the briefs and affidavits before that time, I will let you know in writing well in advance. Any questions, Counsel?"

"No, Your Honor," three voices chimed at once.

"Fine, the court will be in recess."

The gavel hammered down hard.

WASHINGTON, D.C.
May 16, 2005. 9:00 A.M.

The tall mahogany doors swung open slowly. *Solid construction—no hollow-core here,* Cooper thought. "Baxter, Connolly and Suskins" was emblazed in gold leaf on the frosted glass wall that ran for thirty-five feet to the right of the reception desk. A variety of leather seating choices was strategically placed throughout the ample waiting area.

"Good morning, sir, may I help you?"

Cooper had seen blond receptionists before. And he had seen perfect smiles before. But being greeted by a smiling, blond receptionist who just happened to be male was a new experience.

"I'm Cooper Stone—here for some depositions with Mr. Suskins," he answered.

"Oh yes, Mr. Stone. You are a little early," the young man with the smile said. "You'll be in conference room 4, just down this hall to your left. You'll find some coffee and light snacks there if you want to go ahead."

As he walked down the hall, Cooper began to doubt his decision to come alone to the depositions. He felt alone and ill at ease in the posh surroundings. He set his large litigation briefcase under the wall of windows that looked out onto Dupont Circle. He placed his notebook, legal pad, and pen in position on the massive wooden table, which gave the glow of a professionally administered shine. Coffee was next.

As he stirred in some flavored cream, he heard the door open, and he expected to be greeted by Suskins' secretary or one of the younger associates from the firm. But a half-dozen people streamed through the door in crisp precision, taking their places around the table with smiles and silence all around. Cooper scanned each face, hoping for at least one face he recognized. Not one. One had a court reporter's transcription machine and a notebook.

"Did I get the wrong conference?" Cooper began, just as the door opened again, revealing Suskins and two women.

"Good morning, Mr. Stone," Suskins said, with a courteous smile and an extended hand.

Cooper recognized one of the two women with Suskins as Melissa VanLandingham, who had sat with the senior lawyer at counsel table in their first hearing. The attractive brunette in a formfitting, pale blue business suit on Suskins' left was new to him.

"Hello, Mr. Suskins," Cooper replied.

"Please be seated, and let's begin," Suskins replied.

"Is our witness here?" Cooper asked. "I am sorry, but I don't know who is in the room, and I haven't met Ambassador Easler before."

"I'm Jody Easler," the woman in the blue suit said, with a warm smile and a nod from the other side of the table.

"Madam Ambassador," Cooper replied, nodding in reply and bowing slightly.

"Well, shall we begin?" Suskins asked again.

Cooper took his seat, realizing that Suskins had no intentions of engaging in any preliminary small talk, nor of making any introductions of the other three women and two men seated around the table.

"Fine," the young lawyer answered. He turned to the court reporter on his left. "Can you swear in Ambassador Easler as the witness, please?"

When that was done, with an oath that omitted any reference to God, the reporter nodded silently at Cooper.

"Please state your name and position for the record," he began.

"Jody Easler. Dr. Jody Easler, I guess I should add, since this seems relatively formal. I am the United States ambassador to the United Nations delegation in Geneva."

"Thank you, Ambassador Easler." He paused a moment, looking first at his notes and then back at the people seated around the room.

"Madam Ambassador, my first question is this: Who are all the people with you here in the room? Since no one has introduced them to me, I ask you who is who for the record."

Suskins rolled his eyes and flipped his silver hair with his left hand for the first, but certainly not the last, time that morning. "Well, Mr. Stone, perhaps I should help you out with this. In addition to myself and Ms. VanLandingham, whom I believe you have met, we have five of our associates who are working on the case with us. I am sure that you will find this all in order."

"Not a problem with me," Cooper replied. Suskins' brusque attitude caused him to replace some of his uncertainty with a flash of annoyance that tended to clear his head a bit. "Let's just get their names for the record. I don't want to have to guess which of your two hundred associates they might be."

Suskins gave Cooper a look of disdain. "All right, Mr. Stone. But let's move quickly after this. I have a pressing schedule, and I do not intend to turn this deposition into a social occasion. We will get along just fine if you ask pertinent questions with all deliberate speed. But because you seem intent on knowing the names of our associates, well, now, Melissa, why don't you tell Mr. Stone which associates are here this morning?"

Cooper noticed a slight reddening of embarrassment on the cheeks of one of the young female lawyers on Suskins' right. He suspected that the senior partner didn't know their names well enough to introduce them.

"Starting on my right, Mr. Stone," she began, "is Nicholas Drake, then Sarah Henderson, and Tracy Thornton. On my left are Mason Higgins and Christina Cooke."

"Thank you," Cooper replied. He studied the outline of questions in the notebook in front of him for only a few seconds, collected his thoughts, and launched into his planned examination. An hour and twenty minutes later he was done. He had anticipated three hours. But Easler's words were like her hair—professionally arranged and not a single one out of place. Suskins had prepared her well.

"Perhaps a ten-minute break before we proceed with Ms. Stoddard," Suskins announced. It was obvious to Cooper that

Suskins was accustomed to controlling every aspect of depositional procedures.

The deposition of Nora Stoddard went almost as smoothly as Jody Easler's. Stoddard had also been well coached, but her personal ability to deliver smooth sounding answers was not quite as good as the higher ranking witness who had preceded her.

Before he knew it, he was done and had been escorted to the elevator by one of the silent associates who had done nothing but scribble notes at a furious pace the entire morning. Nick Higgins or Mason Drake or Drake Higgins or . . . Cooper struggled in vain to try to remember the man's name.

Cooper looked at his watch as he exited the building. Foot traffic was a little light for the middle of the lunch hour, he thought. He was surprised when his watch informed him that it was only 11:45.

He found himself mentally replaying the morning's testimony. He was the only one who had been asking questions. Suskins had rarely objected. But the witnesses seemed to have been prepared on how to answer every single specific question with such aplomb that he felt that it had been Suskins who had actually controlled the depositions.

Perhaps one of his buddies on the Senate staff would like to go to lunch. Cooper pulled out his cell phone and struck pay dirt on the first try. He quickly hailed a taxi. It would be easier to come back for his car in the garage here than try to find a parking spot near the Capitol. He didn't miss his Senate job that much, but there were times when he wished he was back on the Hill if only for that garage pass.

Back upstairs, Dr. Jody Easler and Nora Stoddard waited patiently in Melissa VanLandingham's office while the two lead lawyers gave instructions to the five associates. That done, the female partner rejoined her clients for a quick debriefing.

"You both did very well," the attorney said with a knowing smile. "So well, one would think that you had been given the questions in advance."

Nora looked nervously at Dr. Easler and then back at her.

"Rest easy, Ms. Stoddard," Melissa replied. "No one knows."

"Too bad Mr. Stone is on the other side," Dr. Easler intervened. "I kind of like the way he looks and conducts himself."

"Well, I'll leave that observation alone," the lawyer replied. "But I do agree that he was well prepared and ad-libbed quite professionally from his script on a few occasions. He is not a bad lawyer for a small-town, small-office practitioner."

"Yes, I think we need to keep an even closer eye on Mr. Stone," Jody Easler said, with a soft laugh.

PURCELLVILLE, VIRGINIA. *May 15, 2005. 7:00 P.M.*

The Garvises and Deanna were talking quietly in the living room. Rick Thomas watched from his covered front porch as the fourth and final car, Cooper's old Buick, dodged potholes on the gravel driveway before parking next to the house.

Cooper got out of the car and walked slowly toward Rick. He started to greet his host in good-buddy racquetball banter, but lightheartedness seemed inappropriate. The look on Rick's face told him he was right to refrain. He smiled weakly at his friend, the embattled father, and said nothing.

"So how did their depositions go this morning?" Rick asked. Even though he was talking to Cooper, Rick looked ahead, in the direction of the Blue Ridge Mountains. His hands gripped the front porch railing.

"They were OK," Cooper replied, "but the other side was extraordinarily well coached."

Cooper waited for Rick to either speak again or invite him inside. But his friend appeared lost in thought. Almost a minute of uncomfortable silence went by before Rick spoke.

"Just tell me one thing before we go inside, Cooper. And I want the truth."

"Sure, Rick," he replied softly.

"Are we in over our heads?"

"Do you mean me or you?" the young lawyer replied, sighing after he answered.

"Oh, I don't know. I guess I mean both of us. Can you handle this guy Suskins and can I afford to fight this?"

"I think so, Rick, and I don't know—in that order."

Rick didn't say anything for several minutes. "Cooper, I have to tell you that I'm afraid."

"Which part scares you?"

"Afraid for my son, that's first. And, yeah, I'm worried about the money. And I'm afraid—I don't know how to say it—I guess I'm afraid for our country. It seems we are about to lose everything that's important, and my family is at the center of it. I feel both hopeless and responsible if anything goes wrong," Rick replied.

Cooper walked over and put his arm companionably around his friend's shoulder. "Me, too," he agreed. "But there is one thing I think I can assure you of. You are not going to lose custody of your son. That is not even a remote possibility."

"Yeah, maybe," Rick replied, shuffling away from Cooper's arm. "Layton may be allowed to live here, but that woman Stoddard will be his real parent. I won't have any meaningful say anymore."

"Let's go inside, Rick," Cooper replied. "I think we need to have this talk with everyone. I want you all to be just as prepared as the duo I faced today."

"I don't want Deanna to hear how I am feeling," Rick answered quickly. "I have to be strong in front of her. She is so afraid and angry that she is about to lose any semblance of rational control. So please don't go anywhere with these comments from me. If others raise their own fears, so be it. But I am going to pretend not to be bothered. I just wanted you to know that, in reality, I am scared to death. OK?"

Cooper breathed deeply. "Sure," he nodded. "Let's go in and get started preparing you for tomorrow's depositions. OK?"

Three hours later, a very tired Cooper stood alone on the porch. The headlights from the Garvises' car could still be seen as the car headed down the gravel road back toward the village of Lincoln. The private conversation with Doug and Jeanne about the costs of the case had gone reasonably well. The front door opened and closed, and he expected next to hear Rick's greeting, as he came outside to discuss finances.

"Cooper?" He turned quickly around to see Laura facing him on the darkened porch.

"Yes, Laura," he replied, feeling suddenly energetic again.

"I just want to tell you that I really admire what you are doing for these families," she said softly.

"Thanks," Cooper whispered, as he stood quietly in the warm country evening.

Laura looked down at her feet and back up at Cooper. He was still gazing at her, yet had not said a word. "Well, that's all I had to say," she faltered, "just that, and thank you for helping them."

Cooper hesitated as he searched for the words to prevent another lapse into awkward silence. "That's just what lawyers do."

"I don't know that much about lawyers, but I doubt that many of them have been with their clients this late at night after a full day—and if I am not wrong about interpreting some of the things I heard—without really being paid anything so far."

"Yeah, I guess the not being paid part is a little different from your typical lawyer. But for me, I finally feel like I am getting to do something that seems important to God's kingdom. So much of what I do is just solving messes that people get themselves into, largely because they ignore God. In that sense it is a nice change of pace for me."

Laura smiled and looked at Cooper with an expression that was totally unguarded. Cooper began to lose the battle with his arms, which ached to reach out and bring her into his embrace. His right hand found her left shoulder in the dark. She didn't move away, and perhaps she even inched a little closer to him. But she spoke instantly.

"Cooper, I can't . . . I think I . . . Oh!" she said in a frustrated tone. "I can't do this."

His hand returned to his side. His stomach felt as if it had dropped somewhere in the vicinity of his knees, and a slow burn of embarrassment crept unseen across his cheeks.

"Terry Pitkin?" Cooper asked dejectedly.

"Pip-kin," she corrected. "Yeah. I've considered myself committed to him for years."

"Are you engaged?"

"No, not really," Laura said, shaking her head. "Oh, we've talked about marriage since we were sixteen or seventeen, but he has never really asked me to marry him."

"Is he waiting on something in particular?"

"I wish I knew. For a long time we were waiting until he graduated from college. Even though we are the same age, he graduated three years later because he did some short-term missions work and then switched majors twice." In the lights that radiated from the family room, Cooper saw plainly the pained expression on Laura's face. "He's a first-year teacher now at Broad Run High School. American history. He says that he wants to earn more than me before we get married, but I am ahead of him in the school's pay system by three years, so he's going to have to leave teaching if it is that important to him."

"So how do you feel about him right now? Do you really *want* to marry him?"

"It's just that I gave him my heart so many years ago that I don't even know how to think in any other way. So, yes, I have wanted to marry him for years and I still do. In fact, I feel really guilty every time I'm with you."

There was a momentary silence before Laura spoke again. "Well, that's not exactly right. When I am with you I am all mixed up. But as soon as I leave you I feel very guilty, like I've cheated on Terry by just talking with you." She shook her head and moaned aloud. "Oh, I can't believe I am saying these things to you. We should just—"

A tap on the oval glass in the front door stopped her. Rick tapped again and opened the door.

"OK if I come out?" Rick asked, sounding a little embarrassed.

"Uh, sure," Cooper said. "We were just—"

"I was just leaving," Laura said abruptly. "Night, Rick," she said matter-of-factly. "Goodnight, Cooper," she said, in a much softer voice.

The two men listened silently as her car door slammed shut and did not speak until they saw the Honda's red taillights recede in the distance. "Sorry if I interrupted something," Rick said.

"If you had come out two minutes earlier I would have felt like killing you. As it was, I'm grateful you came out when you did."

"Do you want to explain that?"

Cooper shook his head. "No, not really."

"OK, then," Rick replied. "Well, shall we talk about finances?"

"Whatever," Cooper answered. A moment of refocusing pulled him back to his duty with his client. "Well, here's what I told the Garvises. I think this case has a lot of potential for getting support from some of the Christian organizations. But until that happens, I am going to need to be paid something, just to keep the minimums going through the office. They were going to pay me five thousand dollars from their savings. It seems like a crime that either of you have to pay anything for this . . . ."

"You know that I would give you anything I have if you could make this go away and give me back control of my son's education," Rick said with an audible sigh. "But we can do the same as

Doug and Jeanne, that's for sure. And, please don't count on this, but Deanna's parents have a fair amount of financial ability, so we can probably get some more help there if we have to."

"That is fine for now. Ten should satisfy my partner and allow me to continue until we can see if we can get some outside help. You are taking on a battle for the whole nation. I think there are a lot of good people who would be willing to support your case because in the long run it affects them as much as it does you."

"Who do you have in mind?"

"From my experience on Capitol Hill, I think one of the most reputable groups is Concerned Women for America. That's where I'd like to go first."

"Sounds good to me," Rick replied. He managed to smile at his friend. "But . . . what if I could clear a path for you and Laura. How much would you charge me then?"

"I'd do the whole case for a buck and half." Cooper laughed, but it was only funny on the surface. His insides ached.

"Thought so," Rick replied, placing his arm around the shoulders of his racquetball buddy.

ASHBURN, VIRGINIA.
May 17, 2005.

The silver Jaguar pulled to a stop under the covered entryway just as Cooper opened the door to enter the grand lobby of the Lansdowne Resort Hotel. Randolph Suskins exited the car and nodded politely in the direction of his legal adversary, while taking the valet parking ticket from a young man with a trim haircut and a forest green uniform. The parking attendant quickly scampered around to the other side to open the door for a woman passenger who waited patiently in the front seat.

Cooper paused in the doorway, waiting to shake hands with Suskins and his co-counsel. The car door opened to reveal a pair of shapely legs swinging out of the camel-colored leather bucket seat onto the pavement. Jody Easler slid elegantly out of the Jaguar and turned to pull the seat forward so that Melissa VanLandingham could climb out of her uncomfortable position in back.

Ambassador Easler, dressed in a stylish black and grey suit, saw Cooper in the doorway. As Melissa struggled out of the car, the ambassador strode quickly to the front door and extended her hand and a smile to the man who had taken her deposition yesterday.

"We're going to have to stop meeting like this, Mr. Stone," she said, with a laugh in her voice.

"Good morning, Ambassador Easler," Cooper replied politely.

"Jody, please," she corrected. "We are not in Washington or Geneva, thank goodness, and so just let me be Jody for the morning, OK?" Her voice exuded pure friendliness.

"Oh, OK . . . Jody," he said, a bit bewildered.

Suskins stood silently by, waiting with his briefcase in his right hand. "Mr. Stone," he said, nodding with a formal air. "Are your clients here? We need to proceed precisely at 9:00 A.M."

"I saw their cars in the same row where I parked out in the lot," Cooper replied. "I think we should be on time. Just the three of you today?"

"No, Mr. Stone, our support team should already be in the conference room. That is the reason, as you probably recall from your conversations with Ms. VanLandingham, that we couldn't use your office conference room. Not enough room for all the people we need at the table."

"Yes, Mr. Suskins, I do recall those details."

Jody Easler, who had moved to the left and behind Suskins, rolled her eyes at Cooper, as if to say, "What made him so uptight on a beautiful spring morning?"

Suskins and Melissa headed down the hallway leading off from the right of the dark marbled entryway. Cooper and the ambassador seemed to naturally fall into step, walking a few paces behind the two lawyers.

"It is so beautiful out here in Loudoun County, Mr. Stone," she said. "Have you always lived here?"

"Actually I was born here, Madam, I mean, Jody. But my family moved to Washington State when I was very young. I really grew up out in Washington and came here about seven years ago to work in the Senate."

"Yes, I heard that you had worked for Senator Parker. I attended a few hearings of your committee about a year and a half ago, and I am pretty sure I remember seeing you across the hearing room."

"What bill brought you to our committee?"

"It was the State Department budget hearings. I was a career officer at the time," she answered truthfully. Her remembrance of Cooper was a diplomatic invention of convenience.

Suskins and Melissa disappeared inside the door to the Lansdowne conference room.

"OK, ready to put on your formal face?" Easler whispered.

"I guess," Cooper whispered in return.

Cooper's four clients sat silently along the back wall of the windowless room. They brightened considerably when their own lawyer entered. Still, with seven opposing lawyers and a U.S. ambassador in the room, their glum facial expressions suggested that they felt hopelessly out numbered.

A tap on the door announced the arrival of Rachel Hennessey. "Morning, everyone," the children's guardian ad litem announced in a pleasant voice. Hennessey had waived the right to sit in on the depositions of the government officials. "Too much law and too little facts," she had said. She was only interested in witnesses who were going to talk specifically in regard to their knowledge of the children. And the parents of her two young clients certainly fit that description.

Within three minutes everyone was ready to begin, and an impatient Randolph Suskins began the questioning. "All right, Mrs. Thomas. I think our notice said that you would be the first to be deposed today. So if you would like to move over here closer to the court reporter, she will be able to hear you better."

Deanna got up, revealing no emotions in her steely expression, and walked to the short side of the table, to the left of where she had been. Cooper moved next to her. The court reporter was just to her right, and Suskins sat on the other side of the reporter.

"Mrs. Thomas, I will not make this a long affair today. I have just a few questions."

Suskins had skipped the usual informal instruction that typically precedes a deposition. He stated nothing to Mrs. Thomas of the purpose of the deposition. Fortunately, Cooper had covered the ground with her earlier.

"Do you spank your son, Layton?"

"Yes, sometimes."

"When was the last time you did this?"

"Last Sunday afternoon, as I recall."

"Did you use an implement to beat your son?"

"I didn't beat my son, Mr. Suskins, sir. I *spanked* him."

"Ms. Thomas—"

Deanna interrupted. "Sir, I will ask you to call me *Mrs.* Thomas if it is not too difficult for you. We are in Virginia, not Washington, D.C., and many married women in Virginia still like to be called 'Mrs.,' not 'Ms.'"

Suskins seemed taken aback, and he paused a moment. "All right, Mrs. Thomas, that will be fine.

"In any event, 'beating' means to strike a child for punishment. How does spanking differ from that?" Suskins continued.

"They sound the same by that definition, but I believe that there is an emotional difference between beating and spanking. Beating implies a cold heart. Spanking implies, to me, a loving heart, one that wants the best for the child."

"So you agree with the best interest of the child standard found in the UN Convention on the Rights of the Child?" he asked.

"Objection," Cooper replied. "Whether Mrs. Thomas agrees with the law as a matter of abstract philosophy is not a factual matter and, therefore, is not a proper inquiry at a deposition."

"All right, Mrs. Thomas. Let me ask it this way. Do you intend to obey the UN Convention, since it directs all parents to cease the use of corporal punishment for their children?"

"We do not concede that the Convention automatically achieves that result, Counsel," Cooper objected. "But if your question is presumed to be a hypothetical question, she may answer whether she intends to obey the law, if it is so interpreted by the relevant courts of the United States."

Deanna looked at Cooper with confusion. "Go ahead and answer, Deanna," Cooper whispered to her. "I've got the right guardrails built around your answer."

"Well, Mr. Suskins, I guess the answer is no. If the UN tells me I cannot spank Layton or any of my children, then I do not intend to obey the United Nations."

"That is very interesting, Mrs. Thomas. What if an American court directs you to stop spanking your children?"

"Which court?"

"Well, let us assume that the order is final. All appeals have been exhausted, and you are commanded by our judicial system, after it has interpreted the UN treaty, that you cannot spank your children. Under that scenario, will you stop?"

"No, Mr. Suskins, I will *not* stop because God directs me to discipline my children in this manner."

"I will return to your view of religion in just a moment, but let me finish the line of questions about spanking first," Suskins said, leaning forward in anticipation of Deanna's next damaging admission.

"If a final court order were to say, 'Stop spanking Layton or you will lose custody of your son,' what would you do? Would you stop spanking him then?"

"They can't do this, can they, Cooper?" Deanna asked, with an audible quiver in her voice.

"Deanna," Cooper whispered quietly into his client's ear. "These are just hypothetical questions. I have established that. You can answer."

"But are they truly just hypothetical, or could this happen?" She said in a whisper low enough that no one else heard.

"It *could* happen, but it is very unlikely, in my view. Not in Loudoun County, Virginia, anyway," he replied quietly.

"And what is the verdict after all that whispering?" Suskins asked. "Would you obey the court order if the price of refusal was losing custody of your son?"

"I don't know what I would do, to be honest, Mr. Suskins. Perhaps we would move to another country."

"But every nation in the world has also ratified the treaty, Mrs. Thomas, except Somalia. Would you go there?"

"You mean you can't spank your own child anywhere in the world?"

"No, Mrs. Thomas, you may not. And when you have reached the end of your legal rope here in the United States, is it your testimony that you are uncertain of whether you would obey the law and the court order that was entered concerning the law?"

"I guess that is what I will have to say. I am uncertain what I would do in that scenario."

Suskins looked down at his notes, flipped his silver hair off his forehead, wrote briefly on the notepad, and laid down his pen. "All right, Mrs. Thomas, I think we have covered the issue of spanking sufficiently for my purposes. Let's turn to the question of home schooling. Under what legal authority do you home school your son, Layton?"

"I have to object to the question as asked," Cooper said. "It calls on her to interpret the Constitutions of the United States and the Commonwealth of Virginia, as well as numerous statutory provisions."

"All right, let me rephrase the question," Suskins said irritably. "Does your family file any papers, give any notice, or receive any permission from some agency of government relative to your home schooling?"

Deanna looked at Cooper for permission to answer. He nodded.

"We have taken the steps to obtain a religious exemption under Virginia law," she answered.

"And what are these steps?"

"We wrote a letter to the school board explaining why we believe that God requires us to home school Layton, and they sent us a letter in reply, recognizing that we are exempt under Virginia law."

"And that was it? Just an exchange of letters?"

"Yes, sir."

"Did anyone look at your curriculum?"

"No, sir."

"Did any official observe your instruction?"

"No, sir."

"Are any achievement tests required?"

"No, sir. We do give achievement tests. They seem to make my parents happy, but we are not required to do so legally."

"Does anyone from any government agency review your ability to teach Layton?"

"No, sir."

"Does anyone from the government perform any social evaluation of Layton's education program?"

"No, sir. I am not sure what a social evaluation means, but no one from the government interacts with our home schooling at all, so the answer is no."

"So this means that there is no psychological assessment of Layton that is required to determine the affects of home schooling on him. Is that right?"

"That is right."

"How do you assess Layton's progress academically?"

"He is doing very well. Our achievement tests show that he is testing well above grade level and in the highest percentiles in just about every subject except spelling. I think he may have been born without a spelling gene."

"I see," Suskins replied, nodding to his team of young lawyers who were furiously making notes on each of their respective legal pads.

"And what are you doing to remedy this 'missing gene,' as you call it?"

"Drill and memorization for the most part. That and phonics," she replied.

"Fine. What about social progress?"

"He is doing well socially. He is a normal little boy with a lot of friends. He is in sports and Cub Scouts and church. He also plays with the kids in the neighborhood nearly every day."

"And I assume that you will say he is doing well psychologically, as well."

"Yes, indeed. Anyone who knows Layton would certainly say that he has his head screwed on straight."

"Interesting, Mrs. Thomas," Suskins said, leaning forward in his chair as if he were about to pounce on her. "And is there anyone who knows Layton well who would say that he would be better served by a more traditional form of education?"

"No . . . I can't think of anyone who would say that."

"No one?"

"Not that I can think of."

"What about your own parents who live in Richmond? Isn't it true that they believe that Layton would be better off in a private school they have recommended to you?"

"Where in the world did you hear such a thing?" Deanna said angrily.

"Mrs. Thomas, my job is to ask the questions. Your job is to answer." Suskins stared hard at her with his thin lips pressed together, with a hint of a smirk evident in their curvature. "So what is your answer? Don't your own parents think that it would be best for Layton to attend a private school?"

"Well, Mr. Suskins, the last time they mentioned such a thing it was in the context of this case. They said that if he were in a school, we probably wouldn't have been challenged in court. But that doesn't mean that such a school is actually best for him academically. It would just remove one element of the threat that you have brought into our family."

"And they never said such a thing to you before this case was filed and served on you?"

Deanna sighed heavily. "My mother had made such remarks. But I think she believes this way because home schooling is different from what she did with her own children."

"Do you think that your mother loves Layton?"

"Yes, I am certain of that."

"Does she want what is best for Layton?"

"Yes, her desires for him are certainly what she believes is best."

"So it would be fair to say that if there were a review of what is best for Layton that there would be a divergence of views right within your own family."

"Yes, if you look outside of the parents to whom God has entrusted the authority over children, then I guess you are right."

"Do you think there are home schooling families in Virginia where the husband and wife disagree over the choice of home schooling?"

Cooper spoke quickly. "Object to the speculative nature of the question."

Suskins brushed his hair back once again. "Do you *know* any home schooling families in Virginia where the father and mother of a particular child disagree over home schooling?"

Deanna thought for a second and then looked down at the table. "Yes, I do."

"More than one such family?"

"Yes, I know more than one."

Suskins smiled thinly. "Thank you, Mrs. Thomas. I think I will reserve my questions about religious matters for your husband."

"Let's take a ten-minute break. OK?" Cooper asked.

"Five should be sufficient," Suskins replied. "Everything is so compact here at this facility."

"Have it your way, Mr. Suskins," Cooper responded tersely.

"Indeed," the older lawyer replied.

૭ ૭ ૭

Exactly five minutes later, Suskins had the court reporter administer the oath to Rick Thomas.

"Mr. Thomas," he began, "have you been here the entire time your wife was testifying during her depositions?"

"Yes," Rick answered, with a puzzled look on his face.

"Is there anything that she said with which you would disagree?" Suskins asked.

"I don't think so. But I wasn't keeping track of exactly all the things you asked her."

Suskins waited for a moment. "All right, Mr. Thomas, I think that will serve as a sufficient affirmation—"

"Objection to your summation, counsel. He said that he wasn't keeping track of your questions, at least not exactly. If you want him to affirm a specific question, you will need to ask him yourself."

Suskins looked at Cooper disdainfully, and then glanced first at his watch and then back at Cooper. "Oh, never mind, let's just move on," he said.

"Mr. Thomas, can you please tell us briefly about your religion? What is your affiliation?"

"We are members of the First Baptist Church of Leesburg if that is what you mean," Rick replied cautiously.

"Is that a Southern Baptist church?"

"Yes, it is."

"Does the Southern Baptist church have an official doctrinal stance on corporal punishment of children?"

"I don't know."

"I thought your wife said that your religious faith required you to spank your children," Suskins asked with a narrowing of his eyes and the pursing of his lips, mannerisms that suggested he believed he was about to trap a witness in a contradiction.

"That's what she said and she is correct."

"Well, Mr. Thomas," Suskins said with a bemused expression, "how can she be correct if there is no official doctrinal stance on the point from the Southern Baptist organization?"

"Mr. Suskins, it seems you don't understand how the Southern Baptist church and, I guess, many other evangelical churches work. We don't have official doctrinal papers adopted by some centralized group convened to vote on what is right or wrong this year. We just believe the Bible on matters of right and wrong and faith and practice, and many other areas of life as well. And the Bible tells us that good discipline of children includes spanking of children."

"All right, the Bible says this, you contend, and not some church doctrinal paper. But, isn't there an official church interpretation of the Bible that gives you the authoritative view on what the passages are supposed to mean?"

"Mr. Suskins," Rick said smiling, "if you are really this interested in church doctrine, and so on, why don't you enroll in the Sunday school class I teach? We would be glad to have you attend. Mrs. Stoddard seemed to enjoy herself when she attended our son's class."

Rick's jovial banter was interrupted by a glance at his wife. Deanna sat frozen in her chair. The smile evaporated from Rick's face. "If you attended our classes, you might find more lawsuits you could file against people for their faith in God."

Suskins flipped his hair off his forehead, put down his pen, and spoke in measured phrases. "Mr. Thomas, I am not amused. And it is the purpose of these depositions to ascertain the facts surrounding this case. I would direct you, sir, to answer my question. And the question was: Who gives you the authoritative interpretation of the Bible relative to corporal punishment of children?"

"No one, sir."

"So spanking is not a tenet of your religious faith?"

"Yes, it is."

"How can it be a tenet of your faith if there is neither a church doctrine nor an authoritative interpretation of the Bible?"

"In the Southern Baptist church and many other evangelical churches, we believe in the priesthood of the believer. This means that each believer is responsible before God to study and know and live according to the Word of God. The Bible directs me to discipline my children in this way. I must make that call, and I must live according to the plain meaning of the Bible as I interpret it. I need no hierarchy to tell me what to do—neither church officials nor the United Nations. God holds me responsible for the interpretation of the Word and the upbringing of my children."

Deanna breathed a satisfied sigh. Just knowing that they were getting a chance for the truth to be said out loud was a relief to her soul.

"What do you teach your son relative to other religions?"

"What other religions do you have in mind?"

"Islam, for example," Suskins said.

"We teach Layton pretty much what Islamic parents teach their children. We teach him that Christianity is the only true way to God. Islamic parents also teach their children that theirs is the one true faith."

"How often is this attitude of intolerance taught in your church service or Sunday school classes?"

"Intolerance? What are you talking about?"

"You have just said that you teach your son that all other religions are wrong. My question is how often is Layton exposed to such intolerance?"

"Objection," Cooper said. "You appear to be operating with a different meaning of intolerance than Mr. Thomas. Historically, intolerance has to do with the refusal to allow another religion to have legal right to exist on an equal basis. You have asked no question that could lead you to conclude that Mr. Thomas teaches his children that Islam should be banned or suffer any legal disability."

Suskins shook his head and smiled with his practiced look of condescension. "Come, come, now, Counsel. History has demonstrated that if a person believes that another religion is wrong, then the natural outflow of such a belief is to seek to ban that religion, or at least that component of the other religion that manifests itself in a way that is contrary to your own views."

"Hm-m-m-," Cooper mused. "I guess that does make sense, given your presuppositions. You are trying to use the UN treaty as a vehicle to ban religiously motivated behavior like spanking and home schooling. So for a person who thinks like that, I guess it is reasonable to suppose that other people would try to use the law to ban religious views they don't like as well. But you have not established that Mr. Thomas thinks like that, so if you want to know if he embraces the philosophy of intolerance that is the predicate of your lawsuit, then you are going to need to ask him that directly and not merely assume that he shares your attitudes."

Suskins glared at Cooper. Shaking his head, he replied, "I thought that Virginia lawyers were better trained than to attack other counsel on a personal level during a deposition. We will have to see what the Virginia Bar Association's disciplinary committee has to say about your little tirade, Mr. Cooper."

Cooper's stomach muscles clenched tightly, but he spoke with a voice of complete calm. "Do what you like, Mr. Suskins. I am certain that truth is a defense to any charge you may wish to pursue."

"If the court reporter could mark this interchange, please. We would like this portion of the transcript expedited," Suskins replied. "Five-minute break," he announced suddenly.

He pushed his chair back and left the room quickly, with all his materials spread open on the table. "Watch my things," he said gruffly, in the general direction of Melissa VanLandingham.

She shifted nervously in her chair while watching Cooper and his four clients as they rose slowly from their places to leave the room. She leaned over to Jody Easler and whispered, "What a jerk that Stone is."

"It's hard to believe that a guy who looks like that can be such a right-wing extremist," the ambassador whispered in reply.

Rick, Deanna, Doug, and Jeanne were huddled just outside the door when Cooper emerged. They grinned at him excitedly. Rick grabbed him around the shoulders. "Way to go, Mr. Lawyer Man!" he said with a hushed intensity, lest one of the five young lawyers clustered about twenty feet down the hall overhear their conversation.

Doug spoke next in quiet tones, but his deep bass voice echoed with obvious emotion. "Cooper, that was very encouraging. Thank you. We feel like we've been on the defensive the whole time. Finally you and Rick have had a chance to say some things that put *them* on the defensive."

Cooper's mind ran down the path of the threatened bar sanction. He himself was likely to be playing defense on another front before too long. But he curbed the temptation to express these thoughts with his exuberant clients and just said "thanks" with a shrug.

When Suskins resumed the depositions, he flew through a few more questions with Rick and went over essentially the same list of questions for the Garvises. The only real differences between the two families' depositions were the education questions. Jeanne Garvis answered a series of questions about their desire to exclude their daughter from the sex education course in the local public school, instead of the home school questions that Suskins had posed to Deanna.

Suskins finished Doug's deposition just a few minutes after noon. The two groups reached a quick agreement to take a lunch break before Laura Frasier's one o'clock deposition.

Deanna found Laura seated outside the conference room on a small, upholstered bench. Three of the associates had exited first and were already well down the hall. Doug and Jeanne, who were holding hands, then followed through the doorway. Two more associates exited next. Ambassador Easler was right behind them but paused in the doorway, waiting. Laura studied her from the top of her well-coiffed head to the elegant black slings that caressed her toes. She heard Dr. Easler laugh melodiously and turn as Cooper walked out next to her.

Cooper caught Laura's eye and smiled. "Ambassador Easler," he said politely, "this is Laura Frasier, who is our witness for the afternoon."

"Ms. Frasier," Dr. Easler said, with a practiced diplomatic nod.

"Hello," said Laura, with a flat tone and a slight smile.

The three stood awkwardly for a few seconds until Rick and Deanna came out of the room. "Hey, Laura, you should have heard old Cooper here give these UN guys a taste of their own medicine," Rick said, with a voice of hushed excitement. But he had not lowered his voice enough to keep Jody Easler, whom he hadn't seen, from hearing.

"I had better join our people for lunch, Mr. Stone," she said politely, before slipping away.

Cooper motioned with his head, and the five others began to follow him toward the restaurant. Laura and he walked together, following the other two couples in pairs down the hallway.

As they turned the corner of the conference area, Cooper and Laura saw the ambassador turning right in the lobby area just ahead of them.

"Who is that woman?" Laura asked.

"Her name is Jody Easler. She is one of the U.S. ambassadors to the United Nations. She is in charge of our delegation in Geneva and is an expert on children's rights."

"So she's on the other side?" Laura asked incredulously.

"Yeah, sure," Cooper said. "Why not?"

"Well, she just seemed so buddy-buddy with you that I thought that she must be on our side of the case somehow."

Cooper blinked nervously, like he used to do when his mom was quizzing him about missing cookies from the cookie jar. "Well, she is definitely more friendly than anyone else on that side of the case, and I am at a loss to explain it."

Deanna paused at the top of the long staircase leading down to the hotel's two restaurants. "I think she thinks Cooper is cute," she drawled. "And you should have seen him a little earlier today, Laura. He was great! He let that Suskins have it. It was the only fun I have had during this whole case. Maybe she likes strong men, even if the guy is calling her and her friends religious bigots."

Laura started to tease Cooper about Jody's friendliness but quickly stopped herself. She realized that anything she might say, however lighthearted, might be misinterpreted. She just held her tongue and descended the stairs toward the huge modern fountain resting between the hotel's two restaurants.

"Let's go to the buffet restaurant," Rick suggested. "The steak house will be too slow."

The group sat close to the windows looking out at the seventeenth hole of the Lansdowne Golf Course. The tee box was about fifty yards away from their table with the par 4 hole sloping magnificently down a steep hill to a protected green. The Potomac River ran silently past the property beyond the green.

The eight people from the other side of the case were seated at a large table on the other side of the restaurant, near the back windows that looked out on the lobby and fountain. Rachel Hennessey and the court reporter had found a table about halfway between the two warring factions and seemed to be having a nice lunch, chatting about nothing in particular.

Cooper went over a few issues with Laura in anticipation of her deposition. The conduct of the morning's questioning had already confirmed that his instruction from the prior night had been essentially accurate, so he felt confident that she merely needed a brief review before they reconvened.

The two married couples were fairly animated in their lunchtime conversation, but a growing uneasiness kept Cooper and Laura relatively silent as they sat next to each other. Neither wanted any reminder of the conversation from the night before. Once Laura caught Cooper stealing a glance at her out of the corner of his eye. She smiled weakly. He shrugged but said nothing.

Fifteen minutes later, Laura raised her right hand and took an oath to respond truthfully to questions to be posed to her by Randolph Suskins.

"Ms. Frasier, you are a public school teacher at Paeonian Springs Elementary, is that correct?"

"Yes, sir."

"And you also teach Sunday school at Leesburg Baptist Church?"

"Yes, sir."

"Emily Garvis is in both of your respective classes. Is that right?"

"Yes, sir."

"Are there any other students in your public school class who are also in your Sunday school class?"

"No, sir. Emily is the only one."

"Which came first, Emily being in your Sunday school class or in your public school class?"

"I am not sure how to answer that," Laura said, looking at Cooper for help. "They both start in September, and she was just there, assigned to each of my classes."

"Let me ask it this way. Did the fact that you were Emily's public school teacher in anyway influence the decision for her to attend your Sunday school class?"

"Oh, I see. No sir, there was no connection. The Garvis family has been at our church for years. If anything, it was the other way around. The Garvises had been thinking about putting Emily in a Christian school or home schooling her. But when they found out that I would be her teacher this year, they decided to opt for another year of public schools."

"Is that right?" Suskins asked stroking his cheek. "How do you know that?"

"They told me all this last June when they got their end of the year report card for Emily, which assigned her to my class for this school year."

"Where did you have this conversation?" Suskins asked.

"In the hallway at church."

"Don't you find this mixture of public school issues and church issues to be just a little troubling, Ms. Frasier?"

"No," she said shaking her head with a puzzled look. "Why would it be troubling?"

"You have just admitted that you had a conversation about Emily's public schooling at church. Don't you consider that to be an improper mixture?"

"I would never have thought of it that way, Mr. Suskins."

"Don't you respect the separation of church and state? A conversation about public school matters while in a church seems to be an inherent mixture of church and state."

"Well, Mr. Suskins, here is how I think about it. I live in a small community. I see many of the school families out and about in the community. Nearly every time I go to the grocery store, I see a family of one of my current or past students. I don't consider talking to a family at church to be a mixture of church and state, any more than talking to a family at Safeway is a mixture of groceries and state."

"Well, Ms. Frasier, perhaps your school superiors should give you some direction explaining the constitutional difference between grocery stores and churches. We may pursue that later. But that is for another time. Today my concern is this—"

"Mr. Suskins!" Cooper exclaimed angrily. "You can threaten me with bar proceedings if you like, and that is your prerogative, I guess. But I will not let you intimidate a witness like that and get away with it."

"Intimidate a witness, Mr. Stone? I have not intimidated Ms. Frasier. Have I intimidated you, Ms. Frasier?" he asked, looking at Laura.

Cooper put his hand on Laura's arm to stop her from speaking. "No," he said, "you are dealing with me for now, not her. You have made an implied threat to involve her superiors at the school to seek to reprimand her for some constitutional violation that you have concocted in your own mind. I want your agreement on the record *right now* that you, Ms. VanLandingham, all of your army of little helpers here, and everyone associated with your firm or any of the parties that you represent, that every last one of you will refrain from making any contact with any person connected to the Loudoun County Schools concerning Ms. Frasier. I want your statement, in writing, and I want it now!"

"Your request, Mr. Stone, is both factually preposterous and without legal merit. I was not threatening Ms. Frasier with the school authorities, but if I chose to contact one of them with information concerning the legal implications of her conduct I would be perfectly within my rights in doing so. You cannot demand otherwise."

Cooper stood up. "This deposition is over! I will be seeking a protective order from Judge Holman barring you from contacting the school district regarding Miss Frasier. Good day, sir!"

"If you walk out of this deposition, Mr. Stone, I will seek sanctions against you for the delay."

"Try it!" Cooper growled as he gripped the edge of the table with both hands, looking Suskins straight in the eye.

The color had drained from Laura's face. Instinctively she reached out to grab Cooper's arm. She caught it just inside the elbow.

Suskins looked at his watch. And sighed. He hated to lose the point, but he also hated to lose the time that a rescheduled deposition would take, even if he got sanctions. He would try another tactic. "Ms. Hennessey, you are a bit more detached from this matter than Mr. Stone. Do you believe that Judge Holman would grant sanctions against Mr. Stone if he left?"

"Not a chance," she replied. "I am before Judge Holman at least twice a week on something, and even though I cannot say for sure, I think your chances are essentially zero of getting sanctions. On the other hand, I think that Cooper will get his protective order in a heartbeat. But I am only a solo practitioner and not a big firm lawyer from Washington."

Suskins blushed and brushed his hair away. "Well, Mr. Stone, let me make you a compromise offer. Let's continue the deposition, and I will agree to your stipulation for now. And I will not go to the school authorities unless I bring a motion asking for permission to do so from Judge Holman."

"No way," Cooper replied instantly. "Even that is a lingering threat against a witness. You have got to decide which case you want to try. If you want to try this case against the Thomas and Garvis families, then you must leave Ms. Frasier alone. If you want to pursue Ms. Frasier's alleged constitutional violations then you can do that. I will not let you do both."

"Oh, Mr. Stone," Suskins sighed. "I remember being young and full of passion, just like you. Sit down. I will agree to your stipulation so long as the record reflects that I think it entirely unnecessary and silly. I had no intention of going to Ms. Frasier's superiors until you made such a scene over the issue. But, to avoid a waste of time, I will agree to your request. Shall we proceed, Mr. Stone?"

Cooper looked at Laura, who was still gripping his arm. He leaned toward her, so that he could speak with her privately. "OK to go forward? If they even chat with the school people, I will nail them for contempt. OK?"

Laura nodded and relaxed her grip on Cooper's arm a little after he sat back down.

"All right, Ms. Frasier, let me focus solely on your role as Emily's teacher at church. What do you teach Emily and Layton about other religions?"

"We don't talk very much about other religions. At this level, we are basically trying to teach the children about the basic principles of Christianity."

"Isn't it true that you were talking about other religions on the day that Ms. Stoddard visited your class?"

"I don't recall any mention of the beliefs of other religions in that lesson."

"Didn't you tell the students that people from other religions were going to hell and that these children had a responsibility to convince them to switch their religion to your brand of Christianity so they would go to heaven instead?"

"Well, that is a strange way of looking at it, but yes, that is essentially what I said, even though I would have never used the words you just used. I don't think of it as discussing other religions. It is just what Christians believe."

"What words would *you* use to describe this teaching?"

"We just teach the children that Jesus said 'I am the way, the truth, and the life, no man comes to the Father but by me.' We tell them that this means that unless people know Jesus they cannot truly know God. And Jesus is the only way to forgive their sin. And unless they know Jesus personally and ask him to forgive their sins, they will end up in hell. And everyone in the world is just like they are. Everyone must receive Jesus for forgiveness of sin or go to hell for those sins."

"So you place this extraordinary burden on children. In fact, a double burden. First they must rescue their own souls from hell by believing what you tell them. Then you tell them that they must change the religious beliefs of every other person on earth, lest they end up in hell also. Do you think that carrying the burden for the eternal destiny of every person in the world is fair to a child and doesn't it teach them religious intolerance? Do you really believe that such a view is in the best interest of the child?"

Cooper started to object, but Laura reached under the table and grabbed him by the wrist and squeezed hard to stop him. "I want to answer this one," she whispered.

"Yes, Mr. Suskins, I believe, in fact, that it is in the best interest of the child. It is the best for the child because it reflects the truth. The truth is that some people die young. It is sad, but it is true. And if a person dies without Christ that person is going to hell. So as to the first half of the so-called double burden you say we are placing on the child, it is not a burden but a lifeline. And as far as the second half, telling others about Jesus, it is a simple act of love. I think that it is always right to teach children to do things that show genuine love toward others. If we know something that will save another from hell, it is the most loving thing in the world to tell people. You may call it intolerance if you will, Mr. Suskins, but I call it love."

The senior lawyer laid his pen on the table and just stared thoughtfully at Laura for several seconds. "Fascinating, Ms. Frasier. Utterly fascinating. You have given me all I need. Thank you very much. I have no more questions."

LEESBURG, VIRGINIA.
May 19, 2005.

"Cooper," Nancy said on the intercom, "Jacob Purves on line 3."

"Don't know a Jacob Purves," Cooper replied without looking up from the papers in front of him. "Is he a reporter or something?"

"He said he is with the Center for Constitutional Litigation."

"Wants to talk about the UN case," Cooper mouthed silently in unison with Nancy, as she drawled the now familiar words.

"Good morning," Cooper said, after punching the appropriate button.

"Mr. Stone, my name is Jacob Purves. I'm deputy general counsel with the Center for Constitutional Litigation. We're a conservative group based in Wash—"

"I know the group well," Cooper replied. "I was a Senate staffer for six years. You can't work in the Senate and not hear of you all."

"Very well," Purves replied. "And I hope that your impression was favorable."

"Your organization does outstanding work," Cooper said warmly.

"Well, as you might expect, we are interested in your UN case. We have been following it and have decided that we want to get involved to assist you in the litigation. That is, of course, if you and your clients are interested in our help."

"Quite possibly," came the tentative reply. "What do you have in mind?"

"In a case of this magnitude, we would expect that there are tremendous expenses. We would like to take care of those expenses, within reason, of course."

"Yeah, of course," Cooper replied brushing the papers in front of him aside as he grabbed a clean pad and pen.

"Do you have any idea how much you have incurred to date?"

"I think it is something around thirty-five thousand. About a third of that goes toward costs for depositions. My clients have paid me ten thousand."

"So you are in the hole at least a couple thousand for just the costs and you haven't been paid anything for your time at all. Did I do the math right?" Purves asked.

"Yeah, you've got it pretty close."

"Well, I am virtually certain that we can get you twenty-five thousand dollars to take care of what you are owed. Would that be acceptable to you?"

"Sure, that would be a great help." Cooper hesitated a moment. "Is there any possibility that you would want to help with the ongoing expenses?"

"Yes, indeed. Our plan would be to fully cover all costs from this point forward."

"That is very generous," Cooper replied. "That would leave us only with the responsibility of raising the money to pay for my time because you would be handling the out-of-pocket costs."

"Oh, Mr. Stone, I guess I jumped the gun in my assumption when you said that you were familiar with our organization. When we enter a case, we take it over. Our attorneys will serve as lead counsel and will handle all aspects of the case."

"Oh, I see. You're right, I didn't understand that."

"Is that acceptable?"

"Well, you are asking the wrong person in the final analysis. My clients will have to agree. Obviously, there is a powerful reason for them to say yes. You are great lawyers, and you will do it for free. But I will have to ask them."

"Sure, Mr. Stone. That is the proper way to proceed. Would you like to call me back in a day or two?"

"Yeah, that seems about right."

Cooper hung up the phone slowly, sat back, and stared for a long time out the window. Suddenly, he reached down and picked up the phone and punched eleven numbers.

"Peter Barron & Associates," Sally's familiar voice rang out.

"Well, Miss Sally, just as pleasant as always," Cooper said.

"No one else could call me Miss Sally and live, Cooper Stone," she laughed. "How are you anyway?"

"I am doing great over all, Sally. A little busy with this UN versus the parents case. I think you may have heard about it."

"Oh yeah, big time. I have seen it in *World Magazine* on a regular basis. And it is a favorite with my chat friends."

"Chat friends?" Cooper asked.

"You know—chat on the Internet. I go to this chat room on *Crosswalk.com* all the time. You know, gives me something to do at night."

Cooper hadn't had the courage to ask Sally if she were still single, but he did not need to, for her answer gave her away. "So what do they say about this case in chat?"

"Well, the parents want to talk about the case. The dads are furious, and the moms are scared."

"I can understand that," Cooper replied.

"And the single women . . ."

"Yes?"

"They just want to know if I can get you to come to the chat room somehow. Ever since your picture appeared in *World* all they want to talk about is you. A few of the single guys give us a hard time. They say that we are lusting after the nonexistent perfect Christian man—Billy Graham in the thirty-year-old body of Matt Damon."

"That so?" Cooper laughed, unable to find the right word.

"I tell them that description fits you perfectly, and they all go nuts."

"Well, I certainly got more than I bargained for when you answered the phone. Mind if I talk to Peter?"

"Sure, I'll get him. But, can I ask you . . . you wanna join my chat room and make me a hero?"

"Just transfer the call, Miss Sally," Cooper said with a laugh.

"I hear a rumor that the most eligible bachelor in Loudoun County wants to talk with me," Peter Barron said with a chuckle. Cooper could picture him rocking back in his chair.

"You mean the most rejected suitor in America, don't you?" His voice lacked any indication he was kidding.

"Oh, boy," Peter said soberly. "Sorry, Cooper."

"Oh, don't worry about it," Cooper replied. "I called to ask for your help on a case."

"The UN case? Yeah, sure, whatever I can do."

"I just need some advice."

"Shoot."

"Well, I just got off this call with a guy from the Center for Constitutional Litigation, who offered to take over the case and pay me everything that is owed to me so far—about twenty-five grand."

"And I take it that you haven't gotten independently wealthy from some unknown source since I last talked to you."

"No, not hardly. The firm *could* use the money. I am still driving my aunt's car if that gives you a hint."

"OK, so you've got an offer for money from the CCL, but there is evidently some catch, or you would be calling to celebrate, not to ask for advice. Right?"

"Right. They want to take over the case. They come in. I go out."

"Whoa. *That* kind of generous offer."

"I guess I can understand it from their perspective," Cooper replied. "If they are going to invest their money into a case, they want to do it with the people they rely on day in day out. I'd probably do the same thing."

"I can understand that, too, I guess. But you really don't want to give up the case, I take it."

"No, I don't. It is not just pride, at least I don't think so. I think I am supposed to do this case."

"You mean from a spiritual perspective?"

"Yeah," Cooper answered.

"Well, that's hard for me to analyze, especially from a distance. Let me ask you some more traditional questions. Anything wrong with this litigation group, other than wanting to butt into your case?"

"Not really, they have a very good reputation in Washington."

"I know I have heard of them, but do you know if they are a Christian group?"

"Secular. In fact, they are a libertarian group. They hate any kind of government regulations, including several categories of regulation that you and I wouldn't find excessive or intrusive."

"Like what?"

"Well, they are in favor of the legalization of drugs, for example."

"Oh . . . *that* kind of libertarian," Peter replied. "Well, do you think they would do a good job on this case?"

"I think they would, for the most part."

"What part do you have questions about?"

"They would do fine on parental rights for spanking. And home schooling, they'd be fine. But, they are not real advocates of religious freedom. So I think they would give lip service to the right of parents to teach their children, but I don't think their hearts would be in it."

"Well, that is a valid, objective reason for hesitation. I suggest that you tell it just like that to your clients and let them make the decision."

Cooper sighed. "Yeah, I guess I need to tell them. I was debating it a little."

"No debate. You've got to do it. They will probably want you to stay in the case if there is any kind of chance that their religious freedom claims won't be litigated as vigorously as you would do for them."

"You would definitely be right if there weren't so much financial pressure. Neither family can really afford to fight this."

"Have you tried to contact any other organizations in Washington for financial help?" Peter asked.

"I plan to call Concerned Women for America. They have a great reputation. But I keep putting it off. Guess I am a little chicken just to pick up the phone and ask for money."

"Pick up the phone, Cooper. You need to do it so your clients know if they have a choice other than the CCL."

"Thanks, Peter, that's another piece of sound advice. By the way, how are Gwen and the three kiddos?"

"Doing great. Can you believe that Casey is a teenager?"

"Man, time flies when you're havin' kids, my friend. That is incredible," Cooper replied.

"Hey!" Peter suddenly exclaimed. "Gwen and I are coming to the East Coast in a couple weeks. New York, to be specific. I've got a conference I have to attend, and we are staying over Memorial Day weekend to see some plays on Broadway. How about you join us for an evening during that trip? We'll go out to dinner and just talk."

"Maybe I will. I don't really have anybody to talk to here."

"Hey, Coop. Serious for a minute. What was all this about being the world's most rejected suitor, or whatever it was that you said when we first started talking? Is it still Sophie? Are you still that hurt over that whole thing?"

Cooper didn't answer for a moment. Breathing hard, he laughed ruefully and shook his head. "Sophie still hurts at times when I think about it. But there are fresh wounds also."

"You know, strange as it may sound, Coop, I am kind of glad to hear that. Not that there are wounds, but that there is anything fresh going on with you."

"Well, nothing is going on with me now. I was hoping there would have been, but I have managed to fall in love with someone who is taken."

"Cooper! You fell in love with a married woman? What?" Peter exclaimed loudly.

"Hush!" Cooper replied. "Sally will hear you and come to the entirely wrong conclusion. There is no married woman—you know me better than that."

"Oh man, you had me scared for a second. So what's the deal? Is she engaged or something?"

"It's one of those 'or something' situations. Her name is Laura, and she is a witness in this UN case. She's a public school teacher with one of the kids in the lawsuit in her class and is also the Sunday school teacher for both kids."

"So how is she taken?"

"She has been dating the son of her pastor since she was sixteen or seventeen. He's supposed to marry her but just hasn't got around to asking her."

"Well, that is not 'taken' in any kind of official way, and you have done nothing wrong."

"She believes she is taken, and that is all that matters. She told me she had given her heart away to this guy years ago."

"And now you gave your heart away to her. Ironic."

"I didn't say that," Cooper replied, uncomfortable with the way Peter had summarized the situation.

"You said you fell in love with her. I think that's the same thing."

"Did I say that?" Cooper asked incredulously.

"Yeah, I even wrote it down on the legal pad in front of me."

"Wow. I am surprised I said that. I have never admitted that before, even to myself."

"So what are you going to do?"

"Nothing. There is nothing to be done. Except make a couple phone calls about getting some financial support for this lawsuit and collect enough money to pay my secretary and light bill. See you, Peter," Cooper said abruptly. "I've got to go. I guess I will see you in New York. Fax me the details."

Peter looked at the phone for a few seconds after the line went dead. He put the receiver back into the cradle, got up out of his chair, placed his hands on the windowsill of his fourteenth floor office, gazed out at Riverfront Park, and prayed for his friend twenty-five hundred miles away.

GENEVA, SWITZERLAND. *May 20, 2005. 10:00 A.M.*

The boardroom at the UN office building was beginning to seem familiar to Ambassador Easler, but the cast of characters still unnerved her at times. The fight for children's rights evoked in her feelings of pastels and whites and brightness, not the black and charcoal and dark purple tones that colored every jacket, every pair of pants, every painted lip, and every head of tinted hair. Her tan pantsuit, subdued red lipstick, and light brown hair were the only ways in which she felt she could deviate from the norm.

Erzabet Kadar scribbled a note to her assistant, sending her off on an apparent mission. "All right, it is time to begin," she announced.

Fine coffee cups on fine china saucers clinked and spoons rattled as the standing coffee klatch seated themselves around the massive table.

"We are to hear this morning from Dr. Easler, who has just returned from the United States to report on the progress of our case against the two fundamentalist families." She paused and surveyed each face around the table to ensure that every eye had been focused where she intended it. "Fine," she concluded. "Dr. Easler, please begin."

"Good morning, Dr. Kadar and members of the committee." She paused, expecting a return of greeting. Only the gentleman from Great Britain raised his eyebrows slightly and moved his lips in a nearly imperceptible move in the general direction of a smile.

"Well, yes," she said with a sigh, "I arrived yesterday afternoon from Washington. Our case is proceeding a bit slower than might be expected in some nations, but by American legal standards it is moving right along. We expect the major hearing at the trial court level in about ten days.

"Our lead counsel, Randolph Suskins, is a former White House counsel and is leading a highly skilled team from one of the major law firms in Washington. He is opposed by a young lawyer from

Leesburg, Virginia, who is in a two-person law firm with his uncle. But he is not entirely without experience because he was counsel for a United States Senator for six years. He was assigned to the Foreign Relations Committee.

"The local judge is a bit of an unknown at this moment. He is very aggressive and doesn't seem to like our counsel, but he has publicly stated that he intends to follow the law, even if he doesn't like it. And I guess it is fair to say that he has made it clear that he is surprised and somewhat dismayed at the allegations in our complaint."

Easler looked at the list of topics that Kadar had given her to cover. "Oh, yes, the media," she said, smiling. "We have been getting favorable press on a very widespread basis. They are playing this case as an anti-spanking case. The home schooling and religious issues we are pleading are potentially much more controversial, but the mainstream media have placed these issues strategically near the bottom of all reports or have simply omitted them all together. As a consequence, the vast majority of the American public is only passively interested in this case because the spanking controversy was the core issue during the ratification fight and people seem to feel that this is only the natural progression of affairs."

Raisa Kreshnikov raised her hand and Kadar nodded. "So does this mean that the American public now fully supports our ban on corporal punishment?"

"No," Easler said with a warm yet condescending smile aimed not at her Russian committee member but at the unthinking Americans who still believed to the contrary. "The ban on spanking is still opposed in some quarters. There is more a sense of resignation than of agreement among such people. However, the other aspects of the case would be perceived as new issues and, thus, have the potential for much more upheaval in public opinion. The press, which strongly supported ratification through priority news coverage and editorials, has the desire to keep public opinion managed so they don't have to explain to angry readers why they supported the children's treaty in the first place."

Easler looked around the table for signs of further questions. "Anything I need to add, Dr. Kadar?"

"Will we win?" came the terse question.

"I cannot say what will happen in the trial court, but that is of only momentary consequence. Mr. Suskins, who counts three members of the Supreme Court as close friends, assures me we have at least a bare majority on the Court. It is the Supreme Court that matters in the final analysis."

"Thank you, Dr. Easler," Kadar said, while looking at her notes.

The meeting lasted another forty-five minutes, as Kadar put a number of others through the paces of reporting on tasks she had given them. As the meeting was breaking up, Kadar's assistant slipped a note to Easler. "Dr. Kadar would like to meet briefly with you in her office," it read.

Easler nodded and gathered her papers.

At the end of a long hallway, Easler knocked and was summoned into a spacious office. The furniture was modern and the paintings were postmodern and dark. But the views of

Lake Geneva and Mont Blanc overshadowed Kadar's attempts at decorating.

"Just one additional thing," Kadar said as she motioned for Easler to be seated. "We want to take every step that is humanly possible to ensure that we win this case."

"Dr. Kadar, I assure you that we are doing this. Suskins is a very good lawyer, and we are giving him every support we can."

"Yes, we are also aiding Suskins in additional ways. But we need to go further. You are familiar with the way American politics works, are you not?"

Easler's answer was yes, but her tone of voice implied, "I have no idea what you are talking about."

"The stakes are too high to simply leave the result to the normal routines. This is a tactic that your nation has embraced for some time now although we in the former Eastern bloc had perfected long before. You do not merely beat your enemy in the courtroom or in the legislative chamber. You do everything you can to discredit your enemy outside of these arenas to make it easier to win inside the arena."

Easler nodded, only beginning to see what Kadar had in mind.

"We want to ensure that we gather information about Mr. Stone outside the courtroom that will make it easier for us to win inside the courtroom. Mr. Suskins informs us that you seem to have a natural affinity for Mr. Stone, so you are being enlisted for this additional aspect of the endeavor."

"What are you asking me to do?"

"Nothing you have not done before, Dr. Easler," Kadar said, with a wicked smile.

"I don't think I—"

"Dr. Easler, there is no thinking to be done. We have the co-operation from the highest levels of your government. You have been given this position and you claim to believe in our cause. If you value each, you will do whatever is necessary for the good of all."

Easler said nothing.

"It will not be that distasteful, Dr. Easler. He is a handsome man. I have seen the photographs myself."

LEESBURG, VIRGINIA.
May 20, 2005. 10:00 A.M.

Cooper gathered his courage as he prepared to pick up the phone
to make that call that he had promised Peter he would make to
Concerned Women for America. Nancy's voice on the intercom
interrupted him.

"Randall Wasson on line 2 for you, Cooper. Says he's with the
Washington Star but is not a reporter."

"OK, Nancy. Put him through."

"Mr. Stone, thank you for taking my call. My name is Randall
Wasson, and I am an associate publisher of the *Washington
Star.*"

"Good afternoon, Mr. Wasson. Mind if I ask a silly question? I
am not sure what an associate publisher does at the *Star.*"

"I could dress it up and make it sound fancy, but what it really
means is that I am a secondary owner of the *Star*. My father bought
the newspaper three years ago and promptly passed away. He left
my older brother the majority interest. He is publisher, and I am
the associate."

"Thanks, that seems quite straightforward. What can I do for you, Mr. Wasson?"

"I'd like for you to come see me so we can talk about your UN case."

"Is there any particular aspect of the case you want to talk about? Do you write stories or editorials as well?"

"No, I don't write anything at all. I want to talk to you about the funding of your fight. I may be able to be of some help. But I really don't want to say more than that over the phone."

"I can't see any reason I wouldn't say yes to that. Sure, I would be very happy to come see you, Mr. Wasson. When do you have in mind?"

"Eight o'clock sharp next Thursday morning. I understand that Thursday is the day after your hearing. Am I right?"

"Yeah, that's right."

"Well, I am leaving town until the day before your hearing, so I assumed that you wouldn't really feel free to meet with me until the day after. I am not in town all that much. I actually live in Asheville, North Carolina."

"Eight o'clock. I guess I can make that. It is mighty early coming from Leesburg, but I will do it."

"Yes, Mr. Stone, I understand it is early, but there is a good reason for it. The *Star* is a morning paper, so most of the activity around here starts later in the day. Deadline is at 10:00 P.M. for national news. So if I can get you in here at 8:00 A.M. and out by 9:00, there is little chance that anyone in our editorial or news departments will see you. Normally that wouldn't be a concern, but you will be a major news figure the day after your hearing."

"Sure, no problem. Eight o'clock sharp. Can you tell me why—"

"I am afraid I must hang up," Wasson interrupted in a whispered voice. Immediately, Cooper heard only a dial tone.

WASHINGTON, D.C. The Capitol Beltway. May 20, 2005. 6:45 P.M.

The white Grand Prix moved skillfully through the sluggish traffic. Terry Pipkin hit the accelerator just enough to move to the far left lane without giving the maroon van he pulled in front of an opportunity to pull ahead of him.

"So have you decided where you would like to stop after the concert?" he asked.

Laura said nothing for several seconds. "I guess the Golden Diner," she replied. "I know we always stop there, but I like it. Why try something new if you've found something you like?"

"Sure, why not?" Pipkin replied.

The conversation once again lapsed into uncomfortable silence, as it had so often lately. Pipkin negotiated a complicated lane change to head south on I-95 toward Woodbridge. Eventually Terry spoke.

"So why is it so hard for us to talk lately? I seem to be doing my normal part, but you seem so distant."

Laura turned and looked at the man she had dated for seven years with a big smile, but there was sadness in her eyes. "I . . . I . . . just have a lot on my mind."

"Are you thinking about the Thomases and Garvises again? That case seems to have taken over your life. Are you still worrying about that Suskins guy ratting on you to the school authorities?"

"Oh, I don't know," she answered with a sigh. "I guess not. I think Cooper scared them off that idea."

"Cooper. That's it," Pipkin snorted in disgust. "He did ask you out that one time—I had forgotten about that. So, what's up between you and Cooper?"

"Nothing, Terry. Nothing at all. Cooper did express interest in me. But I told him that I am in love with you."

"What did he say when you told him that?"

"He asked a very natural question."

Pipkin waited to see if Laura would volunteer the next bit of information, but she said nothing. He asked, "And that question was?"

"He wanted to know if we are engaged. Actually, he asked if you had asked me to marry you."

"Oh," he said, adding a short grunt. It was Pipkin's turn to sit for awhile in silence. Finally he spoke. "So what did you say to him?"

Laura looked at her boyfriend with incredulity. "What do you think I said? I said no. What other answer is there?"

It seemed that they had passed ten thousand cars before Terry spoke again. "So what would you say if I asked you?"

"I refuse to answer that question," Laura said bitterly.

"What? Why do you say that?"

"Because you are not asking me to marry you. It is simply a hypothetical question that you have asked me a dozen times over the years. And I refuse to answer it again."

"Well, maybe it isn't hypothetical anymore."

Laura's stomach fluttered. She looked at Terry, refusing to

believe the words, yet desperately wanting to do so. He saw the vulnerability in her eyes.

Pipkin spoke quietly. "For a long time I think I have been scared to ask, but I always knew you would say yes. For the first time I don't know what your answer will be. Ever since you have been hanging around with this Cooper guy . . . I dunno."

He flipped the turn signal on and exited the freeway at the exit for Hylton Chapel, where the concert would begin in twenty minutes. He pulled silently into the parking lot and turned off the car. Neither person made any move to get out.

"Laura," he said, in a soft and kind voice, "I am afraid of what you'll say, and I can't bear the idea of you rejecting me now after all these years."

Laura's mind was going down so many different tracks at once it was impossible to stay with one idea long enough to come to a conclusion. "I guess I have to admit that I have been more confused since I met Cooper, but, even so, all I have ever gotten from you is hypothetical questions, not the real thing."

She started to speak again but then shook her head and just sat quietly.

"Well, I guess there's nothing I can do but ask you."

He paused and reached in the left outside pocket of his sports coat, and pulled out a small jewelry box. He laid the box on the center console and took both of her hands into his, and looked her straight in the eye. "Laura Frasier, I love you. I have always loved you. I want you to be my wife. Will you agree to marry me?"

Tears welled in her eyes. She was still confused, but her traditional patterns of thought were gaining ground. She thought briefly of Cooper, felt a pang of embarrassment for thinking of him at all, and dismissed it out of her mind. She sighed. She smiled. She pulled her right hand free to wipe away her tears and then willingly returned her hand to his. "Yes, Terry, I will marry you."

For the next two hours, Laura Frasier sat cuddled against the shoulder of her fiancé. Maybe no one else saw it. But to her, the diamond on her hand glistened brightly in the darkness of the concert hall.

CHAPTER 12

LEESBURG, VIRGINIA.
May 23, 2005.

Deputy Micah Daniels called for reinforcements early. He would need three extra sheriff's officers to serve as bailiffs. He wanted to ask for five, but Judge Holman told him that the hordes were only reporters not accused felons—although, Holman sardonically added, it was hard to tell the difference by the way they dressed. Daniels had rolled that comment over in his mind at least fifty times as he issued passes to the various members of the press corps that started lining up next to the folding table he had installed at the bottom of the outside steps.

Daniels began a mental game of assigning felony charges to each of the reporters as he signed their passes. Print reporters were generally burglars. Radio reporters were armed robbers. On-camera television personalities were embezzlers. Every cameraman wandering around the courthouse square was an accused rapist, and this jury of one was almost certain to convict.

Holman had given each of the legal teams twenty passes. The parties and witnesses didn't need a pass although the judge had demanded an exact count twenty-four hours before the hearing.

Every space was taken nearly forty-five minutes before the gavel fell at nine.

The courtroom began to go through noise cycles about twenty minutes before the hearing. Chatter began to crescendo. Deputy Daniels, now inside and firmly in control of his team of armed assistants, walked down the aisle with his hand conspicuously on his sidearm. The noise would dissipate for several minutes but then the buzz would begin to rise again, and Daniels would decide to take another stroll among the "felons."

Cooper, the three Garvises, and three Thomases sneaked through a side door about ten minutes early. Cooper glanced into the sea of reporters to see if Laura had arrived. He had not seen nor talked to her since the depositions. His first level of consciousness said he was just looking for his witness to show up. But his second level of consciousness accused the first level of prevaricating. The second level prevailed on the motion.

A few minutes before nine, he saw her slip into her assigned seat on the second row. He smiled and returned to the task of flipping through his trial notebook for the seventeenth time that morning. He did not see Terry Pipkin, who had been parking the car, slip in beside Laura a minute or two before nine.

No one but Daniels heard the judge's tap on the courtroom door. No one else needed to. "All rise!" the deputy cried in an unmistakable voice. He glared at the audience to see if any of the "accused" failed to stand up with the promptness he believed was appropriate to the occasion.

Judge Holman took his seat and announced, "This is the time set for the hearing in the matter of the National Education

Association and the Children's Defense Fund, petitioners, versus Richard and Deanna Thomas, parents of Layton Thomas, and Douglas and Jeanne Garvis, parents of Emily Garvis. It appears to me that all counsel are present and unless there is objection I assume that all of you are ready to begin." He paused briefly, looking for any sign of objection from Cooper, Suskins, or Rachel Hennessey.

"All right, here is how I intend to proceed, Counsel. I have studied each of your briefs and have reviewed the deposition transcripts you all have provided. It is my opinion that there is not really any dispute over the facts of this case. Therefore, it is my intention to treat this matter as the juvenile court equivalent of a motion for summary judgment. This is a battle over the meaning and applicability of the law. No one disputes the key facts. Unless there is sound objection, I intend to enter the following brief findings of fact."

Judge Holman turned and nodded to Deputy Daniels, who distributed a two-page document to each person seated at counsel table, including all four of the parents. "All right," the judge continued. "First, I find that these parents engage in traditional forms of corporal punishment. There is no evidence that either set of parents has ever abused their children as this term was understood in our law prior to the ratification of the UN Convention on the Rights of the Child. But, these parents fully intend to continue to administer such a discipline in a manner that is reasonable and moderate by historical standards."

He looked up from the paper and departed from the written text. "This is not to say, Counsel, that this means that spanking is now lawful or unlawful. I am just entering findings that help to focus our inquiry. The question for me to decide is a legal one. Can any parent spank their child—ever? The petitioners claim that the answer to my question must be no, as an effect of the new treaty. And, of course, this being a lawsuit, the respondents dispute that claim."

Holman looked carefully at all the main counsel. "Any of you dispute the factual issue or my statement of the legal question to be decided?"

"No, Your Honor," came a chorus of jack-in-the-box attorneys, who spoke quickly on their way up and down in their chairs.

"OK. Let's move to the second finding, which has two parts. It is my finding that the Thomas family is home schooling their son, Layton, fully in compliance with the law of Virginia. It is my further finding, although this is a mixed finding of law and fact, that the procedures in place in Virginia do not require any government official to review the process of home schooling at any point during the process. Home schooling is entirely separate and apart from the government in the manner practiced by the Thomases. Although there is another branch of the home schooling law that requires some level of interaction, the Thomases have lawfully chosen a method of compliance with the law that gives no government agency an opportunity for review for any purpose.

"It is also my finding of fact that Layton appears to be well educated academically, and the evidence seems clear that he is socially and emotionally a fine young man. There is not a single piece of evidence in this record to the contrary. Thus, the issue appears to be nothing more than a question of whether the absence of a government agency to review the parents' choice of home schooling is a fatal legal flaw under the UN Convention.

"I also find that the Garvises have removed their daughter, Emily, from the sex education course called 'Family Life Education' in full accord with the law of Virginia. No harm has been shown that Emily has suffered as a result of her parents exercising their rights under Virginia law. Any objection to this finding and issue statement?"

The chorus said they had none.

"My third finding enters an incredibly sensitive area concerning the religious beliefs of these families. I find that these families are Protestant Christians, Southern Baptists, specifically, who describe themselves variously as 'born-again' and 'Bible-believing,' using these terms to distinguish themselves from other branches of Christianity. They believe that any person who does not, to quote one of the depositions, 'accept Jesus Christ for forgiveness of sins' will go to hell. Therefore, I find that the petitioners are correct in their allegations that these children are being trained in a theology that contains an inherent criticism of other religions and which could affect the manner in which these children think and behave toward people of other faiths. These factual findings do not resolve the important legal issue that remains. This is the issue before this court: Does this teaching content in any way violate the rights of these two children under the treaty?

"Mr. Stone, this case is so sensitive," Holman continued, "that I want to ask you specifically, do you understand what I am finding? I want you and your clients to know that I in no way criticize the way these children are being taught. I am just summarizing the content of the teaching. Specifically, I noted with great interest the colloquy during the depositions that addressed the issue of whether these children were 'loving others,' as you all contend, or 'learning to hate,' as Mr. Suskins contends. I am not making any finding that in any way agrees with either side on that point at this time. I may well have to decide that later. But for now, I am only deciding that the teaching will, in fact, change the way these children look at people of other faiths. Whether they are being taught to love or hate others is an important, and I don't mind saying, somewhat troubling question. So, Mr. Stone, any objection?"

Cooper rose slowly. "No, Your Honor, I think we would all agree with your summation as you have delineated the issue. As long as we get to argue all of the legal points we have raised on the matter, I see no problem with any of the factual components of what you have said."

"Miss Hennessey?"

"No objection, Judge."

"And Mr. Suskins?"

"We are in full agreement with the findings and your issue statements, Your Honor. And let me say I appreciate the way these findings have definitely streamlined this hearing in a most helpful fashion."

"Glad you concur, Counsel," Holman said, with an ironic smile.

"Finally, one very brief factual finding concerning the respondents. I find that both the National Education Association and the Children's Defense Fund are, as alleged, properly qualified nongovernmental organizations recognized by the United Nations. Now the legal question of whether these groups have standing to bring actions such as this one is a very important question of law that I must resolve. I assume there is no objection to this finding. Correct, Mr. Stone?"

"Agreed, Your Honor. Both are affiliated with the UN, as the petition alleges."

"All right, Counsel, with that we are almost ready to begin your oral arguments on the law, with one brief prior extraneous matter that I noted when reading the depositions. Is Miss Laura Frasier here in the courtroom?" Her face flushed, but her hand went up.

"Miss Frasier, can you come forward just very briefly? You are not in any trouble of any kind. I found your testimony to be most helpful, and it was in large part the reason I felt so secure in making my findings concerning the academic success of Layton Thomas. Your observations as his Sunday school teacher were strong confirmations of the testimony of the parents. But there was one other matter, if you wouldn't mind just stepping forward and approach the bench for a brief second, Miss Frasier. Counsel, I would like you to approach, as well."

Laura lost her fear of punishment, but the fear of being the center of attention had gripped her heart like no other moment since the seventh grade when she had fallen flat in the middle of the class play in front of all the students, parents, and teachers.

"Yes, Your Honor," she said nervously, after the swinging rail closed behind her.

The judge leaned forward and spoke in hushed tones so that no one could hear other than those in the tight circle around his bench.

"Miss Frasier, a matter arose during your deposition concerning some possibility that there might be some form of retaliation against you concerning your activities in this case. I want you to have my personal assurance that if any person undertakes any action against you arising out of this case, I will hold such person in contempt of court, be they party, counsel, or otherwise. I do not countenance intimidation of witnesses in my court, and although the circumstances were somewhat ambiguous, I wanted you to have my personal assurance of your safety in this regard."

"Your Honor, I assure you—" Suskins began.

"Mr. Suskins, as I stated, the threat was ambiguous. If it were not, contempt proceedings would have already been commenced and completed. I want this young lady not to suffer any sleepless nights over this lawsuit."

"Thank you very much, Your Honor," Laura said, brushing her hair nervously away from her face.

As she did, Cooper noticed the diamond on her left hand. The heat of disappointment made the room suddenly seem warm and stifling. He tried to force himself to refocus on the hearing, but instead his eyes wandered through the audience until he noted Terry Pipkin sitting next to the empty spot where Laura had been sitting.

"Well, if there is nothing else, Counsel," Holman continued, "I think we are truly ready to begin."

All returned to their seats. To Cooper, each step toward counsel table felt as if he was walking with a fifty-pound weight on each leg. And his head seemed to pound. *Oh, Lord God, please help me to focus on this case,* he whispered in his soul. He smiled bravely to Rick as he sat down.

"Are you OK?" Rick asked. Cooper nodded. Rick picked up the pad that Cooper had provided. "What happened up there?" he wrote.

Cooper took the pad and his own pen. "The judge just wanted to make sure that Laura knew that Suskins better not retaliate against her." Rick nodded, but his expression showed that he wondered why this interchange would drain the color from his lawyer's face.

"Counsel," Holman said as Laura finally sat down, "I want to address each of these issues in order. I will give each of you whatever reasonable time you need on each of the four issues. Mr. Suskins, you are the moving party and have the burden of persuasion on all these matters, so you can go first. My only time limit will be for rebuttal. On each of the issues, Mr. Suskins, you may have a one-minute rebuttal, and that is it. You all have briefed this case very professionally, and there is no need for extended rebuttals."

"Very well, Your Honor," Suskins said, as he stood. His silver suit was a perfect match to his hair color. One might also guess that his pale blue tie had been dyed to match his eyes or that he had purchased color contacts just for the occasion. "If it please the court, I would begin with the issue of the status of the law of corporal punishment as this has been affected by the ratification of the UN Convention on the Rights of the Child.

"Article 19 of the Convention requires all nations to 'take all appropriate legislative, administrative, social, and educational measures to protect the child from all forms of corporal and mental violence.' This provision has been authoritatively interpreted by the ten-member Committee on the Rights of the Child as a ban on corporal punishment.

"Insofar as the issue is whether or not the Convention actually prohibits corporal punishment, there can be no doubt. The only question that has been challenged by Mr. Stone is whether the treaty is a self-executing treaty on this point or whether implementing legislation is required.

"As we wrote in our brief, a self-executing provision of a treaty is one that requires nothing more than the treaty language itself. If the treaty language standing alone contains all the necessary rules, then it is self-executing and, thus, becomes the law automatically, without any need for Congress or the state legislature to pass new laws. If the treaty language is incomplete and there are details to be furnished, then that portion of the treaty is not self-executing and requires new laws to be enacted."

Suskins had shifted into a law school professor lecture mode. His age, stature, and experience became evident to every person in the courtroom. Holman was taking notes and occasionally nodding. Cooper was equally intent on Suskins' every word. He had forgotten for the moment the third finger on the left hand of a certain witness in the second row of the courtroom.

Suskins continued. "Corporal punishment or spanking provides a splendid example of the difference between a self-executing provision and one that is not self-executing.

"To end corporal punishment there can be two different kinds of laws. One is just a simple ban. No punishments. No sentences.

No fines. Just a straightforward ban. The other kind of law to stop spanking would be like the law passed in Sweden. In that country, it has been made a crime to spank a child.

"The UN Convention contains the straightforward ban on spanking. Article 19 bans all 'physical violence' against children, and the UN Children's Committee has officially interpreted this phrase to prohibit all spanking. There is nothing that either Congress or any state legislature needs to do to clarify this ban. Spanking is prohibited—end of story. That much of the treaty is most certainly self-executing and, thus, a valid part of our law today.

"Now, there is nothing in our pleadings requesting any kind of punishment of the parents in this case. We are just asking for an order directing them to stop spanking their children. If we were trying to secure felony convictions or jail terms, then we would be required to get legislation passed by Congress. And certainly such legislation will come in due season. Whether Congress chooses to treat spanking as a federal misdemeanor or felony is a matter for future political debate. But we don't have to wait for Congress to get only an order banning spanking."

Suskins paused, looked at his notes, and pushed his glasses back to their proper spot on the bridge of his nose. "So, to sum up, Your Honor. Banning spanking is automatic—it is already the law of the land by virtue of the treaty because nothing needs to be clarified, funded, or defined. This portion of the treaty is clearly self-executing." As Suskins sat down, Melissa VanLandingham nodded approvingly while mouthing the word *excellent.*

The judge addressed Cooper. "Mr. Stone."

Cooper stood and pushed his chair back from the table to give himself a little room to move as he talked. "Our overall position today, Your Honor, is to argue for the intent of the Senate. And this has particular bearing on the issue now before the court. The law of self-executing treaties that Mr. Suskins has argued is absolutely correct as far as he goes. However, there is one major principle he failed to discuss. And that is, if the Senate makes it clear that a provision in a treaty is non-self-executing, then the intent of the Senate is to prevail over all other considerations.

"We believe that the Senate has made it clear that not a single provision in this treaty is to be considered self-executing. We have filed with the court voluminous citations to the record that demonstrate time after time that numerous senators have made statements for the record showing that they considered every matter in the treaty to be non-self-executing. Over twenty-four separate statements appear in the *Senate Journal* concerning the fact that the ban on spanking was intended to require additional legislation and not be automatically thrust upon the American public by the act of ratifying the treaty.

"There were some fifty-eight senators, both Republicans and Democrats, who went out of their way to point out that various provisions in the treaty were not self-executing. And thirty of these same senators explicitly stated that the entire treaty was non-self-executing.

"Therefore, Your Honor, we think that the conclusion is clear. Unless and until Congress specifically bans spanking through ordinary legislation, it is still legal to spank one's child in the United States. Since Mr. Suskins' clients know full well that they are on shaky ground politically, they are trying to get this court to circumvent the process outlined in our Constitution. Courts are to implement existing law, not make up the law out of thin air. We urge the court to dismiss this portion of the petition."

"Thank you, Mr. Stone," Holman said. "Ms. Hennessey, anything from you on this point?"

"Not based on all legal theory, Your Honor. It is just my position on behalf of the children that no one should hit them. I can't imagine how spanking ever teaches anything to children other than more violence. That's all I have to say."

"Well, Ms. Hennessey, that certainly is the philosophy behind this treaty," Holman replied with a reflective look in his eyes, as he rubbed his glasses on the edge of his robe. "My parents certainly wouldn't have agreed with it, but neither my philosophy nor that of my parents is relevant to the legal issue before me. Mr. Suskins, your one-minute rebuttal, please."

"Thank you, Your Honor. The answer to Mr. Stone's argument is really very simple. The intent of the Senate is not to be gained on this issue from reading speeches and counting inferences. There is only one way for the Senate to officially designate a portion of a treaty to be non-self-executing. They have to take a vote. Normally such a vote would come on a formal amendment to the treaty, called a 'reservation.' There are other conceivable ways to take a vote. But the answer is still the same. Without a vote of the Senate declaring a provision to be non-executing, the normal rules of law that I argued initially apply. There is no such vote. Speeches are simply fluff that senators put in the record to appease their constituents. If they want to make a law, they need to take a vote."

Deanna's heart was in her throat. Suskins had convinced her that he was right about the law. She could only hope that the judge found Cooper's arguments to be stronger. Rick squeezed her hand under the table. Doug and Jeanne couldn't bear to look even at each other, much less the judge.

"I intend to reserve ruling until the end of the hearing, in case any one was wondering," Judge Holman said. "So, Mr. Suskins, why don't you move on to the issues of home schooling and the removal of the young girl from the sex education course?"

"Yes, Your Honor," Suskins said confidently. "We contend that the Virginia law that allows home schooling without direct government regulation is a violation of the clear provision of the treaty."

"Mr. Suskins, let me interrupt you for a minute. Are you contending that home schooling is always a violation of the treaty?"

"No, Your Honor. We don't go that far although we do caution that there are strong indicators that it would not be in the best interests of the child in most cases. We concede that under rare circumstances it might be approved."

Holman rocked back in his chair and looked over the top of Suskins' head at the back wall of the courtroom. "Now, you are contending that there must be some governmental review and approval process, right?"

"Correct, Your Honor."

"Which provision in the UN Convention is the source of your authority for this argument?"

"Articles 28 and 29 are the principal sections that deal with education, Your Honor. But there are implications that arise from other articles, as well. Perhaps the most important provision is the last paragraph of Article 29. This paragraph explicitly recognizes the 'liberty of individuals and bodies to establish and direct educational institutions,' but there are two major conditions that affect the right to establish such schools.

"This means that home schooling, by its very definition and its location within the home, is suspect from the beginning because the right of private education is limited to the establishment of 'educational institutions.' Under the interpretation this phrase has been given by the Committee of Ten in Geneva, there is no way that a home school, which by definition is noninstitutional, would be routinely approved under this exception.

"Additionally, Your Honor, there are five criteria that all education must meet, whether it occurs in a public, private, or even a home school. First, there must be focus on a full development of the child's abilities. We will not engage in a debate on that point relative to home schooling.

"Second, there must be proof that the values of the United Nations Charter are being taught in the schooling. There is no evidence that the Thomases' home school meets this criteria.

"Third, there must be instruction that teaches respect for one's own culture and the culture of others. Like the religious question that we will deal with next, Your Honor, there is serious doubt that Christian home schoolers are teaching respect for the culture of Islam or Buddhism, for example. They teach that adherents of these religions are in error and must adopt Christianity.

"The fourth criteria requires, among other things, instruction in tolerance and equality among the sexes. Specifically required is tolerance of other lifestyles and social groups. The principles of tolerance are not exactly the mainstay of the Christian home school movement. For example, our research has disclosed that homophobia and intolerance of alternate lifestyles are strong motivating factors in why people like the Thomas family choose to home school in the first place. Tolerance education is sorely missing from the Thomas home.

"The fifth criteria is instruction in respect for the natural environment. Mr. Stone has not supplied us with any evidence that this goal has been met by the family's home schooling program either."

Judge Holman began talking even as he was still writing on his legal pad. "So we have the rule requiring institutions, and these five standards you say are missing—or at least unproven. Was there another rule also?"

"Yes, Your Honor, that is right. I probably should have brought it up relative to our argument about the rule requiring an institutional school. But in any event, the very last sentence of Article 29 contains this additional requirement. Private institutions 'shall conform to the minimum standards as may be laid down by the state.' As we have already established and as you have ruled, Virginia does not directly regulate the Thomas home school program. Even if a home school can qualify under the convention, an unregulated home school can *never* qualify. Thus, the Virginia law in question is clearly illegal."

"Mr. Suskins, I have another question for you. In your first argument you contended that self-executing provisions within the treaty are the ones that don't require any explanations or funding or the like. Doesn't that defeat your argument here? If you contend that Virginia law needs to have regulations of home schooling added, isn't it up to Virginia's General Assembly to pass these regulations?"

"More likely Congress, Your Honor," Suskins replied.

"OK—or Congress. But my point is basically the same. Details are needed. This is, therefore, not a self-executing law. What do you say to that argument?"

"If the Thomases were home schooling under a law that already provided detailed governmental review, but we were contending that a new review process was needed, then your point would be well taken, Your Honor. However, Virginia has no regulations at all for religious home schoolers. Nothing is needed beyond the text of the treaty itself to determine that a state that offers essentially unregulated home schooling is in violation of the treaty."

"What about the removal of Emily from the sex education class?" Holman asked.

"This is parallel to the removal of Layton Thomas from the entire school day. If a child is to be removed from any aspect of the public school program, someone for the government must be responsible to review the parent's judgment to make sure that the decision is truly in the best interest of the child. Virginia law provides no such review. Therefore, the removal is a violation of Emily's rights under the treaty. She is entitled to be protected from the homophobia of her parents, or whatever factors have motivated them to remove Emily from the course. Such motivations violate the provision of the treaty requiring an education in tolerance."

"All right, I believe I understand. Mr. Stone, I think it is your turn on the education issues."

"Your Honor, we have two quite different arguments on the issue of home schooling, which are also parallel to our position on the sex education question. First, we contend that a treaty may never violate the express constitutional rights of Americans. And it has been the law in the United States for nearly one hundred years, since the early 1920s, that parents have the right to direct the education of their children. Although parental rights are not specifically mentioned in the Constitution, the Supreme Court held in *Pierce v. Society of Sisters* that they are reserved rights."

"But, Counsel, what do you say about *Missouri v. Holland?* Mr. Suskins points out with some force in his brief that if we are talking about an unwritten constitutional right, then a treaty wins. The Missouri case held that a state's reserved rights under the Tenth Amendment took second place behind a treaty. So, wouldn't a parent's reserved right to direct a child's education also take second place to a treaty?"

Cooper pondered the content of Suskins' argument for several seconds before answering. "Your Honor, nothing occurs to me on how to answer that question, other than just saying that *Missouri v. Holland* was a wrong decision and it should be overturned."

"Perhaps it should be, Counsel, but you need to talk to the United States Supreme Court about that one. They made that particular decision, and they are the only ones who can reverse it."

"Well, our other argument regarding education is that the treaty is non-self-executing in this regard. As Mr. Suskins has argued, if a treaty needs details to be enacted, then the treaty cannot be enforced until Congress or the states pass a law filling in all of the necessary details.

"He has argued that a law is needed that requires a detailed review by the government of the parent's choice to home school Layton or to take Emily out of one class. Laws are needed, he contended. Just by saying that simple sentence, he has indicated that it should be apparent that this aspect of the treaty is non-self-executing. Thus, until either Congress or the General Assembly of Virginia acts, these parents may continue to direct their children's education." Cooper nodded at the judge and sat down.

"Ms. Hennessey, anything from you on this point?"

"No, Judge Holman, all I can say is that I agree with the findings of fact that you made on this point. I think Layton is doing fine in home schooling. I have no contentions one way or the other on the nature of the treaty. I just think this court has a present duty to look at the education of Layton, and I think you have correctly concluded he is doing well academically, socially, and emotionally. Perhaps we should return to this court for an annual evaluation of his progress. He may be doing well now in the elementary grades, but especially as he gets into the middle school years I would worry about him socially. Then when he gets into high school, I think there would be a need to check on him academically, as well.

"So, whatever else happens with this case, I hope that you will retain ongoing supervisory jurisdiction over the family. However, I think it would be best to override the removal of Emily from the family life education course. Other than homophobia and a desire to enforce somewhat Puritanical ideas relative to reproductive matters, I see no motive for removing Emily. She should stay in the class."

"Well, Ms. Hennessey," Holman replied, while stroking his chin in serious contemplation, "the ongoing review you request for Layton would be appropriate if we were in the sentencing phase of a child abuse case. Why are you requesting ongoing supervision now, since you agree that the family is doing nothing wrong at the moment?"

"Your Honor, the reason is pretty simple. Under the law before the treaty, the best interest of the child standard was a part of the law that we applied only to broken families. If there was a conviction of child abuse, or if there was a divorce, then the court had to decide what was in the best interest of the child.

"But now, the treaty implies that the government has the duty to intervene for the best interests of every child and not just children from broken homes."

Judge Holman shook his head and rolled his eyes in exasperation. "I have to be candid with you, Ms. Hennessey. Even though you may well be right on your analysis of the treaty, I cannot believe that the Senate of the United States would force the juvenile court judges of this country to supervise the best interests of the child for every single family in America. But, that does appear to be what they have done. I just hope they are ready to fund a whole bunch of new juvenile judges."

Hennessey smiled as she sat down. "I'm available if you need help in Loudoun, Your Honor."

Holman laughed softly while glancing at his watch. "It is 10:15 now. Anything else, Mr. Suskins? Mr. Stone?" Both counsel shook their heads negatively. "All right, the court will stand in recess for fifteen minutes."

A general hubbub erupted as soon as Judge Holman disappeared through the door, and even Deputy Daniels realized that he couldn't demand immediate silence for the moment.

Doug Garvis tapped Cooper on the shoulder. "Is there any reason that Emily has to listen to this?"

Cooper saw the obvious distress in his face. "Let me send a note in to the judge. I think he will excuse her and Layton. This is not about them individually, in any normal sense of the word."

"It's only going to affect the rest of their lives," Doug replied bitterly.

Cooper looked at his client sympathetically. "It's going to be a battle until they're eighteen, that's for sure."

"And after they become parents, as well."

"I'm afraid you're right," Cooper replied dejectedly. "Let me get a note to the bailiff for you. Is there someone here to take the children?"

"I am sure my mother would rather be outside with Emily than in here listening to all of this. And she would be happy to watch Layton, as well."

"Good plan," Cooper replied.

The noise began to dissipate as the courtroom emptied out the back doors onto the grassy square. A mass of reporters was assembled at the bottom of the steps waiting for any of the principal players to emerge.

Suskins was the first person they nabbed. He deftly answered the half-dozen friendly questions shouted in his direction, and then suggested that Ambassador Easler might be willing to offer her comments. She seemed happy to field additional questions, spinning the proceedings and the treaty in a way that made them sound reasonable and moderate.

As she was talking, Emily's grandmother tried to slip quietly out the front door holding the hand of each of the two children. Seeing Emily and Layton, nearly all the photographers and about half the reporters abandoned Easler's impromptu press conference and focused on the children.

At the first shouted question to the children, one of the deputies guarding the door stepped forward.

"There are to be no questions for these children. Judge's orders." One reporter started to protest, but the deputy cut him short. "Take it inside, bud. See Deputy Daniels. My directions are to keep all of you from asking these kids anything." He said nothing, however, about the army of camera operators and photographers that gathered rolls of footage as Emily's grandmother negotiated the children past the statute of George Marshall, Loudoun County's hero from World War II.

Cooper just sat at his table, ostensibly looking over his notes. It was a convenient place to be to avoid having to see Laura.

As Deanna and Rick emerged, they were greeted with a chorus of shouted questions. "We would prefer that you talk to our lawyer," Rick replied, smiling.

"Is he coming out?" one of the television reporters called out.

Deanna looked around for Cooper and saw Laura in the middle of the doorway. "Laura, would you go tell Cooper that he should probably come out and answer these questions?"

Laura paused for a second, nodded at Deanna, and disappeared. She walked through the nearly empty courtroom and leaned against the railing. "Cooper," Laura called softly. He turned and looked up at her in surprise. "Deanna asked me to tell you that the reporters want to ask you some questions."

"Oh, all right," Cooper sighed. "I guess I need to do that." He stood and pushed open the gate, falling in by Laura's side as they walked down the center aisle of the courtroom.

"I see from your hand that congratulations are in order. You are engaged; that's wonderful." At least his voice sounded cheerful.

"Thank you, Cooper." Laura started to add something, thought better of it, and simply said "thank you" again.

As they emerged through the door, Cooper was instantly engulfed in the media madness. Laura slipped away quietly to join Terry, who was standing next to the two couples under attack. Terry's father, the families' pastor, stood to the immediate right of Doug Garvis in unspoken support.

Laura found herself focused on Cooper, as he dodged and smiled, and attacked and smiled, and spun and smiled, and sighed his way through the press questioning. "He's doing a good job," Pastor Pipkin whispered to the group. "Under real attack, but he's handling it well."

The Thomases and Garvises both mumbled their general agreement. Laura and Terry said nothing. Laura moved slightly closer to her fiancé, and with the arm he already around her shoulders, he, in turn, squeezed just a bit tighter.

෴

It was nearly 10:40 when Deputy Daniels signaled to the judge that the courtroom was in proper order. Holman resumed the bench quickly.

"Sorry for the delay. We have a lot of people to move back in here in the space of fifteen minutes." He picked up his glasses, where he had left them on the bench. "All right, Mr. Suskins, let's get started on the third issue. If you expect me to interfere in any way with the religious instruction of these two families, you are going to need to show me in some considerable detail what your authority is."

"I am prepared to do so, Your Honor," Suskins said with a confident smile, as he stood in place behind the counsel table. "But let me make one clarification as we begin. We are not in any way suggesting that these parents cannot teach these children whatever they like about their own religion. If they want to teach their children that their particular faith is the best way to God for them, there is no violation of the UN Convention. It is their tendency to attack other religions that we are concerned about.

"If we are to live in a world community with peace, human rights, and reasonable harmony, then we must put an end to the era in which one religion thinks that it has an exclusive corner on the truth. The vast majority of people are willing to simply say, 'This is what I believe. I do not intend to suggest that you must believe the same.'

"I am reminded of that famous old tale of the blind men and the elephant, Your Honor. Each found the elephant and, being blind, contended that the elephant was like the part of the body they could feel. One thought the elephant was just a tail, another a trunk, and another believed the elephant was a massive leg. But, the truth was that each had an individual perspective on the truth and none of them were wholly right nor wholly wrong. So it is with theology. Each has his or her own perspective. We need to honor the right of others to be different."

Holman sighed and shook his head. "That's interesting philosophy, Counsel. But I am not a philosopher nor the son of a philosopher. I'm just a trial judge from Leesburg, Virginia, who must make a determination about what the law of this country now requires. There are generations of Virginians who have gone before us who would rue this day if they knew that this question had found its way into a courtroom of this Commonwealth and that a serious argument was being made that the government had any control whatsoever on the point. But, let's try to leave the philosophy if you don't mind, and, instead, just show me the provisions in the UN Convention that you believe require me to intervene in the way you have proposed."

"Fine, Your Honor," Suskins replied. "Article 14 contains the general provisions concerning religious freedom. First, I would note that there is a balance between the rights of the child and the duties of the parents that are carefully considered in this article.

"Paragraph 1 contains a general declaration that the *child* has the freedom of thought, conscience, and religion. The second paragraph notes the right of parents to provide direction for children on matters of religion, but there is a limitation on this right. It says that such direction must be 'in a manner consistent with the evolving capacities of the child.' Let me dwell on that one for just a moment. Child psychologists have determined that a child's own capacities to determine truth start very early—certainly by the time the child enters school. These children are both in the third grade, and studies show that many views, prejudices, and opinions have developed by the time a child is in the third grade. A child in the third grade is old enough, for example, to be taught that it is important to respect people of a different race. If that is true, then it should be evident that a child who is able to be taught about racial discrimination has evolving capacities for understanding, and it is no longer the parents' sole right to simply tell their children what they must believe about religion. They can offer ideas to their children, but it must be done in a way in which the child is truly free to make up his or her own mind. If children are told, 'This is the one true religion,' then they are not free to decide their own destiny. After all, the ultimate principle in this treaty is to protect the freedom of conscience of the child, not the parent."

Deanna closed her eyes and wished very hard to disappear off the face of the earth. She then amended her wish and willed the disappearance of the rest of her family with her. A mental image of pioneer life in a log cabin about 150 years earlier suddenly seemed very inviting.

"But it is the third paragraph in Article 14 that is the most important in light of the information in the record. It teaches that religious belief may be limited if 'necessary to protect . . . the fundamental rights and freedoms of others.' We believe this implies a duty to refrain from teaching that Islam is wrong or Buddhism is wrong or that Jews need to accept Jesus. An attack on the religious freedom of others is inherent in such an exclusivist approach to matters of faith.

"We also return to Article 29 as it pertains to the matter of the religious education of the child, in Sunday school for example.

This article requires that all education of the child must teach tolerance for other religious groups. The Sunday school lesson taught by Miss Frasier clearly failed that test when she taught that other faiths were destined to hell. Article 29 also requires instruction in respect for the principles of the United Nations. The instruction of this church is that world governmental agencies are dangerous and must be watched, lest they become a direct instrument for Satan, who will try to use them to dominate the earth."

An undercurrent of snickering could be heard from the press scattered throughout the room. Deputy Daniels looked at the judge, who was already reaching for his gavel. "Quiet!" he thundered. After ten seconds of glaring at the audience, he turned to Suskins. "What is it that you want me to specifically order in this regard?"

"That these parents see to it that these children are not exposed to any religious teaching that teaches that other faiths are wrong," the silver-haired lawyer replied.

"Is that it?" the judge asked.

"That and refraining from teaching that world government somehow relates to Satan."

"OK, Counsel. I understand your request. Mr. Stone, what do you have to say about all of this?"

Cooper tucked his colorful red and blue tie back inside his navy suit jacket as he took to his feet. "Your Honor, this is perhaps the most solemn responsibility I have ever had to assume as a lawyer. Perhaps the most serious argument I will ever need to make in my whole career." He stood grasping the back of his chair with both hands as he talked.

"I renew the argument that I made relative to the right of parents to home school their children. It is our position that if the treaty is interpreted in this way, then it is in violation of the First Amendment of the Constitution's clause that guarantees the free exercise of religion. And even if this court holds that parental rights are not explicitly delineated in the Constitution concerning matters of education, religious freedom is in the Constitution for everyone to see in unmistakable black and white.

"The cases we have cited in our brief make it clear. A treaty provision that violates any provision of the Constitution is unconstitutional."

Holman smiled and twisted his pen in his hands as he began to speak. "Yes, but, Counsel, how do you answer the argument in Mr. Suskins' brief to the effect that religious freedom in the Constitution doesn't decide whose religion is to prevail, the child's or the parents'?"

Cooper continued, for this was a question he had anticipated. "Your Honor, the other side contends that we must understand the UN Convention according to the spirit of those who wrote it. And they have their Committee of Ten to provide such 'expert' interpretation. I cannot argue with their theory of how legal documents should be interpreted. By the same token, however, we must interpret the United States Constitution according to the spirit in which it was written. Not in an evolving manner, as Mr. Suskins has argued in his brief, but according to the meaning intended by the men who wrote the document. I would suggest that there is little question that if you asked James Madison, who shepherded the First Amendment through Congress, or George Mason, who lobbied for the Bill of Rights, or Patrick Henry, whose insistence that the Constitution not be ratified because of the absence of a bill of rights, each one of these men would answer that parents have the right to direct the religious upbringing of their children and no government should ever be allowed to interfere in matters of belief."

Holman was taking notes without looking up.

"Thus, it is our core contention that even if this treaty is self-executing it is unconstitutional when it comes to matters of attempting to regulate the religious instruction of children, whether by their parents or in Sunday school."

Cooper paused and reached down for his copy of the UN Convention. "Your Honor, I sincerely hope we don't get to the point where there is any reason to try to discern the meaning of the UN treaty language. We want a win on a constitutional basis, not some mere technical victory. But, as a lawyer, I have a duty to bring all of our defenses to your attention.

"If you look carefully at the language of Article 14, paragraph 3, you will see that the rules for limiting religious instruction are not quite what Mr. Suskins stated. He mentioned that religious instruction must protect the 'fundamental rights and freedoms of others.' However, he failed to emphasize the first half of that same sentence. It says, 'Freedom to manifest one's religion or beliefs may be subject only to such limitations as are prescribed by law.' What law has prescribed the limitations Mr. Suskins seeks? There is no such law. We need no rule of construction or inference to determine whether or not there needs to be implementing legislation on this point. Article 14 explicitly says that such legislation is necessary.

Without a law, no such restrictions are possible. Now, it is true that this treaty may put an obligation on Congress to pass a law banning so-called intolerant religious instruction. But until that day, this portion of the lawsuit must be dismissed for now."

Cooper looked at his clients as he sat back down. For the first time that day, they seemed to have a little color in their faces, rather than pale blank stares. All four managed slight smiles in Cooper's general direction.

Without being asked, Rachel Hennessey popped to her feet. "I don't have anything to say on this point, Your Honor."

"Thank you, Ms. Hennessey. And Mr. Suskins, I see no need for rebuttal on this point. I think I've got the drift of your position." Holman looked over his pages of notes. "I guess that leaves just the issue of standing of the two NGOs to file this litigation. You both have briefed this very well and have covered the points you would make in oral argument on this one. Any additions to the formal arguments?"

Cooper and Suskins both shook their heads, indicating that they would both stand on their written arguments.

"All right, in that case, I am ready to rule on all aspects of the case. The oral arguments have been very helpful, very helpful indeed. In fact, Mr. Stone, you changed one of my intended rulings with one of your last arguments."

Rick and Deanna squeezed each other's hands upon hearing at least a little encouragement from the mouth of the judge.

"First, let me say something as a citizen and not a judge. I think I have hinted at it several times, but I want to be explicit. It is an unbelievable day in America that the United States Senate has ratified this treaty that is so invasive of the traditional rights and responsibilities of Americans. But I believe in the rule of law; and if the proper authorities have made a law, even when I believe it to be unwise, it is still my solemn responsibility to enforce it. And that is what I am required to do.

"I will begin with the issue of the standing of the NGOs. Article 45, paragraph (a) contains the following language. 'The specialized agencies, the United Nations Children's Fund, and other United Nations organs shall be entitled to be represented at the consideration of the implementation of such provisions as fall within the scope of their mandate.' The NGO status of the NEA and the Children's Defense Fund is unquestioned and both have a mandate reflected on the face of their NGO certificates to involve themselves in the education, physical, and emotional welfare of children. Therefore, I am required to conclude that the National Education Association and the Children's Defense Fund are proper agencies to bring this lawsuit."

Cooper took notes but didn't have the courage to even glance in the direction of his clients.

"Now, let's get to the substantive issues. And as long as I started with the fourth issue, let me just keep going in reverse. On the third issue, I have to say that I am very relieved that Mr. Stone pointed out the language in the treaty concerning the need for implementing legislation that delineates what steps religious instruction must take to teach tolerance and respect for the religions of others. I came to this hearing with a heavy heart on this matter, and I have been shown a way so I don't have to become the first judge in America to order a restriction on Sunday school lessons. Those of you who support this treaty, you are going to need to go to Congress and see if you can get yourself a statute that gives you the request you make. Now, it would appear that they might be obligated under the treaty to pass such a law. But, you haven't even tried yet, so I will entirely deny the request of the NEA and the Children's Defense Fund to circumscribe the religious instruction of these children."

Cooper was able to sneak a look at Rick and saw a smile starting to spread over his face.

"Now on the issue of home schooling. I reach a similar result. Mr. Suskins has presented a very scholarly brief, nearly a treatise, on the subject of self-executing treaty provisions. And according to his own brief, if any provision of a treaty needs details to be filled in by an additional law, then that provision of the treaty is not self-executing. There is no escaping the nature of the argument. If you want home schooling to have more regulations, then you are asking for an additional law. Accordingly, the request to control the home schooling of the parents is denied. Go back to Congress on this one, as well. Again, Congress may be obliged to pass a law that trumps Virginia statute. But until then I cannot, myself, add or subtract from existing laws."

Even Deanna managed to smile at this statement.

"Finally, we reach the issue of spanking. And I know this is quite a controversial topic. The young people I see in juvenile court routinely appear to me to need more discipline, not less, but I am not free to do as I wish on this matter.

"Mr. Suskins has been quite convincing on this point. Spanking is banned by the UN Convention. There are no conditions needed.

There is no funding needed. There are no implementation rules required—although it is possible to go further and criminalize parents who, in fact, spank their sons and daughters. But such a request is not before me. I am simply asked to implement a provision of a duly ratified treaty."

Holman looked up from his notes and looked down at each of the parents. "Mr. and Mrs. Thomas and Mr. and Mrs. Garvis, this gives me no pleasure. My parents spanked me, and I spanked my children when they needed it. I turned out well and so did my kids, and I am sure that you are good and loving parents. So there is no condemnation at all in my order. But I am required by law to order you to stop all spanking of your children, and such an order will indeed be entered. Mr. Stone, please prepare the order because you prevailed on at least some of the issues today."

Holman abruptly stood, left the bench, and disappeared.

"This court is adjourned," Daniels proclaimed with his hand on his gun, lest any of the "felons" decided to charge the bench.

13

LOUDOUN COUNTY, VIRGINIA.
May 24, 2005.

The traffic was light on the Dulles Greenway. After all, it was only 6:30 A.M. But the heaviness of Cooper's heart was more than sufficient for the moment. He had slept little the night before. He could never quite remember the dreams that kept waking him up, but he knew intimately the thoughts that popped into his head as soon as he was awake.

He had replayed every word of the hearing in his head so many times that he had lost track. There were at least twenty things he accused himself of doing poorly. Arguments he could have made. Points he could have raised. Engagement rings he wished he hadn't seen.

He clicked the radio on to WTOP, the all-news channel. It was a mild distraction until he heard Suskins' voice on the radio. He had watched all the clips of the news he could stand. Listening to another story on the radio was out of the question. He hit the button for the Christian station. Preaching. Not now. He hit the switch for his aunt's favorite oldies station. Love gone bad. He told the car to just shut up and drive.

The *Washington Star* lay on the seat next to him. He was the winner, more so than Suskins, the paper had declared in its lead editorial—all pending appeal, of course. His picture was on the front page, his voice was on the radio, his image had been all over the national nightly news, CNN had been re-running the story throughout the night, and yet, in the light of a glorious morning in late May, Cooper Stone felt abandoned and alone.

The recurrent theme of the discovery of Laura's engagement resurfaced in the midst of traffic, both mental and motorized— Cooper was now at the Beltway. "Why did you let me discover *that* during the hearing?" he cried aloud to the Lord.

Cooper closed his eyes for a split second and then sighed heavily. He was mad at God. He had to recognize his attitude for what it was. It wasn't Suskins. It wasn't the judge. It wasn't the United States Senate or even the foolish voters who had put the current politicians into power. Well, maybe he was a little mad at the voters, but God could have even overridden them. It was God's fault. It was God who didn't seem to care. It was God who had abandoned him. As bad as he felt about his own situation, when he skimmed away all of the surface hurts and thoughts, he was even more troubled that God appeared to have abandoned America.

You've got to help me, God. I can't carry this alone. He repeated the prayer several times. As he prayed, he reflected on the thoughts of his hurried prayer during the hearing the day before. He hadn't thought he could get through oral argument after seeing Laura's ring, but he had. In fact, as he signaled to exit the Beltway onto the beautiful George Washington Parkway, he realized that he had not thought of her engagement at all during the argument itself. That realization initially encouraged him, but he was intent on feeling upset, so he didn't chase the thought down to the comforting conclusion that might have awaited him.

About thirty-five minutes later, he pulled into a parking garage that was about a block from the massive offices of the *Washington Star*. He found the corridor to which he had been directed without difficulty. He knocked on the correct door at 7:55. A short man in his late forties or early fifties opened the door.

"Mr. Stone? I'm Randall Wasson."

"Yes," Cooper said, smiling and extending his hand.

"Great, you are a little early—so much the better," he called out over his right shoulder, as he guided Cooper through the outer secretarial office into his large private office. "I have assumed that you are a coffee drinker, and there is some over there," he said, pointing. "Grab a mug—in fact, keep the logo mug; you have helped us sell a few papers this morning. Come on over and let's talk."

Cooper helped himself at the small table that was placed snug against one of the side walls. He added sugar and just a touch of the amaretto creamer. "Thanks. After driving for an hour and a half in Washington traffic, it's just what I needed."

"Good, good. Please come sit down as soon as you are ready."

Wasson was about five feet six, with salt-and-pepper hair and a trim beard. He wore a black cashmere camel hair sports jacket, grey tweed pants, a button-down oxford white shirt, and a dark red tie patterned with charcoal-colored diamonds. His demeanor seemed energetic and friendly, not rushed.

"Well, how did we do? Did our reporters get the story right?"

"It wasn't bad. In fact, it was probably one of the better articles your paper has done on the case," Cooper replied, as he sank down in one of the saddle-colored stuffed leather chairs.

"That's sounds like you haven't been particularly pleased with our coverage up until this point."

"Well," Cooper said, wanting to be diplomatically truthful, "I haven't felt that the *Star* was the *most* favorable paper on the issue. In fact, the editorials have been harsh at times."

"Harsh? I wouldn't call them harsh," Wasson replied. "'Disgusting' is the word I would use."

"Disgusting?" Cooper replied incredulously. "Why would you say that about your own paper?"

"Ah, Mr. Stone, as you are about to learn, I may own a piece of the *Washington Star,* but I am not enamored with our positioning. Its editorial stance leans too far to the left for my taste."

"I can't wait to hear the rest of this story," Cooper replied, with a big smile.

"Well, it's pretty simple. Like my father and brother and three generations of Wassons before me, I went to Princeton. Our father did well in business, and he intended for both of his sons to follow in his footsteps. And to a degree, all worked out well on a surface level. But, while I was at Princeton, I managed to fall in with some wrong company from my family's perspective. A friend of mine was a part of Campus Crusade for Christ, and next thing any of them knew, their son who had been raised in a strong secularist tradition was suddenly a born-again Christian."

"Wow," Cooper replied. "And I take it your family was not too pleased."

"Exactly. Oh, they put a brave face on it. And they tried their best to find ways to dissuade me from using the family fortune to advance opinions they find to be anathema, but they have not been particularly successful in keeping me out of the family business altogether. For reasons that no one seems to understand, including me, I have been pretty successful in giving advice and direction to a variety of ventures and have been more or less tolerated for my religious views because they like the money they think I bring in."

Cooper just listened in total fascination.

"For my own part, I would say that I was more lucky than good in these matters—that is, I would say that if I weren't a Christian. I think that God has chosen to bless me in giving me good ideas and a clear head, so that there is a witness to my family. God has used me as a life lesson to my family to demonstrate that he is a rewarder of those who diligently seek him."

"This is one of the most interesting stories I have heard in years," Cooper replied. "I feel encouraged."

"Well, I think you deserve to feel encouraged on more counts that just listening to me. You did pretty well in the hearing yesterday also. You knocked out their attempts to stop the home schooling and, more importantly, the whole effort to regulate the kids' Sunday school class. Yeah, I know you lost the spanking point, but that is not the biggest of the three. And then there are appeals."

"Yes? Well . . . I was glad that we didn't lose all three of the points. But, as you said, there are appeals and, for good or bad, either the Supreme Court of Virginia or the U.S. will settle this case in the final analysis. And even if we are affirmed on those two points, all that has to happen to overturn both of those victories is for Congress to pass a new law on either or both points, and then we are dead in the water."

"That is very true, of course," Wasson said, touching his beard thoughtfully, "but we serve a big God and who knows what the final outcome will truly be."

"You can't imagine how much I needed to hear that," Cooper replied. "And I think if my pastor or one of my regular friends would have said such things to me I would have thought, yeah, yeah, more Christian platitudes. But hearing them here in the offices of the *Washington Star* after listening to your story . . . well, they are exactly what I needed to hear."

"Great!" Wasson said, with a quickness in his voice. "I would like us to get to the reason I asked you to come see me. You really need to be out of here as soon as possible. Here's the deal. I am ready, willing, and able to give you $250,000 for this case. But there are a couple of provisos."

"You definitely have my undivided attention," Cooper replied.

"The money will come from my personal lawyer in Asheville. You will receive an initial check for $100,000 from his trust account in three or four days. You should send your billings to him. He will instruct you on how to draw additional amounts once your normal billings would exceed that first $100,000. Everyone tells me that this case is headed for the U.S. Supreme Court and that $250,000 is a reasonable minimum figure. I am afraid it is my maximum figure, as well.

"But, here is the real stipulation. If the news of my gift becomes public, I won't be able to give you another dime. I am trying my best to gain influence here at the *Star* on more than just the business end of things. And if I am seen as a conservative ideologue, my brother will do everything he can to exclude me completely. I want to win the battle on a lot of fronts, so it is important to me that I be able to do this anonymously. You can't tell anybody where the money came from."

"Wow," Cooper said trying hard to breathe as fast as Wasson moved. "Sure, I understand. Whoa, there is one problem. I think under the rules of legal ethics I am required to tell my clients who is paying their bill. There is always the possibility that a person would listen to the person paying the bill, rather than the clients' own best interests. So, as long as I can tell my clients—and they can be instructed to keep their mouths completely closed—then I think we can do this."

Wasson thought for a moment. "All right. Done. The first check will be at your office right after Memorial Day weekend."

"This is so generous, thank you."

"It is God's money, and I just try to follow orders on how to spend it," Wasson replied, standing up. "You really need to leave, but let me quickly pray for you."

Wasson walked over and laid his hands on both of Cooper's shoulders while the younger man was still seated. "Lord God, give this brother strength for the battle, courage for the moment, and purity in his daily life. Encourage his heart that the battle is indeed yours and not his. In the name of Christ Jesus I pray. Amen." Wasson smiled as he motioned for Cooper to rise and leave quickly.

"Blessings, Brother. I'll be praying. But I won't be checking in directly. I'll stay up with the case in the press. Talk to my personal lawyer if you need any specifics. He is a fellow elder in my church in Asheville. He is totally trustworthy."

Less than two minutes later, Cooper stepped onto the sidewalk in front of the *Washington Star* building, filled with thoughts of happiness, anticipation, and relief.

NEW YORK, N.Y. May 27, 2005.

The taxi pulled to a stop in the middle of Central Park. Cooper glanced at his watch. Five minutes late. He shrugged and pulled out his wallet to pay the driver.

The hundreds of miniature white lights that outlined the exterior of the Tavern on the Green were a mere preview of the greater number that festooned the huge central dining area. As he stood admiring the lovely setting, he heard a woman's voice calling his name.

"Gwen!" Cooper exclaimed, as he turned around to see a familiar face. "You are looking fabulous as always," he said after giving her a brotherly hug.

"We are really glad that you are able to join us tonight, Cooper."

"Speaking of 'us,' where *is* Peter?"

"He's up at the stand checking on the reservation. We got here a bit early, but they seem to be running behind schedule and Peter is just confirming how long the wait is supposed to be."

"What have you been doing while Peter has been at his conference?"

"Our youngest is three, Cooper. A mother of a three-year-old sleeps whenever she has a chance."

"And does just enough shopping to keep New York merchants from becoming destitute," said another familiar voice from behind Cooper's back.

"Peter!" he exclaimed. "You don't look as good as Gwen, but you are still reasonably well preserved for an old geezer. Let me look at you," he added, suddenly leaning back an extra six inches. "Well, at least you still have all your hair, so you haven't had to resort to parting your hair under your left ear or anything," Cooper said, laughing.

Peter smiled warmly as he reached out for Gwen's hand and drew her to his side. "Our table is ready," he said. "Let's continue this as we eat."

The table for four was nearly in the center of the domed dining room. The thousands of small twinkling lights made the May evening seem like a scene from a romantic 1940s movie. But, the sense of romance soon evaporated for Cooper as the busboy carefully removed the fourth plate, the fourth place setting, the fourth napkin, and the fourth crystal goblet from the table.

"We saw you on CNN while we were on the airplane," Gwen announced, with a satisfied smile. "I am surprised that you haven't been asked for your autograph here in the restaurant."

"I already gave three autographs at the train station," Cooper said nonchalantly.

"Really?" Gwen replied, with a note of glee.

"No," Cooper replied, embarrassed that he had fooled her so thoroughly. "The only autograph I have been asked for all day was in Washington, when the ticket salesman asked me to sign the credit card slip."

"Were you satisfied with the result of the hearing?" Peter asked.

"No, but we couldn't have asked for a better judge. He made it very clear he thinks this UN treaty is awful, but he said he had a duty to enforce the law even though he didn't like it."

"Why is it that our side of these cases is always the one addicted to the rule of law? When judges on the other side don't like the law they always find a way to avoid it or to find it unconstitutional," Peter said shaking his head.

"Tell me about it," Cooper said.

Gwen became suddenly still. "Cooper," she said quite seriously. "How bad is it going to get for families like ours? We spank when our kids need it. We have home schooled. We haven't taught that the UN is a satanic organization, but since this case has started it seems like we should. What is going to happen to our nation?"

Cooper sighed. "Gwen, I really can't predict the eventual outcome. If the decision of the trial judge is ultimately affirmed, then we have lost on the spanking issue in the short term, but we have gained a little time on the other issues. Nothing more than a little time to stall though. Congress is going to start passing and implementing legislation little by little. By the time your youngest is in high school, every bit of this treaty will probably be firmly in place."

"And what will that mean for our family and others like us?" Peter asked.

"Well, everything they asked for in this case and more. No home schooling for people like you and me not committed to their ideas of tolerance. No spanking—well, that is gone already. Your children will have the ability to access whatever information they want and parents will be unable to stop them. Our freedom to share our faith will be left in shambles. We can teach that Jesus is one way to God, but if we teach that he is *the* way, *the* truth, and *the* life and that no man—or woman, got to be inclusive and tolerant—comes to the Father but by him, we are toast."

"Do you really think it is going to get that bad?" Gwen asked, with a panicked look on her face.

"Given the political leanings of most of our lawmakers? I would say that the answer is yes."

"Well, what other good news do you bring us from Washington, Mr. Stone?" Peter asked with an attempt at a smile.

"I'm finally getting paid for this case," Cooper replied brightly.

"So you called CWA?" Peter asked.

"No, I had the phone in my hand ready to keep my promise to you, as a matter of fact, when I got a call from . . . someone who must remain anonymous. I can't tell you exactly the details—but let's just say I am being completely taken care of for any predictable costs."

"But," Peter probed, "you can't say what the deal is."

"No, I have been sworn to absolute confidence on the subject. And even if I could tell you, which I can't, I certainly wouldn't say anything here in this public restaurant. But you should be happy that I was planning to keep my promise to you and even happier that I'm getting paid."

"Just like a true lawyer," Peter replied. "American liberty is coming to an end, and you are happy because you got paid!"

Cooper winced. Not at Peter's joke—that didn't bother him at all. But the idea that American liberty was coming to an end in a case he was litigating. It hit him with a sense of enormous responsibility.

"Man, when you say it like that," Cooper replied, "it makes me feel too young, too little, to handle something of this magnitude."

"James Madison was about your age when he shepherded the Constitution through the convention in Philadelphia," Gwen said.

Cooper looked at her with raised eyebrows and a smile. "Very impressive, Mrs. Barron."

"Home school moms know things like that," Peter replied, giving his wife an extra hug. "I just bring her along to show off because my lawyer friends don't know as much about American history, the Constitution, and the law as she does. She really can be the life of the party until she starts lecturing the lawyers on some of her favorite founders."

"Oh, stop it," Gwen said, nudging her husband playfully.

Peter looked into Gwen's eyes just as she did that, and a moment of strong magical emotions passed between them. The exchange wasn't lost on Cooper Stone. The single lawyer suddenly felt intensely lonely and even a bit jealous. He sighed, forcing himself to put his longing away for the rest of the evening.

The trio walked through Central Park back to the Palace Hotel, where they were all staying. Cooper and Peter agreed to meet to work out in the morning at 9:30, and Cooper bid his friends goodnight. As he got off the elevator on the fourth floor, the smile on his lips vanished. No need to hide his loneliness any longer.

He turned the corner and saw a beautiful woman appearing to have trouble with the key but definitely trying to get into his room. He had a instant thought that she was a mirage, but a quick re-examination revealed that she was having trouble getting into the room next door to his. As he walked closer, not only did she look more beautiful in her short, glittering evening dress, but he thought she looked familiar. He suddenly realized that he knew her.

"Ambassador Easler?" he asked, astonished. "What are you doing here?"

"Cooper?" she responded, with a melodious laugh. "Me? What am I doing here? It's New York, and I am assigned to the UN. I stay in this hotel ten or twelve times a year. The question is what are *you* doing in my hotel?" It sounded like she was talking to an old friend from college and not to the lawyer who had argued forcefully against her position earlier in the week.

"Well, I guess the reason I am in *your* hotel, Madam Ambassador, is to teach you how to use your key to open your door. Here, let me help you."

She handed him the key and leaned playfully on the door. "Go ahead, Mr. Lawyer, let's see you do it. I've been at this for five minutes. And hey, by the way, I thought I told you to call me Jody and to lose this 'ambassador' nonsense."

"You explicitly said that you wanted me to do that because we were not in Geneva or Washington but Leesburg. I figured that New York falls into the category of Geneva or Washington, rather than the Leesburg group of cities."

"Well, actually, Cooper," she said with a quiet warmth, "whenever we are alone, please just call me Jody."

A surge of adrenaline sent shivers throughout his body and a knot into his stomach. Her hair was perfect. Her face was gorgeous.

And her body, in that dress—he stopped himself at that. The spiritual and legal mess that she represented wasn't worth it.

The door clicked open on his fourth or fifth try. "Oh, you did it," she exclaimed, with glee. "I didn't want to have to traipse down and get a bellman to come up here. Thank you so much."

She pressed hard up against his body and gave him a quick kiss on the cheek. Suddenly he began to wonder if the spiritual and legal mess that she represented might be worth the risk.

"Would you like to come in for a minute? I mean, if you are alone, that is."

"I am alone, but I think I shouldn't," Cooper protested.

"So what's a great looking guy like you doing in a fancy hotel in New York on a weekend night all alone?" she asked coyly.

"I guess the same thing a beautiful ambassador is doing all alone on that same weekend night." Cooper wished he could have the words back as soon as he had said them. He realized that he had just stepped up to the edge of the precipice and kicked away about six inches of dirt, leaving himself a bare toehold.

"Remember, I work here," she replied, with an infectious smile. "Really, Cooper, what *are* you doing here? Tracking me?"

"No," he laughed. "It's nothing like that. In fact, I came to New York partly to get away from the case and— Well, let's just say I wanted to get away from the case. And some great friends of mine from Washington State were here for a few days, and they asked me to join them tonight. And so, here I am. Nothing that exciting."

She let go of the door handle and took a step closer to her legal adversary. Maybe it was her perfume, and or perhaps the radiance of her smile, but something was making Cooper feel foggy and weak-kneed.

"Cooper? Can I tell you something? I would have said the same thing about my evening—nothing that exciting—until I bumped into you. Somehow, this seems terribly exciting to me."

She reached out and touched his cheek with the tip of her finger. He stood still and did nothing to stop her. "Why don't you come in for just a little while, Mr. Stone? I can't stand the idea of another movie in another hotel room all by myself."

He reached up and gently took her hand away from his face, but she held on to his hand and he didn't let go. Her fingers quickly laced themselves inside his fingers.

Suddenly, he gave her a gentle tug away from the door while holding on to her hand. "I've got an alternative suggestion," he said, while every muscle, every tendon in his body seemed to be shaking. "Why don't we go for a ride in one of those horse-drawn hansom cabs? I have always wanted to do that, but I never had anyone to do it with. I can't come into your room, Jody—that's just not me. But come for a ride in the park with me."

She smiled brightly and closed the door behind her, never letting go of his hand, even for a second. "Sure, Cooper, I would like that very much."

She snuggled as close to him as she dared, as they walked down the hall hand in hand. They entered the elevator alone, and she gave him another kiss on the cheek as the doors closed behind them. "This seems very romantic, if you don't mind my saying so, Mr. Stone."

Cooper knew inside that there was something wrong, very

wrong with all of this, but he didn't *want* to just walk away. He would stay out of her room; his resolve was steel on that point. And she was just a witness in the case, not technically the opponent. So there were no true legal ethical barriers to spending a romantic evening with a United States ambassador. His spirit told him to run the other way. But he told himself he just couldn't bear the loneliness any longer.

The horse-drawn cabs were waiting right outside the hotel's exit onto Fifty-seventh Avenue. Cooper helped Jody as she climbed up the steps and onto the wooden seat. As he sat down beside her, he realized that even though it was a warm May night, her sleeveless black dress might feel a little cool as they rode though the park.

"Would you like my jacket?" he asked.

"No, Cooper, just put your arm around my shoulders. I would like that a lot better," she replied, with a voice as sweet as any he had ever heard.

He felt he had no choice. He put his arm around her, and as he did she turned and kissed him passionately. He didn't break away—at least not until it was too late to prevent the photographer sequestered on the fourth floor from getting at least six good shots of the kiss with his high-tech camera, outfitted with full capability for shots taken in the dark.

There were no more kisses that evening, but Cooper could hardly sleep knowing who and what was available right next door.

The following morning he found a handwritten note on hotel stationary slipped under his door. "I had to leave unexpectedly. Good-bye, Cooper Stone. I wish things could somehow be different." It was unsigned.

14

LEESBURG, VIRGINIA.
May 31, 2005.

"*Today Show,* line 1," Nancy's voice announced to Cooper.

It was the seventh press call of the morning. The media interest in the case only intensified after the hearing was over. Fox News had broken ranks with the rest of the national networks and had begun to cast the story as an attack on Sunday school, rather than just a lawsuit on spanking. Once that story penetrated to the public at a significant level, every media outlet felt obliged to carry the story, all the while attempting to spin it in a pro-UN Convention direction.

"Morning, this is Cooper Stone," he said, cradling the phone on his shoulder while he reached for his *Washington Star* coffee mug.

"Mr. Stone, I am Danielle Sabella. I'm an assistant producer for the *Today Show.* We are interested in doing a segment on your UN case for Thursday's program. And we would like to talk with you about the guests we bring on the show for your side of the story."

Cooper assessed her age to be early twenties, from the sound of her voice. "And who are the guests for the other side of the story going to be? I gather you are planning to invite someone, from the way you asked the question."

"Sure, we have to be fair. We are asking a representative from Children's Defense Fund, along with Rev. Matt Manilow from Americans United for Separation of Church and State, and we are also working to find an expert on children's rights—perhaps a child psychologist. But, of course, the names are all subject to change."

"I see," said Cooper, sipping his coffee.

"We wanted you to join us, perhaps with one of the couples you are representing. We would like to be able to interview both of the couples by phone to see who would do best for television and then to pick the most appropriate."

"That won't be possible," Cooper replied quickly.

"Any of it or just the telephone interview?"

"I am available to be on your show, but both of the families have decided that they do not want to do any media at all. They feel that this is a time in which they have to be very protective of their privacy. So they aren't doing anything."

"But this is the *Today Show!*" the producer exclaimed, as if Cooper had declined to have his clients receive a million dollars or a new car.

"Yeah, and they have turned down other national talk programs as well. I am afraid you are stuck with me."

"We have to try to get someone else associated with the case to come on as well. Do you have any suggestions?"

"What exactly is the angle you want to explore on the segment you are producing?"

"We are looking at the whole question of Sunday school—how much influence it has on children, what is taught, and so on."

"Why don't you get a professor of Christian education from some seminary? You know, someone who can talk knowledgeably about Sunday school practices on a widespread and maybe even historical basis."

"I don't think we can do that. My directions are not to use any experts, but to get people who are actually involved in the case."

"But I thought you said you were getting experts from the other side," Cooper protested.

"Oh, that's different."

"Why is that different?"

"Uh . . . well, the other side of the case has organizations and so on. There are no ordinary people personally involved in the case. Just groups and stuff. We have to go with them. But you have real families and kids and . . . . Say, what about the kids' Sunday school teacher? I read that there was some episode with her in the courtroom. Would she come on the program?"

"I don't know, but I can ask her. That is the first time that the question's been raised about Laura."

"What's Laura's last name, and do you have her number?"

"Her last name is Frasier, but I think I will need to call her myself."

"OK. Can I call you back in half an hour to find out?"

"Miss . . ." Cooper looked down at his notes, where he had jotted down the name of the producer. "Miss Sabella, Laura is a public school teacher and right now it is the middle of the school day. I don't know if I can reach her that quickly."

"Which school does she teach at? Oh, never mind, I can find that out if she teaches for the public schools. We'll contact her directly then."

"Look, Miss Sabella, I don't want to be rude, but I really don't think you should do that. In fact, if you contact the public schools about this first, I don't think that either of us will be available for your show. Let me contact her. I will drive over to her school at lunch hour and call you around one o'clock. OK?"

"I guess . . . sure, that will work."

"If this works out, you want us on Thursday morning?"

"Right. You would be filmed in our Washington studio—in fact, I think all of the guests are based in Washington—so we aren't going to bring you to New York. We're pretty sure about that."

"What time would that be?"

"You would need to be at the studio at 6:45. Your segment would air around 7:15."

"Oh, all right," Cooper said, rolling his eyes at the five o'clock wake up call he had just agreed to. "I'll call you back after lunch."

PAEONIAN SPRINGS, VIRGINIA.
May 31, 2005. 12:15 P.M.

Cooper pulled his newly purchased sports utility vehicle into the far corner of the elementary school parking lot. He got out and admired it for the third time that day and the umpteenth time since buying it three days earlier. Wasson's check had indeed arrived, and after paying his bills and expenses, he had had enough left to buy the three-year-old GMC Jimmy.

He pulled his sun glasses up away from his eyes just to check. Yes, the indigo blue color seemed to radiate a deeper hue in the sunlight, just like the salesman had promised. He turned slowly away from his new car and headed toward the school.

The school secretary checked him in and called Laura on the intercom. Third door on the right. He remembered the way, even though he had only been to Laura's classroom on one prior occasion, about a week before her deposition.

Cooper didn't like to think about Terry Pipkin asking Laura to marry him. He couldn't stand the idea of her saying yes. He didn't want to think about them together in any way. Instead, he had connected seeing Laura's ring with the courtroom. Rather than seeing her ring as a symbol of her promise to marry another man, Cooper had coaxed his own mind to look upon her ring as merely a tangible reminder of his loss in the courtroom. Lawyers lose in the courtroom on a regular basis. It's just part of a litigator's life. Summary judgment granted. Laura must wear a ring. You lose. On to the next case.

The door was open when he arrived in room 12. He paused in the doorway. She was sitting at her desk, head buried in some student papers. A cup of yogurt was in one hand and a spoon in the other. The sunlight cast a soft shadow across her face and she looked . . . Cooper stopped, searching for the right adjective to describe her beauty, forced his hand to reach up and tap quietly on the open door.

"Laura?"

She looked up with wide eyes, and her face broke into a quizzical smile. "Hi, Cooper. So what brings you here today?"

"I have come to talk to the most sought after Sunday school teacher in America."

"Me?" she asked, shaking her head.

"You can't believe all the media calls I am getting. Ever since the hearing, there has been more and more focus on the limitations on religious freedom that Suskins is seeking. I am doing as many interviews as I can to try to get the truth about this treaty out to as many Americans as possible. But some of the shows don't want me alone, and the *Today Show* has insisted that they want you on the program. They have also insisted that I get an answer for them today."

"I guess they take the name of their show seriously—they want everything today," Laura replied with a smile. "But why me? Why not the families? Why not you?"

"They wanted the families, but neither of them want to do any media at all. And I am supposed to appear on the program with you."

"Oh, I see," Laura replied. She shook her head and smiled. "I guess so. I would certainly like to help expose this treaty for what it really is. Is there any reason I shouldn't want to do this?"

"Well, the only thing I can think of is if doing the show with me would make you uncomfortable in any way."

Laura looked down at her desk, but Cooper could see her smiling. She looked up confidently. "Cooper, we never did have a chance to talk about my engagement to Terry. He just finally asked me to marry him. And that is what I had wanted since I was seventeen years old. There was nothing to do but say yes. I never wanted to hurt you. I hope I didn't do anything to lead you on. I know you liked me . . ." Her eyes looked down at her papers again. "Liked me a lot, perhaps. And I guess I got a little confused about how I felt. And I am really sorry if you got hurt. And I think you are a great guy. But . . ."

She shook her head and pressed her lips together as she examined the young lawyer trying to smile bravely at her. "Are you OK?" she asked.

"Sure," Cooper said with the hint of a laugh. "I feel great today."

"I am not talking about just today. Are you OK generally?"

"Laura, I don't know how to answer that question 'generally.' But I can answer it as it pertains to you. I am OK. You are a great young woman and a real delight. But, you were very up-front with me about Terry, and if I let my emotions run down the wrong track for a little while, it certainly wasn't your fault. You never led me to believe otherwise. So, I am OK . . . no, I am *more* than OK about your future. If God wants you to marry Terry, and because you said yes, I believe that must be what he wants, then that is what I want for you too. That's as honest an answer as I know how to give."

Laura smiled, looking relieved. "I have to tell you that I have been dreading this conversation. But you have made me feel much better. Thank you." She bit her lip, which was starting to quiver a little. "Thank you very much, Cooper."

"So, what about the *Today Show?*" he asked, happy for an opportunity to change the subject.

"I'd be happy to do the *Today Show* if you think it will help the cause. What do I need to do?"

"Bad news on that point. You need to be in the studio in downtown Washington at 6:45 A.M."

"In the morning?" she asked.

"'Fraid so."

"I am not sure the cause needs that much help! I hate driving in Washington rush hour traffic."

"Well," Cooper said, "since we are all settled with each other, I don't see how it is wrong for a lawyer to drive a witness to a television interview."

"I guess that would be fine." Laura scrunched her face in mock pain. "But what time would you need to pick me up?"

"5:30 A.M."

"I was afraid of that. But . . . it's all for the cause. See you Thursday morning."

"Bye," he replied.

Cooper was tempted to linger and look at her, but he wisely turned quickly and headed for the exit gate.

LEESBURG, VIRGINIA. May 31, 2005. 1:00 P.M.

The notice of appeal and motion for expedited consideration was waiting on his desk when he returned from Laura's school. A messenger service had hand delivered the package to Nancy, catching her at lunchtime between bites of her turkey sandwich.

Cooper flipped through the eighteen-page brief accompanying the motion. Suskins spent that many pages just arguing why the case should be considered quickly. His brief on the merits would be the maximum length of fifty pages, unless he secured approval for a longer brief. Must be nice to have all that help, Cooper mused.

He spent the afternoon drafting an appellate strategy. He saved the four-page outline of arguments and strategy to his hard drive and then attached it as a file to an e-mail that he sent to all four of the parents—the two dads at work and the moms on their home computers.

He recommended that they consent to the motion for expedited appeal. His friends on the Senate Judiciary Committee were hearing rumblings about a conservative Supreme Court justice who was thinking of retiring. It was likely that a new administration would appoint a justice who was supportive of the treaty.

He asked for and received quick e-mail agreement from all four clients. By four o'clock he was hard at work on his notice of cross-appeal and designation of transcript.

CHAPTER 15

LEESBURG, VIRGINIA.
June 2, 2005.

Laura thought she heard knocking on her front door. She glanced at her watch through eyes that felt bloodshot but looked clear in the mirror. But then again, she was looking through sleepy eyes, and so she couldn't be sure that she saw everything correctly. She and Terry had planned to go to a movie last night, and she hadn't had the courage to tell Terry that she needed to cancel the evening to get up early to ride with Cooper to do the *Today Show.*

She hopped a couple steps through her living room as she struggled to get her high heel on her right foot. "Morning, Cooper. Come on in. I'll be just a minute," she said retreating for her bathroom and one last effort with the curling iron.

"OK," he replied, nervously glancing at his watch. He walked around the living room looking at the photographs that were on display on her walls, desk, and both of the end tables.

"Looks like you have a nice family," he called out in the general direction in which she had disappeared.

"Thanks," came the reply, mumbled over hairclips that she had stuck in her mouth moments before.

"Where do your parents live?"

"Floor-duh," he thought she said. He deciphered her next phrase to mean "they're retired," although he had to struggle a bit before he deciphered the meaning from her muffled sounds.

She appeared in an inner doorway. "OK, I'm ready."

Cooper said nothing but smiled and opened the front door for her. The Jimmy was sitting with the engine running and the lights on, parked right at the end of her walkway.

"You got a new car, Cooper. When did you do that?"

"Last week," he answered, as he opened the passenger door. He shut her door and looked at his watch again as he hurried around to the other side. *Eight minutes late,* he thought.

"It's really nice. I like the smell of the leather seats," Laura remarked, as Cooper was fastening his seat belt.

"Yeah, after that old thing of my aunt's, this seems like a whole new world. But it's just a car." The second sentence may have been true for some people, but in Cooper's case, it was, at minimum, an understatement. "I was really glad to get something more of my own style," he said more truthfully.

"I guess you are doing OK financially on this case now. You told me that the reason you kept driving your aunt's car was because of the expenses of a private law practice."

"Yeah, I'm doing fine with the case right now."

"Well, that was really great what that guy did from the *Washington Star* to underwrite the case."

Cooper turned white. "Guy from the *Washington Star?*" he asked innocently.

"Yeah, you know the publisher's brother or something. Deanna told me about the situation."

"Deanna told you, huh? It was supposed to be confidential."

"Yeah, she said that, too, but I was asking her about the case one night. Frankly, I was worrying about both you and them. I didn't know how either of you could afford to keep going. I guess I was pretty persistent. And she figured that because I had been kind of an insider on the case from the beginning, she could tell me."

"Well, as long as it doesn't go any further," Cooper replied, still breathing a bit heavily from the shock of the subject being raised at all. "If it goes public, then I'm dead in the water, and a really nice man will suffer for it."

"Oh, I promise not to tell anyone at all about it." She reminded herself to be sure and tell Terry to also be quiet about the money. He had been by her side when Deanna had explained the whole situation. Laura thought it not necessary to mention that fact right then.

Several minutes passed and then they fell into lighter conversation about the end of the school year. Laura told Cooper about her plans to visit her family in "Flor-i-da," and they laughed about her mumbled pronunciation earlier in the morning.

For the first time, they also told each other about their childhoods and families. They had each progressed up through their college years when Laura fell a little silent for a minute.

"Cooper? Can I ask you something a little personal?"

"I guess," he replied hesitantly.

"You are thirty, right?"

"Yeah."

"Never been married?"

"Right."

"Why not? Have you ever been serious with anyone?"

"I was engaged once," he replied. His voice told her that he was not going to volunteer anything more until she asked another question.

"So, what happened?"

"She broke it off. We were a month from the wedding."

"Another guy?"

"No. Not at the time, but she's married now. She just said that something wasn't right about everything."

"How long had you been dating?"

"Since high school. All she would say is that she felt like we started off too young. And that was it."

"Oh . . ." Laura's voice trailed off. She closed her eyes and leaned against the window of the car, wishing she had never brought up the subject. She became quiet, and eventually Cooper turned on the radio news to cover the awkward silence that filled the car.

Despite the late start, they arrived at the studios right on time. A guard at the front desk of the office building hustled them up to the tenth floor, where they were to go for makeup. Cooper had gone through these paces five or six times by now and had adjusted to the idea of wearing makeup, so long as they removed every vestige of it as soon as he stepped out of the studio.

He and Laura were in side by side swivel chairs with a pair of makeup artists working over them both. Laura's artist pronounced her "nearly perfect in every way" before she started, just needing a little powder here and there. The woman working on Cooper squeezed large amounts of tan looking goo onto a sponge and wiped it all over his face, just like the prior occasions. He hated the feel of it, but he had to admit it did make him look better on video.

Danielle Sabella came in with her clipboard during the makeup process and reminded them that they had only eight minutes and there were a total of four guests, including them, not counting "the talent."

The makeup artist handed Cooper's jacket back to him instantly as he stepped down from the stylist's chair, and they were both hurried to the studio waiting area. The door to the green room opened, and they could see the back of a woman with light brown hair in a green silk suit who was engaged in friendly conversation with another person. Her head turned toward the sound of the opening door, and Jody Easler smiled her warmest and friendliest smile.

"Mr. Stone, good to see you again," she said extending her hand as she remained seated on the couch.

"Good morning, Ambassador Easler," he replied, trying to get his bearings. "I think you may have met Laura Frasier previously at Lansdowne," he said politely, gesturing toward Laura with a calmness that masked his turmoil.

"I think we saw each other in the hallway, but I don't believe we were actually introduced," Jody replied. "I am very happy to meet you, Ms. Frasier," she said, with a nod.

"I'm happy to meet you, too," Laura replied uncomfortably.

Cooper was saved from having to think of what to say next by the young woman with the clipboard. "All of you need to come with me, right now."

There were five chairs on the set. Jared Andrews, the "talent," sat on the far left. Rev. Matt Manilow, from Americans United for Separation of Church and State, was seated next. Jody Easler was in the center. Cooper was next, and Laura was on the far right.

Microphones were attached, coffee mugs full of water were set in front of each guest, and there was a general commotion that suddenly died when a red light flashed on top of the camera marked "3."

"Should children's Sunday school classes be regulated under the new United Nations children's treaty?" Andrews intoned, in the manner that had brought him to the top of a profession that valued more the ability to project concerned winsomeness than to show actual intelligence. "That's our topic this morning on the *Today Show*'s 'Insight on the News' segment."

He turned on cue and squared his shoulders to look straight into camera 2. "A test case concerning the meaning and implementation of the UN Convention on the Rights of the Child is underway in Loudoun County, Virginia, a bucolic suburban area on the far western edge of the Washington, D.C., metropolitan area. Two families in this case are on trial, in part, because of what their children learn in Sunday school."

His shoulders swiveled once again. Camera 3. "We have several of the participants in that trial as our guests this morning, but I want to begin with the Sunday school teacher accused of violating international law by what she teaches to third graders on Sunday morning. Laura Frasier, good morning, and welcome to the *Today Show*."

Laura winced at the introduction but smiled and replied, "Good morning."

"Ms. Frasier, I think that everyone in America wants to know why you think it is necessary to teach that other religions are wrong. We certainly understand everyone teaching in their own faith tradition. But, why does your denomination insist on telling young children that people who follow other faith traditions are going to hell?"

Laura's ears burned. She had had no idea she was going to be attacked like this. "Mr. Andrews, all I can say is that it is the truth."

Andrews was not prepared for the answer. Sensing as much, Manilow intervened. "Here you have a perfect illustration of the dangers of fundamentalist thinking. We are right; everyone else is wrong. It is this kind of assertion that has kept the world at war over religious questions for centuries. I am sure that Ms. Frasier here means well, but at some point in time we have got to stop the bloody feuds over religion."

"Let me turn to an expert on children's rights," Andrews said, again pivoting toward the correct camera. "Ambassador Jody Easler is with us this morning. Dr. Easler is a world-renowned expert on children and is the American representative to the UN at Geneva. She also serves on the official Committee of Ten for the implementation of the treaty. Good morning, Madam Ambassador."

"Good morning, Jared, it is great to be with you again."

"Madam Ambassador, let me ask you how the kind of rigid fundamentalist teaching we have been discussing affects the lives of children in the long run."

"Well, Jared," she said with a perfect smile that seemed genuinely warm, "I know that every parent and, I am sure, every Sunday school teacher wants what is best for the children.

Ms. Frasier is certainly a person of good will and has the best of intentions for the children in her class. But, here is my concern. Very subtly, and perhaps unintentionally, a child is harmed by the kind of lesson we are talking about. When we teach a child that one's religion is truth, I think everyone benefits. Faith is such a noble thing. But when we teach children that their religion is *the only* truth, an insidious change takes place. Such children learn to look at others as lesser in value. Such ideas lead to disharmony, and potentially conflict, and ultimately violence. We simply are trying to learn to teach children about matters of faith, without planting seeds in their hearts that will ultimately lead to violence."

"Thank you, Ambassador Easler. That was very helpful," Andrews said.

His earpiece told him, "Go after the lawyer. Camera 2."

"Now, let's focus on the court action. With us this morning is Cooper Stone, who is the attorney representing the parents. Mr. Stone, can you tell us what legal rights you believe are invaded when parents are simply instructed to teach their children to be tolerant of others?"

"Well, Mr. Andrews, I agree with the statement of Miss Frasier. I think parents have the right to teach their children the truth. Truth has been the highest goal of our legal system since the inception of our country. If parents are foreclosed from teaching their children the truth in the name of political correctness, then we have lost the fundamental rights and values that have made this nation great."

Manilow pounced. "There they go again," he groaned. "You can't have a conversation with a fundamentalist without him whining about the Founding Fathers. Let's face facts. The founders were deists not Christians. And simply put, we are not locked in a time warp of 1789 or 1776, or whatever year Mr. Stone thinks it is. This is 2005, and it is high time we recognize the nasty reality that fundamentalism is a danger to us all. We are being nice to simply ask parents to refrain from teaching a small portion of their traditional hate-based doctrines to their children. We should probably think long and hard about doing more. Just leave other people alone. That's all we're asking, just leave other people alone."

"Well, there you have it," Andrews concluded triumphantly. "It's an interesting story and we'll be following it closely."

"Clear," the producer called from the sidelines.

A phalanx of technicians descended on the guests, removing wires and urging them to move off the stage and out of their lives.

"What was that?" Laura whispered to Cooper.

"That was a shark feeding, and we were the fodder, I think," Cooper replied quietly, shaking his head. "Let's get out of here," he said.

Laura took the lead heading back to the makeup area so that Cooper could have the goo removed. As they neared the door leading from the darkened off-camera area of the studio, there was a tap on his shoulder. He stopped, turned, and looked Jody Easler straight in the face.

"Sh-sh . . ." she whispered. "Listen. Sorry about today. I am sorry about a lot of things." She started to say something else, but after a quick glance off to her left suddenly smiled and started talking in a normal voice. "Mr. Stone, I guess we will see you soon in the Virginia Supreme Court. Good day," she said, extending her hand.

Cooper shook hands with her and felt a small scrap of paper pressed into his palm. He slowly stuck his hand into the outer pocket of his suit jacket and said good-bye with no elaboration.

Upon reaching the makeup area, he asked the makeup artist to wait just a moment and stepped into the adjacent rest room. As soon as the door closed, he retrieved the paper from his pocket. A small yellow note read: "Don't use e-mail to send your clients case plans. Be careful, Cooper. I wish . . . ." That was all.

Neither Cooper nor Laura said much until they were inside the car.

"Cooper, I am not blaming you, but I have to say that I can't believe I got up at 4:15 this morning for that!"

"I don't think they treated us very fairly, that's for sure," Cooper replied ruefully.

"Fair? A crooked sheriff with a speed trap and a brother-in-law for the judge is a paragon of virtue compared to those buzzards!"

"Laura Frasier! Where did you learn to talk like that?"

"It's one of my dad's favorites. I brought it out special, just for the occasion," she said, with a teasing look in her eyes.

"You are really something," Cooper laughed. "I am finding out all kinds of things about you this morning. Good thing Suskins was in a hurry when he was taking your deposition. Who knows what he might have found out?"

"Speaking of my deposition, *Mister Stone*. What's with this ambassador woman? You two seem particularly friendly with each other!"

"I can't tell you because I can't figure it out myself," he answered honestly.

"If I didn't know better, I would say she has a crush on you."

Cooper couldn't think of what to say, so he said nothing and just shrugged and rolled his eyes.

"Cooper? What is going on? Does she have a crush on you?"

"Oh . . . I am sorry, I didn't realize you were serious. How would I know that? But come on, you heard what she said. How could I ever be attracted to a woman who is so . . . so, I don't know. Liberal . . . I guess that word is the only way to describe her."

"I hadn't considered the possibility of you being attracted to her for that very reason, plus it seems pretty evident that she is not a believer. I was only thinking about her liking you."

"You asked me a personal question this morning. Can I ask you one?"

Laura swallowed hard and wished again she had never brought up the question about his past. But she felt compelled. "I guess so, but if it is too personal, I am going to decline to answer."

"It is just this. Why all the sudden interest in whether Jody Easler has a crush on me? What brought that on? I don't get it."

"Isn't it obvious?" She asked, as much of herself as of him. "Just being protective of you. I wouldn't want you to fall into the hands of a 'liberal,' as you described her. A pretty liberal, perhaps, but a liberal, nonetheless."

"OK, OK . . . I was just asking."

As Cooper navigated the highway on the Virginia side of the Potomac, Laura stared out the window at the array of monuments on the other side of the river.

"Lots of weather we've been having lately, don't you think?" she asked.

"Another one of your dad's favorites?"

"How could you tell?"

"My dad used the same line whenever he wanted to change the subject."

They both laughed, and by unspoken mutual consent, left all of the difficult subjects of the world behind.

WORLDWIDE WEB. *June 2, 2005. 11:00 P.M.*

Cooper still couldn't believe that he had agreed to do this on the same day that he had to get up so early for the *Today Show*, but Sally had practically begged him. And, well, she was a good friend, and he had committed himself.

He logged on the computer and followed the directions Sally had given him to get into chat on *Crosswalk.com*.

The screen read:

You are entering the News Room as CooperStone.

Sally had decided he should just use his real name for this special event. He hit the "enter" button.

Welcome to our Special Event. Cooper Stone, Esq., who represents the two Virginia families in the UN children's treaty test case, is our special guest.

Cooper read the screen and watched information start to scroll past his eyes at a speed he could barely follow. He watched a variety of names appear on the screen: Cryllic, contentmomma, notreally, Katie_host, sancty-fried, Angelic, MissSally, nana, firemomma, FiddlersPapa, and others. The screen told him that thirty-two people were in the chat room, the vast majority with strange names like the first handful on the list.

Miss Sally: Cooper!!!! You made it. Welcome to our chat room.
Angelic: Hey Cooper, welcome.

FiddlersPapa:	Thanks Cooper, Sally has told us about you, and we wanted you to come anyway.
Cryllic:	LOL fid, be nice he just got here.
CooperStone:	Thank you . . . I think. Sally tells me you all have been praying for me and the case, thanks!
Katie_host:	Mr. Stone, thanks for coming. I will try to keep these chatters in line . . . That is a dubious task, but I think I can guarantee that it will be nicer for you than the Today Show this morning. Sally told us you were going to be on and many of us watched. Who watched?
Nana:	I watched . . . boo @ Today Show.
Firemomma:	I watched . . . bunch of vipers
SandeeBeach:	I watched . . . but I hit the mute button . . . just wanted to see if Sal's friend was as cute as she keeps bragging.
DamonDude:	Are we going to do this cute lawyer business all night or are we going to ask real questions about the UN?
CooperStone:	I sure hope the UN.
MissSally:	Coop, can you tell us what the status of the case is?
CooperStone:	Sure. The trial court has issued its final order and the first appeal has been filed by the other side. We are getting ready to cross-appeal.
FiddlersPapa:	Why are both sides appealing?
Sancty-fried:	Because our side has a cute lawyer and their side has a drop-dead gorgeous ambassador . . . not that I pay attention to stuff like that.
Firemomma:	Not that kind of appealing, lol.
Sancty-fried:	So you don't think he is cute, fire?
Firemomma:	You are trying to get me in trouble, Sancty . . . I refuse to answer that question . . .
Notreally:	Good for you, fire, that Sancty can never be serious. I mean how can a liberal be drop-dead gorgeous? Beautiful, maybe, but not gorgeous, only conservatives can be gorgeous.
Katie_host:	Raises her eyebrows at Sancty and Notreally and warns them within an inch of their lives
Sancty-fried:	gets out tape measure

CooperStone:	Appealing . . . why are we appealing? Because neither side liked what the trial court ruled. Both of us had some part of the case we want the Virginia Supreme Court to overturn.
Nana:	How can we pray for you, Mr. Stone?
Cryllic:	Yeah, we have been praying a lot for you.
CooperStone:	I would appreciate prayer for my ability to concentrate in the next month. I have to write the appellate brief pretty much by myself. The other side has a huge team of lawyers at their disposal.
Firemomma:	Will pray.
Nana:	I will pray daily.
Sancty-fried:	Why do the other lawyers stand around a garbage disposal?
Notreally:	Because their briefs are a bunch of trash.
Katie_host:	Oh, you two, can't we ever have a serious minute in here?
Angelic:	I will pray even though I am Canadian.
MissSally:	Cooper, you mentioned distractions. Any thing specific you want to mention about that?
CooperStone:	not really
Notreally:	You rang?
CooperStone:	No, I was just answering Sally's question.
Notreally:	Happens all the time. I have the most bruised ego in chat. No one ever means to call on me . . .
Katie_host:	Notreally!! Stop it. This poor guy has no idea what you are talking about.
Sancty-fried:	Neither does notreally.
Katie_host:	Oh that's it.

CHATMASTER moves Sancty-fried to JAIL <secured>

CHATMASTER moves Notreally to JAIL <secured>

Katie_host:	Sally, watch the room for me.

CHATMASTER moves Katie_host to JAIL <secured>

MissSally:	Cooper, sorry about all this. Our two resident jokesters were just up to their normal tricks. But Kate took them to our chat jail. They won't bother you anymore.

CooperStone:	No problem. I was just a little confused at times. But it wasn't the first time today.
MissSally:	At the risk of being nosey, are the distractions you are concerned about female?
CooperStone:	I'd rather not go into it.
SandeeBeach:	I'm willing to be a distraction if you are taking volunteers.
Angelic:	Me too, even though I am Canadian.
CooperStone:	How do you blush in chat?
MissSally:	You catch on fast, Coop. We will pray for you. Anything else we can do?
CooperStone:	not really.
CooperStone:	Not, you sir.
Firemomma:	It's OK, Notreally is in jail.

CHAPTER

16

PURCELLVILLE, VIRGINIA.
June 3, 2005.

"Layton, come down here right now!" Deanna called out loudly. It was her third attempt.

No answer.

"Layton!"

No answer.

"LAYTON WILLIAM THOMAS, *you get down here this minute!*"

Deanna stormed up the stairs and flung open her oldest son's bedroom door.

"Layton," she said, her voice back under control. "What are you doing? I was calling you real nice for the last ten minutes, and then I tried yelling, and you still didn't come down. I want to know what is going on!"

"Nothing."

"Nothing? What do you mean nothing, young man?"

"I dunno. I was just in my room."

"What exactly were you doing in your room?"

Layton hung his head. "I was playing a video game."

"With the ear phones on?"

"Yes, ma'am."

"You know that I have told you that you can't play video games on school days. Come on. There are only three more school days left in the year. Why did you do it?"

"I just wanted to. I don't feel like doing school work."

"You don't feel like doing school work? I am afraid you don't have a choice. You will do school work, like it or not."

"Well, next year I won't have to do school work."

"What are you talking about?"

"You know the case. You can't spank me, and you can't make me do school work. I will get to do what I want."

Deanna felt like she had been punched in the stomach. She steadied herself, grasping the doorframe with her left hand. Her hand was shaking, not in anger at her son, but at the looming sense of helplessness.

"That's not what the judge said," Deanna said, with as much control in her voice as she could muster.

"That's what the guys on my soccer team told me. It's been in all the newspapers."

"I don't care what the newspapers say. I am still your mother."

"Yeah, but moms can't make us obey anymore. Talk to me if you want. But right now I want to play Nintendo."

"Layton," she said with a veil of calmness, "that is just not acceptable behavior. I am afraid I am going to have to spank you."

"You can't."

"Oh yes I can."

Deanna held her son firmly by the arm and marched him down to the kitchen where she kept a yard stick for just such occasions, although it had been three months since the last time she had to use it. Layton was required to touch his knees, like always. She gave him three quick swats, like always. And then she gave him a hug, like always.

"Layton, you know we can't tolerate such behavior," she said calmly.

Layton looked at the floor a long time. Slowly he raised his head. Even more slowly he lifted his eyes to meet his mother's gaze. Deanna could tell he was fighting back the tears. "Mom, I'm sorry," he said softly.

"I know this whole thing has put a lot of stress on you, and this may not make sense to you, but I think this Nintendo business was just your way of testing me."

"Maybe," Layton replied, still very quiet. Suddenly tears started welling up in his eyes.

"Layton, you said you were sorry. I have forgiven you. Are you OK?"

"Mom, it's just that—"

"What, Layton, what is it?"

"What am I supposed to tell Miss Hennessey?"

"What do you mean, Son?"

"She saw me with Emily's grandma outside the courthouse the other day and told us both that she would be calling us from time to time, and that if our parents spanked us we were supposed to tell her."

Deanna's heart began to beat faster and faster. "Are you sure she said that, Layton?"

"Yes, Mom, she did."

"Layton, let me talk to your dad and Mr. Stone. Please don't say anything until we talk to them."

"What if she calls today?"

"Don't lie to her, Son, but just say that you can't talk. Oh . . . I don't know . . ."

Deanna sat down on a chair in the kitchen and covered her face with her hands. She began to sob uncontrollably.

"Mom, I am really sorry about the Nintendo. Please don't cry."

Deanna Thomas grabbed her son into her arms and held him. "It's not you, Layton, honey. I'm not upset with you anymore. I just can't believe what is happening to us."

PURCELLVILLE, VIRGINIA. *June 7, 2005. 2:00 A.M.*

He had gone to bed about 11:30 after a seventeen-hour day, eleven hours at work. At first Cooper had dozed right off, but at about 11:50 he stirred and his mind sprang fully back to life. And the scene that troubled his mind began its nightly visit to his memory. The incident with Jody Easler rewound itself until he once again clutched the note she had slipped to him on the set of the *Today Show.*

There was the warning. Someone had apparently intercepted his e-mail. But what could he do? Who could he tell? How could he get help? Anyone he would tell about the e-mail intercepts would also have to be told about Jody Easler, and what would he say about her? He was paralyzed first by worry, then by fear, then by guilt. Sleep had been elusive for several days.

Tonight would be no different.

If only. If only. The words ricocheted around the walls of his mind like a well-hit racquetball shot. But the ball never stopped bouncing.

He finally fell into a dreamless hard slumber sometime after 4:30.

17

PURCELLVILLE, VIRGINIA.
June 9, 2005.

No one had seen or heard the car coming up the driveway. But the doorbell rang anyway.

"Layton, please go see who it is."

"Sure, Mom," came the reply, followed by the clamor of feet coming up the basement stairs.

A minute later Layton appeared at the laundry room door. "Mom, you need to come to the door."

"Who is it?" Deanna asked.

"It's that lady—you know the one who visited here after she came to my Sunday school class."

Deanna leaned over and grabbed the washer to steady herself as a flash of anger and fear swept over her body. "Are you sure?"

"Yeah, Mom. It's her. And there is some other woman with her."

"Well, if she thinks she is getting in here again, she is crazy. You go back in the basement and play with your sister. Trent is still asleep, isn't he?"

"I haven't heard him since you put him down for a nap."

"OK, you go play, honey."

Deanna followed her son until he disappeared down the basement steps. She could see Nora Stoddard through the oval glass window. And indeed, there was another, younger woman with her.

She opened the door about six inches. "Yes? What do you want?"

"Mrs. Thomas, I think you remember me—Nora Stoddard from the Children's Bureau."

"Yes, I certainly remember *you*."

Nora Stoddard turned and nodded in the direction of the young woman, who was dressed in a black pantsuit. "Well, actually, Ms. Donner here from Loudoun County Social Services is officially in charge of this visit. May we come in?"

"No."

Stoddard seemed a little surprised by the simplicity of the answer. Estelle Donner stepped forward. She was clasping a black vinyl binder in front of her. "Mrs. Thomas, we need to come in. I am the social worker assigned to monitor your family. It is just routine after there has been a supervisory order entered by the court in a juvenile matter. We just want to check on Layton and the other children to see how the adjustments are going."

"Well, Miss Donner, I have no intention of letting you in my house."

"I am afraid you have no choice. This is a requirement."

"I do have a choice. And this is it." Deanna closed the door, locked the deadbolt, and left two dumbfounded women standing on the porch.

She grabbed the phone handset off the wall in the kitchen as she headed through to the laundry room. She dialed Cooper's number. Just as Nancy answered the phone Deanna saw Stoddard and Donner walk past the laundry room window in the direction of the driveway. She wasn't sure if they saw her through the window before they disappeared from her line of sight.

"Nancy, this is Deanna Thomas. I need to speak to Cooper on an urgent matter."

"Certainly, Mrs. Thomas. He is with some clients, but if it is urgent I'll go slip him a note."

"Please do, Nancy. Tell him that Nora Stoddard is here at my house with a Loudoun County social worker, and they are demanding that I let them in my house and . . ." Her voice started to break. "They want to question my children."

"Yes, Mrs. Thomas, I am sure he will take the call." Nancy's voice sounded more than a little concerned.

Almost immediately Cooper came on the line.

"Deanna, you have Nora Stoddard and a social worker in your house?"

"No, Cooper, they are outside. I wouldn't let them in. But they demanded to come into the house and question Layton and the other children."

"I can't believe they would do that! Did they show you a court order or anything?"

"No, nothing like that. They just said it was routine in a case where the court had entered some kind of order. I don't remember the exact words."

"Where are they now?"

"I think they are sitting in my driveway in their car."

"Your kitchen phone is portable, isn't it?"

"Yes . . . why?"

"I want you to go outside and hand them the phone and let me talk to them. Will its range go that far?"

"I think so," Deanna replied. She had regained her surface calm with Cooper now engaged in helping her, but her stomach felt queasy and her heart seemed to be ready to explode.

She opened the door between the laundry room and the garage. Stepping out onto the landing, she hit the button activating the garage door opener. As the door began to open she saw that they were still there in a white Taurus, parked right in front of her garage door. Stoddard was in the passenger's seat talking on a cell phone.

Deanna walked to the driver's side and tapped on the window. Donner hit the button and the window came down.

"Mrs. Thomas, have you changed your mind?" she asked.

"No, ma'am. My lawyer wants to talk to you," Deanna answered, as she thrust the phone through the open window. "Now."

Donner took the phone while looking toward Stoddard for directions. Stoddard nodded affirmatively and appeared to be trying to terminate her cell phone conversation.

"Hello," Donner said tentatively into Deanna's phone.

"Hello, this is Cooper Stone, the attorney for the Thomas family. Who is this please?"

"My name is Estelle Donner. I am with Loudoun County Social Services. I've been assigned to the Thomas family for routine follow-up."

"Frankly, I don't think there is anything very routine about this case, Miss Donner. In fact, Mrs. Thomas told me that you have Nora Stoddard from the federal government there with you. Is that routine?"

"No, that part is not routine, but we always come out for these visits whenever the court enters a finding in an abuse or neglect case."

"But there has been no finding of abuse or neglect."

"Well, um, yeah. But Ms. Stoddard has advised us that our duty under the UN treaty is the same as in an abuse or neglect case. If there is a court order against the family, then we have to supervise. We are only treating the order as the equivalent of a finding of abuse or neglect and doing our routine follow-up."

"I will be direct with you," Cooper replied. "There are a lot of assumptions built into your decision that we will just have to have Judge Holman resolve for us. So unless you have an order from him, I am going to instruct my client to continue to deny you entry. Why don't you both go back to your offices and tell the attorneys who advise you what I have said, and let them take it from there."

"It sounds like we have no choice. However, I will have to talk to Ms. Stoddard to get some direction."

"Fine," Cooper said. "Can you give the phone back to Mrs. Thomas?"

"Sure," she responded, handing the phone back through the window.

"Deanna," Cooper advised her immediately, "go back inside and shut the door behind you. I don't think they are going to do anything right now, but I don't want them to hear our conversation, so just say nothing until you are back inside. I'll wait."

Deanna dutifully walked back through the garage. She hit the switch again, and Cooper could hear the sound of the garage door opener as the door closed out the intruders.

"OK, Cooper," she said, pausing on the landing on the top of the steps that led to her interior laundry room door. She stood there motionless as Cooper briefed her on his side of the conversation with the social worker.

"Is there any reason we have to stay here?" Deanna asked.

"No, what did you have in mind?"

"My parents have been pestering me to bring the children for a visit for a few days since school is out. I don't think I have done a good job of honoring my father and mother. I believe I should go to Richmond for a few days and remedy my error."

Cooper laughed. "It is always a good idea to honor one's father and mother. Have a nice time in Richmond. Make sure that you give your number to Nancy before you leave."

"Thank you, Cooper. I am really glad you were there for us today."

"I still have to stop them on a more permanent basis but glad to help for now."

PURCELLVILLE, VIRGINIA. *June 9, 2005. 11:30 p.m.*

The emotional signals that this was going to be another sleepless night were already apparent. Rather than fight it, Cooper got up and pulled on his sweatsuit that he had neatly placed on the side of the bed only thirty minutes earlier.

He switched on his television and flipped through all the channels three times, pausing for an extra ten seconds on any show that gave evidence of a ball being kicked or thrown or bounced. Nothing. He clicked off the power.

The computer beckoned next. After a warm-up that seemed to take forever, he was able to hit the necessary keystrokes and log on to the Internet. He checked the weather for Loudoun. Sunny, hot, and humid. And then, just for fun, he checked the weather in Spokane. Sunny and warm. No humidity. *Lucky Peter. Lucky Gwen. Lucky Sally.* Thinking of Sally gave him an idea.

He pulled out of the drawer a paper that Sally had sent him, which listed the steps to log into the chat on *Crosswalk.com.* He looked at the directions closely, to make sure he understood the part about how to create a new account. He didn't want to appear in the room as CooperStone.

He thought that Rocky was a good alias for a guy named Stone, but plain old Rocky was already taken as a screen name, so he kept trying variations until he got something he could use.

About two minutes later, he hit the "enter" button and the screen read:

You are entering the News Room as RockyofVA.

He waited for names to come rolling across the screen but no one was in the News Room. He hit the button to "pick a room." Mars Hill had seventeen people. He hit that button.

You are entering Mars Hill as RockyofVA, the screen read.
You see here: Angelic, Anxious4Jesus, RevBill, FiddlersPapa, Katie_host, Notreally . . .

The list continued until all seventeen names had scrolled across. He thought he recognized about half of the names from the earlier chat session. MissSally was not logged in.

RevBill:	So those who believe in OSAS are clearly in the better position if you take that passage seriously.
Wesleyan:	Yeah, if you just look at THAT passage, perhaps. But what about the verses I mentioned a minute ago?
Anxious4Jesus:	I just got here. What's OSAS?
FiddlersPapa:	Welcome Rocky. Isn't it a little late to be up in Virginia?
Notreally:	OSAS=Once saved always saved. It's our nightly debate on eternal security, to be predictably followed by our nightly debate on tongues . . . etc. etc.
Firemomma:	My three year old son said the cutest thing today . . . anyone want to hear?
Notreally:	The thing we should really be debating is OCAC.
Angelic:	OCAC?
RockyofVA:	Thank you FiddlersPapa.
Notreally:	OCAC=Once a chatter always a chatter. I think the real issue is addiction to chat rooms.
Saddlepal:	Anything other than RevBill and Wesleyan yelling at each other about eternal security again. Perhaps CatholicLady is right. Maybe there really is a purgatory and watching them debate the same thing night after night is it.
Angelic:	LOL@saddle
Cryllic:	So why are you up so late, Rocky? You didn't answer that part of Fid's question?
Firemomma:	Thanks for asking to hear the cute thing my three year old said. He crawled up in my lap and said: Mama, why do you have a flat lap but Grandma's lap is fluffy?
RockyofVA:	To tell you the truth, cryllic, I am having trouble sleeping so I thought I would try this chat room.
RevBill:	Don't any of you ever want to discuss anything serious? Have all Americans had their brains turn to mush? All I

	see is this jabber and jokes unless my friend, Wesleyan and I mix it up on eternal security.
Angelic:	I like serious discussions, even though I am in Canada.
Katie_host:	Why are you having trouble sleeping, Rocky? Anything we can pray about?
Firemomma:	Did anyone see what my three year old said? No one replied. Is this thing working tonight?
Notreally:	We saw it, fire, we just thought it was so precious that to recognize the brilliance of your three year old with a mere LOL or even a ROFL would be like saying, "Nice picture" in front of the Mona Lisa. True brilliance needs more than faint praise.
Firemomma:	Are you joking, Notreally?
Notreally:	not really.
Saddlepal:	Notreally's always joking, Firemomma, you know that. I thought the fluffy comment was indeed cute. I was just thinking about Rocky's sleepless in Virginia problem.
Cryllic:	Rocky? Are you there? You haven't said anything.
RockyinVA:	I am trying to think of how to respond.
Notreally:	Oh . . . my . . . we may have hit an actual human need. (Rocky, I am serious. Please feel free to share prayer requests, etc. We are more sane than we sound.)
RockyinVA:	I would like prayer, but I am trying to think of how to tell you what to pray for delicately. I can't come out and just say the details. It's too sensitive.
Katie_host:	We are all listening, Rocky. Even Notreally.
RockyinVA:	Well, I am having trouble sleeping because I am basically afraid and guilty.
FiddlersPapa:	Go on Rocky, we really do care.
RockyinVA:	It sounds worse than it probably is when I see what I typed on the screen. But I can't shake this thing.
Notreally:	Are you a believer, Rocky? Do you know Jesus as your Savior?
RockyinVA:	Yes, Notreally, for a long, long time. Which is why this is so bad, I should know better.

Cryllic:	What can you tell us?
RockyinVA:	I guess I can say this much . . . I did something I shouldn't have done . . . I feel guilty about it.
Firemomma:	Have you confessed it?
RockyinVA:	Thousands of times, it seems.
Angelic:	Then why is it still on your conscience?
RockyinVA:	Because I am afraid that people are going to find out.
Notreally:	Is there any reason that people will find out? Or are you just torturing yourself with false guilt over sin that has already been forgiven?
RockyinVA:	I don't want you all to think I have done something horrible. By the world's standards I didn't do anything bad. But I should have known better.
FiddlersPapa:	I'm glad to see that you recognize that sin is sin.
RockyinVA:	But to answer Notreally's question, there is a reason that I actually need to tell somebody about the whole thing. It's a big mess and too complicated to explain.
Saddlepal:	Do you need to confess the sin to someone whom you have wronged?
RockyinVA:	Oh, this is so hard. I will just tell you. I kissed someone I shouldn't have kissed. That's it. But I learned something from her that I need to tell someone else about. I can't really do what I need to do because of all this. There, there is my whole dirty laundry out in front of you all.
Katie_host:	What was wrong with kissing her? Are either of you married?
RockyinVA:	Goodness, no. I wouldn't have done that.
Firemomma:	So you're both single?
RockyinVA:	Yes.
Angelic:	Does she think it was wrong to kiss her? Do you need to apologize to her?
RockyinVA:	No . . . in fact, it was her idea. To be precise, she kissed me. I just didn't stop her.

Notreally: If you don't want to say, don't, but why was it wrong to kiss her if you are both single?

RockyinVA: It is real complicated. I can't tell you any more details. I just can't. But I would appreciate your prayers.

Katie_host: We will pray for you, Rocky.

Cryllic: Yes, we'll pray.

Notreally: Yes, Rocky, we will pray. But let me share just one idea from Scripture with you. Is that OK?

RockyinVA: Sure, Notreally.

Notreally: Here let me cut and paste the passage a verse at a time. It is Hebrews 9:11-14, directly from the NIV.

Notreally: 11When Christ came as high priest of the good things that are already here, he went through the greater and more perfect tabernacle that is not man-made, that is to say, not a part of this creation.

Notreally: 12He did not enter by means of the blood of goats and calves; but he entered the Most Holy Place once for all by his own blood, having obtained eternal redemption.

Notreally: 13The blood of goats and bulls and the ashes of a heifer sprinkled on those who are ceremonially unclean sanctify them so that they are outwardly clean.

Notreally: 14How much more, then, will the blood of Christ, who through the eternal Spirit offered himself unblemished to God, cleanse our consciences from acts that lead to death, so that we may serve the living God!

Notreally: I really wanted you just to see verse 14, but the rest of the passage helps to give you the context.

RockyinVA: Thanks.

Notreally: Here's the point, Rocky. We need to see that a clean conscience is a result of Christ's blood. He not only forgives our sins and cleans our hearts. He cleans our consciences as well.

RockyinVA: Yeah . . . I see that in the verse.

Notreally: Even if you had done something that deserved death . . . the Apostle Paul certainly did . . . I mean the deal with the stoning of Stephen. No matter what you have done . . . and kissing someone you shouldn't have certainly isn't a crime that deserves death . . . it is under the blood and you have a clean conscience as a result of Christ's blood, not as a result of you doing penance or something.

RockyinVA: Wow! That is really good.

Notreally: Rocky? You said that you feel like you can't do what you need to do because of this whole kissing thing? Right? And you didn't want people to find out?

RockyinVA: Right.

Notreally: There was a time I was struggling with false guilt. I kept feeling that I was disqualified from serving God even though I had confessed my sin and taken care of it as best I knew how. I felt like Satan kept playing tricks with my mind and, like you, I couldn't sleep—which is why I stopped joking around when I saw what you were talking about.

RockyinVA: listening.

Notreally: If Satan is telling you that you can't do what you need to do because someone might find out and that would be embarrassing to you because you are a Christian, just do what you need to do and don't listen to Satan's lies. If God wants it to come out publicly, it will be for your good. But either way, just respond to your clear duties and let God worry about what the consequences are.

RockyinVA: That is just what I needed to hear. Thank you so much, Notreally.

Notreally: No problem, glad to help. And it saved all of us from RevBill and Wesleyan's 17th round of the same old fight.

RockyinVA: Thanks again, all of you. I still need your prayers. But I have a good idea of what I need to do. It was good to see you guys again. Goodnight.

Katie_host: Goodnight, Rocky. Blessings.

Firemomma: Nite, Rocky.

Saddlepal:	We'll pray, Rocky.
Angelic:	I'll pray in Canada, Rocky.
RockyinVA leaves.	
FiddlersPapa:	Again? Did he say good to see you again? Anyone else ever see him before?
Firemomma:	Not me.
Cryllic:	Not me.
Anxious4Jesus:	Me either.
Angelic:	I've never seen him, but I'm from Canada so I'm not here all the time.
Notreally:	You all sound like my kids when I asked them who broke the vase.

The chat room soon progressed to other topics. But Cooper Stone fell on his knees, grasped the chair he had been sitting on, and cried out in thanksgiving to God. He asked for strength to carry through. He vowed to call Peter Barron in the morning to tell him his whole story and seek help.

Cooper slept soundly for seven and a half hours.

CHAPTER

18

LEESBURG, VIRGINIA.
June 10, 2005.

Cooper woke up refreshed, anxious to get going. It was a great
change of emotion. He wanted to call Peter first thing, but there
was a three-hour time difference between Washington, D.C., and
Washington State. More to the point, he had legal work to do. The
social workers' visit from the day before required attention.

He realized that it was probably not best to sit back and wait for
Suskins or the county attorney to initiate contempt procedures
against Deanna. So his task for the morning became the preparation for a motion for a stay of judgment. Before noon Judge
Holman would have this request to stop all enforcement until the
appeals were final.

Cooper decided to immediately seek an emergency stay to stop
Loudoun County Social Services from enforcing the order. The
only problem—an emergency request required him to serve the
papers on Suskins in person.

He called Jeanne Garvis to see if she could deliver the papers.
Dentist appointments for three kids. Deanna had already left for

Richmond. He called Rick on his cell phone to see if he could help, or if he knew of someone who could. "I'll have someone there at 11:45 sharp, even if I have to do it myself," was Rick's reply.

By eleven o'clock, all the papers were ready and it was 8:00 A.M. in Spokane. After a time of prayer, Cooper walked out of the office to call Peter from a pay phone across the street.

"Morning," Peter answered the phone cheerfully.

"Good morning, Peter. It's Cooper."

"Hey, Coop. You in the neighborhood and want to come to dinner tonight?"

"No, nothing like that."

"Too bad. Gwen and I had a great time with you in New York, and we both said it would be great to see you more often."

"It was a night I'll never forget," Cooper bantered.

"Cooper, it was pretty fun, but a night you'll never forget?" he teased. "That's pretty strong. Just say you had a good time and leave it at that. I have warned you that people don't trust a lawyer who exaggerates." Peter was laughing.

Cooper paused before answering seriously. "Well, Peter, for reasons I am about to tell you it really was a night I'll never forget."

"Sounds like a confession coming up. I think I'll sit down," Peter said soberly.

"I don't know what you're thinking I am about to say, but there is no way you can guess."

"Does it involve a woman?"

"Yes, Peter, but let me explain before you get too far down the wrong track."

"Sure, I'll listen."

"There is a woman on the other side of this UN case named Jody Easler."

"Name sounds familiar," Peter replied, not able to just listen for very long.

"Probably should be if you read the news. She is the U.S. ambassador to the UN in Geneva. Technically, its an under-ambassador position, but she has the title of 'Ambassador.'"

"Was she the one on the *Today Show* with you?"

"Yeah, that's her."

"OK, I can see why there might be a problem. About your age and very attractive."

"All right, I guess that does save some of the explanation. Anyhow, she has always seemed real friendly to me. Too friendly in retrospect. I first noticed it a little when I took her deposition in Washington. The next day, she came to the depositions of our clients at this fancy hotel out here in Loudoun. She was real chatty—well, actually, she was real flirty with me there. Some of our people commented on it. Thought it was strange. I shrugged it off. Although, being candid, I kind of liked the attention."

"Thanks for being honest. That helps me see where you are spiritually on this. Keep going."

"Anyhow, nothing else really happened until I walked out of the elevator with you and Gwen that night in New York. When I turned the corner, there she was. She was supposedly having trouble opening the door of the room right next to mine."

"Boy, that's a pretty strong coincidence," Peter said.

"Yeah, well, I opened her door for her and she invited me in."

Peter held his breath for a moment.

"I refused to go in."

Peter breathed again.

"But to say she was flirty then would be the understatement of all time. There is little question but that she was trying to get me into her room, and well, you know—"

"Yeah. Did she?"

"No. I never went in her room, nor did she come in mine. But let me keep going."

"OK. Sorry."

"Well, the fact is, I tried to manage the temptation rather than run from it because—again to be candid, I didn't want to be alone. I had just been with you and Gwen and saw you two so much in love, and that is so great. But I was feeling all alone, and Laura, you know the teacher I told you about? I had just learned she had gotten engaged. And Jody *is* nice to me. And she is, quite frankly, gorgeous."

"Sounds like you're laying the foundation for an excuse."

"Peter!" Cooper said, with just a touch of exasperation. "Can't I just tell my story for once! It's not excuses. I know I did the wrong thing. I was just trying to help you see why I felt vulnerable."

"Cooper," Peter replied softly. "I'm sorry—really. Please keep going."

"So where was I? Oh, yeah, I was trying to manage a temptation. So to try to get her away from inviting me into her room, but not really wanting to be alone, I suggested that we go for a ride in Central Park in a hansom cab. So we did. It was a little cold. She had a sleeveless dress on. Well, to make a long story short, I put my arm around her to keep her warm and she kissed me—I mean *really* kissed me."

"And you didn't stop her or protest."

"No. I kissed back." Both were silent for a few moments.

"I don't want to interrupt again, Coop. Are you through?"

"Yeah. That was it, at least as far as that kind of stuff goes."

"One kiss and a ride in the park? Nothing more?"

"Nothing more."

"Well, Peter, I don't think that spiritually you should be feeling like this is a major tragedy. I take it she's not a believer and you think the relationship is wrong. I would agree, but I have to believe there is more to this story or you wouldn't be calling me about it."

"There is more. But no more romance."

"Keep going."

"Well, the morning we were on the *Today Show,* and I was there with Laura—talk about being whipsawed emotionally—Jody was there also, as you apparently saw. She was friendly and nice but not openly flirtatious, at least not that I noticed. Laura actually thought that she was and said something to me about it afterward. But, anyhow, the important thing that happened was when we shook hands. I came away with this piece of paper in my hand that she gave me secretly. She acted like she was being watched or something. I went into the bathroom and read it. It says in so many words, 'Be careful, Cooper Stone. Don't send your plans to your clients by e-mail. I wish,' and then it just trailed off. That may not be the exact wording but it is pretty close."

"Oh, my!" Peter exclaimed. "Now I understand why you need some advice."

"Good. So what do I do?"

"Not so fast, a few questions first.

"Is she actually a party to the litigation?"

"No, she's technically just a witness—although she is pulling the strings to some degree for the other side."

"But it sounds like somebody else holds the real power."

"I guess so," Cooper replied, glad for a chance to think a little more clearly about her. Somehow it made him feel a little less guilty.

"And it is pretty obvious that she wasn't at your hotel and right next door just by accident. That was planned by somebody."

"Hmm. I guess you are right about that too."

"So somebody had this whole romantic evening thing planned for you, and the only logical conclusion is that you were being set up. And it seems pretty clear that the setup was designed to make you look bad to hurt the UN case somehow. But it would seem to make her look bad, too, so I don't get that part of it. But you were definitely set up. Photographers probably awaited you in her hotel room. Are you sure you stayed out?"

"I am sure!"

"So she has given you a warning to not use e-mail. Did we use e-mail at all to set up the trip to New York?"

"Yeah. Sally e-mailed me your itinerary and the time to meet you."

"And had you sent your clients any plans prior to the *Today Show*?"

"Yeah—a day or two before I had e-mailed them my appeal strategy."

"You definitely have a security problem, friend."

"So what do I do about it? Go to the FBI?"

"With this president in office? Not on your life. The FBI may be the one intercepting your e-mails."

"So who do you suggest?"

"I've got a friend out here. Computer whiz. He helped me unravel a deal in a prior case. I'll call you back if he has any ideas. By the way, you should probably think about being careful of what you say on your telephone."

"I thought of that. I'm calling you from a pay phone."

"Good job."

"I'm not a total idiot."

"No, but I'm trying to decide what to call you, a moron or a fool, for going for a romantic ride in Central Park with a U.S. ambassador who is on the opposite side of the biggest case in your life."

"Point noted," Cooper admitted.

"Hey, Cooper," Peter said seriously. "I know you did the wrong thing here, but I want you to know that I still love you like a brother. We are OK. You understand?"

"Yeah, Peter. Thanks."

"Let me talk to Aaron, and I'll get back with you if he has anything."

"Bye."

Cooper hung up the phone, looked both ways before jaywalking, and headed back to his office. As he entered, he was surprised to see Laura sitting in his waiting room.

"Laura? To what do I owe this pleasure?"

"To the fact that your friend, Rick, talked me into driving to Washington, D.C., for him this afternoon. You needed something delivered?"

"Yeah, but . . . well, thanks," Cooper stammered.

Cooper walked down the hall and went behind his desk, determined to be all business.

"This is a motion for a stay and for an order for immediate protection. I suppose you heard about the social worker and that Nora Stoddard woman showing up at Rick and Deanna's yesterday?"

"Yeah, Deanna told me about it before she left for Richmond. But, Cooper, I am dying to ask you something. Can I?"

"Is it personal? We haven't had too much success with personal questions lately."

"I don't know. It's not personal with me. I am just really curious."

"OK. Try me."

"Why were you across the street using a pay phone?"

Cooper spoke slowly and deliberately. "So like I was saying, if you just hand this manila envelope to the receptionist at Suskins' office and say that this should be given to Mr. Suskins right away, that's about it. Then just call me when you're done, and I will know that I can go before Judge Holman."

"OK . . . I think I've got it."

"You know how to find K Street?"

"Yeah, I have lived in the area my whole life, remember?"

"That's right—just checking."

"And you want me to call you as soon as I am done?"

"Right."

"Where do I reach you? Here or at the pay phone across the street?"

"Get out of here, Miss Frasier."

She was laughing as she left the office with the papers.

LEESBURG, VIRGINIA.
June 10, 2005. 3:00 P.M.

"Judge Holman will see you now," Deputy Daniels said, hanging up the phone. "Where's your D.C. buddy?"

"You mean Randolph Suskins?"

"Yeah, that's the guy. The one with the thousand-dollar suits and the ten-dollar haircut."

"Ten-dollar haircut?" Cooper asked, laughing.

"Yeah," the deputy said with a grin. "Haven't you ever noticed how his hair keeps flopping down on his forehead and he keeps flipping at it? I can't tell you how hard it has been for me to stop myself from going over there with some scissors and just snipping it off."

Cooper chuckled again. "Actually, Mr. Suskins is not here today. But the judge may choose to call him and do a phone conference."

"Good luck."

Cooper walked into the inner chambers of Judge Holman, who was seated at his desk in his shirtsleeves. The air-conditioning worked, but not that well.

"Come in, come in, Cooper. Good to see you."

"Thank you, Judge. Did you have a chance to look at my papers?"

"Yes, I did. And we will need to call Suskins and Hennessey in just a second. But before we do that, I just wanted to tell you that I thought you presented your arguments well in the hearing—and also in the briefs. We both know that you are up against the big boys, and I am proud to say that our hometown boy did a more than honorable job."

"Thank you, Judge. It's been a lot of work."

"I'm sure it has," he replied. "I know this is none of my business and will have no bearing on any aspect of anything that comes before me, but I am just a little concerned for you—are you getting paid for this?"

"Yes, Judge, fortunately I am. It wasn't that way at first, but now I am."

"Good. Don't tell me anymore. Let's call Suskins and Hennessey," the judge said, picking up the phone.

"Rachel Hennessey told me that I can inform you that she waives her right to participate. Said she didn't have a dog in this particular fight."

"All right. With a local lawyer, I'll accept your word on that. But, Mr. Suskins we are going to call."

"I agree, Judge."

After the typical transfers and delays, the judge finally got Suskins on the phone.

"Good afternoon, Judge Holman," Suskins said.

"Afternoon Mr. Suskins. Mr. Stone is here with me in my

chambers and has informed me that you were served with his motion about two hours ago. Is that right?"

"Yes, Your Honor. We haven't had a chance to thoroughly analyze the papers, but I have been able to skim through them quickly."

The judge raised his eyebrows at Cooper, as if to say, "I doubt that because you have dozens of law clerks available for this kind of work."

"Well, Mr. Suskins, give me your current position on it."

"Well, obviously, we think the social worker's visits are in the best interest of the child and simply a part of the routine procedure that accompanies juvenile protection cases at this stage of litigation."

"Yes, Mr. Suskins, but what about the point that Mr. Stone raises that in the other cited cases there has been finding of abuse or neglect before there are such visits. There has been no such finding here."

"That is true insofar as it goes," Suskins replied. "But the alternative is simply to allow these families to openly flaunt your order, which you concluded was required as a matter of international law."

"There are actually two issues rolled into this," Holman said. "One is whether they must obey the order to not spank the children in the interim. The other is whether you can send social workers into their home."

"That is true, Your Honor. And we believe that the order should be enforced in the normal fashion in both respects."

"Fine," Holman replied. "Mr. Stone, obviously I had the benefit of hearing from you in writing. Do you have anything to add?"

"No, Your Honor. You clearly understand our position."

"All right, gentlemen, here's what I am going to do. I am going to grant part of the emergency application, deny part of it, and schedule both requests for a hearing on the request for a permanent stay. The order is stayed insofar as social workers' automatic access into either of the families' homes. Now, if they have actual evidence that anyone is violating my order, then I will certainly entertain an enforcement motion in proper sequence. But, absent such hard evidence, leave these people alone.

"On the motion to stay the order banning spanking, I am denying that for now. You can argue this out in a hearing." He paused to look at his calendar. "I'll set it for ten days from today at 8:30 A.M. Now if you two can present me with an agreed order on temporary matters, I will most likely sign it. Any questions?"

"No, Your Honor," Cooper said.

"Thank you, Your Honor," Suskins added.

Hanging up the phone, Holman looked up at Cooper. "Sorry, Cooper. I feel my hands are tied. The whole world is watching everything each of us is doing in this case, and we have to be absolutely clean on it all. You know I hate this treaty. An unbelievable group we seem to have in the Senate. But I am going to have to call every point absolutely according to the law. No hometown favoritism."

"I understand, Your Honor. I wouldn't want it any other way."

"I believe you mean that, Cooper. That's the way of a Virginia gentleman."

Cooper smiled as he reflected on that compliment while driving back to his office.

LEESBURG, VIRGINIA. *June 10, 2005. 7:00* P.M.

"Terry, can you close the sliding glass door?" Laura called. "Smoke's getting in the kitchen."

"Sure," he replied, loud enough to be heard. "These steaks will be done in just a couple minutes anyway."

Laura moved about the kitchen quickly, shaking sesame seeds on top of the mandarin orange salad—her favorite, which Terry had grown to like. She was taking the baked potatoes out of the microwave when her fiancé opened the sliding door with the platter of steaks in his right hand.

"Ah, nuts! Microwaved baked potatoes. I thought you promised me you would bake them in the oven once school was out."

"Yeah, I did, and most of the time I will do that. But I had a busy day and just didn't have time."

"So what were you up to?"

"Oh, just this and that, some running around."

"You weren't going to check out more bridal registry stuff at the mall, were you? You know we agreed that we wouldn't begin doing all that until we set a firm date for the wedding."

Laura saw her chance for escape from Terry's line of questioning. "I wasn't at the mall, but," she glanced at him hard, "when are we going to set the date? I agreed to *marry* you, not just get permanently engaged."

Terry saw his chance for escape. "We've been over all that before. But where were you all day if you weren't at the mall?"

"Just running errands."

He could tell she was being deliberately evasive.

"Do I have to play twenty questions, or are you going to tell me?"

"Rick Thomas asked me to do a favor for his family. He needed some papers delivered, so I took them where they needed to be."

"Now we are getting somewhere. Where did you have to go?"

"Into Washington."

"Really? What kind of papers did Rick need to get into Washington?"

"They were legal papers, Terry. Why the inquisition? I didn't ask you to account for every minute of your day."

"What I want to know is why the evasiveness? I don't suppose that you got the legal papers from Cooper Stone and you didn't want me to know, did you?"

She popped up from the table. "Forgot the salt and pepper," she mumbled.

"Laura! What are you hiding?"

She turned with her hands perched on her hips and her jaw jutting forward, like it always did when she was mad. "I am not *hiding* anything. I was just trying to avoid another fight with you. Anytime the name Cooper Stone crops up in a conversation, you get upset with me. I am sensitive to it, and I am tired of fighting about it. But why you pick on me about it, I don't know. I told you I want to marry you. What are you so jealous about?"

"What am I so jealous about?" he asked shaking his head in mock disbelief. "You can't be that dense."

"Oh, now you've done it. I think you had just better leave! If we are going to resort to an evening of name-calling, I have already done my quota of those for the month. Why don't you just come back another night when you are prepared to be civil to me?"

Terry closed his eyes and leaned his head forward.

"Laura, I am sorry I used the word *dense*. But you have got to understand my perspective on this whole Cooper Stone business. I am not blind, nor am I an idiot."

"What are you talking about?" she demanded.

"I have seen the way he looks at you. And even though you don't exactly return the looks, I can tell that you know what is going on inside of the guy."

His choice of words hit her hard. Laura stared at the floor as she responded softly. "Whether I can tell what he is thinking or not— and I never claimed to be a mind reader—the important thing is what is going on inside of you and inside of me. I think I know what is going on inside of me, but I am not sure anymore what is going on inside of you. I don't know what your intentions are toward me."

"You've got a ring, don't you?"

"Yeah. That proves only that you had the intention of buying me a ring."

"What are you talking about?"

"Terry, we are not nineteen-year-olds anymore. We aren't waiting to get married until we are finished with our braces or acne treatments. We're not even waiting to be finished with college. We've been there. We have done all of those things."

"We didn't have acne treatments," he replied, with a smile.

She relaxed a little. "Yeah, I know, Terry, honey," she said, much more kindly. She spoke again with a quiet intensity. "I am trying to tell you that we are not kids anymore. We are very much adults. And you're over here for dinner nearly every night. I am not just tired of waiting. I want to know what the deal is with you, to make you want to wait and wait and wait. You said you think I can tell what is inside of Cooper. Like I already said, I want to know what is inside of you."

"In other words," he said bitterly, "you want to know if I really love you like Cooper Stone does?"

"I didn't say that," she said truthfully. But suddenly, as Terry himself pointed out Cooper's obvious love for her, she felt the impact of the words with a force she would not have anticipated.

"Maybe you didn't say it, but it is what you meant."

"No . . ." It was all she could manage to say, as she bowed her head in defeat, her arms limp at her side.

"I think you're right. I think I need to leave, maybe for good." It was not the first time he had threatened this during their previous, much milder verbal scuffles over the same subject.

"No . . . please," she protested again, a bit stronger this time. She walked toward Terry and put her hands on his shoulders as he still sat dejectedly at the kitchen table. He reached up and took one hand off his shoulders and then the other.

"Yes . . ." he said, in quiet bitterness. "I need to leave." He left without another word.

GENEVA, SWITZERLAND.
June 18, 2005.

There were aspects of life in Europe that she did not particularly like, but driving was not one of them. It was Saturday, and she had no official receptions until evening. She had given her driver, her guard, and her role as ambassador the day off. Today, she was just going to be Jody and her sunglasses and her Mercedes convertible.

She could have taken the freeway most of the way to Avenches, but she enjoyed the curves and climbs that the backroads offered on the way to the Roman ruins. The UN staff had kindly prepared a map for her, marking with a yellow highlighter the local suggestions for the most scenic drivable route to the historic destination.

It was a beautiful summer day in the French-speaking portion of Switzerland. The Alps were visible only as long as she followed the road by Lac Leman, the lake that English-speaking people insist on calling by the far less romantic name of Lake Geneva. "Lac Leman." She repeated the name over and over to herself. She liked the sound of it. It sounded, well, excitingly romantic.

The wind whipped her shoulder-length hair only moderately, as her designer sunglasses and scarf kept her hair more or less in place. She would have preferred to have it blowing more wildly in the wind, but then she couldn't see to drive. Of course, she could have let it blow free if she were in the passenger seat and a handsome man were behind the wheel to escort her through her planned agenda for the day.

Oh, there were plenty of men who were handsome in their own way, but they were mostly the hired help. The diplomats that were in her wider circle of friends were mostly paunchy, balding men whose intentions for her were usually suspect.

Both her mind and her Mercedes took twists and turns and curves and hills as she thought through the possibilities. As had been the case for many of her lonely moments—and she had far more such moments than she had ever contemplated before joining the diplomatic corps—the meanderings of her mind managed to linger in the general vicinity of Leesburg, Virginia, or on the carriage ride in New York and the company that had been so, so, oh . . . pleasant, that May evening.

As she slowed to about thirty kilometers per hour to negotiate a traffic circle about seventy kilometers south of Avenches, she noted a white cargo van parked about two hundred meters down the eastward spoke of the four-way circle. The driver, a man in a dark suit and dark glasses who was leaning on the side of his vehicle, spoke into a cell phone. She watched him watching her as much as she could without being obvious. As she cleared the circle, she glanced back over her right shoulder. He jumped into the van, which did an immediate U-turn and headed back toward the thoroughfare.

Probably a coincidence, she wanted to believe. But diplomatic training had encouraged her to be alert to such behavior because of terrorism and kidnappings.

About ten kilometers further north, she saw a sign announcing the boundary of a small village. Beside it was a sign with a round red "50" in the middle, with the word "Generale" surrounding the numerals. She slowed her speed to fifty kilometers per hour.

The few dozen people who were walking, lingering, or bicycling through the village were dressed in a variety of casual clothes, some modern, others in a manner that always evoked images of World War II in her mind. But there was only one man in a business suit. He peaked at her from behind the raised hood of a gleaming black Mercedes that seemed to have mechanical troubles.

Her own Mercedes appeared to possess some type of recuperative power for its sister vehicle, for as soon as she passed by, the hood was quickly closed and the stalled car's engine started at once. The larger, darker car stayed about a quarter mile behind the ambassador's convertible, never seeming to gain or lose ground, as the curves and hills swept under the gleaming chassis of the two autos.

She suddenly decided that the Roman ruins in Avenches would have to wait until another time. Lunch in Murten seemed much wiser at the moment. She hit the accelerator hard, heading for the ancient walled town that was only seven kilometers ahead.

The driver of the big Mercedes kept pace without appearing to even breathe hard. However, Jody's own breathing was sufficiently increased to supply more than enough oxygen to both vehicles and both drivers.

She relaxed only a little as the signs of modern civilization greeted her at the outskirts of Murten. She turned left at the co-operative grocery store up the hill, inside the walls of the town. Normally, the center street was off limits to those from outside the town, but her diplomatic license plates would result in a waiver of all such formalities.

She parked in front of the store with a large green cross, the European symbol of an apothecary. But it was the restaurant just to its left to which she headed. A public place seemed safest for the moment. If she saw one man in a suit and sunglasses inside, she had every intention of calling diplomatic security back in Geneva. A helicopter and armed marines were but minutes away if she felt the need.

The lunch was pleasant and light. Good bread. Good wine. Good salad—as long as you like plain lettuce, but the white dressing that the locals called "French" was superb. The *poule* was a little tough, but it tasted fresh and natural. And the view through the wall of plateglass windows was peaceful. A small lake surrounded by hills was nothing like Lac Leman, with its surrounding fifteen-thousand-foot peaks descending to the very shoreline, but it was serene and safe looking.

She asked her waitress in French if there were a way to walk along the top of the wall without going back out into the center street. The waitress brought her the busboy, who was willing to take her through the kitchen, down an alley, and up a hidden set of stairs. Jody was delighted. Maybe the CIA might need her talents after she finished with the diplomatic corps.

She walked north toward the gate opposite from where she had entered. A large, medieval clock tower guarded that entrance to the town. Its face had recently been repainted. The colored pattern and the gilded hands were spectacular in the sunlight.

The small lake lay off to her left. Fields with cattle and a few sheep dotted the three or four kilometers between the city wall and the water's edge. To her right there was a clear view into the center street and the storefronts along the side opposite her restaurant. The wooden walkway on top of the city wall was covered with the original peaked roofing. Archers used to peer over the gap at the top of the solid railing wall as they guarded the city from attack. The short wall blocked any view of Jody from the shoulders down.

She walked slowly toward the clock tower. Every car, every store, and every person got her careful review. There were no footsteps on the wooden wall save her own.

As she approached the clock tower, the wall curved sharply to the right, affording her for the first time a view of the open highway to the north of town. She looked carefully up the road, and even though she tried to convince herself that she was mistaken, the big Mercedes and the white van were parked on opposite sides of the highway facing north and south respectively. Their drivers were about three feet apart standing in front of the van, both talking on their cell phones.

She watched them carefully for a long time. Suppressing a sense of panic, she calmly retraced her steps back toward the restaurant and its hidden steps. She glided down the steps without incident and into her car.

She hit the accelerator hard as soon as she reached the main highway heading south just past the grocery. No sign of either the van or the Mercedes.

She decided that the freeway might be a wiser choice for her return. Five minutes off a feeder road she merged into the three lanes headed toward Geneva. The traffic grew more and more congested as she approached Vevey and then drove back along the northern edge of Lac Leman. The charms of Lake Geneva, and its romantic French name of Lac Leman, eluded her this time.

The guard was on duty in front of her residence, and she was never so relieved in her life as when she pulled inside the gate and saw it close behind her.

She went into her personal office. A note was strategically placed in the center of her otherwise empty desk. "Hope you enjoyed your ride. Murten is beautiful this time of the year." She had told her staff she was going to Avenches. How would anyone know about Murten?

She couldn't be sure, but the handwriting seemed familiar. She found a file folder of party invitations and mementos she kept in her bottom left-hand drawer. A note from Erzabet Kadar welcoming her to Geneva was near the bottom. The handwriting matched perfectly.

PURCELLVILLE, VIRGINIA. *June 18, 2005.*

Rick had insisted that everyone associated with the case come over for a barbecue dinner that Saturday evening. Holman had signed the order on Friday making the stay against the social workers permanent. Deanna and the kids were returning from Richmond Saturday morning. In celebration, Rick wanted to cook dinner for everyone. That is what he told people, but his definition of "cooking dinner" was barbecuing the hamburgers. Deanna fixed the potato salad, the fruit salad, sliced and sweetened fresh straw-berries to go on the ice cream, and prepared the lettuce, onions, and other condiments. She even took the raw hamburger meat and shaped it into patties so that her husband could "cook dinner for everyone." But she was glad to be home, and she didn't mind in the least.

The Garvises arrived first with their six children. Cooper's sec-retary, Nancy, her husband, and their nine-year-old grand-daughter, Kristen, came soon after. Nancy had answered the phone, as usual, when Rick had called to invite Cooper. Rick realized that she had typed a lot of papers for them, so he invited her as well.

Cooper showed up about ten minutes late and noticed immedi-ately that Laura was not there. He dared not ask if she was coming. But he did make sure that he took Rick out to the driveway to see his new SUV. It was a sunny day, and he wanted to make sure that his friend saw how the color looked under such conditions.

Just as Rick was dutifully looking under the hood—yup, the engine was still there—they heard the sound of a car slowing on the gravel road in front of the Thomas home and turning onto the driveway. It was Terry Pipkin's burgundy Grand Am, and there were two people inside.

"Hi, Laura," Rick called, as she stepped out of the car.

Terry immediately was at the side of his fiancée. He put his arm conspicuously around her shoulder.

"Thanks for coming, Terry," Rick said.

"Sure." The curt answer was all Terry offered.

"Hey, you two!" Cooper called out closing the hood of his Jimmy.

"Hi, there," Laura replied in a singsong voice without any enthusiasm.

Doug Garvis and Terry got involved in a long conversation about the deacon board at church toward the end of dinner. It was the first time he had said more than five consecutive words all evening. Laura used the opportunity to escape the discussion by helping Deanna, Nancy, and Jeanne clean up.

As they were finishing, Emily and Kristen called Jeanne and Nancy outside to watch a trick they had learned to do on the trampoline. Laura lingered to help Deanna.

"So, what is it with you and Terry tonight?" Deanna asked in a quiet voice.

"What do you mean?"

"Come on, Laura, something is obviously wrong. Have we done something to offend you all, or are you having a fight or something?"

"Oh, you haven't offended us at all," she answered, deliberately avoiding the rest of the question.

"So you're having a fight, I take it."

"Well, not exactly a fight—at least not today. We had a whopper a couple of days ago, and it is still a sore subject."

"Does the sore subject have anything to do with all the time you have been spending helping our family?"

"No . . . no, it has nothing to do with that. Terry wants you to beat these UN people—he's a strong supporter of what you're doing, just as his dad is."

"If you want me to stop bugging you I will, but it just seems that there is something that is making both of you very uncomfortable. The way you all reacted at dinner was just . . ." Deanna's voice trailed off for a moment as she thought. "It's Cooper, isn't it? He's the sore spot."

"I didn't say that."

"You didn't have to. I should have figured it out. When Rick suggested that you deliver the papers—"

Her thought was interrupted by the telephone.

"Hello," she drawled. Something about talking on the telephone seemed to intensify her Southern accent, as if she didn't want to be caught talking "Yankee" in case a loyal son or daughter of the South happened to be on the line.

"Good evening, this is Michael Gilmore with the *New York Times*. I am in the Washington Bureau. I was wondering if—"

Deanna stopped him. "Mr. Gilmore, no one in this family wants to talk to a reporter, and if you are selling subscriptions, we aren't interested."

"Wait!" he begged. "I am not trying to interview you. I am just trying to locate your lawyer, Cooper Stone. I'm working on a deadline for our Sunday paper. I can't find a home number for him, and no one answers at the office."

"Well, Mr. Gilmore, this is your lucky day because Cooper Stone is standing in my backyard talking to my husband. I'll get him for you."

"Reporter—*New York Times*," Deanna whispered to Laura, as she walked to the back door. "Cooper," she called. "There's a reporter for the *New York Times* on the phone for you."

Cooper came bounding in the back door a moment later. He smiled at Laura as he headed for the phone. "Cooper Stone," he said cheerfully.

"Mr. Stone, this is Michael Gilmore with the Washington Bureau of the *New York Times.* I'm on deadline for a story for tomorrow's paper. I want to ask you a couple of questions about your UN case if I may."

"Sure, shoot," Cooper replied.

"The area of inquiry concerns how you are being paid for the case."

Cooper suddenly froze. "Yes?" he responded cautiously.

"Well, to get to the point, are your fees being paid by Randall Wasson, the associate publisher of the *Washington Star?*"

Laura thought she could see the color drain from Cooper's face. There was no mistaking the fact that he had grabbed hold of the edge of the kitchen desk, as if to steady himself.

"Now where would you hear something like that, Mr. Gilmore? Besides, my clients haven't authorized me to talk about their financial obligations."

"So you refuse to confirm or deny that point?"

"Mr. Gilmore, lawyers are under ethical rules regarding confidential communications. We do not discuss the fees we charge our clients or the manner of the payment of such fees."

"So your clients are personally paying you?"

"Mr. Gilmore, I am not going to answer any questions you have concerning the payment of my fees in this case. Do you have any other subject you were calling about?"

"Not really," Gilmore admitted.

"Then, I think we are finished, sir. Good-bye."

Cooper hung the phone back in the receptacle and leaned hard on both of his hands, which he had placed palms down on the desk.

"Cooper, who was that?" Deanna demanded.

"I can't believe it," Cooper moaned.

Deanna began to panic, thinking that some order had been issued affecting her children. "What is it, Cooper? Is it about Layton?"

He shook his head vigorously from side to side. "No, it's not about Layton and Emily." He looked up to see who was in the room. Seeing only Laura and Deanna, he continued. "This guy from the *New York Times* wanted to know if Randall Wasson was paying our attorney fees in this case."

It took a moment for the meaning of the question to sink in, but both women understood the implications at about the same time. Deanna sat down hard in the nearest kitchen chair. Laura turned bright red.

"I can't imagine how he found that out," Cooper remarked.

"Well, I didn't tell him," Deanna said quickly.

Laura said nothing. Cooper tried to sneak a look at her; when he did, their eyes met.

"No . . ." she said quickly, shaking her head. "Me neither."

"There are only five people other than Mr. Wasson and me who knew this, and they are all here," Cooper said slowly. He stopped and turned to Deanna. "Laura told me that you had let this fact slip out in some conversation. I don't mind that much your telling her. Just as long as neither of you told anyone else."

"No, no, not a soul," Deanna replied, with a clear conscience.

Laura knew that she should remind Deanna that Terry was also in the room when the matter had been discussed initially, but she just couldn't bear the thought of another fight erupting between the two of them. And she had warned Terry to not let it inadvertently slip out. "Cooper, I want you to know that I have not told a soul about this," Laura promised him.

"I believe you both, but we have a real problem here and I think we should ask everyone who knows about this to meet us in your living room. Is that OK, Deanna?"

"Sure. I'll go get Rick and the Garvises."

Laura and Cooper didn't say anything for a moment. "I promise you that I didn't tell anyone," Laura said, as if she was begging him to believe her.

"Laura," he said kindly, "I believe you."

Laura could hear Terry and Doug talking as they came in the front door from the porch where they had been conducting their impromptu deacon's meeting. Their voices trailed off just a moment later as they entered the living room.

"I suppose we should go into the living room," Laura said to Cooper, not wanting to be caught by standing alone with him by her fiancé.

"Sure," Cooper replied, his thoughts still concentrating on the reporter's phone call.

Rick and Deanna came in the back door as Laura and Cooper walked single file across the kitchen. "Nancy and her husband were nice enough to watch the kids, in the backyard. I told her that you took a press call and asked to meet with all of us," Deanna said.

"That's fine," Cooper replied.

As they entered the room, Cooper noticed immediately that Terry was sitting on one of the two green chairs located near the front wall of the room. "Terry, I hate to be rude, but we need to have a very confidential meeting for just a couple minutes. Maybe you could help Nancy and Fred in the backyard with the kids."

Terry said nothing but stared at Laura. He then walked out without a word, glaring at her.

"I don't know how to say this," Cooper began, "but we have sprung a leak somewhere on a matter that was supposed to be extraordinarily confidential." He described the phone call to them, and each person denied having told a single soul.

"Well, I don't know if they are going to publish the story or not, but we have to assume that they are going to call Mr. Wasson and ask him the same question. I am sure that he will refuse to answer also. But just because someone is asking, he will know that the matter had gotten out and our source of funds for this case may well be gone."

No one said anything for a long time. "So what are we going to do if he does withdraw?" Doug finally asked.

"The only thing I can think of is to go back to the Center for Constitutional Litigation and ask them to take the case. I know of no other way to raise the money at this stage of the case."

"There's got to be some alternative," Deanna said.

"I'm sure there must be," Jeanne chimed in. "We want you to keep fighting for us, Cooper."

Neither husband said anything, thinking over the financial implications in addition to the need to protect their children.

"I don't know of anything," Cooper said. "At a minimum, you all need to meet with the lead attorney from that group. Maybe you will like him after all."

"But he's not a Christian, is he?" Jeanne asked.

"Not that I know of. And given his position on a few other issues, I would be surprised if he is."

"I'll meet with him, but I can't imagine someone who is not a Christian being able to really fight for us, especially on our rights to teach our children that there is only one true faith," Jeanne said earnestly.

A thought suddenly hit Cooper. "Did I ever send you an e-mail about Mr. Wasson?" he asked.

"No," several voices said at once. "Why?"

"It's just that e-mails are not truly confidential over the Internet," he replied. "But if I didn't send one, no problem."

Eventually they all agreed to meet with the Center's lawyers. Cooper was to arrange the time. Everyone sat quietly for nearly a minute. Finally Rick said, "Let's pray."

The living room was visible from the backyard through a set of glass doors on the back of the house. Terry could see the group standing, holding hands in a prayer circle. His slow burn increased significantly when he noted Laura standing next to Cooper.

When the prayer was over, the Garvises announced that they should be leaving. Laura whispered a quick good-bye and thanks to Deanna and headed for the backyard to retrieve her jealous fiancé.

"What was that about?" Pipkin demanded angrily as they headed toward his car.

Laura stopped immediately. She turned, took both of Terry's hands, and looked him straight in the eye.

"I have to hear this from you. There has been a breach of confidence in this case, and I think Cooper is going to be replaced by other lawyers. No one seems to remember that you were in the room when Deanna said something she shouldn't have told us.

"So I just want a yes or no answer from you. Did you talk to a reporter about Cooper's fees being paid by that guy from the *Washington Star?*"

"No!" Terry replied vigorously. "I haven't talked to anyone about that."

"OK," she replied, searching his eyes carefully. Satisfied, she turned and they resumed walking toward the car.

"So why is Cooper leaving the case?" he asked, as soon as they fastened their seat belts.

"It's not for sure. But I guess there is no other way for them to pay for this case, and this group has offered to do it for free. You remember all that, don't you? Deanna said that when she told us about the guy from the *Star*."

"Oh, yeah," Terry replied. "That's right. I remember now."

Pipkin's mood brightened considerably for the rest of the evening.

CHAPTER

21

LEESBURG, VIRGINIA.
June 20, 2005.

There had been no article in the Sunday *New York Times,* but Nancy announced a call from a lawyer in Asheville, North Carolina, promptly at nine o'clock.

"Good morning," Cooper announced, trying to sound upbeat.

"Good morning, Mr. Stone. I assume you know why I am calling."

Cooper swallowed hard. "I guess Mr. Wasson got a call from a *New York Times* reporter."

"Actually, Mr. Wasson didn't talk to him, but the attempt was made."

"I am very sorry about this, but I have questioned each of my clients, and they all say quite convincingly that the information didn't come from them."

"I am sure that is the case," Tim Ballard replied.

"I recently found out that there was a leak to a key witness in the case, Laura Frasier—the children's Sunday school teacher. Mrs. Thomas apparently told her of the situation, but Miss Frasier has assured me repeatedly that she told no one."

"I hope that is the case also," Ballard said kindly.

"I thought I should mention we have reason to believe that the other side has managed to intercept our private e-mail messages. I have checked the file thoroughly, and I did not put any information about Mr. Wasson in any e-mail. But, perhaps there are other levels of espionage going on here."

"Perhaps so."

"None of this is going to change anything, is it?" Cooper asked.

"Yes, Mr. Stone, and I am sorry. The *New York Times* reached Mr. Wasson's brother at home. And his brother called and yelled at my client, demanding to know the truth. Mr. Wasson told him that he refused to answer the question unless his brother was willing to disclose what charities he supports with his own personal funds. But even so, the matter has erupted, and Mr. Wasson feels led to terminate the relationship. Too many other goals are jeopardized."

"I understand," Cooper replied.

"Thank you for your cooperation, Mr. Stone."

"Actually, I should thank you and Mr. Wasson profusely. He has taken us this far. My brief for the Virginia Supreme Court is practically done, there is enough money left to pay for the printing of the brief, and I have been paid everything owed to me so far. How can I do anything other than say thanks?"

"That is very gracious of you under the circumstances, and I will tell Mr. Wasson," Ballard said.

Cooper thought he might as well get the inevitable over with. He called the Center for Constitutional Litigation next. They were delighted to hear from him and agreed to come to his office the following afternoon to meet with all of the clients.

He continued to edit his brief for the Virginia Supreme Court until just before lunch. Then he was finally able to make the call he needed to make to Peter.

"Peter Barron & Associates," Sally said.

"Morning, Miss Sally," Cooper said.

"Good morning, Cooper," she laughed. "I assume you want to talk to Peter. But tell me quickly, did you enjoy yourself in chat the other night?"

"Oh . . . you mean the first time," he said, after a brief pause. "I thought it was fine. Those people are a little crazy, but they seem like a good group."

"First time? Have you gone back a second time and didn't tell me?"

"Well, yeah. I was having a hard time sleeping one night so I thought I would try it."

"What room did you go in?"

"I think it was called Mars Hill."

"Cool. What was going on?"

"Just two guys arguing over eternal security."

"Must have been RevBill and Wesleyan," Sally said confidently.

"Yeah, I think you're right," Cooper replied. "You act like you know these people."

"Well, I do. At least, sort of. It is kind of a weird experience in chat. You talk to people you would probably never give the time of day to if you saw them first. You know, you just don't like their looks or something. But, then you get to know them a little in an environment where looks don't count at all, where just what you say matters. I kind of like that."

"I think that makes some sense," Cooper agreed.

"So did anybody recognize you from the first chat?"

"No. I used a different screen name."

"What name did you use?"

"Do I have to tell you?"

"Only if you want me to transfer your call to the world famous Peter Barron," Sally teased.

"Rocky."

"Rocky? That can't be; we have another guy named Rocky. He's twice divorced and keeps asking every woman if she is single."

"Well, actually it was Rocky with 'ofVA' on the end of it."

"Oh, OK. That makes sense. Do you think you will do it anymore?"

"Maybe. You know us bored single people; we have to have something to do."

"I am transferring your call now, Mr. Stone," she said with mock frigidity in her voice.

Cooper only heard a few seconds of "hold" music before Peter answered the phone.

"Good morning, Cooper. How's everything?"

"Well, that is a complicated question. Or do you want me just to say 'fine' so we can go on with business?" Cooper asked, laughing.

"Whatever you would like," Peter chuckled.

"Here's the problem of the day I need you to help me solve. I just lost the funding for my case."

"And so you are calling me for a donation."

"Not a bad idea," Cooper laughed. "How about fifteen thousand dollars? That would tide me over until dinner."

"All right, time to get serious, Cooper. What's the deal?"

"Well, we had an outside contributor who was willing to pay for everything, provided that it remained absolutely confidential. I could tell my clients and no one else. But both he and I got calls over the weekend from a reporter for the *New York Times*. And, now—zip, the money is gone."

"Did they publish a story?"

"No, at least not yet. The reporter told me it was for yesterday's paper."

"Man, that's too bad. Do you have any idea how the reporter found out?"

"None. Unless someone is reading my e-mail or tapping my phone."

"Oh yeah, I talked to my friend, Aaron, the computer whiz. He said that there are a number of ways to intercept e-mails, and that you shouldn't put anything truly sensitive through an account they know about."

"Thanks. But I probably won't be on the case much longer anyway."

"So what contingency plans do you have?"

"I have the Center for Constitutional Litigation coming to meet the clients tomorrow night. They are still willing to take the case."

"You're close enough to being done with your Virginia Supreme Court brief. Why don't you just talk to them about doing the U.S. Supreme Court appeal if that becomes necessary."

"It'll be necessary. If we lose, we will definitely go on up. And you can be guaranteed that the NEA and Children's Defense Fund aren't going to stop either."

"Good point."

"But that is good counsel. Even if I have to volunteer my time for the Virginia Supreme Court oral argument, it won't be more than three or four days of my time. I can spare that at this point. But, I couldn't even pay my share of the overhead, much less any salaries, if I had to do the next level for free."

"I understand," Peter replied. "Well, let me think about this some. Is it OK with you if I tell some people about the need? I might be able to get you a few donations."

"Sure, tell whoever you want. I didn't share with you who the original funding source was, but that is the only detail that was confidential," Cooper answered matter-of-factly.

"It's probably best just to say that more funds are needed."

"I like that," Cooper said. "Thanks a lot, Peter. I really appreciate your counsel."

22

WORLDWIDE WEB.
June 21, 2005.

You are entering Mars Hill.

Contentlady:	I don't believe that we should give up on our country just because of the current bunch in DC.
Sancty-fried:	Are you saying that our government is bananas?
Firemomma:	Courtesy laugh to Sancty. Ha.
Abba4JC:	They may not be bananas but they are nuts if they think I am going along with this one.
Angelic:	Has something new happened in America? I am in Canada and I don't hear everything that is going on.
Notreally:	Our newly elected president has decided to eliminate tax deductions for more than three children in a family. So if you have a big family like me, you are toast.
Angelic:	Why are they doing that?
Notreally:	You have to understand how this crowd thinks, Angelic.
Sancty-fried:	We think Notreally? Since when do we think? I thought we just hit random letters to see what happened.
Contentlady:	LOL @ Sancty.
Notreally:	I wasn't talking about US thinking. Come on. You know better than that. I was talking to Angelic about learning how our new leaders think. They think like China does. Too many kids. Have only one. It's Thursday. Time to eat rice again.

Sancty-fried:	Thanks, content, that is the first time you ever laughed at one of my jokes.
Contentlady:	I didn't laugh on purpose. I just hit the keys randomly and LOL @ Sancty was just what came out. Strange coincidence, that's all.

MissSally ENTERS

Abba4JC:	Hey, Sally. How's the west coast tonight?
MissSally:	I'm doing great although I was told that the only reason I chat is because I am a bored single person.
Notreally:	What idiot told you that?
MissSally:	Some brilliant lawyer.
Notreally:	Like I said, who was that especially bright person who made such an astute observation? (He won't sue me for calling him an idiot will he?)
Contentlady:	LOL @ notreally
Notreally:	Another set of random key selections, content?
Contentlady:	No, notreally, actually I just dropped something on my keyboard.
Abba4JC:	ROFL@ Content
MissSally:	Actually, this brilliant lawyer who made the snide remark about me chatting needs our help. He doesn't know he needs our help but he does.
Sancty-fried:	I think that would describe half of the population— they need our help but don't realize it. I wonder how we could get them to realize it. Then we could all be rich instead of just being thin, good looking, brilliant, witty, and humble.

Saddlepal ENTERS

Abba4JC:	Hey, saddle, Sally is about to tell us how some brilliant lawyer needs our help but he doesn't realize it. I think a classic chat moment is about to arise.
MissSally:	Oh hush you guys I am serious. Remember Cooper Stone? He's the lawyer for the parents in the UN Children's Convention case. He did a guest chat a couple weeks ago.
Firemomma:	Wants to hear about Sally's idea.

Abba4JC:	Me too.
Saddlepal:	Promises to listen.
MissSally:	Well, here's the deal. There had been a donor helping to underwrite the families' defense of this UN case. And for reasons which I am not at liberty to share (because I haven't got a clue) that resource has come to an end.
Firemomma:	Bummer.
MissSally:	And because of this, there is a strong likelihood that a group of non-Christian lawyers will take over the case because they are willing to do it for free.
Sancty-fried:	Why are the non-Christians willing to do it for free but the Christian lawyer wants to charge money?
Notreally:	Because there are so few Christian lawyers and so many non-Christian lawyers? Law of supply and demand? Christian lawyers are very, very rare.
Abba4JC:	I met a Christian lawyer once.
Firemomma:	I saw a picture of a Christian lawyer in a book.
Saddlepal:	I hope none of you guys ever come in here with a serious idea and want help. Sally and I will do nothing but crack jokes about you.
Notreally:	I resemble that remark, saddlepal.
Sancty-fried:	Notreally stole my thunder.
Saddlepal:	You guys never quit. Go ahead Sally, ignore the rabble.
MissSally:	The reason the non-Christians can do it for free is that they are a part of a big legal foundation which has a big budget and a lot of donors. The Christian guy, Cooper Stone, used to be an attorney in the same law office I work in as a legal secretary. Now he is in Virginia and is just starting private practice and he has got to pay his basic bills like rent, supplies, furniture, and that all important paycheck for his legal secretary.
Contentlady:	That makes sense Sally. But why is it so bad for the non-Christian lawyers to do the case?
Abba4JC:	I know the answer to that one. Remember the Sunday

school deal. The UN people are arguing that kids cannot be taught that Christianity is the one true faith—that we have to respect others by being willing to say that Christianity may be true for us, but it is wrong to say that it is THE truth. Do you think that nonbelievers even understand the importance of this much less agree with us?

Notreally: Can't imagine most lawyers understanding anything that involves common sense.

Sancty-fried: I agree with Sally. And Abba. And especially Contentlady who either has brilliant taste in jokes or the most amazing luck in random keyboard whacking experiments.

Angelic: So what can we do to help him Sally?

MissSally: Don't laugh. I want us all to send him money.

Firemomma: LOL @ Sally

Abba4JC: ROFL @ Sally

Contentlady: lolololol

Notreally: Hey Sancty, do you think Sally is going to have to get a chat humorist union card with that one? That was a stroke of a true journeyman joker. I have never seen such progress. We have spawned comedic brilliance.

Sancty-fried: Can we get a commission?

Saddlepal: Calm down you bozos, I think Sally is serious.

MissSally: Thank you, saddle, you are really nice tonight. I AM serious. But I know that none of us have very much money. But all of us could probably afford $25. Who in this room could afford $25 to help save American Christian families from takeover by the UN?

Abba4JC: I would give $25.

Sancty-fried: I would give $25 if Sally promises to tell me her humor secrets. (Seriously, I would give for this cause).

Notreally: You cheapskates, I will give $27.50.

MissSally: I will hold you to that Notreally.

Notreally: No problem.

Firemomma: But even if we all gave $25 that wouldn't be enough would it?

MissSally: No, but how many people do you have in your e-mail directories? How many are Christians who would probably agree with us?

ContentLady: I have 276 people in my directory.

Saddlepal: 459 in my directory.

MissSally: Enough examples. I think we would easily have 4,000-5,000 people in our directories. And some of them would pass it on to their directories. Before long I think we could get the message to over 100,000 people. If just a few thousand send $25 we can raise all the money we need.

Saddlepal: I will do this Sally. I can't think of anything more important.

MissSally: smiles @ Saddlepal and glares at the rest of the room until they also agree.

Notreally: We all agree. Anyone who disagrees, say so now. We have to get this over with quickly so we can go back to having fun. Why waste time saving America and our religious freedom when we can crack jokes in chat?

RevBill ENTERS

Wesleyan ENTERS

Notreally: Oh, nevermind about going back to our normal chat. Hey RevBill and Wesleyan, Sally has the floor and we have preempted all other debating topics for the next six hours.

RevBill: I can only stay a couple hours.

Sancty-fried: You catch on quickly, RevBill.

MissSally: OK, I will start the e-mail chain. I think I have all your addresses. If not, send me your address to MissSally@crosswalk.com. I will e-mail out all the info and directions and addresses and you all just snowball it to your lists. And send your own $25 as soon as you get the e-mail from me which will be in about 20 minutes.

Notreally: OK, we will send our $25.
MissSally: Notreally, you gotta send $27.50.
Notreally: Oops. I meant that.

23

PURCELLVILLE, VIRGINIA.
June 23, 2005.

He couldn't help but look back as he walked away from the parking area near the bike trail. That salesman *was* right. The paint on
his GMC Jimmy really did seem to change color in direct sunlight,
albeit early morning sunlight.

But how was he going to make the insurance payments? He had
been so focused on the UN case that he had started turning down
other clients. His uncle had warned him about that, but the money
seemed so certain.

Cooper saw no one else on the WO&D jogging trail for the first
half-mile of his run. It was good. He wanted to be alone and think.
Somehow at his place with the television and the computer right
there, he couldn't find real solitude. Focus. That's what he needed.

The meeting had gone reasonably well. Brandon Powell had
been very convincing. And the Center for Constitutional Litigation
had substantial Supreme Court experience. Neither Deanna or
Jeanne wanted to switch attorneys, but their husbands convinced
them that the financial realities left them no choice. The papers

specifying a change of attorneys would be filed right after the oral argument took place in the Virginia Supreme Court on July 1.

The corn in the fields Cooper passed on his left was about waist high. The trees formed a perfect canopy over the trail for a couple hundred yards at a time. He ran through this pattern of sunlight and shadow for the next four and a half miles while he circulated these same thoughts through his mind.

He was tempted to leave the trail when he crossed the main village road in Paeonian Springs. The elementary school was just a quarter-mile south, but the building was empty and he would feel rather ridiculous staring into the empty classroom that Laura occupied during the school year.

He steeled his resolve, turned, and headed west on the trail back toward Purcellville. He suddenly had one simple but important thought. He had to forget everything that would distract him from the oral argument in the Virginia Supreme Court. The lost cause with Laura? That was for starters. Being replaced. Yeah, and even his financial woes. Focus. Prepare. Win.

It became a mantra that he recited in a rhythm as his feet pulsed against the asphalt trail. Focus. Prepare. Win. Focus. Prepare. Win.

He had just begun his chant for about the fifteenth time when the cell phone ringing in the pocket of his running shorts startled him. He fumbled to pull the phone out. He flipped it open and said "Hello" into the wrong end. He turned the phone over and tried it again as he reluctantly slowed to a stop.

"I'm looking for Cooper Stone," the female voice said.

"This is Cooper," he said, standing still, with his free hand perched on his hip.

"Sounds like you are out of breath. Is this a bad time? This is Amanda Chism with the *Washington Times*."

"I am in the middle of running, but I can stop and talk for a couple minutes."

"You sure?"

"Yeah. What's up?"

"We hear that you are stepping down from the UN case. I'm calling to verify that and ask why, if it is true."

Cooper started to laugh incredulously. "Who told you that?"

"Well, I suppose I can tell you. He didn't say it was confidential. Someone named Terry Pipkin. Is he connected with the case? He claimed to be on the inside somehow."

"I see," Cooper said, the blood running hot through his veins. "Terry Pipkin. That man is incredible."

"So is it true?" she persisted.

"Can I talk to you off the record?"

"Sure."

"We had a meeting last night where this idea was discussed. And, yes, replacing me is a possibility. But not right away. It would be at the U.S. Supreme Court level. Getting a new lawyer for the U.S. Supreme Court happens a lot. So it is no big deal."

"It's not because you ran out of money?"

"Is that what Pipkin told you?"

"He said that there had been a major donor who bankrolled the case, but he got spooked for some reason and has bailed out. Any of that true?"

"I don't want to talk about my clients' finances, even off the record."

"So is there anything you want to say on the record?"

"No."

"So I stumble into an exclusive story and you confirm it but won't go on the record at all?"

"Listen, Amanda, I'll make you a deal. If and when it comes time for me to be replaced, I will give you a one-day advance notice before any other reporter. I'll talk on the record. I'll give you anything you need."

"Fair enough."

They hung up.

"I'll also give you the exclusive story of how I am going to beat the tar out of a creep named Terry Pipkin," he promised, not into his cell phone but in the general direction of the cornfield.

SPOKANE, WASHINGTON. *June 23, 7:00* A.M.

"Hello," Peter mumbled, scrambling to pick up the bedside portable phone and get into the bathroom before Gwen was awakened.

"Did I wake you up?" Cooper asked.

"No . . . not really . . . my alarm was set to go off in five minutes. What's up, Cooper?"

"I need a good lawyer," he replied.

"What?"

"I think I am going to commit a crime of violence, and I want someone to represent me."

Peter said nothing.

"I am kidding, of course."

"I knew that," Peter replied.

"Well, at least I am kidding about doing it. I am not kidding about being that mad." He told Peter about the conversation with the reporter.

"So do you think that this Pipkin guy is the one who called the *New York Times* about your donor?"

"I am certain of it."

"Is that from your gut, or do you know something else?"

"Well, I guess I would say it is a educated gut reaction. I mean, he said most of the same things to this reporter. It's got to have been Pipkin. He wants me off the case."

"So he can keep you away from his girlfriend," Peter concluded.

"Fiancée," Cooper corrected.

"Oh, yeah," Peter replied.

"How did Pipkin know this? Was he at the meeting?"

"No."

"Was Laura there?"

"No, but she knew that last night's meeting was happening."

"Did Laura know about the donor?"

"Yeah, Deanna told her. She thought it was OK. But Laura swears that she didn't tell Pipkin. I asked her point blank, and she kept assuring me that she hadn't told him."

"It seems pretty obvious that one of your clients either told Pipkin directly or told Laura, who then told him."

"So should I ask Laura?"

"What would your motive be for asking her?"

"To find out who told Pipkin."

"And?" Peter pressed.

"I dunno, just to find out."

"So you can be mad at more people or perhaps more knowledgeably mad at him?"

"I don't know . . . this is so confusing to me."

"Cooper, let me be straight with you, OK?"

"You will, whether I agree or not," Cooper laughed.

"You're probably right. I think your reason for asking Laura about this would be to bring Pipkin down in her eyes. And then, things might go bad between them. And then she would be available. And then, hey, surprise! You are available also. Nice and convenient. Isn't something like that rumbling around in your brain?"

Cooper sighed before answering. "Yeah, I guess that's about it. But so what? I don't want her marrying this guy."

"You don't want her to marry him even if he is the greatest guy on earth, right?"

"Objection, Counselor," Cooper replied. "Assumes facts not in evidence. He's a jerk. Not the greatest guy on earth."

"All right, he's a jerk. But is this the way you want to have a foundation for a relationship? Do you want to win her heart by simply being better than some creep? Don't you want her to want you just because she loves you and thinks you're the right guy for her?"

Peter let Cooper sit in silence for nearly a minute. "Are you still there, Coop?"

"Yeah. I'm just thinking."

"Sure, go ahead and think."

Another minute passed in silence before Cooper spoke. "I suppose you are right. But what if she marries him without knowing this?"

"When's the wedding?"

"Oh, they haven't set a date. My guess is that he is just stalling."

"It sounds like she has plenty of independent evidence that he is a jerk."

"You finally see my point!"

"Well, Cooper, I would let God take care of protecting Laura from Pipkin, at least for now. If there were an actual wedding date maybe someone should talk to her father—not you—but someone. If her father knew, I would guess he would intervene. But, as it is, I think it is in God's sphere of responsibility."

"Yeah, OK. But it's easy for you to say."

"I know. Believe me, I know. This has to be very hard for you. But there is one thing you should do. You should let your clients know about this so that they will keep their confidential communications away from Laura because they have a habit of winding up with Pipkin."

"Good idea. I'll call Deanna. She is the source; there is no question about that."

"Let me know if I can help."

"Will do. Thanks again, Peter. Did you think you were signing up for counseling duties when you hired me as an associate?"

"Not really. But it is what I do, not because you were in my law firm, but because we are brothers in Christ."

"Thanks a lot, Peter."

༄ ༄ ༄

Deanna was horrified to learn of the call from the reporter. And she said she was very, very sorry to have forgotten that Pipkin had been in the room when she originally told Laura about Mr. Wasson's donations. And she promised not to say anything more of a confidential nature to Laura. And she promised not to tell Laura about this call from the reporter. And, again, she was very, very sorry about the whole thing.

Deanna sat stunned for the next thirty minutes, reviewing every detail of her conversation with Cooper. She *was* very sorry she had been the source of the leak. And she would indeed keep her promise to Cooper not to tell Laura anymore confidential information about the case. But she just couldn't keep her promise about not telling Laura of Pipkin's behavior. That wasn't about the case. She just couldn't let her friend marry a man who was not to be trusted.

༄ ༄ ༄

That afternoon, Nancy brought Cooper three checks that had arrived in the mail without explanation. They were made to Jameson & Stone, in care of Cooper Stone. They were designated for "the UN Case." Two checks were for $25. One was for $27.50.

GENEVA, SWITZERLAND.
June 27, 2005.

The regular meeting of the Committee on the Rights of the Child
had bogged down in the details of the national reports from
Southeast Asia. Jody Easler was bored. When she first arrived in
Geneva she had engaged herself in every detail of every report with
the same kind of passion that had energized her ten-year career. It
was the fight for "the children," and she cared. Something in her
feminine instincts cared very deeply.

While some others believed that maternal feelings were an
antifeminist deviation from the truth, she had been very carefully
taught that feminine instincts were quite powerful, even spiritual
in a nontheistic way. Some of her mentors might even say that
truth was bound up in the Goddess—and she respected that,
though Jody herself had never gone down that path.

At their foundation, Jody's feminine instincts were for the children, not for the politics and power and position. Yet, the longer
she stayed in Geneva, the more she understood that the top leadership was all about the power and not about the children.

She did a mental inventory of the ten members around the table. Three of the committee were married. Two had children. The married woman from China had one. The single woman from Nigeria had two. She wasn't opposed to having children herself. But there simply hadn't been either the time or the right partner.

After three tortuous hours, the meeting was finally over. Jody cleared her things into her briefcase quickly and was headed out of the conference room. "Dr. Kadar would like to see you in her office," the ubiquitous aide whispered discretely in the American's ear. Jody nodded and headed down the hall.

She was made to wait for fifteen minutes in Kadar's outer reception area. She was fuming by the time the same aide opened the inner office door, beckoning Jody to join them in the room.

The aide sat off to the side and behind Kadar against the window wall, pen and pad in hand, just in case. "Thank you for coming Dr. Easler," Kadar said with a tone that was supposed to sound friendly, but the pursing of her lips and a slight squint of her eyes gave the opposite impression.

"I have only come as requested," Jody replied tersely.

"Actually, Dr. Easler, I think I have some good news for you."

Jody's tensed muscles relaxed only slightly. "Good news? I am ready for some good news."

"Your friend Cooper Stone appears to be ready to step out of the litigation."

"Why is that good news?"

"It may or may not be good news from the perspective of our litigation strategy because his apparent replacement has substantial

Supreme Court experience. But I thought it would be good news for you personally."

"Why so?"

"Because we won't have to use the photographs of the two of you in New York. We had planned to release them a week or so before oral argument in the Supreme Court to throw the other side into confusion. But if he is withdrawing, then there is no need to print the photos."

"What photographs? He never came into my room!"

"Our photographer caught the two of you in a nice romantic embrace in some carriage. We thought you had adapted to his refusals quite nicely."

"No one told me that we were being photographed outside the room. And what is this about printing the photos? Are you all crazy? I knew you planned to blackmail him quietly but to use them in public? That would drag me through the mud as well."

"Well, Dr. Easler, you know how we feel about these things. If one of our own gets a little mud on them, so what? No one cares. It is Mr. Stone's side of this battle that cares about such indiscretions. And besides, if the photos had been as we had planned, no paper would publish them. But a beautiful couple locked in a romantic kiss, well, that is front-page material when the man and woman are on opposite sides of a major event."

"Just a minute! I care! I care a great deal! I don't want to look like your cheap tramp. If it is published, it will look like I trapped him into kissing me."

"Isn't that what you did? The kiss was simply your adaptation of our original plan, was it not? Or were you actually succumbing to the charms of Mr. Stone?"

"You are crazy if you think I am going to dignify that with a response."

"We have noticed that you seemed especially solicitous of Mr. Stone. Whispered conversations in television studios and the like. But that seems to have died down. We have detected no recent content."

"You have *detected?* You admit you are spying on me? I have suspected it, but I never believed you would admit it."

"Oh come now, Dr. Easler—you know the rules of engagement. Nothing is left to chance. The loyalty to the movement on the part of one of our key players is always essential."

"Which movement? The movement to help children? Or the movement to gain political power?"

"You said it yourself. I am not going to dignify that comment with a response. Good day, Dr. Easler."

LEESBURG, VIRGINIA. *June 27, 2005.*

Nancy tapped on Cooper's door. "Mail call," she sang out.

"Oh, I was coming to get it in a minute. You didn't have to bring it in," he said, clearing his desk for a new client meeting scheduled in a half-hour.

"I thought there were some things you'd want to see right away," Nancy replied.

"More twenty-five-dollar checks?"

"Yes, some of those. Eighty-five to be exact. One check for one thousand dollars also."

"Isn't that our highest so far?"

"Yes, we had sixty-three yesterday. So far, we have $7,235. Almost always twenty-five dollars but a few odd amounts."

"I wish I knew who is at the bottom of this."

"There was a note with one of them today," Nancy said handing him an envelope. "Something about word being passed among some chat room people and e-mail. I don't get it."

"What?" Cooper asked, his mind racing immediately to *Crosswalk.com*.

He grabbed the envelope eagerly from Nancy. While he was tearing it open, Nancy extended her hand, holding another envelope. "I thought you would want to see this one right away also." She quickly turned and left.

Cooper glanced briefly at the second envelope as he eagerly unfolded the first letter. The return address on the second envelope caught his eye. *Laura Frasier, c/o Mr. and Mrs. Edward Frasier.* Laura had written from her parents' home in Florida.

"When did she go down there?" he asked out loud, as he sat the first letter aside only partially opened.

Dear Cooper,

I am writing to you to apologize for breaking a confidence. As you know, after you met with the four parents, Deanna told me about the results of the meeting. I in turn told Terry. Terry then told the *Washington Times*. It was never my intention to hurt you or to cause any difficulties for the case.

Terry made it plain that his motive was simply to

keep me from having contact with you. He apparently felt that until the announcement was public, that there was always a danger you would stay on the case. I am certain that he told the *New York Times* about the earlier matter, though he refuses to give me a straight answer on the subject.

In any event, will you forgive me?

I shouldn't give you any more problems in this regard in the future for two reasons. One, I have come down to Florida to stay with my parents for the rest of the summer, so I won't be around to mess things up. Second, Terry and I have broken off our engagement, so there won't be the need to tell him of such matters in the future.

Again I am sorry.

Blessings,

Laura

Deanna had to have told her. He didn't even bother to call to yell at her. *Come to think of it, why would I yell at Deanna?* Maybe he should just be relieved.

Cooper dialed directory assistance and got the phone number for Laura's parents by using the address on the envelope. He paused, thought better of it, and hung up the phone. He would wait for at least twenty-four hours before calling. It would give him time to think and pray about what he hoped would be one of the most important phone calls in his life.

WORLDWIDE WEB. *June 27, 2005. 11:00* P.M.

You are entering Mars Hill as CooperStone.
You see here Abba4JC, Contentmomma, cryllic, Angelic, Firemomma, Sancty-fried, Notreally, MissSally, Saddlepal . . .

There were thirteen chatters in all.

MissSally:	Cooper! What are you doing here?
CooperStone:	I want to come and say thanks.
MissSally:	So you are getting our $25 checks?
CooperStone:	Mostly $25, some for some odd amounts—one was for $27.50, that seemed strange.
Notreally:	blushes
Saddlepal:	You did it. You came through.
Abba4JC:	What kind of amount would notreally have sent other than a strange amount? It seems so natural.
Contentmomma:	LOL@ abba (on purpose).
MissSally:	So how much have you gotten so far?
CooperStone:	Over $7000.
Angelic:	How much from Canada?
CooperStone:	Yeah, that was one of the big surprises. We have over $1000 from Canada.
Firemomma:	Angelic, take a bow.
Katie_host:	So we have raised about ten percent of our goal. I guess that is good.
MissSally:	It has been only about a week. I think it is pretty good.
Saddlepal:	I think it is great. I am in the mail business here in Montana, and I think that you can expect a lot more.
MissSally:	You are in the mail business in Montana? I thought you were a cowboy from Texas. I'm so bummed.
Saddlepal:	I ride horses and I am from Texas. But I have lived in Montana for three years and I direct a mail shop. So what's wrong with that?
MissSally:	Oh, I don't know but it seems less intriguing to be chatting thousands of miles away with a mail shop guy than with a cowboy.

Firemomma:	Anyone wanna hear the cute thing my seven-year-old daughter said when I told her about this fund-raising idea?
Saddlepal:	But I am not a thousand miles away, only about 150 from Spokane.
CooperStone:	I would like to hear your story, firemomma.
Sancty-fried:	Somebody tell the new guy not to encourage the cute kid stories—unless of course, RevBill and Wesleyan are debating again.
MissSally:	Really, saddle? Do you ever get to Spokane?
Firemomma:	OK, then, Sancty, I WON'T tell it.
Notreally:	Oh fire, don't listen to Sancty. He is so mean at times. Please feel free to tell us your story.
Firemomma:	Thank you notreally that is nice.
Notreally:	No problem, fire. I hear you make good oatmeal and raisin cookies, I would like two dozen please.
Saddlepal:	In fact I am coming to Spokane next week to pick up a new folding machine.
MissSally:	Really? Can you email me with the details? I would like to make you dinner to thank you for helping me with this project.
Abba4JC:	raises her eyebrows at MissSally's forwardness.
CooperStone:	Do you all do this every night?
MissSally:	takes her tweezers and plucks out Abba's eyebrows.
Sancty-fried:	Do what every night? Conduct an altruistic campaign to raise enough money to save America from the evil empire? Normally we don't do that every single day . . . just those days ending in y.
Notreally:	Yes, what was it last week, Sancty? Oh yes. The Heartbreak of Psoriasis Foundation. Raised 10 million for them, wasn't it?
MissSally:	They are joking, Cooper.
Cryllic:	Not that they are funny, Cooper. It is a statement about their character, not their actual ability to be humorous.
CooperStone:	I think this is all hilarious.

Notreally:	I knew I should have sent $27.95. A really smart man like Cooper deserves my very best.
Contentmomma:	So are you going to stay on the case, Cooper? Have we raised enough? $50K should do it for sure.
CooperStone:	Well, I can sure stay in for a while longer. If you keep going, there is no doubt.
Abba4JC:	If you will come chat with us once in awhile then we will keep it up for sure.
MissSally:	But if you come too often, Cooper, I will tease you about being a bored single like me.
CooperStone:	Looks to me like you are doing your best to not be a bored single. Dinner with saddle? Looks promising to me.
Katie_host:	LOL @ Cooper.
Sancty-fried:	Congratulations Mr. Stone, that is your first LOL in chat. You should print this page and frame it.
Notreally:	The boy catches on fast. Sancty, can you believe him? A lawyer, and a Christian and a chat jokester. A true Renaissance man.
CooperStone:	LOL@ notreally.
Firemomma:	Don't encourage his jokes, Cooper. It is a downhill slide from there. Jokes, then puns, then seedy little tales, and before you know it . . . boom . . . you are at the bottom, telling cute things your kids have said.
Sancty-fried:	Ouch!
Notreally:	Humbly begs Firemomma's forgiveness and asks her to please tell her story . . .
Firemomma:	OK
Notreally:	. . . as soon as RevBill shows up.

Cooper logged off the computer and made his way quickly to bed. He reset his alarm for 6:00 A.M. He would only get six hours of sleep as it was. His slow rhythmic breathing underscored a level of contentedness that had evaded him so completely just a few weeks ago. His mind began reviewing the events of the day yet again, but a little more slowly each time. He was in the twilight between sleep and consciousness when his bedside phone shook him quickly to full wakefulness.

He grabbed the phone perfectly with a strong swoop of his arm. "Yep," he said. It seemed like the right way to answer the phone at midnight.

"Cooper?" It was a female voice that sounded only vaguely familiar.

He sat up. "Yeah? Who's this?"

"Jody."

His mind raced for only few seconds until concluding it was *that* Jody. "Where are you, Jody?"

"Geneva."

"What time is it there?"

"Six."

"In the morning?"

"Yeah, I wanted to call you when I was alone," she said. She had sequestered herself in a secure diplomatic office with lines that were regularly screened for espionage interference.

"I have to say I never expected it would be you calling me. What's up?"

"I have to meet with you. It is very important."

"Can't you tell me over the phone?"

"No."

"Is it business important or personal important?"

"Both."

"So when and where?"

"You'll meet with me?" she asked.

"Yeah. Why not?"

"Well . . . it's just . . . I'll tell you when I see you. I fly to Dulles today. Arriving at about 3:00 P.M. your time. Some place out of the way. I can't be recognized. Lansdowne at seven?"

"The hotel? I don't think—"

"No, the restaurant."

"I'm not sure that the restaurant is all that out of the way. Too many D.C. types there."

"Any other suggestions?"

"Al's Pizza in Purcellville. Nobody from D.C. would ever think to look for a U.S. ambassador there."

"See you at seven."

Around two he got exhausted from trying to unravel everything and fell sound asleep.

ROUTE 7, WEST OF LEESBURG, VIRGINIA.
June 28, 2005.

Preparing for oral argument had been more than a little difficult that day. The mantra Focus-Prepare-Win had had no effect whatsoever.

Cooper had thought about calling Peter about the evening's rendezvous but couldn't bring himself to do it. There was a certain excitement about seeing Jody again, but Cooper felt that he didn't have any improper motive. *I don't have any motive at all for meeting. It was her idea.* He had told this to his conscience about a half-dozen times during the course of the afternoon.

There was only one word that Jody had used that really troubled him. *Both.* What did she mean? "Business or personal?" he had asked. "Both," she had said.

Cooper convinced himself that he would have declined the meeting if she had merely said "personal." But deep in his spirit, he knew that it would have been a struggle to say no.

He prayed for protection for about the twelfth time as he exited the freeway and headed south on Route 287. A beautiful little college lay off to his left.

He turned right on Main Street and was in the parking lot of Al's a minute later—6:40, his wristwatch informed him. He went inside, took a table in the far back corner away from the pinball machines, and waited for ten minutes. He walked to the counter and ordered. Large. Half Hawaiian. Half bacon, mushrooms, and onions.

A taxi pulled up at 7:03. She walked in, not in a fancy dress as he had imagined, but wearing a red T-shirt with a modestly scooped neckline and a pair of jeans. She gave no signs of being an ambassador, other than her purse and belt, which appeared to be expensive Italian leather. Her hair was pulled back in a loose ponytail.

Cooper's self-confidence was crushed. He wanted her to look like the ambassador of the Evil Empire. Then she would be easy to resist. But she looked like the girl next door—provided that her daddy had a little extra money to throw around on leather goods. She was far more beautiful than he had dared to remember.

There was a giggly group of twelve- and thirteen-year-old girls from a softball team who focused on them like radar. Good looking guy. Great looking woman. And a taxi at Al's Pizza in Purcellville, which was by far the most titillating thing they had seen in weeks. The girls took an immediate poll as to whether the man would kiss the woman as soon as they saw Cooper get up and head in the direction of the front door. Only three had voted "no kiss."

A chorus of disappointed "ahs" erupted when Cooper said, "Hi, Jody," and warmly shook her hand.

"Hello, Cooper," she replied with an effusive smile. "It's really good to see you again."

A whispering campaign erupted among the girls as to whether a delayed kiss counted. Al caught Cooper's eye and gave him the combination of raised eyebrows and extended lower lip, which is the universal signal between men meaning "nice catch." But what he said was, "Pizza is ready, Cooper."

Cooper took the aluminum platter and escorted the ambassador back to the corner seat, where a pitcher of Diet Coke and two tall plastic glasses awaited their dining pleasure. Their corner booth was next to the window, with Cooper facing toward the front of the restaurant.

Jody looked at him and with apparent seriousness said, "Ambassadors aren't allowed to eat pizza off of the platter."

Cooper looked up with concern for his breach of etiquette, but the smile that erupted on her face told him that she was joking. "When was the last time you had a pizza?" Cooper asked.

"You know, I can't tell you," she replied. "That's a horrible sign of how messed up my life has become."

Cooper breathed deeply, realizing that he was going to hear some portion of that tale. He only hoped that her messed up life wouldn't involve him too much.

"Can I pray for the food?" he asked. Jody nodded. "And maybe I can pray for you too."

"I would like that," she said softly.

He covered both concerns briefly and sincerely, and then asked her which kind of pizza she wanted. He was astonished to learn that she had never even seen pineapple on pizza, much less eaten any. He offered his opinion that the State Department's cultural education program obviously left something to be desired.

"Well, shall I tell you my tale of woe?" she asked, trying to remain cheerful. The light-hearted banter for the last five minutes was the only moment of emotional respite she had had in a long time.

"Sure, might as well," he replied.

"I guess I'll start off with the worst thing. I came to New York that weekend to compromise you. And blackmail you. It was all a plan we had hatched to use against you in the lawsuit if and when it was needed. Our side plays politics for keeps."

She paused to gauge his reaction. To her amazement, he seemed unchanged. To *his* amazement, he was still sitting on the bench across from her.

"But obviously, none of that happened. I have assumed your refusal was because of your moral convictions because I didn't exactly get the impression from you that you think I am ugly."

"You are far from ugly," he replied. *Was that OK to say?* he asked himself, wincing inside. He felt he had to say something.

"When you asked me to go with you for a ride in the park, I was going because I wanted to. When you refused to come in the room, as far as I was concerned, my assignment was over."

"But then . . ." he encouraged her.

Her eyes dropped in embarrassment. "But then, I found out, just a few days ago, that there was a photographer nearby who captured us kissing on camera. And I was told that our forces intend to use it if you remain on this case."

"Whoa," he exhaled as he shook his head in disbelief. He sat there thinking for a moment. The pizza was getting cold. "So have you been sent here now to deliver this message to try to get me to pull out of the case?"

She looked at him with hurt in her eyes. "No, Cooper," she said, "I came to warn you and try to help you—and me, as well. Besides, I have been told that you are leaving the case after the Virginia Supreme Court oral argument."

"I don't know who told you that, but it is not necessarily the case. I would say that I am undecided."

"Well, that is an important factor that our people don't seem to know, and I hope they will stay off the trail of the truth."

"So why are you trying to help me?"

"I don't expect you to believe me, but I really care about what happens to you."

"Isn't that just what the double agent is supposed to say?" he replied sarcastically.

"Perhaps so. But it is true."

"Fine. Let me ask you this: Why do you care what happens to me?" He had already assured himself that if she said that she loved him, or anything that resembled that, he wasn't going to believe a word she said from that moment on.

"I guess it is just a late blooming sense of decency. Mainly from watching your decency. You took this case without knowing how you would be paid, out of a sense of dedication and, well, decency. You stayed out of my room out of a sense of decency. The restraint you showed in the carriage ride after I kissed you speaks of a man of decency. I have been around a lot of men. No one has ever displayed your kind of decency."

Cooper wanted to believe her. She sounded so sincere. And it had the ring of truth, not something that would have been scripted by a spy master.

"So why do you need help too?"

"Well, for one thing, I don't want to see our picture on the front page of the *Washington Star* anymore than you do. Can't you see the headline? 'Embracing the Enemy.'"

"Yeah, I think that's about what it would say."

Cooper watched three or four girls in red, white, and blue softball uniforms sneaking up the sidewalk outside the building to get a closer look at Purcellville's mystery romance. "We had better eat some pizza," Cooper said, breaking the tension as he nodded in the direction of the girls. "The natives are suspicious."

It was her laugh at that moment that told him she was telling him the truth. Something in its music gave him the assurance he needed.

After they had both eaten several bites and sipped at their Diet Cokes, Cooper noted that the girls had retreated. "So what do you think needs to be done?"

"I don't know," she replied. "I guess I had hoped that the intelligence report that you were definitely leaving the case would be true. But there is no way that I want you to leave this case now. Maybe there are other good reasons, but for me it is good enough that Erzabet Kadar wants you off."

Cooper had seen the name in print but had never heard it correctly pronounced before, and so he paused for a beat or two before understanding who she was talking about. "Well, I don't want to leave the case. And money has begun to come in from another source so I may not have to leave. But I have no idea of how to blunt the effect of Kadar's decision to publish our picture. Do you think she is going to do that immediately?"

"Not as long as they think you are withdrawing. Does anyone know differently?"

Cooper thought of the chat room. Every one of them could be spies. "Notreally," he replied, with no intention of telling her about the chat room member who would have appreciated that private joke with no small amount of mirth.

"Well, when the case gets before the United States Supreme Court, we should both expect the photo to go public if you are still on the case."

Cooper shook his head like he had just remembered something. "I have been so thrown off by this blackmail scheme that I forgot to ask you about the note you gave me about my e-mail being intercepted. What is going on with all that?"

"I am not supposed to know anything, and I really know very little. One day I was sitting in Suskins' office." She paused and smiled ironically. "Actually, we were plotting against you—court-room plotting, not skullduggery, when a call from Kadar came in. The conversation was mostly one-sided because Suskins just nodded and spoke briefly ever so often while he was making notes. I can't remember the exact words, but the words *plans* and *e-mail* were mentioned in connection with you. I just put two and two together and gave you the note."

"So Suskins is involved in all of this? Is he the one leading the charge?"

"He's involved, but he tries to keep his hands as clean as possible. There is no question as to who is really in charge—Dr. Kadar calls the shots."

"So nothing happens until the Virginia Supreme Court decides?"

"That's what I've been told."

"By then I will pray that we will find a way out of this," he said, "and that we both do the honorable thing, even if we can't."

"Please pray, Cooper. If God shows you a way out of this mess, you may make me a believer in the power of prayer." She certainly sounded convincing.

"Well, that is a great challenge. But I know a great God," Cooper replied.

"So . . ." Jody said, in a tone meaning that she had been in Al's Pizza as long as she could take it, "how do I catch a cab to take me to my hotel?"

Cooper smiled. "You're serious? Catch a cab? In Purcellville?"

"One dropped me off here."

"Right! And unless another dignitary decides to come to Al's Pizza or maybe Food Plus across the parking lot in the next few minutes, you will have to call one to come from Dulles airport. It'll be thirty minutes—minimum."

She looked distressed.

"Where's your hotel? I'll take you if it is not too far."

"Lansdowne. I liked it there when we had the depositions."

"Yeah, it is the nicest place in the county. In fact, I am a member of their health club there. It's where Rick Thomas and I play racquetball."

Cooper grabbed his car keys and cell phone from the table. "All right, Madam Ambassador, I think it is time for me to take you back to the Lansdowne, but there is only one condition. I will not even step one foot outside the car when we get there."

"I understand, Cooper. I am not trying to tempt you."

His mind said, *You don't have to try very hard.* But his spirit overrode his mind. "I didn't think you were," he replied out loud.

During the twenty-five-minute drive from Purcellville to the Lansdowne, the conversation was light, but the emotional energy was charged. Both of them recognized it but said nothing.

Cooper extended his hand when it was time for her to go. She took his in both of hers and squeezed tightly for just a minute. "You're a good man, Cooper. Goodnight."

"Goodnight, Jody." Cooper drove away immediately.

LEESBURG, VIRGINIA.
June 30, 2005.

His briefcase and file boxes were nearly ready to take to Richmond.
Cooper was reviewing his checklist to make sure he had everything
when Nancy buzzed in. "Rick Thomas on line 1."

"Cooper, we need to talk. When are you headed for Richmond?"

"I was leaving in about five minutes. Do you want to talk now
or when we have dinner at the hotel tonight?"

"We need to talk before you go. Just you and me."

"Sure, Rick. Is something wrong?"

"Yeah, at least it appears to be."

"Do you want to give me a clue?"

"I'll be there in five minutes—I'm calling you on my cell." Rick's
voice sounded either scared or mad. Cooper couldn't be sure.

Cooper couldn't imagine what the problem might be that
was so important on this day before the oral argument in
Richmond. But it had to be something. Fortunately, he didn't
have long to stew about it. Rick appeared at his office door right
as promised.

"Come on in, Rick." Cooper noticed a grim look on Rick's face and a manila envelope in his right hand.

"Cooper, I am really sorry to do this to you just before oral argument, but I need to show you something. Deanna opened it up when it arrived in the mail earlier today, and . . . before I say more, you take a look."

He had a premonition that sent a hot wave of embarrassment through his body. He pulled open the silver clasps and removed a stack of photographs. The hot wave became an inferno. He thumbed quickly through the photos, nodding and muttering as he went. His face was bright red.

"That's what I was afraid they were when I saw the envelope," he said. "But I didn't expect it to really happen."

"You knew about these photos?"

"Yeah," he nodded. "I had been warned."

"By who?"

"Jody Easler—the woman in the pictures."

"You can guess how Deanna reacted when she saw this, can't you? Our lawyer embracing the leading American proponent of the UN treaty. How do you think it made her feel? How do you think it made *me* feel?" With each word, his growing anger caused his voice to become louder and louder. "The Garvises got an identical envelope. Doug was so upset he couldn't come with me."

Cooper felt leveled by Rick's anger. "Would you like to hear my explanation, or do you just want to vent at me? Not that I blame you."

"Sure, I would love to hear an explanation. I hope it is a good one. I hope it makes me believe that I can still trust my lawyer and my friend." His tone was still pretty hot.

"You're going to have to be the judge of all that."

Rick nodded, somewhat calmed by the humility of Cooper's reply.

"Actually, I've got an idea. I want you to talk to my old boss in Spokane, Peter Barron. I've told you about him before."

"Yeah, you mentioned him. What does he know about this?"

"I was up in New York to visit Peter and his wife that evening. And basically I was set up. Peter knows nothing about the photos. I confessed everything to him and sought his counsel before I knew anything about any photos. But, I think it might have more credibility if you hear the story from him."

"All right, we can start there," Rick agreed.

Cooper called Peter's office and after only a brief delay got the Spokane lawyer on the phone. "Peter, I need you to do me a very big favor. I want you to tell one of my clients about my activities in New York City after I left you and Gwen in the elevator."

"Are you serious?" Peter asked.

"Dead serious. I can explain later, but I think it would be best if you just tell him what you know about my actions, without me saying anything more right now."

Cooper's voice was extraordinarily subdued. Peter decided to simply follow his friend's request. "OK. Put him on."

"This is Rick Thomas, one of the fathers in the UN case," Cooper said to Peter before handing the phone over to Rick.

"Hi, Rick, my name is Peter Barron. Cooper used to work in my law firm here in Spokane, and we have stayed in touch. He has called me for advice several times on your case."

"He's mentioned you to me, Mr. Barron."

"Well, this is a little unusual, but let me just plunge in and tell you what I know.

"First of all, it was my idea for Cooper to come to New York. He and I were on the phone talking about your case, and I felt he needed cheering up a bit. Things weren't going so well with the case at that moment, and he was struggling with his feelings for a girl named Laura—I take it you know her. And I just thought it would be good for him to come to New York, visit with my wife and me, and go to dinner—that sort of thing.

"So he came. We had a good time. And, I don't know, maybe at 10:30 or so, he left us. He was staying on a lower floor and just got off the elevator on his floor."

Peter told him how Jody was waiting in the hall, how she tried to coax him into her room, how Cooper suggested the carriage ride instead, and how she had kissed him, even though Cooper had clearly cooperated.

"The bottom line, Mr. Thomas, is that Cooper is a human being, a man who made a mistake. Not the worst mistake in the world but clearly an error in judgment, and I guess we should say it is a sin. But there is no question in my mind that he is 100 percent loyal to you and your case. And it is my judgment that he was probably set up—that her being there was no coincidence. But I don't have any hard evidence of that."

"Well, we've got some hard evidence of part of the story," Rick replied.

"What do you mean?"

"There was a package of photos mailed to my house showing Cooper and that ambassador woman kissing in the carriage," Rick said, without any heat.

"Oh, no!" Peter exclaimed.

"My wife opened the package and was devastated."

"Oh, my! You've got to be kidding."

"So he hadn't told you anything about any photos?" Rick asked.

"No, I just learned about them from you."

Rick glanced at Cooper uncomfortably and looked away. "He just told me that the ambassador had warned him that there were photos." Noting Rick's embarrassment, Cooper tapped Rick on the shoulder and motioned that he was going to leave the room so that Rick and Peter could talk more freely.

Peter spoke. "Well, he didn't tell me anything about that. But he did say that she had slipped him a note with a message warning him that his e-mail was being intercepted. I think she gave it to him after the *Today Show.*"

"All right," Rick acquiesced.

"I'm sure that you are worrying about trusting him."

"You should hear my wife," Rick replied.

"I don't even want to *think* about that," Peter assured him. "But, Mr. Thomas, I believe that Cooper is absolutely trustworthy."

"Really?"

"I would trust him with my life."

"I am trusting him with my kids, and it's about the same thing."

"Probably more important than your own life, in some respects," Peter replied.

"Thanks, Mr. Barron," Rick said sighing. "You've helped a lot."

"Glad you called."

Rick walked to the door and beckoned Cooper back into his own office. He reached to shake Cooper's hand. Cooper gladly reciprocated, with a mumbled thanks. "So where are we?" he asked.

"Well, we are a good way down the road. But I still have more questions."

"Fair enough," Cooper replied.

"This ambassador—what's her name?" Rick asked, tired of calling her "that ambassador woman."

"Jody Easler."

"Ambassador Easler gave you some kind of note warning you that your e-mails were being intercepted?"

Rather than answer him, Cooper reached over and pulled an envelope out of his center desk drawer. He handed it to Rick.

After examining the note, Rick asked, "Why didn't you tell us about this?"

"I didn't want you all to freak out about espionage." Cooper paused, strengthened his resolve, and continued. "Honestly, though, that is the lesser reason. The main reason was that I felt it would lead to questions that would ultimately expose my behavior that you have now seen in these photos. I was embarrassed to tell you about that."

"I guess I can understand that. Doesn't make it right. But I can understand."

"So are you promising me that the only thing you did with this woman—with Miss Easler—is this one kiss?"

"It's not the only thing, but it was the worst thing. I held her hand, but I didn't do anything worse than what you have seen."

"Nothing is going on between you and her?"

"That's right."

"So why were you having dinner with her at Al's Pizza a few nights ago?"

Cooper felt like he had been kicked in the gut. "Man, 'be sure your sin will find you out,'" Cooper said. "Not that I am saying I sinned with her that time."

"Keep talking," Rick said.

"Well." Cooper breathed slowly, trying to think of where to begin. "She called me from Geneva the night before we met at Al's. She said she had to talk with me.

"She refused to talk over the phone, hinting that the lines might be tapped, and suggested we meet at the Lansdowne. Well, I wasn't about to meet with her in a hotel, so I suggested a place that I thought would be out of the way, where no one would recognize her. But obviously someone did."

"Yeah, one of the girls on the softball team that was in the restaurant is a friend of Emily Garvis. The friend's mom had watched the *Today Show,* and when she came to pick up her daughter she saw you both. She called Jeanne to ask her about it. Jeanne called Deanna. They both figured that it must have been someone else and couldn't have been the ambassador. But after seeing these pictures, both women concluded that she had been with you at Al's."

"Man, I cannot believe how big of a mess I have managed to get myself into," Cooper said dejectedly. He gave Rick a full accounting of the evening, including how grateful she had seemed when he prayed for her and how he had later left her at the Lansdowne without getting out of the car.

"Please tell me there are no more surprises," Rick pleaded.

"I've told you everything there is to tell."

"All right, Cooper. I believe you, and I trust you. But I have just one more question."

"Yeah?"

"How do you feel about Jody Easler now? If she is secretly on our side, then the need to stay away from her is far less."

"Maybe, but that's not a certainty, and, more importantly, she's not a Christian."

"But it sounds like she is starting to open up to the things of God."

"Yeah, and I am really glad about that. But still—" Cooper hesitated.

"Let me ask you this way, Coop. If she became a Christian, what would be your intentions toward her?"

"I would be thrilled if she became a Christian. But even though I find her very attractive . . . maybe in a weak moment, too attractive . . . the fact is that I'm in love with Laura."

"Bummer."

"Bummer? Why do you say 'bummer'?"

"Because Deanna called Laura in Florida and told her about the photos."

Cooper searched vainly for words for a moment and then gave up. When Rick left a few minutes later, Cooper remained sitting in his office with his eyes closed, in an attitude of prayer.

CHAPTER

RICHMOND, VIRGINIA.
July 1, 2005.

The prior evening's preparation had not been what Cooper had planned. The two couples met with him in the home of Deanna's parents for a time of crying and hugging and praying, and even a little singing—if one could call the sounds coming out of Doug's mouth "singing." The sense of reunion was strong and the fellowship sweet. Although no one mentioned the incident with Easler directly, they reaffirmed their belief in Cooper's loyalty in the face of the efforts to tear them apart. Deanna didn't say a word about having informed Laura of the photo. Cooper was uncomfortable with bringing up the subject, but he sensed her confidence in him had returned and that was enough for now.

There was a long line outside the courtroom when Cooper and the families arrived together. There were no less than five television broadcast vans with their huge antennas already extended, prepared to shoot a signal straight to satellites when the coverage began.

The crowd parted to allow the small group, led by a young man in a navy suit, to pass through. They had done the same thing when a larger group, led by an older man in a charcoal suit and a silk tie, had come through five minutes earlier.

Cooper saw the back of Jody Easler's head in the front row of the courtroom as soon as he entered. "She's here," he whispered to Rick as they walked down the center aisle. "We say nothing." Rick nodded.

Once inside the bar, Cooper politely said hello to Randolph Suskins and Melissa VanLandingham. As the lawyers continued to unpack their briefcases, a clerk opened the double doors in the back, and the crowd began to quickly fill the empty seats of the marbled chamber.

Seven identical tall black leather chairs loomed behind an elevated mahogany bench that stretched for nearly thirty feet. The clerk worked his way down the row, fixing each chair in its precise location.

The emblem of the Commonwealth of Virginia, a maiden dressed for battle, holding her foot on the chest of her fallen opponent with her sword at his throat, suggested a value system that esteemed freedom even more than the famed Virginia cordiality. *Sic Tempus Tyranus* read the motto—"Thus Always with Tyrants."

Rick turned to his father-in-law and whispered from their front-row seat, "Ever notice that the Virginia seal has a picture of Deanna about to slit the throat of the UN Secretary General?" He smiled in reply and patted Rick on the leg.

Since the courtroom contained only two counsel tables, Cooper and Rachel Hennessey sat at the counsel table on the right. Suskins and VanLandingham occupied the left table, amid a row of a dozen matching black notebooks that contained a full copy of every case cited by either side. Five associates from Baxter, Connolly, and Suskins sat in the front row alongside Jody Easler and a half-dozen high officials from the Children's Defense Fund and the NEA.

Cooper decided there was no point in trying to cram another fact or citation in his head. He spent the last few minutes in silent prayer just asking God for help for himself, for the families, and for future generations.

A trio of court officials slid quietly into their slots at five minutes before nine. At 9:00 A.M., the harsh sound of a wood gavel striking a hardened base was immediately followed by the cry, "Oyez! Oyez! Oyez! The Supreme Court of the Commonwealth of Virginia is now in session. All having business before the Honorable Supreme Court draw near. God save the Commonwealth and this honorable court."

A line of seven judges appeared to Cooper's right and filed silently behind their respective chairs. There were five men and two women. Even though Virginia had had a steady stream of Republican governors since 1993, the legislature appoints judges at all levels. The GOP had taken over the legislature in the 1997 elections. Four judges were Republican Party appointees; three were pre-1997 Democratic Party appointees.

"Please be seated," Chief Justice Herrick directed.

"This morning's case is Children's Defense Fund and others, petitioners versus, Richard and Deanna Thomas and Douglas and Jeanne Garvis, respondents.

"We have doubled the allotted time we normally grant for oral argument due to the significance of this case, as well as to the novelty of the legal issues before us. Each side will have one hour.

Counsel for petitioner has reserved ten minutes of that time for rebuttal. Miss Hennessey has informed the court that she will be available to answer any questions that the court may have for her in her role as guardian ad litem for the two minors. We have allotted a maximum of ten minutes for such questions, which will come after Mr. Stone completes his argument.

"Mr. Suskins, if you are ready, you may begin."

"May it please the court, I am Randolph Suskins, appearing for the two official UN-sanctioned organizations, the Children's Defense Fund and the National Education Association. As longtime respected child advocacy organizations, these two UN non-governmental organizations have brought this litigation to advance the implementation of the UN Convention on the Rights of the Child, a treaty that they helped to create and worked to ratify through the United States Senate."

"Counsel," Justice Haven, seated next to the end on the left-hand side of the bench, interrupted, "doesn't it strike you as more than a little odd that lobbying organizations have been empowered with duties that have been historically performed exclusively by government. Do you think, for example, we could privatize the prosecution of armed robbery and allow counsel for the National Rifle Association to summon people into court?"

"Your Honor, while it may be unusual, it is neither unconstitutional nor unlawful for these organizations to bring this litigation. First, unlike a criminal prosecution for armed robbery, juvenile litigation of this character is essentially civil in nature and commenced for the best interest of the child. Allowing private parties to commence civil litigation for the protection of the public interest has been of long standing. For example, the Sierra Club, a lobbying organization, has been allowed to file cases to enforce the environmental laws that they helped to create. It would seem odd that our legal system would allow private parties who lobby for trees to be able to bring civil enforcement litigation but deny the same privilege to organizations that lobby for children. Abundant legal decisions support the right of the Sierra Club to do so, and we ask for nothing more than an extension of that principle."

Justice Bonicelli, a balding Democrat famed for liberalism on the substantive law but a conservative stickler on every matter of procedure, leaned forward toward his microphone. "But, Counsel, how does this kind of litigation conform to the standards of Article III of the U.S. Constitution on standing? As you know, Virginia courts follow essentially the same rule. If you have the right to bring this lawsuit today, show us the case. Aren't you really asking us to invent a new rule of standing?"

"No, Your Honor, we are just asking for an application of an existing rule to a new fact situation. Courts routinely apply old rules to new facts, and we ask nothing more."

"Perhaps, Counsel," Bonicelli continued, "but I think you gloss over too quickly the truly civil nature of environmental litigation and the quasi-criminal nature of these proceedings. This case has all the trappings of a child abuse case, which is far more criminal than civil in nature. How do private parties have standing to litigate a quasi-criminal matter like this one?"

"The short answer, Your Honor, is that they have been given this standing by the text of the UN Convention on the Rights of the Child."

"So then it is your contention," Chief Justice Herrick asked, "that the UN treaty overrides the standards of the U.S. Constitution on standing? Does it override the Constitution on anything else?"

"Your Honor, we do not think that the UN treaty overrides the U.S. Constitution, rather it supplements it in this and other ways. It is clear from Article VII of the Constitution that once a treaty is ratified it is a part of the highest law of the land."

Herrick leaned back in his chair as he continued to question the silver-haired lawyer. "Your definition of 'supplement' is an interesting one, Counsel. Your claim appears to be that you can supplement the Constitution by adopting a rule that is just the opposite of what the Constitution demands. That seems more like overriding to me, doesn't it to you, too, Counsel?"

"No, Your Honor. We do not think that what we ask is opposite of what the Constitution demands."

Hearing no immediate questions, Suskins quickly decided to change gears. "If I might, I would like to turn to the issue we believe is most significant for the court today. It is the question of whether this treaty is immediately effective, or whether it requires new laws to be passed by either Congress or the state legislatures in order to be implemented. As you know, this is the issue called the 'self-executing treaty doctrine.'

"The clear law on self-executing treaties favors our position on both the home schooling and religious education issues, despite the trial court's ruling to the contrary."

Justice Schwartz, a former Republican state senator, leaned into his microphone. "You admit that either Congress or the state legislatures can pass new laws on these subjects, is that right?"

"Yes, Your Honor."

Schwartz continued. "Before this treaty, Congress couldn't pass laws on education directly. They would have to create funding programs, and if the states wanted the federal money, they had to accept the strings that Congress attached. But we have never embraced the idea that Congress could directly regulate education. How can Congress pass a law regulating home schooling? Home schools don't get federal funds."

Suskins looked at him with the bemused look of a professor who had just been asked the most simpleminded question from a freshman student. "Well, Your Honor, in the very text of the treaty the federal government undertakes certain responsibilities. One of the responsibilities is to make sure that the education system measures up to the standards required by the UN. With this responsibility goes authority. Thus, by ratifying the treaty, Congress has acquired the full legal authority to directly regulate all education in this country.

"But if Virginia says home school is legal under current law and Congress passes a different law saying that home schooling is banned, then which law controls?

"Obviously, the federal law would control under the Supremacy Clause, Your Honor."

"And you think that the United States Senate knew that when it ratified this treaty?" Schwartz asked.

"They should have known it, Your Honor, for it is plain on the face of the treaty—with existing law, starting with *Missouri v. Holland,* to buttress that view."

"Counsel, I would like to explore your understanding of which portions of this treaty are self-executing." Justice Wilhoite, from the far right side of the bench, was speaking.

Suskins nodded. "Certainly, Your Honor."

"Article 13 of the Convention," Wilhoite began, "guarantees children the right to receive and impart 'information and ideas of all kinds.' Let's consider an example where a child wants to receive explicit information about homosexuality and his parents don't want him to do that. Do you interpret this treaty to say that the child would have the final say on this question?"

"No, Your Honor. The child would not have the final say."

Wilhoite brightened. "You mean that the parent would have the final say?"

"No, that wouldn't be accurate either," Suskins replied.

"OK, then, will you tell me how it should work?" Wilhoite asked.

"In the case of a dispute of this nature between the child and the parent, it would be the responsibility of the decision maker to weigh the parents' concerns and the child's desires and make a decision that is in the best interest of the child."

"Who would the decision maker be?" Wilhoite continued.

"Normally, it would be the child's social worker, I would imagine, Your Honor."

"How does the child get a social worker?"

"Under the Convention, every child has immediate access to a social worker for the implementation of the child's rights under this treaty," Suskins replied, with a thin smile.

"So what you are telling us, Counsel, is that the real decision makers in ordinary family disputes are social workers? Mom and Dad no longer have the final say then?"

"Well, you could say that. We prefer to focus on the social workers as guarantors that the decisions made by parents are, in fact, in the best interests of the child."

Wilhoite pulled off his glasses and rubbed his eyes a moment before continuing. "Well, Counsel, that was a long path to get where I had intended to go initially. But, now, we have created a situation in which you say the treaty requires social workers to review a mother and father's decisions. Is that kind of provision a self-executing part of this treaty, or do we need to have Congress pass a new law on this subject?"

"We think this is self-executing."

"No law from Congress is necessary?"

"That is correct, Your Honor. Our argument is that a law is not necessary before the child's right to receive information can be enforced."

"OK, Article 15 gives the child the right to peaceably assemble," Wilhoite said, flipping through a document. "If a child wanted to join the Ku Klux Klan, can a parent stop the child from joining the Klan, or would the social worker get involved in this one too?"

"All disputes between parents and children are potentially subject to government review, Your Honor," Suskins replied.

"So is the right of a child to join a group to which the parent objects a self-executing provision?"

"Yes, Your Honor, it would be."

"Counsel," Chief Justice Herrick began, "do you consider the decisions of the Committee on the Rights of the Child to be binding upon the courts of the United States concerning the meaning of the treaty?"

"Yes, Your Honor. By the very terms of the treaty, this UN committee is given the ultimate authority to determine its meaning. American courts would be required to follow its interpretations on a principle similar to the Full Faith and Credit Clause."

"How does this principle affect any of the issues before us today?" Herrick continued.

"That's an excellent question, Your Honor—"

"Which is why I asked it, Counsel." The courtroom broke out in quiet laughter.

"Your Honor, there have been numerous decisions by the Committee on the Rights of the Child that have repeatedly held that spanking is banned by the terms of the treaty. Decisions against Belgium in June of 1995, Austria in 1999, and Canada in May of 1995—just to name three—all concluded that spanking is illegal under the direct terms of the treaty."

"But, Counsel," Justice Schwartz interrupted, "didn't the committee urge all three of these nations to pass legislation banning corporal punishment to come into compliance with the treaty? Doesn't that demonstrate that our Loudoun County trial court was wrong in interpreting the ban on spanking to be automatic?"

"No, Your Honor, the Loudoun County decision was certainly correct on that aspect of the decision. The reason for the difference is that, unlike Belgium, Austria, or Canada, the United States has a particular provision in our Constitution that creates legal effects for treaties. This type of provision is not found in the constitutions of those three nations.

"When Belgium, Austria, and Canada ratify a treaty, they have created a moral obligation to comply with the treaty. But in the

United States our Constitution specifically says that a ratified treaty is a part of the highest law of the land and thus coequal with the U.S. Constitution and federal laws passed pursuant to the Constitution. Because of that provision of American law, virtually all of this treaty is automatically applicable without the need for new legislation, especially in light of the binding decisions of the official committee."

"Are there other decisions of this committee that you contend that should guide or perhaps even bind our decision today?" Justice Wilhoite asked.

"Yes, Your Honor. In January of 1995, the committee issued a decision concerning Great Britain that we believe settles the sex education question relative to Emily Garvis, as well as the home schooling issue concerning Layton Thomas. That decision held that Britain was in violation of the Convention by its practice of allowing public school children to withdraw from the sex education courses in that school on the mere desire of the parents. The decision held that to comply with the treaty, government officials would need to review the parental request to opt out of sex education to determine whether such a request was in the best interest of the child. But there was more. The committee also held that the practice of allowing parents to withdraw children from the public school for alternative education of any kind—implicitly, private schools or home schools—was a violation of the treaty unless the decision was properly reviewed by government agencies that are given the task of reviewing the decision for the best interest of the child."

Suskins walked to his right a step or two as he continued. "The issue concerning Emily's sexual education class has already been clearly answered.

"There has been some effort by Mr. Stone to focus this court on the unique effects of this treaty on the law of home schooling in Virginia. This is not correct. It is our view that the home schooling and private school laws in every state fail to measure up to the requirements of this treaty."

The reporters scribbled rapidly as this new claim surfaced in open court. "But we should not assume that Mr. Stone is correct in arguing that this amounts to a ban on home schooling. All that is required is that the government reviews the circumstances of each child to determine whether the proposed alternative education was in the best interest of the child."

Justice Vanderleigh, one of the two women appointees, had been silent until this point and, in fact, at times appeared to be asleep. Suddenly she interrupted. "Counsel, do you mean that if I want to enroll my daughter at one of the best prep schools in the state, a government agent must review my decision to determine whether the agent believes that I have made the best decision for my child?"

"Yes, Your Honor. While certainly under the scenario you have painted the approval would most likely be granted, it is simply a check to make sure that parents are not imposing a form of education on a child that is truly out of step with what that child really needs."

Justice Vanderleigh continued. "And would the criteria for determining whether an education is out of step with what a child needs include the factors listed in Article 29? If a private school refused to teach the principles enshrined in the Charter of the United Nations, would that be a negative factor in such a review?"

"Yes, Your Honor, that is accurate. But it is unlikely that any good private school would be adverse to teaching the UN Charter."

Justice Schwartz had waited as long as he could. "Counsel, your time is starting to wind down, and we have not had any discussion of this Sunday school issue. Are there any decisions by your committee that specifically guide our decision on this aspect of the case?"

Suskins flipped his hair off his forehead. "There is no specific decision concerning religious education per se. But we believe the decision concerning withdrawal from public education in Great Britain is informative on the point because those children who are withdrawn entirely from the public schools are so often put into religious schools. Thus, if religious schools on Monday through Friday are subject to the dictates of the Convention, then religious schools on Sunday should also be governed by the standards of the UN."

Suskins flipped through the pages of the notebook that he had brought to the lectern. "However, there are matters within the legislative record that are instructive on this issue. I would direct the Court's attention to page 37 of our brief, where the verbatim statements from Senator Hellman are recorded. He, as you may know, was an opponent of the treaty and voted against it. One of his points of criticism was on the very issue of the potential for the control of religious education. He cited a book written and published by the American Bar Association. It should be pointed out that the ABA supported the treaty and still does. Senator Hellman was alarmed by a legal interpretation of the treaty that the ABA had made. The ABA wrote that a church that teaches Jesus is the only way to God, and there are no other valid alternatives, was in violation of the treaty. The ABA had also written that a Christian school that taught world government was an agency of Satan was also in violation of the treaty. Both of these points have been taught by the Sunday school teacher in this case."

Suskins' voice raised a new level of emotion, sounding more like a preacher than a college professor. "All of this was before the United States Senate. Hellman argued that this was unacceptable. But he lost the vote. Simply put, Your Honor, the Senate had full knowledge of this very issue, and we believe that their ratification vote in light of this information from the ABA is at least persuasive if not conclusive on the point."

"Counsel, did you have a chance to see the large monument across the street in Capitol Square before you came in this morning?"

"No, Justice Wilhoite, I did not."

"Well, I suggest that you may want to stop and take a look later when we are finished. You will see George Washington, James Madison, and Patrick Henry on that sculpture. And you might want to ask yourself the question of what these men would think of the arguments you are making today. Your views are asking for an extraordinary change in both the law and the social structure of our nation."

"Your Honor," Suskins replied kindly, "I *will* go and visit this monument as you have requested. But, I think I should comment on the implication of your question now because I assume oral arguments will end as scheduled."

Chief Justice Herrick smiled and said, "Yes, Counsel, and in your case that will be in about a minute and a half."

"Here is my answer. James Madison and the founders of this country did not put our nation into a lockbox. They left future generations room to maneuver and adapt the law to fit the needs of our society. And one method that they gave to us to accomplish a change in the law was through the negotiation and ratification of treaties. The leaders of our generation have followed this process. The treaty has been negotiated. It was signed by President Clinton nearly a decade ago. It has now been ratified, at long last. We were the only nation on earth other than Somalia that had not ratified this document. We were out of step with the world until then. But we used the founders' own procedures to get in step by ratifying this treaty."

"Counsel, I see that you have used your time. There are ten minutes remaining for rebuttal. We will now turn to Mr. Stone."

Suskins picked up his notebook and yellow pad and walked back to his place at counsel table. He nodded at Cooper in self-satisfaction as the two intersected on their respective courses to and from the lectern.

"May it please the court," Cooper began, "my name is Cooper Stone. I have the honor of representing the two families who have been named as respondents in this case today."

"Mr. Stone, before you launch into your prepared argument, let me ask you to pick up where Mr. Suskins left off," the chief justice instructed him. "You spent a great deal of your brief arguing for the intent of the Founding Fathers in several aspects of this case. Why isn't Mr. Suskins right? If the founders gave us a procedure that allows a ratified treaty to become the highest law of the land, why doesn't that settle the bulk of the questions you have raised?"

Cooper smiled quietly before answering. "Well, Your Honor, we contend that this entire treaty is unconstitutional, if we are to follow original intent of the Constitution. The Founding Fathers never imagined that the treaty process would be used to control the internal politics of the United States. They intended treaties to control trade, boundary line issues, and matters such as fishing regulations on the high seas. The idea that treaties could be used to control family life, spanking, church services, and the like, strikes at the heart of what it means to be a self-governing nation. What would the Founding Fathers say to a treaty that committed us to follow the rules of the king of England on matters of education and family living? They would have said that such a treaty was unconstitutional because it violated the very premise of America as a sovereign nation. There is fundamentally no difference between allowing an unelected king of England to decide policy questions for America and letting an unelected group of ten people in Geneva, often meeting behind closed doors, to decide policy questions for America. If we are going to keep our self-government, we must keep our sovereignty. Americans should be the only ones who make laws for America."

Justice Vanderleigh leaned forward. "Counsel, that was a speech that would make all of the men depicted on the statue across the street very proud of you as their fellow Virginian, but, frankly, that speech belonged in the United States Senate, not here. Unless you can cite a case in which the U.S. Supreme Court has ruled that a treaty that controls domestic policy is unconstitutional, I am afraid that we have no ability to accept your argument. Is there such a case?"

"No, Your Honor. I rely only on the fundamental principles of our nation and have to concede that the treaty process has been used in recent decades for the control of domestic political matters. But just because the Constitution has been repeatedly violated does not make it right. Segregated schools were the practice for generations, but eventually the courts said the words of the Constitution require a different result. That is what I am asking for here."

"Well, Mr. Stone," Justice Vanderleigh responded, "it is a noble pursuit, but you are in the wrong court today to be making that request. You may well get the opportunity to make that argument to the Supreme Court of the United States. What legal foundation do you offer that we can use here in the Supreme Court of Virginia?"

"There are three main points, Justice Vanderleigh," Cooper said, glancing down quickly at his notes. "First, we consider the question of standing. As was indicated by many of the court's questions to my worthy opponent, there are substantial constitutional issues raised when a private party is allowed to assume a function of government. The rules of standing are not mere rules of court procedure. They are rules of federal constitutional law. Treaties can, indeed, supplement the Constitution under the current law. However, it is clear that treaties cannot override the Constitution. And allowing the NEA and the Children's Defense Fund to bring this suit flies in the face of the accepted rules of standing under the Constitution. Mr. Suskins argued that the United States followed the procedural rules of the Constitution when it negotiated, signed, and ratified this treaty. But now he wants to ignore the procedural rules of the Constitution when it comes time to bring an enforcement lawsuit. We say that the rules should be followed here without exception and that this lawsuit should be dismissed."

Vanderleigh leaned forward, looking over her reading glasses. "But what would stop this new federal agency created to champion children's rights from bringing this same lawsuit again if we dismiss this one because the wrong parties filed the papers?"

"You're correct, Your Honor, in suggesting that the federal government could indeed file a very similar case if you dismiss this one. But, it is important that you do so for two compelling reasons. First, it will be of no small consequence to many American families to keep advocacy groups like these from gaining the power to prosecute parenting practices they don't like. Second, there is an automatic check on excesses by the government itself. If federal agencies go too far, there is at least the theoretical ability of the voters to react at the ballot box.

"Moreover, we contend that there is no portion of the treaty in question that is self-executing. We believe that Congress or the legislatures of the states must pass the laws in question to achieve the results that these lobby groups have advanced in court."

"But, Counsel," Justice Schwartz asked, "can you really say that about spanking? Aren't you up against some very plain language on the whole question of spanking?"

"Yes, we concede that the language banning spanking is quite clear. But our defense is that if the committee in Geneva has determined that other nations need to pass legislation to ban spanking, then such legislation is required here also. Mr. Suskins cannot have his cake and eat it too. If the decisions of the Geneva committee are binding about some issues, then the court must treat the committee's decisions as binding about all issues."

"But what about Mr. Suskins' point that these other nations do not have our Supremacy Clause? Aren't we in a completely different position than Belgium and the others? Their politicians ratify an international treaty, and they have only vague ideals to haunt them when they give speeches. Our politicians ratify a treaty, and we are stuck with it as a binding rule of constitutional law. How do you answer Mr. Suskins' point, Counsel?"

Cooper spoke deliberately. He had faced this question in his oral argument preparation. He had asked God to reveal a supernatural answer to him if there was one. Nothing came to his mind.

"I have no answer at the present time, Your Honor," Cooper replied. "But, again, his point is completely eliminated if we prevail on either the issue of standing or the issue of whether it is unconstitutional to ratify a treaty that affects the internal policy of the United States."

"I understand," Justice Schwartz said, with a nod and a condescending smile that caused Cooper's stomach to knot up even tighter.

"I would point out, Justice Schwartz," Cooper said, attempting to recover some lost ground, "that my answer affects only the issue of spanking. The home schooling issue and the religious education issue require additional arguments."

"Yes, Counsel, we understand that," the chief justice interrupted, "but isn't it true, on the face of the treaty, that government review of educational decision making is mandated? Can't we be required to say that the Virginia system of unregulated home schooling is illegal until the state law is amended to mandate more government oversight?"

"Only if you are prepared to say that all private and home schooling laws in the nation are also unconstitutional because, as Mr. Suskins admitted, there is no state law regarding private schools and home schools in the country that meets the standards he says the treaty requires. We cannot believe that the Senate intended to automatically ban all private education."

Justice Schwartz looked gravely at Cooper. "But couldn't we be required to hold, whether we like it or not, that until these new rules are in place that all private education is effectively banned?"

"If you held that, you would be reversing *Pierce v. Society of Sisters,* a nearly hundred-year-old precedent from the United States Supreme Court. In the 1920s, Oregon tried to ban private education, and the Supreme Court ruled that such a ban was unconstitutional. So a ban, even a temporary ban, on private schooling would still be unconstitutional. And the one thing the other side appears to concede is that it cannot directly violate the Constitution. So we believe that if private schooling must be regulated, then these new regulatory laws must be passed before the old laws are replaced."

"You recognize that the Virginia General Assembly may be legally required to revoke our existing laws on private education, don't you?" Justice Bonicelli asked.

"Yes, Your Honor, that may the case, but the details of the replacement law will be very important and until those laws are passed this case is premature."

A pause in the barrage of questions allowed Cooper a chance to glance at his notes. "Finally, turning to the issue of religious education, we contend that this provision of the treaty violates the First Amendment of the United States Constitution. Again, Counsel concedes that the treaty cannot violate the express guarantees of the Constitution. Control of religious teaching is a law against the free exercise of religion, and James Madison carefully worded the First Amendment to say that Congress shall pass no such law."

"But Mr. Suskins argued that there is a distinction between the First Amendment rights of adults and children. If a treaty interferred with the religious rights of adults, it would be quite different. But he argues that all this UN treaty does is to make sure that children get their own right to make their own religious decisions and to keep parents and other adults from poisoning their ability to make an independent choice. What do you say to his argument?" Bonicelli asked.

"Well, Your Honor, let me give you an analogy. One of the most important religious questions ever to be answered is this one: Where did man come from? That question affects the entire system of beliefs about the nature of man and the nature of God. Yet, our public schools for years have taught only one view on this. Evolution is *the* truth, children are told. Why is this not poisoning their minds? Why are children not given freedom of choice on this topic? Why hasn't the Children's Defense Fund brought this question before the Court? If the principle is that adults cannot influence the beliefs of children, then it will be impossible for adults to teach schools."

"Actually Counsel, won't the rule be," Justice Schwartz asked, with a somber look on her face, "that adults who disagree with the

UN won't be allowed to influence the beliefs of children in a contrary fashion. If you agree with the UN, you can 'poison' children's minds with impunity."

"Obviously I agree, Your Honor."

"The only problem, Counsel," Justice Schwartz continued, "is that neither you nor I were in the U.S. Senate when they took the vote on this treaty."

Cooper started to reply, but the red light flashed on the lectern. "Unfortunately, my time is up, Chief Justice Herrick."

"Thank you Mr. Stone. Miss Hennessey, do you have anything you would like to add at this point?"

"No, Your Honor, unless you have any questions for me." All seven justices shook their heads negatively in response.

"Miss Hennessey, it appears that your briefs have been the model of clarity, and we have no questions at this time. We will give Mr. Suskins his remaining ten minutes, with no implications to be taken that his briefs are lacking in clarity."

"Thank you, Your Honor," Suskins said, smiling at the good-natured comment from the chief justice.

"I will only make one brief point and will yield the balance of my time. Mr. Stone argued that it is a violation of the First Amendment to restrict the ability of parents to teach one small aspect of their religious dogma that results in an attitude of intolerance and hate. We contend simply that neither hate nor intolerance are true Christianity, nor are they protected by the U.S. Constitution. Hate crimes have been outlawed in this country for some time. Parents may have the religious freedom to teach love, but the freedom to teach hate is not a value that has been enshrined in our Constitution. With that, I simply ask this Court to grant us judgment according to the prayer of our complaint."

"Thank you, Mr. Suskins," the chief justice said. "Counsel, the case was well briefed and well argued. I don't mind saying that a historic case of this nature requires superior advocacy, and you both have done your jobs with excellence. Our decision will be difficult; but in light of the extraordinary issues involved, we will expedite our decision as soon as is humanly possible. We will be in recess."

"All rise," came the cry.

A tentative silence hovered over the courtroom as the seven justices filed out. The door closed, and the silence instantly was overcome by the sound of excited chatter.

PURCELLVILLE, VIRGINIA.
July 4, 2005.

The day began with every indication that it was going to be a "triple-H" day in the far western suburbs of Washington—hazy, hot, and humid. Deanna was busy about her "do list" just an hour after dawn. She had insisted in returning home, even though her parents begged her to stay awhile in Richmond. The UN was not going to spoil her Fourth of July traditional barbecue. In fact, she was determined that the Thomases were going to celebrate America's birth more fervently than ever before.

Deanna had invited a crowd—nearly a hundred people were expected. Church friends, neighbors, families from Little League, and others who had supported them in prayer over the past months—few turned down her invitation. For Cooper it was a no-brainer. He knew better than to cross Deanna Thomas once she had made up her mind.

Rick asked Cooper to go with him to the Fourth of July parade in downtown Purcellville. Layton and Nicole remembered the bag of candy they got last year, and they talked Trent into wanting to join them. The parade had more fire engines than ever—eighteen from all the surrounding village and town fire companies—and the same number of marching bands—zero. But what it lacked in bands, it made up for in candy thrown from cars. Every driver, whether he or she chauffeured a beauty queen or a politician, or merely represented a limo service advertising its availability, threw candy to the kids.

After the festivities, the trio of children sat happily in the back of Rick's Suburban as they bounced down the narrow, poorly paved road heading south of town. They each had bags full of candy that would last until Christmas, and cheeks full of candy that would last until dinner.

Cooper joined Rick in helping to set up folding chairs rented from Leesburg in a big, double semicircle flanking the back deck. Deanna had asked a family from the church, Steve and Trish Domenech and their eight kids, to play some of their great blue-grass music and to lead the crowd in a few hymns and patriotic songs. Deanna was intent on creating an atmosphere of unadulter-ated American patriotism.

Dinner was to begin at five, so that everyone could get to the fireworks at Franklin Park on time. The crowd started to roll in around 4:30. Food and lawn chairs and infants were lugged across the front yard of the Thomas home after Cooper and two teenaged boys directed them to park in the front field of the three-acre par-cel. After the bulk of the crowd arrived, Cooper left the boys to handle the remainder of the parking duties. He returned to the house to see if he could help Rick in any other way.

The food was great. The kids were manageable. And the chat-ter about the case was nonstop. Cooper was only able to eat when self-appointed expert Belinda Spriggs, who lived on the edge of Purcellville and who had run unsuccessfully for the town council in 1977, began to pontificate on the dangers of the UN. She may have been a bit quirky, but Cooper thought she was extraordinarily well-informed and accurate in her analysis. And her monologues were the only way he was able to down not only a hamburger and about a pound of potato salad but the award winning strawberry shortcake that a self-proclaimed "cranky old grandpa" had offered as his contribution. As soon as Belinda stopped talking, another group of friends wandered up to him and asked, for the tenth or eleventh time, how things had gone in Richmond last Friday.

Finally, it was time for the music to begin. The Domenech family played and sang their best, which wasn't half bad. The crowd got into the clapping and the stomping, and even a little dancing around the edges. The noise and vigor was sufficient to allow a taxi to come up the driveway and drop off a single female passenger without anyone noticing.

She went inside the front door when no one answered the bell. She called out. No one answered. She set her suitcase down in the foyer and headed through the kitchen to the back door. She paused when she saw that the Domeneches were in midperformance, realizing that if she went through the door she would be in the middle of the "stage." She retraced her steps to the front door and walked around the garage into the backyard. She stood quietly on the edge of the crowd next to some neighbors of the Thomases. The neighbors nodded a greeting in her direction, which she returned with a nod and a smile.

"Just before our last song," Steve Domenech announced over his portable sound system, "we want to bring up a man who we need to thank and honor for his courage. Last Friday in Richmond, one of our neighbors and friends stood before the Supreme Court of Virginia and argued a case, not just for Rick, Deanna, Doug, and Jeanne, but for all of our families as well and for the future of our nation. I know a lot of you were praying about this, and I want Cooper Stone to come up here. We've got a little present from all of us to thank him for his great work in Richmond."

Amid the strongest applause of the day, Cooper stepped through the bushes, onto the brick landing and up the wooden steps of the back deck. Rick, Deanna, Doug, and Jeanne all stood on the far end of the deck away from the singers, with a good-sized box wrapped in red, white, and blue.

Deanna insisted that he open the box before saying anything. After a few seconds of effort, Cooper lifted out a life-sized bronze-colored bust of Patrick Henry. Rick walked to the microphone.

"We wanted to give Cooper this reminder of the great orator of the American Revolution, as a token of our thanks for the sacrificial work Cooper has done for all of us. We all think he did a great job last week, and if you read the weeping, wailing, and gnashing of teeth in yesterday's Sunday *New York Times* editorial section, they think he did a great job, too, and they don't like it a bit!"

A huge cheer punctuated with laughter rose from the crowd. "So, Cooper, come say a word to us," Rick encouraged, as he began to clap.

Amidst an enthusiastic standing ovation, Cooper walked to the microphone. "Wow, with all that applause, maybe I should announce my candidacy for some office," Cooper said, with a big smile.

Another big cheer arose with shouts of "Cooper for President" laced through the noise. "I am too young to be president," Cooper laughed.

"And too honest," a voice from the crowd yelled, to approving laughter.

"Well, all I want to say about yesterday is, praise God. I don't know the outcome; no one can predict—not even the *New York Times*. But I want to tell you how buoyed up I felt by the prayers of countless thousands who knew enough to believe that our only real position of strength is to be on our knees before God."

"Amen!" several voices called out.

"Please continue to pray for the outcome," Cooper asked, as he scanned the crowd. "There may be some—" Just then he saw her beaming on the edge of the crowd, and it stopped him dead in his tracks. "Some surprises along the way that I cannot predict. So keep praying, and trust God with the ultimate outcome. Thank you so much."

He smiled, walked back toward Rick and Deanna, thanked them for the nice present, and quickly asked to be excused. He tucked Patrick Henry like a football under his left arm and stepped lightly down the three wooden stairs, to the grassy area off to the left.

She had not stopped beaming at him since he had caught her eye a few moments earlier. "Laura! I thought you were in Florida."

"I was until earlier today. I just landed at Dulles less than an hour ago. Deanna begged me to come to her party, and you know how insistent she is. She wanted everyone here who had helped her."

"Well, that is so great!" Cooper said, knowing that he was rapidly reaching the end of topics that would consist chiefly of pleasant banter.

"Yeah," Laura replied, smiling but saying nothing more.

The neighbors had slipped quietly away toward the food tables when they saw the dynamics of this young couple who alternated between smiling and looking a little uncomfortable.

"Deanna said you did well in court," Laura offered, after a long pause.

"Thanks," he replied, before they both lapsed back into silence.

"Can we?" Both of them had said it at once, and they laughed with enthusiasm and nervousness in response.

"You go ahead," Laura said.

"I was just going to ask if you think we could go for a walk so that we could talk awhile?"

"Sure," she replied, with a subdued smile.

"Well, let me put Patrick Henry away first." Cooper dashed up the steps of the deck, placed the orator of the American Revolution back into his box, and slipped him under the table that held the singers' sound equipment. He was back by Laura's side in no time.

"You ready?" he asked.

Laura nodded and smiled in a way that told Cooper there were some issues on this beautiful young woman's mind. As they began down the driveway, the Thomases' golden retriever dashed after them, always anxious to go for a walk. "Come on, Sunny," called Laura. She had accompanied Deanna many times on this same route and knew that Sunny demanded the privilege of accompanying anyone who wanted to walk in the pleasant Virginia countryside.

"So did you enjoy your time in Florida?" he asked.

"I am enjoying it so far," she replied.

"Oh, so you are going back?"

"Yeah, that's the plan. My car is still down there. I drove down initially, and Rick just sent me a frequent flyer ticket to come up for a couple days."

"Oh," Cooper replied, grateful to Rick but disappointed in the idea of her quick return.

"Do you want to start?" she asked.

"Start?"

"Yeah. I think we both have some explaining to do to each other."

"Oh, boy," Cooper replied with a wave of embarrassment as the topic of Jody Easler swept through his consciousness.

"OK. I guess I'll start," he replied. "But I am going to need some help. I think it has been pretty clear for a long time that I have been interested in you—really interested, it would be fair to say. But, you were reserved about everything—for an obvious reason named Terry."

She nodded her head in acknowledgment. "And I tried to honor the loyalty you showed to him, even though my own feelings toward you were increasing just about every time I saw you."

She nodded affirmatively once again. "Yes, you were pretty good about trying to at least say the right things. But I could still tell."

"Obviously, I have heard that your engagement is off, but I really don't know what that means. So before I go charging down some emotional path, can you tell me whether you are still together and just not engaged, or whether you are broken off completely?"

The rocks under their feet crunched ferociously in the silence that followed. "Well," she explained thoughtfully, "I guess that depends on which one of us you ask. I think Terry would tell you that we are just not engaged but still together."

"And you?" Cooper asked.

"I'm leaning toward it being over, but I haven't officially pulled the plug. I guess that would be the best way to describe where I am. That's why I went to Florida—to think things through."

"Oh," Cooper replied, a bit crestfallen.

"Well, that makes my question all the more pertinent," he continued. "I wanted some kind of preliminary indication from you where you were in your thinking about—well, about the two of us—about me, before I charged ahead. Is that a fair question? You have never really said how you feel about me."

Laura stopped walking just as they reached the three-way intersection at the end of Chapel Hill Road. She reached out and took Cooper's hand in both of hers. "Just look at me, Cooper Stone. Look into my eyes. If you can't see the answer to your question, then you are not the man I have thought you to be."

Cooper sensed that this moment was an opportunity for truth, and anything but looking was out of the question. He lowered his eyes after a few seconds, to temper his emotions that had begun to race out of control.

He sighed deeply and let go of her left hand, while maintaining his grip of her right hand with his left. "I think I see," he said, with a smile that bubbled up from deep within his soul. "Let's keep walking," he said.

"OK, if that is how you feel about me, then why the conflict over Terry?"

Laura's answer was one he expected but not right then. "I could ask you the same thing. If you are so smitten with me, then where did those pictures taken in New York come from?"

Cooper blushed even though he was fully expecting this. "I've never felt so badly about anything in my life. But I thought Rick was supposed to explain what really happened. Didn't he?"

"He did, but I wanted to hear it for myself—at least enough of it to judge your veracity from my perspective. You could fool Rick and your lawyer friend out in Washington State, but I want to hear it with a woman's ears."

Cooper sighed and started to let go of her hand. Laura held on. "No need to let go of me yet. Just start talking, Buster, and I will decide whether to let go of you."

The laughter in her eyes bolstered his courage. "Laura, let me say that I was disloyal in two different ways by allowing Jody—oh, why the defensiveness—by kissing Jody Easler. She kissed me, but I kissed her back. First, perhaps most clearly, I was disloyal to Rick and Deanna and the Garvises by doing anything at all with someone associated with the other side of this case. That was mental disloyalty to them. It should have been obvious to me and I blew it. But I was also disloyal in my heart not just in my head. Even though you were engaged to Terry, I had given my heart to you. I know that is crazy and in some ways wrong. But I had no business doing anything with anybody. Even though I haven't lived this way all my life, I have come to believe that I shouldn't date or pursue or kiss any woman unless I view her as someone I might marry."

Laura knew instantly what she wanted to ask next but waited to speak. Cooper started to talk, but she squeezed his hand in a way that he intuitively understood as a signal to keep quiet.

"So why did you give your heart to me when you knew I was not free to return your love?"

Cooper sighed. "I guess I shouldn't have. From early on, I have been seriously interested in you. There was just this huge roadblock in the way."

His direct statement had a more powerful effect on her than she could have imagined. Her mouth was not about to speak the words she was feeling, but her fingers wrapped tightly around his.

She finally spoke, after spending a few moments looking pensively at the overhanging limbs of the large trees that lined the dirt road. "That is what has been so confusing to me for such a long time. You came into my life just a few months ago. You seemed ready for a serious commitment, not quite from the beginning, but almost. And yet, Terry, who I have been with for seven years has never given me that same feeling even once—at least not with the same intense confidence I got from you. I don't understand all of that."

"I don't know how to analyze the 'Terry' part of that," Cooper replied. He paused as they crested the hill on Hughesville Road. He looked back out across the valley toward the Blue Ridge Mountains, which, appropriately enough, had taken on a rich blue hue as the afternoon haze settled into the last hour before sunset.

"But I sure understand the 'confused' part. You will remember that I, too, was once engaged to my high school sweetheart. And she broke it off with me just a month before our wedding. I didn't understand her at all because I had given her my heart when I was so young."

Cooper motioned Laura to resume walking as he continued to speak. "I can't really explain all that emotionally. But what I can tell you is that I wish I had waited until I was much older before I gave my heart away. Everyone tells you to start dating so young. My friends thought I was an idiot because I waited until I was in high school. But with every date, you give away a little of your heart. And when you go through a longtime early love and it goes sour, you not only give away a piece of your heart, you send it through a shredder. I just think I have learned the hard way that people shouldn't date except at an age and with a person where they both are seriously contemplating marriage."

"Me, too," Laura said instinctively. They walked in pained silence for about three minutes as they both relived the agony of their respective memories.

"Tell me this, Laura. Maybe this will cure the confusion for you. I know it has worked for me. Here's the question you should ask: If you had met both Terry and me for the first time now, at this stage of life, which one of us would you be interested in?"

"You," she replied instantly.

He looked at her hoping for a little longer answer, but the only signal he got was the intensity of the way she held his hand.

"Well, I asked myself that same question months ago, and I reached the same conclusion."

"That you would rather have me than that ambassador?"

"That's not the question. I have never thought about it that way. No, I meant my old girlfriend from Spokane. Even though she is married, I never fully reconciled my feelings because, frankly, I had given her my heart. But I became liberated from the past and all the bitter hurts by asking myself that question. Who would I be interested in if there had been no yesterday and I only knew you both today? You were clearly the one who suits me as the adult I am today.

"I was just too immature to understand all of what was at stake when I was in high school, but no one helped me build fences around my emotions and told me to stay emotionally pure. I got all the standard lectures about being physically pure, and I was, at least from the world's standpoint. But, oh, man, it's just such a crazy system that encourages us to let kids give away their hearts when they still have braces on their teeth."

"That makes a lot of sense, Cooper," Laura replied softly. She smiled. "Can't we sue someone in Christian leadership for malpractice for not telling us any of this stuff? Why would we think that the world's system of dating is God's way?"

"If I knew who to sue, I would do it for you, my dear." He smiled back at her, and they both laughed a little.

Something in the music in his voice seemed to force Laura's free hand to come across and grab Cooper by the arm. She held onto his arm now with both hands and moved close to his side, as they continued down a gentle slope where the dirt road came to yet another intersection.

"So how confused are you right now, Miss Frasier?"

"Not confused at all, Mr. Stone," she replied, smiling demurely.

He slowed to a stop and turned to face her.

"Laura, this may break all speed records of all time. But I love you with all of my heart, and I know I want to marry you. Will you be my wife?"

"I love you, too, Cooper. I think you are simply amazing. There is no question that God has made you to be a perfect fit for the person he has made me to be. But I am not ready to say yes to you."

She let him agonize for only a moment before adding, "But if you were to ask me a different question, say, like, um . . . 'Can I call your father and ask his permission?' Then I would say yes in a heartbeat, and to get Daddy on the line even punch in the numbers on that cell phone you have in your pocket."

They both laughed as he swept her into his arms and just held her for a long time. They pulled back to gaze in each other's eyes. A kiss was inevitable. When it came, it was strong and passionate and pure.

LOS ANGELES, CALIFORNIA.
July 10, 2005.

Laura's father didn't want to give Cooper an answer over the phone. In fact, he wanted him to spend several days, perhaps a week, with the family to have some conversations and get to know each other better. Unfortunately, Cooper had agreed to appear on *Politics and Hollywood,* and the trip to Florida would have to wait. He intended on flying to Tampa straight from Los Angeles.

He landed in Los Angeles at 11:00 A.M. on the first nonstop from Dulles. A sedan service was waiting to take him to the small boutique hotel that the producers used for most guests on the program.

It was a perfect day in Los Angeles, and he had three hours from the time he arrived at the hotel until he had to leave for the studio. The situation called for a trip to the beach to lie in the sun, but there really wasn't time, nor did he think it wise to take a taxi to the beach. So a lounge chair beside the small pool in the interior courtyard would have to do.

The sun felt good to Cooper as he just closed his eyes and laid back. He wanted some sun but actually needed a rest. He was drifting between sleep and wakefulness when he heard footsteps on the pool deck right beside him. He looked up instinctively. A beautiful woman in a red and white striped bikini stood right next to his lounge chair.

"Hello, Cooper," she said quietly.

"Jody!" he replied, much louder, though there was no one else in the courtyard to hear either of them.

"Surprised to see me, I take it." She spoke in a normal tone of voice.

He was sitting up, leaning on his right hand while shielding his eyes from the sun with his left. "You got that right. What are you doing here?"

"Same thing as you," she replied.

"Getting a tan? Isn't this a long way from Switzerland to come for a tan?"

"No," she said, shaking her head and laughing. "I'm on *Politics & Hollywood* with you tonight. I take it the producers didn't tell you."

"No, they sure didn't. They just said they weren't sure who the guests would be, but that I should count on someone who held the opposite point of view."

"Listen, Cooper," she said quietly, "I need to talk to you."

"Uh . . . what about?"

"Can I sit down?"

"Sure."

She placed the towel and beach cover-up she had been holding on the concrete deck in between the two lounge chairs. She placed her cell phone and plastic card room key on the small glass table that was between the chairs. Cooper's phone, room key, and sunglasses were already on the table.

"We are being watched," she said in a very subdued voice. "Smile and nod like things are great."

Cooper nodded and smiled in a manner that would have seemed totally unconvincing to anyone who knew him well. "Where?" he asked. "I can't see anyone."

"He's in the dining room over there," Jody said, gesturing with a move of her eyes.

"How do you know?"

"He's my assigned guard from the UN. Supposed to protect me from intruders and strangers. But he reports to Kadar."

"Since when does the UN assign you a guard?"

"Ever since Kadar and I have gotten crossways on the committee."

Just then one of their cell phones rang. Both grabbed their own phone. It was Cooper's that was ringing. But just as he said "Hello," Jody's phone also rang.

"Cooper Stone," he said quietly, turning his back on Jody.

"Mr. Stone, Jenna Essex here from the Associated Press in Richmond. I just wanted to get your comment on your victory in the Virginia Supreme Court."

"Hello," Jody said into her phone.

"Victory?" Cooper said, in an incredulous but happy voice.

Jody heard a woman's voice. "Madame Ambassador, this is

Corina Driana from Dr. Kadar's office." She glanced at her watch. Two o'clock. Eleven at night in Geneva.

"Yes, the court handed its decision down about ten minutes ago, and you won a unanimous victory," the reporter replied to Cooper.

"Yes, Miss Driana," Jody answered.

Cooper stood up in excitement, raising his arm with a clinched fist in victory. "That is so great! Have you seen the opinion?"

"There was a loss in the Virginia Supreme Court today," Miss Driana said to Jody. "We wanted you to know before you went on the show tonight."

"Yes," the reporter answered. "Let me see . . . It seems that the victory is a little technical in nature. All they have appeared to do is to say that private parties can't bring this lawsuit. There's a lot of discussion about standing. Would you like to comment?"

"Um-hm," Jody replied to Miss Driana. She turned, tapped Cooper on the shoulder, smiled, and mouthed the word "Congratulations," as she continued to listen to Kadar's assistant on her cell phone.

"Wow! I wasn't expecting it this quickly, but they did say that they would try to expedite the decision as fast as they could. But, my first comment is that we are excited and pleased with the decision."

"In fact, Dr. Kadar doesn't believe that it is best for you to go on the show tonight. She thinks that the discussion will be all about the legalities in light of the decision. Dr. Kadar is trying to arrange a law professor from UCLA that she knows to take your place," Driana continued.

Cooper was having a hard time thinking, trying to sound intelligent with the reporter yet straining to hear and understand everything that Jody was saying on the phone.

"Do you feel that this is a complete victory or a hollow victory, since the other side says that even if this decision is affirmed on appeal, the same charges can just be brought again by government agencies? Doesn't this victory really just delay the inevitable?" the reporter asked.

"But I think that we should focus on children, not on the legalities, for an audience like this," Jody replied.

"We are grateful for victory on any grounds," Cooper answered the reporter. "And in any event, we believe that elected American officials like the Commonwealth Attorney in Loudoun County are far less likely to file some of these outlandish complaints."

"Dr. Kadar seems to think that this is best," Corina Driana said flatly.

"So," the reporter continued, "will you be handling the case on appeal to the Supreme Court?"

"But I disagree with Dr. Kadar," Jody answered.

"I have every intention of arguing the case in the Supreme Court as things sit today," Cooper answered.

"I will let her know," Miss Driana continued, "but she has informed me that she wants someone more in tune with the international agenda rather than nationalist views on this particular program."

"That sounds a little uncertain," the reporter talking to Cooper noted. "What's the contingency?"

Jody's face was turning red with anger. "You tell Dr. Kadar that I am an ambassador of the United States of America, the most powerful nation on earth."

"Funding has been an issue for me, but it looks like we've made enough progress so that I can take it all the way through. And let me save you from asking," he added quickly. "I am not willing to answer any detailed questions on fund-raising. All I will say is that members of the public have been providing support on a private basis to my clients."

Corina Driana's voice was pure ice. "I will so inform Dr. Kadar," she said. "One more matter. Dr. Kadar has asked me to let you know that you should expect that the photographs accompanying this story tomorrow will be a lovely picture of a couple in a New York carriage."

"Why would the witch do that?" Jody answered.

Cooper whirled and looked at Jody with raised eyebrows.

"Is there anything you'd like to add, Mr. Stone?" the reporter asked.

"Dr. Kadar believes that it is imperative that the press accounts tomorrow focus on something else other than the Virginia decision. She thought that you, as a loyal member of the international team, would understand the need."

"No," Cooper replied shaking his head with a bewildered smile. "I'm just in a bit of a daze right now. So much happening at once. Thanks for letting me know."

"Tell Dr. Kadar that I am an American, and I will give her suggestion due consideration but will make my own decision. Goodbye." She snapped her phone shut.

"You're welcome. And congratulations," the reporter answered.

Cooper punched the "end" button on his cell phone after saying good-bye.

"Well, that was something," Cooper said to Jody with a smile. "What was going on with you?"

"You have definitely complicated my life even further, Mr. Stone, with that little victory of yours," Jody answered with a wry grin. "Congratulations."

"Thank you," he replied with a deferential nod. "But what was happening with you? Who was that?"

"It was Kadar's chief henchman—her so-called legislative assistant. They want me off the show tonight. At first she said it was because they wanted a lawyer to do the show, in light of the court decision. But the real reason is that they are convinced that I am not enough of an international team player."

"Are they right?" Cooper asked.

"I don't know anymore, Cooper," she replied, her silky hair swaying as she shook her head. "I used to think that the international forum was the best way to achieve our agenda for the children. But, I seem to be the only one in Geneva who cares about anything other than power. It seems—" She stopped short and nodded in the direction of the wall of windows looking into the dining room. "My guard is getting a call from Kadar's assistant."

"How do you know?"

"I see him talking and I just know it's her. They want me off the show tonight, and right now he is being told to keep me off. That's the way they do business."

"Will they hurt you?" Cooper asked.

"Only if they find it necessary or helpful," Jody replied, with a cold surrender that made Cooper's stomach tighten reflexively.

"Listen, Cooper, it is essential that I get on that show tonight. It is essential for you and me and . . ." It seemed strange to her to be saying it, but after a pause she said it anyway. "And for America. But I need your help."

"What do you need me to do?"

"If I go back to my hotel room, I will never make it to the show. He," she said with a nod toward her guard who was still on his cell phone, "will stop me. Here's my plan. But we need to make this look good. Sit up and work with me. Don't worry, I am not going to come on to you again."

Cooper sat up warily and swung his legs over the side, on the edge of the lounge chair. Jody slid over to his chair to sit right beside him. She whispered in his ear for about thirty seconds. They both nodded and she smiled. "It'll work," she said confidently. "See you at the studio. And, Cooper, thanks." She couldn't stop herself from kissing him lightly on the cheek as she stood to leave.

She stood up, put on her beach wrap, picked up her cell phone, and headed immediately across the courtyard in the opposite direction of the dining room, toward the lobby. Cooper saw the guard get up quickly from his table and head toward the door of the dining room.

Jody walked straight through the lobby and, wearing nothing but her bikini, cover-up, and sandals, got into the first taxi in the short line that waited in front of the hotel. "ABC studios, please," she said, after she shut the door.

"Sure thing, lady," the driver replied, his eyes checking her out in his rearview mirror.

Cooper picked up his cell phone and dialed, watching carefully for any sign of the guard. Rick was at home. A happy conversation ensued celebrating the victory, even though the suit had been dismissed on a narrow basis.

He saw the silhouette of the guard as the man headed into the lobby. Twenty seconds later the guard opened the door into the pool's courtyard area. He glanced around, pretending not to see Cooper, and disappeared back into the lobby.

Cooper called the Garvises, still watching the European. He glanced at his watch. Not enough time to call Laura. He got up and picked up his sunglasses, cell phone, and both room keys. He walked straight into the lobby. The guard was not around.

"Did you see what happened to that man in the dark suit and sunglasses?" Cooper asked the middle-aged woman behind the front desk.

"He left about two minutes ago," she answered. "I assume he went in a taxi because I heard one roar off a few seconds after he disappeared outside the door."

Cooper muttered a quick "thanks" and headed off toward the elevators. He went to his room and dressed as rapidly as possible for the program. He glanced at his watch, picked up his cell phone, and called Laura. He basked in her congratulations, and they talked over the details of his expected arrival.

Hanging up the phone, he walked briskly out of his room and down the hall. Halfway toward the elevator he paused and looked up and down the hall. Seeing no one, he slipped into the stairwell and headed up two stories.

He opened the door slowly and peered to his left down the hall-way. Seeing no one, he ventured into the hallway and looked quickly to his right. Nothing. He turned to the left and stopped in front of the third door on his right. As he fumbled for the key in his pocket, a momentary panic hit him in the gut. *What if it was all a charade and she—or someone else—was waiting inside for him?* With grim deliberation, he slid the key into the slot and opened the door. The drapes were open and the sunlight revealed an empty room with a single large suitcase open on the bed. He closed the suitcase, picked it off the bed, and headed quickly back down the hall toward his own room.

The hotel phone rang about five minutes later. "The limo from the studio is here for you, Mr. Stone," the voice said. "They were also supposed to pick up another passenger. She isn't with you, is she?"

"If you mean Ambassador Easley, she is not with me. She should already be at the studio."

"Fine, I will let the driver know," the receptionist said.

Cooper placed Jody's suitcase in the trunk of the limo and made light conversation with the driver during the ten-minute ride. He noticed a taxi parked about a half-block before the gated entry to the studio, and a man in a dark suit and sunglasses was sitting in the back seat.

Cooper thanked the driver and shook his hand after receiving the suitcase back. He reached for his wallet. "No tips, sir," the driver said with a smile. "It's all on the studio."

"Thanks again," Cooper replied.

A young woman with shockingly red hair sat at the front desk. "May I help you?" she said, with a bored expression.

"I'm Cooper Stone, here as a guest on *Politics & Hollywood*."

"Just a moment, I'll let the producer know. You can have a seat over there," she said, motioning toward a series of vinyl chairs.

Cooper sat nervously for about three minutes, looking frequently in the direction of the front door, expecting the UN guard to burst in at any moment. Eventually the studio door opened revealing a young woman all in black—pants, T-shirt, and platform shoes, with black hair to match—holding a clipboard.

"Cooper Stone?" she asked.

"Yes, that's me," he replied, grabbing the suitcase as he stood to his feet.

"Are those the clothes for Ambassador Easley?"

"Yes, this is her suitcase."

"Well, she has been anxious for you to arrive with the suitcase. But our host who met her as she is dressed now has been hopeful that you might forget it."

"I hate to start out disappointing the host," Cooper replied, with a wink.

They walked down a long hall, turned to the right, and then walked down another long hall. The young woman opened a door to reveal a sitting room with a couch and two love seats surrounding a television set in one corner. Behind this grouping was a small kitchenette table with four wooden chairs. A selection of fruit, cheese, and crackers on a large black plastic platter was on the table, still wrapped in cellophane.

"Ambassador Easler is in that dressing room on the right," the young woman said, nodding toward a closed door. "You can take the suitcase in to her, or I can do it if you would prefer."

"You should do it," Cooper said.

"Is it OK if I have a little of this fruit?" he asked, as she walked toward the dressing room.

"Sure, and there are soft drinks and bottled water in that refrigerator in the corner. Make yourself at home," she replied. She handed the suitcase into the dressing room and then quickly exited.

Cooper clicked on the television to the Fox News Channel. The report on his victory in the Virginia Supreme Court aired soon after he turned it on. It showed file footage of the case from both the Leesburg and Richmond hearings. He could see Laura standing behind him in one of the clips from Leesburg. "She knew I was the one even back then," he said out loud, thinking he was talking only to himself.

"Who thought that?" Jody's voice asked from behind the couch.

Cooper's face flushed. "I didn't know you were there," he replied.

"Well, so what? You've said it, and now you have to explain it."

Cooper could see in her eyes that she was having a good time at his expense.

"I was just talking about one of the witnesses," he told her.

"Oh, Miss Frasier," Jody replied. "Are you two?"

"Well, let me just say that I am flying from here tomorrow to meet her parents in Florida."

"That's serious," Jody commented.

"Yeah, I hope it is very serious," Cooper replied.

"Well, it looks like I need to congratulate you for the second time in one day." There was a touch of envy in the tone of her voice.

But Cooper simply replied, "thanks," and tried to think of a way to change the subject.

"I saw your guard sitting in a taxi about half a block from the gate when I came in. My guess is that he doesn't know you are already inside."

"As long as he thinks that for just a few more minutes, I will definitely make it on the air."

"Why are you so set on getting on this show?" Cooper asked.

"There is something I want to say about this whole UN Convention that if I don't say it tonight I might not ever get to say it again on national television."

"So does that make you afraid they are going to do something to you after this show?"

"That is possible, but I hope to actually make it more unlikely."

Just then the door opened, and the producer, Miss Truxell, walked in and stood with her back against the door, obviously holding it open for someone to follow. "Ambassador Easler is right in here, sir."

The guard entered the room, still wearing his sunglasses. "Thanks," he muttered, as she shut the door.

Cooper stood up. "Miss, I think there is some mistake. This gentleman has been harassing the ambassador. I watched him trailing her at the hotel."

"But he said he was her security officer from the UN, and he showed us his credentials."

"Yes, yes," Easler replied. "I had forgotten that Dr. Kadar had promised to send me a new guard. My mistake. But, Miss Truxell, if you wouldn't mind, I think he would enjoy himself most if he was allowed to sit in the studio audience. He is from the Czech Republic, and I am sure has never been in an American television studio before. If you would be so kind to escort him there now, the taping begins soon, doesn't it?"

"Fifteen minutes," the producer replied. "In fact I need to get you both into makeup right now. "Sir, if you will just come with me, I will get you a good seat in the studio audience."

"But . . . uh . . . ," he stammered, struggling not only with a limited English proficiency but with the delicacy of the situation.

Truxell, however, was a pro at getting people in and out of a television studio and knew how to move an unwelcome fan away from a star, and this situation was a perfect occasion to showcase her skills. She gave him no choice but to follow her.

"That was great," Cooper said smiling. "You are quick on your feet."

"American ingenuity," she replied, as the two followed an aide from the makeup department, who led them to a well-lighted room down the hall.

As they entered the room, the makeup artists were just finishing their work on the two other guests for their program. Cooper recognized both of them—Jason Baldwin from the TV program *Chums* and Marina Mansfield, a pop singing star. Jason nodded politely in their direction while Marina just glanced at them and went back to chatting with the makeup artist.

A few minutes later they were sitting on the well-lighted set. There were about 150 people in the studio audience in bleachers. Jason Baldwin and Marina Mansfield were seated on the left-hand side of the set; Jody and Cooper were on the right.

Theme music began to play and an announcer proclaimed, "Tonight on *Politics & Hollywood*—the UN Convention on the Rights of the Child! Our guests, attorney Cooper Stone; pop singer, Marina Mansfield; the US ambassador to the UN at Geneva, Dr. Jody Easler; and from the hit comedy *Chums,* Jason Baldwin. And the host of *Politics & Hollywood,* Greg Maris!"

Maris came bounding onto the set for the first time and smiled as he soaked in the applause, as if the audience had spontaneously yielded to an impulse to engage in a personal act of adulation rather than to the flashing red "Applause" signs in front of them.

The host led off the show with three or four one-liners, two of which fell flat with the studio audience. He quickly made his way to the chair in the center of the set to launch the discussion.

"Well, Mr. Stone," Maris said the second he was seated, "I guess you believe that children belong to the parents like a piece of chattel property—just like in Elizabethan England."

Mild snickers of agreement rippled through the audience dominated by young people. Cooper paused half a beat. "Well, I do think that children need a sense of belonging to something, like belonging to a team. In that sense, I do believe that children belong to their family and their parents. Children certainly do not belong either to the government of this country or to the UN."

"Ah . . . oh . . . uh," Maris responded. "Well, Marina, you have a child, do you think that the UN is a harm to your child?"

"Not at all," she responded, flashing a row of perfect teeth. "I appreciate the help the UN provides to look after the condition of children, to make sure that day care is well-managed, and that children receive the socialization they need."

"Speaking of socialization," Maris interjected, "one of the issues in this case is whether parents should be allowed to home school their children. What do you think about that?"

"Well, I for one think it is an incredibly stupid idea," Jason Baldwin said, leaning forward while resting both forearms on his knees. "I mean, how are these people going to teach, say, physics, for example? If they knew that much about physics, they'd all be physicians."

The studio audience roared with laughter. Cooper thought of making a point but only shook his head and smiled.

"Well, we haven't heard from our distinguished ambassador to the United Nations in Geneva, the very lovely Jody Easler. I am sure Madeleine Albright never stirred the crowd in the UN the way you stirred my staff in the costume in which you arrived here today. You want to tell us about that?"

Jody winced very slightly, but no one could tell from the shake of the head and the confident smile which followed. "Oh, Greg, I just try to explore native customs including costumes and forms of dress, and I was here in southern California and thought I would dress like the locals."

"OK," Maris replied, "I guess we won't go into that right now, but I want to focus on this lawsuit that is going on in Virginia to enforce the UN Convention on the Rights of the Child. There was a victory for Mr. Stone in the Virginia Supreme Court today. What do you make of all this? Is your side going to ultimately be successful in getting our country to come under the authority and guidance of the UN on the issue of children's rights?"

"I hope not," Jody replied with a smile, as she crossed her legs and then her arms, staring at the host waiting for his reaction.

"Just a second folks, let me check my guest cards. Jody Easler, child's rights advocate—pro-UN. That's what the card says." He held the three-by-five card up to the camera for effect.

"All right, Ambassador Easler—what's going on here? You hope that the UN is not going to be successful in gaining compliance with its treaty here? I thought you were one of its strongest advocates."

Cooper, like everyone else watching the program, was riveted in his chair, waiting to hear what Jody said next.

"That's true, I have been one of the leading voices in this country calling for ratification and implementation of the UN Convention for children. I testified for its ratification in the Senate. And I don't want to be misinterpreted in what I am about to say— I still strongly favor children's rights. But, I have come to believe that international law is not a proper tool to control the policies and laws of the United States."

"That is an astounding statement, Ambassador," Maris said.

He turned to face the audience. "You guys may just be here for fun and games tonight, but this is real news. Listen up.

"Well, Ambassador Easler, what has caused you to come to doubt the appropriateness of the UN as the way to advance children's rights?"

"To be honest with you, Greg, it's the people on the UN Committee for the Rights of the Child that I don't think can be trusted. The longer I am around them, the more I am convinced that they simply want political power for its own sake and are willing to engage in power politics no matter what the cost."

"OK. Like what?" Maris asked.

"Well, for example, take Mr. Stone here," she shifted in her chair to face Cooper. She put her hand across the gap between their chairs and laid it on his forearm.

"Mr. Stone is a decent young lawyer just trying to defend a couple of families. He certainly believes in their cause as well, but he is a good man only trying to argue for what he believes. Well, Dr. Kadar, the appointed Hungarian who heads the UN committee, coerced me into trying to compromise Mr. Stone in a hotel room in New York."

The audience erupted in catcalls and cheers.

"Now that's what I call diplomacy!" Maris cried out raucously, eyes gleaming.

"But, I was only able to kiss him once, and he refused my advances!"

The audience booed, then jeered, then laughed. Cooper turned red. Maris laid his head back on his chair. "Hey baby! Just keep talking, honey, my ratings are going through the roof!"

Jody wasn't about to be stopped. "I think the whole thing stinks! The politics of personal destruction have nothing to do with what is good for children! It is critical that the people who make the decisions that control our policy should ultimately answer to the good people of the United States. I don't trust Dr. Kadar, nor anyone else on that committee."

"Are you resigning as UN ambassador?" Maris asked, goading Jody to keep going.

"Now that you mention it, Greg, I guess I am."

"Hey, I was just kidding," he replied. "If you are having a bad day, take some time off."

"No, resigning is a great idea. It is the honorable thing to do. Let me just say one more thing. See that man over there in the second row?" Jody pointed at the dark-suited man. "He is a guard sent here by Dr. Kadar to keep me under her thumb. If anything happens to me, I just want everyone to know that he did it."

A camera crew rushed over and zoomed in on the hapless guard, who sat still for a moment and then abruptly jumped up, accidentally knocked over his chair, and ran out of the studio with a camera crew hot on his trail.

"Well, well, well," Maris said, thrilled with all the mayhem and action, "maybe we should take a commercial break. Maybe one of our other guests will renounce their life's work here on national TV. I don't think I have to remind you to stay tuned."

Cooper looked at Jody with admiration. "That is the bravest thing I think I have ever seen," he whispered, as soon as the production assistant had yelled "clear."

"Or the stupidest," Jody admitted.

"No way," Cooper said. "You were incredible."

"Well, I am dead one way or the other. Either my career is dead, or maybe Kadar will just kill me."

"Do you really think that she would do that now?"

"No," Jody whispered. "Actually the reason I did all this was to eliminate her ability to blackmail me—and you. I remembered a Bible verse I heard as a child. 'You shall know the truth and the truth shall set you free.' I concluded it was my only way out from being bullied by Kadar. If I reveal her nasty little secret, she has nothing left to use against me. And I get to tell the whole story, not just part of it."

"Jody, I can't begin to tell you how proud I am of you," Cooper said, placing his hand on her shoulder.

The producer cried out, "Quiet! Fifteen seconds."

Maris tried to stir things up again after the commercial, but nothing could come close to the pandemonium that Jody had caused in the first half of the show. But she was still smart, glib, and gorgeous as they talked through a range of issues, some important and some foolish. Cooper did well, while the two celebrities threw in a comment or two that seemed like the dullest pabulum by comparison to Jody's insights. As the program ended, Phil Williams, the executive producer of the program, was waiting for Jody at the edge of the set. He introduced himself, shook her hand, and thanked her for the best program in the history of the show.

"Thanks, I guess," she said. "I really don't have an encore."

"I was actually hoping you would do not just one encore but a whole bunch. We have been looking for a female cohost for the program, and I think we have found her. Want to go to dinner and talk about it?"

Jody looked at Cooper as if she were abandoning a good friend. "Go ahead," Cooper said encouragingly. "I need to get going early in the morning to fly to Florida."

"Bye, Cooper," she said.

"Bye, Jody. I'll keep praying for you."

"Please do, Cooper. I'd like that."

TAMPA, FLORIDA.
July 12, 2005.

It had been hard to see them sitting next to each other. She had died a thousand deaths when Jody Easler told the world that she had tried to engage Cooper romantically, and had indeed managed to get him to kiss her. It was even harder to watch the obvious admiration that Cooper had expressed when Jody resigned from her ambassadorship. Despite the pain, however, she also felt considerable respect for Easler's actions. She would just handle this internally. No need to talk it out. It would be all right, she told herself. Her parents expressed words of understanding for Cooper's actions although it was obvious that her father was a little perturbed over the scene.

She spent a fitful night imagining Cooper and Jody in the same hotel, albeit on different floors. There was nothing in his words or his tone that gave her any objective reason for worry, but she concluded that objectivity wasn't the only way to look at a situation.

Nothing in that night of fitful sleep and worry prepared her for the morning. There on the front page of the paper lying on her parents' doorstep was the photo of Cooper and Jody kissing in front of the New York hotel. Worse yet—if it could be any worse—CNN news kept running clips of Easler's on-air resignation, punctuated with regular doses of the New York photo. The media spin—fed by the backroom whispers of Kadar and her allies in the White House and Senate—was that Easler had changed her political position because she had fallen hard for the handsome young lawyer.

Laura didn't want to believe the speculation, but hearing television's "talking heads" discuss it time and again became unbearable. It was only 10:30, and Laura had four more hours to wait before Cooper arrived at the Tampa airport.

She took a walk in her parents' neighborhood; it was unbearably hot and muggy, but sitting in front of the television was far more intolerable. When she walked back inside the air-conditioning felt good for a moment. But that feeling was short-lived when her mom greeted her with the news that Nancy, Cooper's secretary, had called and wanted Laura to call her back about media requests.

She called Nancy solely out of a sense of duty. Nancy told Laura to give Cooper the message that eighteen newspaper reporters, all four television networks, nine radio programs, and the *National Enquirer* had called wanting interviews. The *Enquirer* mostly wanted to know if there were more photographs available.

Laura spoke kindly to Nancy and promised to deliver the message, but what she really wanted was to be delivered from the enveloping horror of living inside a media romance scandal. She headed to her room to take a shower and get ready to go to the airport. Stray thoughts began to run through her mind. She tried to suppress the moments when she began to wonder if she had done the right thing by choosing Cooper.

As she sat in the backseat on the way to the airport, she nearly started crying. If she had been alone, there would have been no doubt of it. For days, she had been looking forward to Cooper's arrival with eager anticipation. But the moment had come upon her with great dread.

They arrived at the gate about fifteen minutes early. Laura didn't think anything at first of the two scruffy guys with a television camera and microphone equipment. They had plopped themselves down in the seating group just opposite where she sat nervously between her mom and dad. But when they were joined by a preppy looking man in his midthirties dressed in a blazer and slacks, she realized that they were probably hoping to interview Cooper.

She said nothing to her parents, but a debate was raging inside her about whether she should just leave the airport and hide someplace safe. The "get-me-out-of-here" side of the debate gained even more ground when a young woman in gray slacks and a white blouse accompanied by a man with photography equipment sat down next to the television crew and greeted them by name.

The gate door swung open suddenly, and the guy with the television camera hopped up, hoisted it up onto his shoulder, and switched on the light. The sound man hit some switches and handed the mike to the guy in the blazer, who in turn busied himself checking his hair for strays and his blazer for wrinkles. The woman newspaper reporter stood next to the guy in the blazer, while her photographer placed himself between the television cameraman and the sound technician.

About twenty people exited before Cooper appeared in the door wearing a golf shirt and slacks.

"Mr. Stone, Mr. Stone, Jeff Findley with FOX 7 News, I'd like to ask you a few questions," the reporter called out.

"Just a minute," Cooper replied, looking to find Laura in the crowd. Seeing her, he burst into a big smile and rushed toward her. If she had been alone, he would have picked her up in his arms and twirled her in a full circle, but a polite hug seemed more appropriate with her parents there.

The moment he put his arm around Laura the camera was on them with a close-up shot. An explosion of flashes followed from the still photographer.

"So, Mr. Stone, a girl in every port? Is that your mode of operation?" the TV reporter said, with a smirk.

Something inside sent a message to Cooper's right arm to smash the square jaw with a clenched fist. Fortunately, however, the desire to make a good impression on Laura's family was stronger. "I have no idea what you are talking about," Cooper replied, his arm still around Laura's shoulders. The flashes continued to burst intermittently.

"Well, from what our sources tell us, it is the ambassador in New York and Los Angeles and this rather attractive young lady here in Florida. I wanted to ask you if your relationship with Miss Easler was the basis for her change of position, but the appearance of this new young lady has added an interesting twist to the story."

Cooper whispered "Excuse me" to Laura and stepped away from her, stopping only six inches from the nose of the reporter. "Hope this doesn't mess up your camera angle, but I want you to make no mistake about my answer. There is no romantic relationship between Ambassador Easler and me. She was assigned to create one, but I refused. That is what she said on national television last night, as I am sure you know. I am here in Tampa to meet the family of a young woman I intend to marry. There is nothing, I repeat nothing, going on between me and the ambassador. Do I make myself clear?"

"Got it," Findley said. "Just a few more questions—"

"No further comment," Cooper said angrily. He turned his back on the blow-dried reporter and stepped back to Laura and her parents. He shook hands with her dad and then her mom, and said, "I am really sorry about all of this. Can we get away from the gate so that we can be properly introduced?"

"Sure," Mr. Frasier replied, "right this way."

The newspaper reporter ran after the group and fell in stride beside Cooper. "I'm sorry that guy was so rude, Mr. Stone. Would you mind if I ask you a couple questions about the court case?"

Cooper glanced at Laura, trying to gauge her emotions. "I guess it is acceptable, especially if you are willing to keep walking until we are at baggage claim. I want to be completely clear of that guy."

"No problem," the young woman said, as she hustled to keep up with Cooper's pace. "Perhaps I could ask you a couple of simple questions while we are walking?"

"OK," he replied tentatively.

"Your opposing attorney has declared that your victory in the Virginia Supreme Court is—let me get his exact words—'just a whistle stop on the way to the U.S. Supreme Court,' where he said he expects a totally different outcome. What do you say to that?"

"Well, Mr. Suskins is probably right that the U.S. Supreme Court is very likely to review this decision. But I think it is a bit presumptuous for either of us to forecast victory. I like my chances just fine."

She wrote as fast as she could while trying to walk. "So, are you going to be arguing the case in the Supreme Court?"

"That's the plan at this point," Cooper replied.

"Do you expect any political or legal fallout from Ambassador Easler's sudden resignation last night?"

"That's hard for me to predict. I hope there would be some political rethinking going on. The best thing that could happen for this country is for the Senate to revoke its ratification as soon as possible."

"Do you think that there is any chance of that?"

"Oh, man, that's hard to say. Not much. I think we may need to get through the 2006 elections for that to be a realistic possibility. If there is a backlash against the Senators who have given away our nation's sovereignty, then it is possible that it will be revoked."

They arrived at baggage claim. Laura's dad and mom quietly disappeared to get the car while she waited with Cooper for his bags to arrive. He tried to hold hands with Laura, but instead of warmly taking his hand, she seemed stiff and distant. Cooper desperately wanted the reporter to disappear so he could talk to Laura, but he didn't know how to end the interview without rudeness.

"So you think the voters can have a real impact on the whole issue of the UN treaty?" the reporter continued.

"There is no question about it. In my opinion voters didn't pay enough attention to a broad range of issues in the last election. They seemed to focus on the campaign like it was a high school popularity contest."

"All right, just one more question, and I really hope you don't take offense at this. I am just trying to do my job. Can I ask who this young woman is at your side?"

She spoke very kindly and Cooper was inclined to answer her, but he wasn't about to do so without Laura's permission.

"That's really personal, and, frankly, we need to talk for at least a few seconds before I answer. Would you mind leaving us alone for only a minute or so?"

"No problem," she answered.

The cameraman started to shoot yet another photo of the two of them discussing the victory, but the reporter squeezed his arm hard to stop, knowing full well that an ill-timed flash would most likely end the interview.

"What do you want to do?" Cooper whispered to Laura.

"I want to get out of here," she pleaded, looking at him with pain in her eyes.

"OK." Cooper was so embarrassed that he had trouble looking directly at her.

"Wait, just a second," she whispered. The expression on his face made her think of something other than her own emotional turmoil for the first time in a few hours. "Do you want to tell them?"

"If it's all right with you. First of all, I think they will find out anyway. We are just too hot in the media's mind. And all those Washington reporters saw you at the hearing. So it's just a matter of time before they figure it out. Second, I like the idea of being linked with you romantically in the press because I think it will help stop all these silly rumors about Jody and me."

"OK. I guess you're right, but please don't call her 'Jody' to me again, OK?"

"You mean that ambassador woman? You got it," he said, with a wink.

Cooper motioned to the reporter to come back over as he saw his bags coming down the belt. "This is Laura Frasier," he said, after retrieving the bags and setting them down.

"Laura, are you from here in Tampa?"

"No," she said, a little surprised to be answering directly. "I live in Leesburg, Virginia. I am just here visiting my parents."

"And you two are engaged?" the reporter asked.

"Not exactly." She thought about two or three vague answers and the possibility of simply not answering, but eventually said, "We're here to talk to my parents about that."

"Oh—good old-fashioned values," the reporter said, with a smile that came dangerously close to a smirk. "So, Mr. Stone, I heard you say that there is nothing going on between you and Ambassador Easley, despite the picture in all the papers today. Were you and Miss Frasier dating when that incident occurred?"

"No."

The reporter expected him to elaborate, but he just stood and smiled.

"OK. So there is nothing to the media speculation that the ambassador has become smitten with you, and that is the reason she has changed her position and suddenly resigned."

"If she is smitten with me she has certainly not let me know," Cooper replied. "And I am not available, in any event. I think that Ambassador Easley gave her real reasons for resigning on the program last night. She simply became disillusioned with the methods of international government. I wouldn't be looking for any hidden explanations other than that."

"All right," the reporter said, glancing over her notes.

Cooper decided not to let her reload with more questions.

"I think we need to be leaving now. Thanks," he said.

He picked up both bags and nodded at Laura to lead the way, which she did with gladness.

The ride in the car consisted of pleasant, light conversation, punctuated by a few moments of awkward silence. Cooper could tell that Laura was still upset about something, but there was no opportunity to probe her emotions while riding in the backseat of her parents' Lexus.

"Are you a golfer?" Ed Frasier asked, apparently trying to lighten the mood.

"I play golf; in fact, I love to play golf. But I am not good enough to be called a golfer."

"You have a handicap?" he asked.

"Two of them—chipping and putting," Cooper replied, smiling. "I shoot in the high 90s mostly."

"Laura, your young man is off to a good start," he said, grinning at her in the rearview mirror.

Ed was an avid golfer, and the fact that Terry hated to play golf was always a bit of a sore spot in that relationship. However, the unreasonable delay in getting his daughter to the altar had grown to be a far bigger concern as that relationship had dragged on for years.

Laura seemed a little happier during dinner and the rest of the evening, but there was no real time for the two of them to be alone for longer than a few minutes at a time. Cooper decided not to broach the subject of her skittishness until he had a longer period of uninterrupted time.

Laura went to bed pleased that her parents—especially her dad—seemed to like Cooper a lot. She just wished that the words "Jody Easler" would leave her mind and never come back.

NEW YORK CITY, N.Y. July 12, 2005. 5:00 P.M.

Suskins exited the cab in front of the elegant office tower on East Forty-Fourth, only a half-block east of UN headquarters. The rapid elevator jetted him to the forty-first floor, where a security guard with a radio waited to escort him down a dark hallway. Modern and postmodern works hung at random intervals on the walls.

The guard came to a stop in front of a door and nodded. Suskins turned the handle and walked into a small conference room with a view over looking the UN building and the East River just beyond. The room was empty.

He opened his thin black leather briefcase, pulled out his memo pad, and placed it on the table. He glanced at his watch and began to fume almost immediately that Kadar was not there to begin the meeting. Less than two minutes later, an interior door opened behind his back. Kadar's assistant, Corina Driana, entered carrying a yellow tablet and was followed by her boss.

Suskins stood to greet her. "Thank you for coming, Mr. Suskins," Kadar said in her thickly accented voice, as she sat down directly across from the lawyer.

"Yes, yes. It needs to be done." He spoke briskly.

"You seem a bit impatient with the person who pays the generous legal fees you have generated in this matter."

Time was important to Suskins, but a paying client was more important. He tried to relax and operate at her pace. "I'm sorry," he replied. "I am just anxious to get this matter before the United States Supreme Court, so that we can achieve the victory that all of us desire."

"A worthy goal, Mr. Suskins. Tell us your analysis of the justices on the Court, and how you predict the outcome of this case."

"Our firm has five attorneys who have clerked for the Supreme Court in the last seven years. We have held extensive sessions with them, and with our three most senior Supreme Court practitioners, and have concluded that there are four solid votes on either side of the case."

"And the ninth justice?"

"Justice Lorence is an unpredictable swing vote. Even his former clerks—and we have two on staff—are uncertain. If the case was purely about the substance of the treaty, he would be on our side for certain. But he is not as predictable on issues like the standing of the NGOs to bring the suit. We just don't know."

"How can we assure a fifth vote for our position?"

"We need one of the four conservatives to retire and have President Rodman appoint a favorable justice."

"Isn't one of them in poor health?"

"Yes, Justice Campbell has had prostate cancer, but the official report is that his surgery in June was a total success."

"Any chance that the actual facts are different than the official report?"

"We have no idea," Suskins replied.

"We will check," Kadar said, nodding to her assistant, who made a notation on her pad.

"As you wish," he replied.

Kadar leaned back in her chair and looked out at the river, lost in thought for several moments. "So, one change of justice is all we need to guarantee a win."

"Yes, one retirement will do it."

"Or death," she said coldly.

Suskins nodded. "Yes, that too," he concurred.

TAMPA, FLORIDA. July 13, 2005.

Ed Frasier was able to get a 7:00 A.M. tee time at his home golf course the following morning. Any later in the day and it would be just too hot to play in July.

It was a beautiful course with magnificently lush greens and fairways. Cooper was a bit nervous and made several jokes about how badly he expected to play.

"Here's the deal," Ed said with a wry grin, as they walked onto the first tee. "I like to win, but I like to win fair and square. So, on each tee I will ask you a difficult question that will determine my willingness to let you marry my daughter. That should give you something to think about besides golf. So you will be able to just play instinctively, instead of getting too concerned about your game."

"Oh, that will help me a lot," Cooper replied, with a chuckle.

Ed walked to the tee box, teed up his ball, and stroked a nicely hit shot 195 yards straight down the middle. Cooper could hit it farther but not consistently and not that straight.

"OK, well here goes," Cooper said as he pushed his tee into the ground.

"As you're getting set up there, Cooper, here's your first question. What makes you think that Laura is the right one for you to marry?"

"You want me to answer that now or after I hit?"

"Oh, after, of course, when we are riding in the cart trying to find the wayward shot you are about to hit."

Cooper had never prayed about a golf shot before that moment. He looked to heaven for help and swung in a slow, sweet pendulum, hitting nearly 250 yards, where it landed on the right side of the fairway.

"Great shot," Ed said, deeply impressed by Cooper's apparent ability to handle pressure. "So why's Laura the one?"

"Well, sir," Cooper said, daring to breathe again for the first time as he plopped down in the golf cart, "let me get the obvious things out of the way first. She is a Christian—and that's essential. I think she's gorgeous—"

"So do I," interrupted her father.

"She has a good heart toward others and wants to serve. I've watched how she has placed her own career at risk to help her friends Rick and Deanna. To tell you the truth, I first started really falling for her when she came to help me with the paperwork for the case late one night."

Ed pulled the cart to a stop in front of his own ball. "You're off to a good start. Keep talking and get out your 7-iron," Ed said.

"Would an eight be OK?" Cooper asked.

"A hundred and forty-five yards with an 8-iron?"

"If I hit it right," Cooper replied sheepishly.

"Oh, to be young and strong," Ed murmured, just before he took his 5-wood and smoothly laid the ball on the edge of the green about thirty feet from the hole.

Cooper walked to his ball and breathed deeply three times, and then took two practice swings—and they were two more than he normally took. He swung, stubbed the shot, and the ball dribbled about ten yards ahead.

"Like I said, *if* I hit it right." He walked forward three embarrassing steps, took no practice swings, and placed the ball not five feet from the hole with a perfect shot.

Ed grinned broadly and shook his head. "Nice recovery."

"Thanks," Cooper replied, greatly relieved.

"As you were saying about Laura?" Ed asked, keen to keep the pressure on this young man.

"Yeah. I was saying how much I admired the way she was so willing to serve others. It showed me a selflessness that deeply impressed me. And when I am with her, I think I can be myself without any pretenses—just who I really am. And she always seems transparent to me too—well, almost always."

"Almost?" Ed asked as they got out of the cart and approached the green, putters in hand.

"When we were in Virginia, I would have said always transparent. Something seems to be bothering her since I have been here, and I can't totally figure it out."

"Let's putt and then talk some."

Ed two-putted for a routine par. Cooper sunk his putt, also making par, which would have been a birdie had he not muffed his second shot.

"Nice hole, Cooper," Ed said, sounding more relaxed than he had been thus far. The two men got in the cart and headed to the second hole. "I think she is worried about that 'ambassador woman,' as she calls her," Ed said. "And . . ." Ed took his foot off the pedal and let the cart coast to a stop, a hundred yards before the next tee. "I guess I need to hear it straight from you. I want you to tell me straight up, man to man. Is there anything going on between you and that . . . that . . ."

"Ambassador woman?" Cooper said, completing the phrase. "There is nothing at all, sir."

"Nothing? Ever?"

"Well, you know that she made her advances toward me in New York, when Laura was engaged to Terry Pipkin. And I have to say I was flattered by her attention. But that was it; even then I wanted no one but Laura, even though I thought it was an impossible dream."

A lot of lies are told on golf courses, and regular golfers can usually tell. Ed Frasier knew that he had just been told the truth. "Good answer, son. Let's play the next hole."

Ed mixed the round with light conversation, along with serious questions about Cooper's faith, his relationship with his own parents, his finances, and his view of children. He was deeply impressed and enjoyed Cooper's company immensely. The fact that Ed won the round by only two strokes didn't hurt a thing.

CHAPTER 31

TAMPA, FLORIDA.
July 13, 2005. 8:00 P.M.

Cooper wasn't sure that he liked the sound of Chuck's Fish Shack, but Laura's dad had insisted they try it. Another test, perhaps. But when Cooper turned the last corner, he saw it was a very elegant, upscale restaurant right on the beach.

The sun hung low and orange, with its bottom edge dancing in the calm waves of the Gulf of Mexico. A few clouds lingered high overhead, promising to reflect any of the glory of the colors the setting sun was about to offer.

A trim woman in her midforties escorted the couple to a quiet corner along the glass wall that looked out over the water. The large room was full, mostly with groups of four or six. Several men in the room watched Laura out of the corner of their eyes, while a number of women looked at the handsome couple as they crossed the room. Several women and at least a few men recognized Cooper and Laura from their front-page photo. Whispers, stares, and few pointed fingers followed them across the room.

The table they were offered was set for four. Cooper and Laura sat side by side looking out the windows at the Gulf, as much for the view as for the fact that their backs would be facing the room full of gawkers.

"Really nice place," Cooper commented as they studied the menu. "Your dad has good taste."

"He really likes you, Cooper. I am happy about that."

"You are?"

"Of course. Why would I not want my father to like you?"

"I've been getting a sick feeling that while your dad and I are growing closer by the minute, I haven't been able to bridge the distance between you and me since I got off of the plane."

Their waitress came up to describe the specials, which sounded wonderful until she announced at the end of her three-minute litany, "And Chuck says to tell you that all the fish are dead." It was a part of her standard recitation.

"Chuck must be a character," Cooper said, shaking his head.

"My dad has played golf with him a couple times since I have been down here, and he always comes home laughing and telling us all the jokes he learned."

"So, do you want to tell me what is going on?" he asked.

"Nothing is going on. Well, at least I—" She stopped, then repeated herself. "Nothing is going on."

"That doesn't sound like nothing," he protested.

"Oh Cooper, this whole thing with you and that ambassador woman"—a term she pronounced as if it were a swear word—"is just so hard to bear. The media keeps saying she changed her view because she has fallen in love with you."

"That doesn't make it true. You know that. Just because the media said it. Why would you believe them?"

"Oh, I don't believe it because they say it. But I am still upset. I saw the way she looked at you on the show that night. It looked to me like they are right."

"I can't help the way she looked at me. How was I looking at her?"

"Oh, I don't know, exactly. I was paying more attention to her, for obvious reasons," Laura replied.

"I don't think that is the way she feels, but even if you're right, I can't help it. I don't feel that way toward her." His voice suddenly lost its defensiveness and took on a much softer tone. "I am madly in love with you."

That declaration was enough to make her smile, but just for a moment. Laura's brow was knotted in frustration a moment later.

"So tell me what's still bothering you," Cooper said.

"I know you love me, and, Cooper, I love you, too, so much this whole thing is killing me."

"If we love each other, then I don't understand what is wrong."

"I don't want anyone else even thinking they are in love with you," she replied.

"Why is that so important to you? If I don't choose her, isn't that the end of the line? Who cares what she thinks?"

"Do you want Terry Pipkin to still think he is in love with me? How would you feel if you saw me on television with him and he kept giving me those goo-goo-eye stares she was giving you?"

Cooper caught his breath, suddenly realizing the impact that the events had on Laura. Just the name Terry Pipkin churned his stomach. He put his arm around her shoulders. "I hate it how the world's system of dating and romance works. All I want is to love only you, and you have said that you love only me. I wish there had been no other girls I had ever cared about romantically. And I *really* wish there had never been a Terry Pipkin in your life. So when you mention him, I finally understand how you feel about Jo—that 'ambassador woman.' But we can't change our pasts, and we can't control the feelings of others. All we can do is to focus on each other and keep everyone else out of our own hearts."

Cooper could feel the stiffness in Laura's shoulders relax a bit. "There is so much pain from early and random romances. Can't you get the Senate to do a treaty banning that?" she asked bitterly, but Cooper could see a smile beginning to emerge.

They both laughed. Laura turned just a little to look Cooper straight in the eyes. She looked at him and smiled, as she leaned against his side as much as she could in the side by side armless chairs. Neither of them said anything for a little while. The sun was ready to slip completely into the watery horizon; the sky was a brilliant deep indigo with vivid streaks of red and pink.

Cooper looked into her eyes again. "I am sure everyone is staring at us or else I would kiss you," he said, with a soft smile.

"I just don't care what they think," she replied, returning his gaze.

TAMPA, FLORIDA. July 15, 2005.

Laura's mom had prepared lunch about forty-five minutes ago. She and Cooper had been chatting in the kitchen all that time, as Laura and her dad had gone for a drive and had not returned.

Bonnie Frasier liked Cooper, but the adjustment had been harder for her than for her husband. Terry's father had been their beloved pastor a long time. She had gladly accepted the role of becoming closely related to the family that had been so important to their spiritual life.

Cooper was talking to Bonnie about his six years in the Senate when they both heard the garage door opener began to whir. "Finally," Bonnie said. "It's a good thing I made salads for lunch. Anything else would have gotten cold or stale by now."

Cooper only smiled, not wanting to say anything negative about Laura having an extended conversation with her dad. Laura walked into the kitchen first. It was obvious that she had been crying, but she was now smiling broadly.

"Is something wrong?" her mother asked. Cooper was glad Bonnie asked the question.

"No, Mom. Dad and I were just reminiscing a little, and talking. I got a little emotional, but I am fine."

"She got a *lot* emotional," her dad interrupted as he entered the room. "But she is not just fine; she is exceptional."

He crossed the kitchen and gave his daughter yet another hug. "Well, Cooper, we are ready to answer the question you have asked the two—I mean the three—of us," he announced.

"Ed, please, let's sit down for this. Don't do everything so abruptly," Bonnie said nervously.

Cooper helped Laura with her chair following the lead of her father, who had done the same for her mother. He looked at her quizzically, and she tried her best to give him a mysterious look, but he could see a smile breaking out around the edges of her mouth and eyes.

"Let me make it official," Ed said, as soon as they all were seated. "Cooper, Bonnie and I are very pleased to give you our permission and our full blessing to marry Laura. This has not been the path we expected, as you know. But we are convinced that this is truly God's will for her and, as best as we can tell, for you as well."

"Thank you," Cooper replied, reaching over to shake his hand. "Thank you so much."

"It feels like someone should sing the closing hymn or let the groom kiss the bride or something," Ed remarked.

"Why don't you just bless the lunch instead, dear," Bonnie replied.

The chatter at lunch was happy and light, but it got more substantive soon when Ed asked when they thought a good time for the wedding would be. Cooper had previously told both Laura and her father that he would like to get married as soon as a wedding could be planned.

They settled on a December date, so that Laura would only miss a week of teaching by having the honeymoon coincide with the school's Christmas vacation. She wasn't sure she would teach in the future, but she had signed a contract for this school year and felt that she should keep her promise.

As soon as that decision was made, Ed and Cooper became innocent bystanders in a wedding frenzy conversation. After a half-hour or so of feeling useless, Ed suggested to Cooper that they leave the women alone to do their planning.

Once away from the table, Cooper told Ed that he needed to get back to work by Monday. He and Ed agreed that he and Laura would drive back together on Saturday and Sunday, spending the night in Charlotte, North Carolina, at Ed's brother's home.

The drive was lighthearted, with much fun and laughter. But the closer they got to Loudoun County, Virginia, the more Cooper began to feel pressured. He was about to be served with a petition for certiorari to the United States Supreme Court, prepared by a group of lawyers who had argued dozens of cases in that Court.

LEESBURG, VIRGINIA. *Late Summer, 2005.*

The petition for certiorari was perfect. Not a misplaced comma. Not a single spelling error. Not an extra space in the numerous strings of numbers and letters that lawyers employ for the citation of cases. And it was convincing. Cooper was convinced that Suskins would win this round of the fight, with his masterful filing to have the Supreme Court accept the appeal of *Children's Defense Fund, et al, v. Thomas, et al.*

He read it through for the fourth time that morning. Why even reply? The court rules didn't require a reply. And they were going to take the case, regardless of what he wrote in a reply brief. So why take the time and effort and, most importantly, the money?

Nancy brought him the morning mail. There were only two envelopes with twenty-five-dollar checks. The grassroots fundraising had slowed precipitously as soon as the "kissing controversy" erupted. A total of $18,346 had been raised, including the $50 in today's mail. It was enough for the printing costs of one brief in the Supreme Court and Cooper's overhead for the next eight weeks. Wasting seventy-five hundred dollars on the printing costs of a brief asking the Court to refuse to take the case didn't seem worth it.

Slowly the word filtered through the Christian community in Loudoun, announcing Cooper and Laura's engagement. Although it didn't happen right away, little by little people started coming to him with their legal problems, as they began to understand that he was innocent in the episode with Jody Easler. By the end of the summer, Cooper's portion of the practice with his uncle had grown enough to support himself and a frugal bride.

The evenings and weekends of the summer were the best that Cooper had ever known. He and Laura went on walks and to outdoor concerts and toured the monuments and sat outside under the stars and just talked.

When the clerk of the Supreme Court didn't receive any opposition by August 15, he circulated thirty copies of the petition filed by Suskins to all nine justices and their army of clerks.

The buzz among the clerks was that this was one of those five or six cases a year where the grant of review was a certainty. It was going to be a done deal when the case was brought on the discussion calendar the day after Labor Day.

The results were made public six days later, on September 10, 2005. The public is never informed of the internal vote on a petition for certiorari. But Erzabet Kadar knew that the petition had been granted, as well as the closeness of the results, within hours of the vote.

On September 27, after being admitted to Georgetown Hospital for a routine checkup of his prostate cancer, Justice William R. Campbell, associate justice of the United States Supreme Court, died of a massive stroke while still in the hospital.

WASHINGTON, D.C.
September 30, 2005.

The White House pressroom was jammed for the expected announcement. The conference was announced for 10:30. It was already 10:45, and the experienced reporters knew that the signs were such that it would be at least ten more minutes.

After a few minutes a young woman walked to the front of the platform, took down the White House oval on the lectern and replaced it with the seal of the president of the United States. Everyone in the room shuffled with reasonable dispatch to the seats assigned to them by tradition.

At 10:58, the White House Deputy Press Secretary stepped to the podium and said, "Ladies and gentlemen, the President of the United States."

Helene Rodman, the first female president of the United States, stepped forward. "It is my profound privilege to announce to you this morning," she began reading from the teleprompter, "that I am nominating Senator Elizabeth Rose for the position of associate justice of the Supreme Court of the United States. Senator Rose has served the people of California with distinction for fourteen years and, as you know, has recently become the chair of the Senate Judiciary Committee, after serving as the ranking minority member since 2000. She was an outstanding trial lawyer for the National Organization for Women before she was elected to the Senate in 1990. I believe and trust that she will be swiftly confirmed for this position so that the Court may perform its important work this term with a full compliment of nine justices." She smiled her perfectly plastic smile and turned to Senator Rose for remarks.

"Thank you so much, President Rodman. It is a great honor to be considered for the highest court of the United States, and I am grateful for this opportunity to serve America in a new capacity if I am confirmed. I have to say, though, that it is with mixed emotions that I have consented to have my name placed in nomination. Although every lawyer dreams about service on the Supreme Court, it has been the highest privilege of my life to serve for fourteen years in the United States Senate. But I believe that Governor Black will be able to find an able replacement for the Senate, and it seemed that I could not refuse President Rodman when she asked me to consider this high position. Thank you, Ms. President. I am honored by your trust."

The two women stood side by side at the lectern for the obligatory pictures, smiling at the kind words shared by each, even though President Rodman knew perfectly well that Rose had employed every political pressure she had learned to coerce her appointment. Ms. Rodman had wanted to nominate Congressman Steve Farenholt, who had been the chairman of her presidential campaign. But the whispering campaign of "betrayal of the feminist agenda" had forced Rodman to pay Farenholt with a promise to appoint him to the next vacancy.

"Any questions will have to be addressed to me," the president stated, as Rose moved a step or two back from the lectern. "Under the traditions of the Supreme Court nomination process, nominees do not speak publicly on their nomination until the confirmation hearings.

"Mr. Baker," the president said, acknowledging the reporter from the *Washington Star*, who had sprung to his feet first.

"Ms. President," he said, using the form of address specified by the rules the White House Press Office issued on Inauguration Day, "other than the obvious compatibility that you and Senator Rose have on the issue of preserving *Roe v. Wade* and a woman's right to choose, are there other issues coming before the Supreme Court that have prompted this selection?"

"Mr. Baker," she replied with a smile intended to look cheerful, "it is an awesome responsibility to select a person to a lifetime position like the Supreme Court. Cases come and go. I was looking for a person with both the intellectual rigor to serve as a justice, as well as a steadfast commitment to the evolving nature of the Constitution of the United States, that great living document."

"So there weren't any cases at all that figured into your selection process?"

"No, I did not ask or analyze her views on this case or that."

Her answer was true in a tricky sort of way. The two women had not talked about cases on a hit-or-miss basis as the term "this case or that" would imply. They had had a sheet of every single case pending on the Supreme Court docket, and Rodman had demanded an answer from Rose as to her intended vote on the entire list. They had spent a full twenty minutes just on the UN treaty case.

"Ms. Anderson," the president said, acknowledging the Supreme Court correspondent for ABC News.

"So you and Senator Rose had no occasion to discuss the impending case from Virginia regarding the UN Convention on the Rights of the Child?"

"As you know, Senator Rose and I have been both strong backers of this treaty for almost two decades. We have talked about this treaty many times and, yes, we talked about the litigation in an informal way before the sudden and sad death of Justice Campbell. But discussions about the political issues surrounding the treaty are quite different from the legal issues that must be addressed in the Supreme Court."

"Mr. Arledge," the president called out in the direction of the *Los Angeles Times* reporter, who had written no less than three flattering profiles of her candidacy in the recent election. "I am sorry I didn't see your hand earlier."

"How long do you expect the confirmation process to take? As you know, the Court begins its term next Monday."

"I know that it may seem quick, but, of course, the fates have determined the order of events not me. I believe it is essential that the Supreme Court be at full strength from as close to the beginning of the term as possible. I have spoken to the Senate Majority Leader, and he assures me that a hearing can be held quickly and a floor vote scheduled in time."

"Will there be enough time for the traditional FBI investigation into the background of the candidate on that time schedule?" Arledge asked.

"I have informed the FBI director that it is his duty to complete this investigation forthwith. And even if it doesn't take the same length of time that has been traditional, we have the assurance that Senator Rose has been through three U.S. Senate campaigns. I am certain that if there were something unscrupulous in her past, either you fine members of the fourth estate or her worthy opponents would have brought it to the attention of the public by now. We think that the deadline is crucial and this administration will do everything it can to see to it that the vote is taken within two weeks."

President Rodman nodded to Senator Rose, and they walked off the stage and out the doorway behind them and to their right. Senator Rose stopped to shake hands with the president as the door closed behind them. The president just kept walking past, pretending that she didn't even see the woman she had just nominated for the Supreme Court.

WASHINGTON, D.C. October 1, 2005.

He knew his way to the back corner of the basement cafeteria without directions. For six years, Cooper had been a regular at the Tuesday morning gathering of Senate staffers who wanted to pray and share a brief time in God's Word. The atmosphere of the group brightened considerably for a couple of minutes on the arrival of their former compatriot.

They subjected him to a little teasing about his season in the tabloids but soon settled into the serious siege mentality that had become the norm since the last election. The announcement of Rose's nomination to the Supreme Court was the realization of their worst fear and most dire prediction. Cooper's arrival only served to exacerbate their feeling of despair because he was a reminder that Matthew Parker was no longer a member of the United States Senate.

Cooper had been asked to come by Marian Nellis, chief of staff to Senator Zach Tyler from South Carolina, one of the most reliable conservatives in the Senate. She had been following his case closely and wanted Cooper to talk with the group about the impact of the Rose nomination on the outcome of his case.

The group shared prayer requests around the tables in as close to a circular fashion as six rectangular tables scooted together would permit, and then prayed together for each need. Afterward, Marian told her colleagues the reason for Cooper's presence.

"I asked Cooper to rejoin us this morning to share a prayer request and maybe an action item that affects the Rose nomination that so many of us are deeply concerned about. Cooper, what do you think the Supreme Court is going to do with your case, and what do you think the timetable will be?"

"I can only make educated guesses, Marian," he replied. "I assume that the other side is going to move with all speed to make sure Rose is on the Court. Their brief is due October 10. I have thirty days to reply. Then they have ten days to reply."

"That takes us to November 20 just to get the briefs in if you take your full time," Marian replied. "Is that right?"

"Yeah, that's right."

"There is no way we can stall her confirmation that long. Anyone disagree?"

A murmur of dejected agreement buzzed through the thirty-member group.

"What is the longest anyone thinks we can stall it?"

Scott Gordon, chief counsel for the Republican leader of the Senate, spoke first. "They want a vote by October 14. It's going to take a miracle to stall it at all because there are sixty Democrats in the Senate. We can't even sustain a filibuster without the support of at least one Democrat. I can't imagine any circumstances in which we can push it past November 1."

It was the right analysis, and everyone quickly assented. "So is there nothing that can be done to try to get Cooper's case to Court before she gets confirmed?" Marian asked.

"We would have to cut twenty days out of the briefing schedule to even have the briefing done before she is on the Court. Then there is oral argument."

"Well, there is a possibility, although it is remote," stated Gordon, who had clerked for the chief justice five years earlier. "If Cooper submits his brief only five days after he gets the petitioners' brief, their reply brief would be due on October 29. The chief justice can schedule oral argument as soon as Cooper's brief is filed. If he announces an argument on October 31 or November 1, then that is the fastest it can be done."

"But there is no way I can write a brief and get it printed that fast," Cooper protested.

"Yeah, not by yourself," Gordon said, "but we can help. And we can get a lot of it done early. There are at least a half-dozen of us here today who have clerked for federal judges. If you give us a list of issues to begin working on, I think we can get it done in four days, and the printer over on H Street can turn it around in twenty-four hours if we give him the text on computer disk."

"Well, if you all would do that for me it might work," Cooper replied. "But I can't pay any of you. The funding for the case is thin right now."

"Cooper, you're a really nice guy and we like you a lot, but we wouldn't do it just for you. We're doing it for America. Who's with me?" Gordon asked.

Eight hands shot up.

"You've got your law firm, Cooper," Marian said. "Put them to work."

"Hold on a minute," Bryce Green, one of the eight volunteers, said raising his hand. "Just one problem. Even if we keep Rose from being confirmed, how do we get to five votes on the Court? We've got the three remaining conservatives at best."

"That's true," Gordon replied. "Maybe we can get Lorence's vote. But that's iffy at best. I don't know how it adds up. I just have this prompting in my spirit that we are supposed to try to do this. If Rose gets on the Court, it will only get worse. We've got to try."

"And we've got to pray," Marian replied, with a determined look on her face. The prayers that morning were fervent, not those of a people under siege but of a unit about to march into battle.

WORLDWIDE WEB. September 30, 2005. 11:00 P.M.

You are entering Mars Hill as CooperStone

You see here 17 chatters: Abba4JC, Katie_host, FiddlersPapa, Cryllic,

Angelic, MissSally, Sancty-fried, Contentmomma, Notreally, Saddlepal,
Firemomma . . .

Cryllic:	So when's the date, Saddle?
Saddlepal:	We've decided on February 14
Angelic:	Valentine's Day!!!!! Way cool.
Katie_host:	Well, if it isn't the star of stage, screen, and tabloid magazines. CooperStone, welcome back.
MissSally:	Cooooooooooooooooooooooper!!!!!!!! What are you doing here?
Cryllic:	Valentine's Day! That's so romantic, congratulations.
CooperStone:	Long time no see everyone. I came to ask for prayer for the UN case.
Firemomma:	Sure, Mr. Stone. We'd also like to hear an update on the case.
Saddlepal:	Thanks, cryllic. Sally and I are very happy and very excited.
CooperStone:	Sure firemomma, but what's this with Sally and Saddlepal?
MissSally:	We're engaged . . . *blush*
CooperStone:	NO WAY!!!!!!!!!!!! That is wonderful.
MissSally:	Thanks Coop.
Abba4JC:	They're our first Crosswalk chat marriage. And unlike so many chatroom romances, they were both single to begin with. We are so proud.
CooperStone:	Congrats, Sally and Saddle. So Sally will your married name be Mrs. Pal?
Angelic:	LOL
Notreally:	Old Joke, Cooper. But a good one.
Sancty-fried:	Saddlepal made the same joke when the engagement was first announced a couple weeks ago.
Katie_host:	So, Mr. Stone, please tell us about the case and this Supreme Court appointment and everything.
MissSally:	And your engagement also, Cooper. Peter tells me that you are getting married in December.
Sancty-fried:	WARNING!! News overload. The ratio of actual news to

mindless blather in this room is reaching dangerously high proportions.

CooperStone: Yes, Laura and I are getting married December 18.

Notreally: You got engaged without it making the National Enquirer?

Sancty-fried: By the way, can we allow a guy who has been shown kissing a UN ambassador on the cover of the National Enquirer in our chat room?

Notreally: checks the admission rules . . . let's see no bores, no humor-impaired, no one from frozen countries in the North . . . I see nothing about kissing ambassadors.

Firemomma: Is Laura the Sunday school teacher or the UN woman?

Sancty-fried: Ouch, fire . . .

CooperStone: Laura is the Sunday school teacher. I was never interested in Ambassador Easler. That was just a press invention.

Sancty-fried: That picture was a press invention?

CooperStone: No, unfortunately not, but it's a long story . . . let's just say it was a one time deal and I was at least partially innocent.

Notreally: An interesting phrase for a lawyer. Judge: How do you plead? Defendant: I plead partially innocent.

Katie_host: Oh knock it off you guys, we have been over all that, it was in the papers. I want to hear about the case and the Supreme Court appointment.

CooperStone: Thanks, Katie. Well, it frankly doesn't look very good. With the death of Justice Campbell we lost a likely vote. Senator Rose is certain to vote with the other side.

Cryllic: How many votes can you count on?

CooperStone: The best estimate is three.

Abba4JC: So that means that five of the existing judges are against you? What hope is there?

CooperStone: Three for sure are against us, and probably four. Justice Lorence is the only one up for grabs. But sometimes he is able to get one of the other liberals to go along with

	him on a procedural matter. Since the Virginia Supreme Court decision is essentially a procedural victory, it is our only real hope.
FiddlersPapa:	But if Rose is on the Court doesn't that doom us?
CooperStone:	Yes. Probably does. That is why I am asking you to pray that her confirmation will be delayed as long as possible.
Firemomma:	How long of a delay would you like?
CooperStone:	Fire, I think I remember that you have a three-year-old. Right?
Firemomma:	Yeah . . . why?
CooperStone:	I would like a delay until he is 18.
Katie_host:	LOL . . . now give us the real answer.
CooperStone:	At least until the first of November. That is two weeks longer than the White House and Senate leadership want.
Cryllic:	Is there anything we can do in addition to praying?
CooperStone:	Yeah, you can all call or e-mail your Senators urging them to demand a complete analysis which will result in at least some delay.
Firemomma:	E-mail? Did you say e-mail? Would you like us to conduct an e-mail blitz campaign? I hope I hope.
CooperStone:	Absolutely. The more contacts the better. Pressure is the name of the game.
Angelic:	Can we do anything from Canada in addition to praying?
Sancty-fried:	Yeah, throw snowballs at the Senate.
Abba4JC:	No, Angelic, throw them at Sancty in Texas instead.
Sancty-fried:	ducks.
Katie_host:	Angelic, you have American friends on your e-mail?
Angelic:	Yes, sure, lots of them.
Katie_host:	Then tell them to call and to pray.
Angelic:	Good idea.
Sancty-fried:	Yeah. That's what I meant. Send out e-mails until the result snowballs.
Cryllic:	Yeah, sure, sancty.

MissSally:	Anything else we can pray for?
CooperStone:	Yeah, To make this work I have to file my brief with the Supreme Court only five days after I get the other side's brief. I need a lot of prayer for that.
Saddlepal:	How is that possible?
CooperStone:	A bunch of my friends who work for the Senate and are lawyers have volunteered to help me. One of them clerked for the Chief Justice. It is the only way this will possibly work.
FiddlersPapa:	We'll pray, Cooper.
Abba4JC:	I'll pray and tell others.
Notreally:	I'll send $27.50.
MissSally:	LOL, Notreally, that was last time . . . but I will still hold you to that. Get the check in the mail.
Notreally:	Me and my big mouth.
Sancty-fried:	You type with your mouth?
CooperStone:	I need to go. Thanks for praying and sending e-mails to the Senate.

CHAPTER 33

LEESBURG, VIRGINIA.
October 16, 2005.

The glow from the lantern-styled street lamp illumined radiance in Laura's face and hair that captivated Cooper's gaze as the couple walked hand in hand down Market Street's red brick sidewalk. The cupola, which crowned not only the county courthouse but the entire core of the historic section of Leesburg, shone brightly in the darkening autumn sky. Cooper's fingers tightened perceptibly around Laura's hand as they passed by the darkened courtroom where he had first discovered her prior engagement ring. He wished he could make such thoughts stay in the corners of forget-fulness, but he could not seem to stop such bitter moments from briefly appearing on the center stage of his memory. Laura chose that moment to look up at him with a warm, loving smile. He tried to create what he hoped was a reassuring smile as he attempted to force his mind to forget about the past.

"What are you smiling at?" she asked, her forehead wrinkled in a quizzical expression.

"Nothing unusual—just thinking how glad I am that you are mine," he replied.

The light changed and they crossed over King Street, past Payne's Biker Bar. "Better Here Than Across the Street," the sign in the window proclaimed, declaring the establishment's patrons' preference for the bar over the courthouse. Cooper opened one of the tall doors of the restaurant next door, housed in what was once Leesburg's finest bank. Laura stepped through the door with Cooper right behind.

"We have reservations at 7:15," Cooper said to the hostess.

"Yes, Mr. Stone, your table is ready. Right this way," she responded to her regular customer.

The Lighthouse Café was the most difficult place in town to get a last minute reservation. But Nancy had called earlier in the day and pleaded with the manager of the elegantly renovated former bank. Cooper had not seen Laura for five days while he and his brief writing team had worked nearly nonstop in the bowels of the Dirksen Senate Building.

The waiter quickly brought two glasses of water and a basket of warm bread as the couple studied their menu.

"It is so good to see you again," he said, looking very tired, despite his best intentions.

"I am so glad you got it done. I guess I really didn't think it was possible."

"The printer told us that it was the fastest he had ever seen one produced, except for the presidential election challenges from Florida in the 2000 elections."

"Well, that is truly an accomplishment. But it is good to have it behind you," she said, hoping that Cooper would be able to think about something other than the brief for at least a little while.

"It looks doubtful that all this speed will do us any good though. The Judiciary Committee hearings on the Rose nomination were scheduled today—they start the day after tomorrow. And the Senate Majority Leader announced a planned floor vote on the twenty-second. It looks like she will be sworn in on the next day."

"So you did all this for nothing?"

"Well, to be accurate, it looks like we did it fast for nothing. But, I am glad to have had the help of Scott Gordon and the others. I'm not sure they would have helped this much if I had been on the normal track of responding in thirty days."

The waitress brought their salads. Cooper blessed the food and prayed for a miracle regarding the Rose nomination.

His mouth was full of endive when the cell phone in his pocket started ringing. Gulping down the salad, he scrambled to pull the phone out before it rolled the call over to voice mail.

Flipping the phone open, he said hello into the wrong end of the phone, realized his error, and turned the phone over. "Hello," he said again.

"Cooper? This is Jody Easler. Is everything OK there?"

"Jody! Hi! Everything is fine. I just answered the phone upside down."

Laura winced when she heard the name "Jody."

"I was wondering if you could help me," she said. "I am coming to Washington tomorrow. I am supposed to testify on the Rose nomination."

"You are? Why?"

"I don't want to say too much about it over your cell phone. Let's just say for now that Senator Marshall asked me to testify."

"Man, I guess that means—"

She cut him off. "Don't. Not over a cell phone. All I will say is that Marshall has to inform the Senate chairman who is on his witness list in about half an hour. When my name is on the list, Kadar will know it within minutes. She will stop at nothing to keep me from testifying."

"What do you want me to do?" he asked.

"I am afraid to make transportation plans or a hotel reservation in my own name or over my own phones. And I don't want anyone from the Senate committee making the plans either. It just can't be kept confidential. Can you get me a place to stay and have someone trustworthy pick me up at the airport?"

Cooper looked at Laura, trying to figure out how to respond. "I have an idea," he replied. "Do you remember Laura Frasier?"

"Your fiancée?"

"Yeah, how did you know?"

"I read the tabloids about . . . well, you know . . . you and me and this whole bizarre case."

"In any event, Laura will be at your gate to meet you. We'll have everything planned without your name appearing anywhere."

"That sounds great," Jody replied.

Cooper took down her flight number and arrival time and quickly ended the call.

"I suppose you are going to tell me what that was all about," Laura said.

"Jody Easler is going to testify for our side on the Rose nomination."

"What does she know about Rose?"

"I have no idea. She was unwilling to talk about it because I was on a cell phone."

"Why not?"

"She's afraid that Dr. Kadar from Geneva will try to stop her, and she wants me to make her hotel and transportation plans secretly."

"I don't get it," Laura said.

"I can only speculate that she knows something that is damaging to Rose. If she does, I want to do whatever I can to help."

"So why am *I* meeting her at the gate?"

"Two reasons. First, Kadar's people aren't as likely to know you as me. And second, you won't have any reasons to be suspicious of me if you are actually the one picking her up."

"Hmm," Laura said, pushing the remains of her salad around on the plate. "I thought we were through with that ambas—with Ambassador Easler."

"Do I need to tell you how much I love you and want no one else?"

"Maybe you don't exactly *need to,* but I sure wouldn't object if you said it right now."

"Laura, you are the brightest spot in my life. Please don't think that anyone else could ever come close to you. I love you, sweetie."

"That'll do for now," she said with a wry grin. "Well, I guess I'll pick her up. Practice another couple creative lines and have 'em ready for tomorrow, just in case I need to hear them."

Cooper reached across the table and took both of Laura's hands in his and smiled at her. They talked no more of the subject that evening, but an underlying tension flitted in and out on the edges of their emotions.

WASHINGTON, D.C., Dulles Airport. October 17, 2005.

Laura arrived at gate C-9 fifteen minutes before the scheduled arrival of the United Airlines flight from Los Angeles. The gate area was already crowded with well over a hundred people waiting to board this same plane as it continued to Paris. Cooper had told her to look out for anyone who could be stalking Easler. Laura spotted at least twenty men who looked suspicious to her and decided to simply give up any amateurish effort at counter-surveillance.

Laura's swirling thoughts led her to silent prayer. *Lord, please help me to be wise and say that which is helpful for the good of your kingdom.*

A flurry of activity by the uniformed airline agents served as an advance signal that the plane was expected at the gate any moment. The door soon opened, and four men in suits, each with a briefcase and a black suitcase on wheels, quickly exited the ramp area, heading toward the shuttle buses to the main terminal.

There was a lapse of nearly a minute before anyone else appeared. The delay was soon explained as a couple in their eighties toiled deliberately up the ramp. Jody Easler was right behind them.

Laura stood up and waited. Jody, wearing a knee length dark skirt and a brightly colored silk top, paused at the doorway. Spotting Laura, she nodded and headed with bold strides in her direction. "Hello, Laura. Thank you for doing this," she said.

Even the simple task of saying "You're welcome" seemed incredibly difficult. "I'm happy to try to help," Laura forced herself to say. "Can I help you carry something?" she added.

"No, I just have this one bag," Jody replied. "I didn't check any luggage either. I plan on a quick turnaround after tomorrow's hearing."

They walked several yards in silence before Laura said, "Cooper is waiting in the car. He said to wait until we got inside to tell you the plans."

"That's wise," Jody responded in a quiet voice. "Did you see anyone who might be watching for me at the gate?"

"There were too many to tell," Laura replied softly. "A least a couple of different men seemed to be watching me closely."

"That could just be the normal crop of creeps and slugs who belong under a rock someplace," Jody replied.

Jody's description made Laura laugh. Jody joined in her laughter, and the wall between the two women began to slowly tumble. The conversation was pure chitchat of the get-to-know-each-other variety as they took the seven-minute ride on the shuttle bus to the main terminal. Laura noticed a man who had been in the waiting area. He was alone toward the back of the huge tractor-like shuttle bus. He was talking nonchalantly on his cell phone.

"Pay attention to that guy back in the corner," Laura said very quietly. "He was by himself in the waiting area and doesn't seem to be with anyone now. If he was meeting someone, where are they?"

Jody smiled with deceptive warmth while casting a wary eye in the direction indicated. "Got him," she replied. "Did you get a look at his shoes?"

"I didn't notice," Laura replied. "Why?"

"European men wear weird, ugly shoes. Even rich men."

The shuttle arrived at the terminal with a grinding of brakes. The automatic doors swung open on each side of the driver's cabin. The two women were near the front and got off as quickly as possible, trying to lose the guy with the cell phone without taking the time to check out his shoes.

"Cooper told me to try something if we thought we might be followed, so bear with me, OK?" Laura whispered.

They walked a couple hundred yards toward the escalators that led to baggage claim and ground transportation. However, rather than go down the escalator, they continued on another fifty yards, pausing in front of the elevator. They punched the button and waited. They took turns glancing over their shoulders to see if the man on the cell phone was still following them. The elevator arrived and they walked in. Laura looked back toward the escalator one more time.

"I saw him pause at the top of the escalator and look over here," Laura said. "He seemed to be headed downstairs in a hurry."

Jody reached out to push the button to go down to the baggage claim level. "No, wait," Laura said. "Cooper's idea was for us to just stand here for several seconds."

"Then what?" Jody asked.

"Then this," Laura replied, hitting the "open door" button and getting out where they walked in. "Follow me."

They walked to their right and quickly headed to the front door at the level reserved for departures. Cooper's Jimmy was only fifty yards ahead, waiting at the far north end of the nearly mile-long terminal.

He jumped out upon seeing the approaching women and greeted Jody with a smile and a handshake. He quickly swept her bag in the back of his GMC. Cooper got back into the front. Laura assumed the seat next to her fiancé—she had no plans to be *that* gracious. Jody took a seat in the back behind Laura.

"Were you followed?" Cooper asked as soon as the doors closed.

"There was one suspicious guy we were watching, but your elevator trick seems to have lost him. He's probably down on the arrivals level looking for us right now," Laura replied.

"It's too bad I'm not in the State Department anymore, Cooper. I could recommend you for a position in intelligence, with good moves like that one."

Cooper laughed. "My next trick is for you to spend the night with Laura. We figured that no one would look for you there."

Jody told them about the invitation she had received to testify from Scott Gordon's boss, Senator Rob Marshall of Virginia. After exhausting that subject, she asked about their wedding plans. She seemed happy for the two of them. Her expressions seemed so real that the walls in Laura's heart began to tumble down even faster.

Cooper asked her about her new career in show business. She was quick to tell him that it was a position in journalism and news commentary, but they all laughed when she said it.

Cooper stopped momentarily at a Chinese restaurant on the eastern edge of Leesburg, keeping the car running as he ran inside. The women waited outside in the growing darkness. He came back quickly with a bulging white plastic bag, which he set on the floor of the backseat. He continued on to Laura's home, parking in front.

He got Jody's suitcase out of the back and the food from the floorboard. Laura stood waiting for him at the front door.

He handed Jody her suitcase and Laura the bag of Chinese food. "Have a great night," he said. "See you in the morning."

Jody looked at him with astonishment. "You aren't going to eat with us?"

"No," he replied. "I figure that if Erzabet Kadar's people lose you at the airport, they may choose to track me as one place to look for you. I don't want my truck sitting out here when they start looking. You two have a great time, and I'll pick you up at 7:15 tomorrow morning to get you to the Senate on time."

The door closed, and since Cooper had shared this plan with Laura, the moment she had truly dreaded had now arrived. She had relaxed considerably about the idea of Jody, but an idea and a flesh and blood person were different in practical terms.

Laura got the dishes out for their dinner and pulled some Diet Coke out of the refrigerator. "So who is on *Politics & Hollywood* for you tonight?" Laura asked as they sat down at the table.

"They don't get a substitute for me. Greg Maris did it by himself before. They figure they can survive for a show or two without me. I'll be back in a couple days, assuming I'm still alive."

The matter-of-fact way she spoke of the question of her own survival momentarily unnerved Laura. "Do you think they would actually . . . actually harm you?" Laura asked plaintively.

Jody nodded. "Only if they felt they had no other choice. But Kadar wouldn't hesitate to order me killed if lesser means failed her."

"What do you have to say that is so dangerous to them?"

"I think it is safer for you to not know. Just in case."

"You seem so calm about it," Laura said, deeply impressed with her guest's demeanor.

"Actually, I am terrified of the prospect of dying. Cooper once told me that he faces the idea of his mortality with real confidence. Being calm about the prospect of death is so strange to me. I have a hard time even relating to it."

Laura silently asked God for wisdom. A door was open and she didn't want to falter. "He's that way because he has confidence he will spend eternity with God. Even though I sure don't want to die anytime soon, I share his confidence."

"That is a very strange way of thinking," Jody said, in a tone that conveyed respect.

"Anyone can have that same confidence if they know Jesus."

"You know I have always wondered what knowing Jesus meant. People have said things like that before, and I've always been baffled by the words."

Laura rested both her arms on the table. "Getting to know God is actually pretty easy once people understand that he is holy and we aren't. Solving that problem is the key."

"What do you mean?" Jody asked.

"The whole point of Christianity is to have a personal relationship with God. God has told us that the relationship he wants with us is like a marriage. In marriage, there has to be a basic compatibility between a man and a woman. With God we have to have basic compatibility as well. The problem is that we are sinners and God is holy. Our sin stands in the way of the relationship he wants to have with us. But God gave us a solution if we will just accept it. The reason Jesus died on the cross was to pay the penalty for our sin. If we simply tell God that we recognize that we are sinners and that we accept the penalty paid by his Son, he promises that he will come to us and live within us spiritually. Our spirits are made new, and it is then possible for us to have a true personal relationship with God."

Jody seemed to agree, but her eyes gave a signal that she was still confused.

"Why would God do all that? Why would he have his Son die for . . . strangers?"

"For the same reason that most mothers are so willing to sacrifice their own lives for those of their children. They love the child they have brought into the world. God created us and he loves us. It breaks his heart to see any of us separated from him because of our sin. He was willing to do whatever it took to give us a chance for eternal life with him."

Jody asked questions for nearly two more hours, but Laura's patient manner and effective use of Scripture began to be used by the Holy Spirit to penetrate a life and heart that had little thought of God until recently.

At 9:45, Jody was ready. She prayed in faith, acknowledging her sin and asking Jesus to be her Savior. Laura wrapped her arm around Jody's shoulder, and the women the tabloids portrayed as rivals in romance became sisters in Christ, bound together by the love of God.

CHAPTER

34

PURCELLVILLE, VIRGINIA.
October 18, 2005.

Cooper didn't see the tan Ford Taurus parked a half-block down Main Street from his home. He got into his Jimmy and headed east—6:45, his watch declared. He went through the drive-thru at McDonald's, getting his regular breakfast sandwich and a large coffee.

The tan sedan waited cautiously in the Food Lion parking lot. "He's stopped at McDonald's," the driver said into his cell phone.

Cooper turned left and drove past Loudoun Valley High School and then down the frontage road connecting to the Route 7 freeway. Cooper's SUV was starting to get too far away as the Taurus hit the ramp. The driver pressed down hard on the gas pedal with his thin-soled Spanish leather shoe.

The Taurus maintained just the right separation to keep visual contact. Even if Cooper had seen the Taurus, there would be nothing to suspect. It was the route that the vast majority of commuters took as they left Purcellville heading to Ashburn, Reston, Tyson's Corner, or Washington.

Eight miles later, Cooper turned left at Sycolin Road. There were two cars between his vehicle and the Taurus. A hundred yards later, he turned left again into Laura's townhome development. The Taurus slowed and followed discretely. Cooper pulled to a stop in front of Laura's home and quickly jumped out, heading for the front door. The Taurus glided past and turned the corner about three hundred yards to the south. The Taurus quickly executed a U-turn. The driver parked his car on the side street, so that the front of the car offered a binoculars-aided view back down Laura's street.

Three minutes later he spoke into the cell phone again. "Easler and another woman just got in the car with him. I think the woman was the one at the airport yesterday."

"Don't let them get here," came the reply. The voice was husky and female, with a Hungarian accent.

"I understand."

Cooper flipped a quick U-turn of his own and headed back to Sycolin Road in a hurry. The Taurus accelerated to keep pace. The Jimmy turned right on Route 7 and exited nearly immediately, onto the crossover ramp that put his vehicle eastbound on the Dulles Greenway.

Cooper, Laura, and Jody had exchanged good morning pleasantries, but Laura was bursting with the desire to tell him about Jody's salvation experience. As they pulled on to the main body of the Greenway, he glanced in his rearview mirror, thinking that he had seen that tan Taurus before—in Purcellville. *Tauruses are a dime a dozen,* he tried to reassure himself.

"So what did you two talk about last night?" he asked.

Laura looked back over her shoulder, seeing if Jody wanted to answer the question herself. Jody nodded at Laura in a manner that indicated *you start*.

"Well, it was a really great conversation. We talked about our lives and our struggles and about you a little bit, but mostly about God. And after a lot of questions and discussion, Jody—" Laura paused and glanced back at the former ambassador, who smiled with reassurance that it was OK to continue. "Jody prayed to receive Christ."

He wanted to shout "Are you kidding?" but stifled the impulse. "That is fantastic!" he exclaimed.

He waited for Jody to speak, but she just sat still, with a shy smile on her face. Cooper was trying to look at her in the rearview mirror and didn't notice the car pulling even with him on his left.

Jody finally spoke. "Well, it just made a lot of sense."

Suddenly, Cooper slammed on the brakes to avoid a tan Taurus that pulled right in front of the car. "That idiot nearly killed us!" he cried. "Why is he in such a hurry to change lanes?"

"Now he is slowing down," Laura said, her attention focused on the near collision.

"I don't know, but I am going to get away from him," Cooper said, as he jammed on the accelerator.

Both Laura and Jody glared at the driver as Cooper sped past the Taurus, which had slowed down considerably. Laura suddenly gasped and turned to look at Jody. "I think it's him, Jody. Isn't that the guy who was following us at the airport?"

"Yes, it is," she said, her voice breaking with fear. "Cooper! You've got to get us out of here."

Cooper pressed the accelerator to the floor. Before long, they were going ninety miles per hour and weaving through traffic. The Taurus was right on their tail.

"Laura, get my cell phone out of my jacket pocket and call 911," he shouted, dodging an angry commuter as they headed under an overpass.

Laura leaned over and dug in his suit jacket frantically, as Cooper continued to dodge and swerve through traffic. Pulling it out, she dialed the number and hit "send."

"Loudoun County Emergency," said the female voice.

"We are being chased by a man who tried to run us over," Laura blurted out breathlessly. "We have a former ambassador in our car. She is likely the target."

"Calm down, ma'am," the voice said. "Where are you?"

"We just passed exit 6 on the Greenway."

"Which way are you headed?"

"East, toward Washington."

"Please describe both cars, ma'am," the voice asked, as calmly as if she were asking a friend for a recipe for macaroni and cheese.

"There are three of us, one man and two women. We are in a 2002 GMC Jimmy. It's dark blue. The car that is chasing us is a tan Taurus."

Just then a loud crash exploded outside Cooper's window. He jerked reflexively to the right. "What in the world?" he yelled.

"Cooper, it's your outside mirror! Look!" Jody exclaimed from the backseat.

The glass of the mirror was completely shattered. A hole about an inch in diameter had been ripped completely through the mirror assembly.

"Laura, tell them that the guy is shooting at us!" Cooper yelled.

"I heard that, ma'am. Just a moment. I need to radio," the dispatcher said. Cooper continued to weave rapidly through traffic.

About twenty seconds later, the voice was back. "I'll stay on the phone with you until we get you some help," she said, with only slightly increased emotion. "How far are you now from the toll plaza?"

"How far from the toll plaza?" Laura panted.

"About five miles," Cooper said.

The traffic begin to be more and more congested. Cooper saw the Taurus gaining on him as he was slowed by traffic. He yanked the wheel hard to the left and drove down the shoulder, regaining speed as he went. The Taurus imitated his move and was soon only a few hundred yards behind. Seeing an opening, Cooper cut rapidly across all three travel lanes, hoping that the same hole in traffic wouldn't be there for the Taurus. He was only partially successful, as he gained only two or three hundred yards after the Ford jammed its way across the path of a half-dozen terrified drivers.

They rounded a big corner, and four police cars were waiting about a quarter mile before the toll plaza. Two brown sheriffs' cars were on the right shoulder, noses facing in the direction of traffic. Two metallic blue Virginia State Police cars were on the left shoulder. Cooper began to slow to a stop after reaching the police.

The Taurus suddenly cut back across traffic to the left shoulder and headed across the median. Reversing directions, the driver headed back toward Leesburg. In a flash, both state police cars had their lights on and their sirens blaring, and their rear wheels flung turf as they accelerated across the median in pursuit of the Taurus.

Cooper hit his brakes hard and came to a stop just past the sheriff's cars.

"Thank you, Jesus," Cooper breathed, leaning his forehead on the steering wheel.

The Loudoun County deputies quickly descended on his car with weapons drawn. Cooper hit his automatic window button. "We're the good guys!" he shouted.

"Probably so," the closest deputy replied, "but why don't you exit the vehicle with your hands in plain view, just so we can make sure."

Cooper slowly opened his door and stepped onto the pavement.

"You're Cooper Stone, the lawyer from Leesburg, aren't you?" the deputy said.

Cooper nodded enthusiastically, putting his hands back at his side. Sliding his gun back into his holster, the deputy walked forward briskly to the car. "You all OK in there?" he asked, sticking his head in the window.

"Yeah, I guess," Laura answered.

Jody, who was quietly crying in the backseat, simply nodded affirmatively.

"Quite a ride you all have had from all the cell phone calls we've been getting," the lead deputy said.

"Someone is trying to stop Ambassador Easler there in the back from making it to the Senate this morning. She is supposed to testify in a hearing on the Supreme Court nomination that starts in an hour," Cooper explained. "They tried to run us off the road and shot at us at least once. Look at my mirror there," he said, pointing at it with his hand.

After a few minutes of conversation, the second deputy walked to the first, who had taken charge of the scene, and whispered a few words to his fellow officer. The first deputy smiled. "Looks like they've got the guy in the Taurus. Hungarian diplomatic passport and a gun with empty casings in the chamber."

After some radio conversations with their office, the second deputy agreed to take Laura and Jody in his vehicle. He would provide them with transportation to the Senate as soon as two additional sheriffs cruisers could join them to provide both a front and rear shield. Cooper moved his car to the parking area reserved for toll plaza employees. He then headed back to Leesburg with the other deputy to write a statement and identify the Hungarian suspect.

Cooper walked over to the two women and gave Laura a hug. "I'll be there as soon as I can," he said softly. Turning to Jody, he started to shake her hand, but seeing her tear-filled eyes, he gave her a brotherly hug. "I'm sorry about all this, but I'm glad that you are OK." She smiled weakly.

"And I'm even more glad about last night's decision. God was certainly looking out for us today," he said.

Laura didn't flinch at all. She watched Cooper's eyes as he talked to Jody. His heart, indeed, belonged to Laura alone.

WASHINGTON, D.C. October 18, 2005.

The Senate Judiciary hearing room was packed to capacity. The news media dominated the left side of the huge, wood-paneled chamber. A row of staffers sat against the wall guarding the chairs of their "principals"—the senators who would conduct the morning's hearing.

At 8:55, Senator Joseph Selden, who would chair the hearing, entered the room with three additional staff. One by one, the senators made their way to their seats on time. Both the promptness of their arrival and having the full committee in attendance were rare. A highly controversial Supreme Court nomination would guarantee a huge television audience, and the egos of the United States Senate would not allow them to miss such an opportunity for national exposure.

Senator Rose went first. The questioning by members of her own party and that of the first three Republican senators was a virtual love fest. Senator Marshall of Virginia was the last Republican on the panel. He was one of only five senators who had publicly declared opposition to the nomination. The news media was expecting fireworks during his allotted ten minutes.

"Good morning, Senator Rose," Marshall began.

"Good morning, Senator," Rose replied.

"I only have a few questions for you today."

A rumble of quiet laughter went through the knowledgeable members of the audience, who knew Marshall's reputation for fighting vigorously whenever he perceived an issue of principle to be at stake.

"My first question is to return to the question you have been asked previously, regarding whether you and President Rodman had discussed any of the cases currently before the Supreme Court. At your announcement hearing, President Rodman said that there were no such discussions. Do you recall her saying that?"

"Yes, Senator, I recall."

"Was she correct when she said it?"

"Yes, Senator, she was correct."

"Did you have discussions about any of the cases at any time since President Rodman took office, in other words, even before Justice Campbell passed away?"

"No, Senator, I had no such discussions with the president about any pending cases at any time since the inauguration."

"Specifically, referring you to the pending case that arises out of my home state of Virginia, did you and the president ever discuss the case which seeks to implement the UN Convention on the Rights of the Child?"

"No, Senator, we did not discuss the case. We, of course, discussed the treaty itself, but we have never discussed the case arising from the treaty."

"What do you think of the request in that case that seeks to impose a ban on spanking?"

"Senator, you know my record on that issue politically. I have spoken on the political point many times in this chamber. Politically, I have supported that position. But as a member of the Supreme Court, I will be asked to make legal, not, political conclusions, and I believe it is improper for me to discuss the legal conclusions I might be required to make as a member of the Court, should I have the good fortune to be confirmed."

"And you have not discussed the legal position on this issue with anyone in the White House?"

"That is correct."

"Again, as to the issue of home schooling, which is another issue in that case, have you discussed the legal issues concerning this portion of the case with any employee of the Executive Office?"

"No."

"And as to the issue of banning children from Sunday school, if their church teaches that Christianity is the only true religion and that all other religions are erroneous, have you ever discussed the legal issues concerning this portion of the case with any employee of the White House?"

"No, Senator, I have not."

"If you had discussed such issues with the administration, would you consider yourself disqualified from sitting on the case when the matter comes before the Court?"

"Yes, Senator. That is the reason I have steadfastly refused to discuss the legal issues concerning any pending case with the president or with any member of her staff."

"Thank you, Senator Rose. Those are all the questions I have."

A disappointed murmur ran through the media. No blood. Not even any testy exchanges to excerpt for the evening news.

After Marshall concluded his questions, the first panel of three witnesses was seated immediately. Jody Easler was the third.

The first two were supporters of Senator Rose. The president of the American Bar Association praised Rose and gave her the organization's highest rating. Rose had worked closely with the ABA in securing ratification of the UN treaty. A professor from Harvard Law School was second, who analyzed Rose's legal writings over her career and pronounced her to be brilliant.

Jody Easler was third because the one slot allocated for Republican witnesses had not been taken by any of the higher-ranking GOP senators. It was Marshall's slot just for the asking. He was allowed to begin the questioning for his witness.

"Ambassador Easler, you were, until July, the U.S. ambassador to the United Nations in Geneva. Is that correct?"

"Yes, Senator Marshall."

"And in that capacity, you were selected to serve as the first person from the United States to serve on the Committee on the Rights of the Child. Correct?"

"That is correct."

"Can you please tell us the function of the Committee on the Rights of the Child?"

"It is a panel of ten experts, Senator. They are chosen by the UN. The United States does not automatically get one of the slots. My appointment was seen as a celebration of the fact that the United States had finally ratified the treaty. The purpose of the panel is to enforce the treaty. In other countries, the nations take the position that the treaty creates only a moral authority. In the U.S., because of the Constitution's Supremacy Clause, the committee is well aware that the treaty creates a legal authority which binds the United States and the individual states in our own courts."

"Senator Marshall," Senator Selden interrupted. "This hearing is about a Supreme Court confirmation not a rehash of the treaty ratification. I fail to see the pertinence."

"You will see it shortly. If I may, Mr. Chairman, it is my time for questions."

Selden bristled but said nothing because he had no power to stop the questions.

"Ambassador Easler, did you ever have occasion to discuss the case that was filed by the National Education Association and the

Children's Defense Fund while you served on the Committee for the Rights of the Child in Geneva?"

"Yes, Senator Marshall, we did. On behalf of the White House, I presented several potential cases to the committee, for its strategic decision as to how to begin implementing the treaty."

"What did you recommend?"

"On behalf of the United States, we had recommended what we viewed to be a less controversial case as the first effort to implement the treaty, but the committee obviously decided to pursue the more contentious case in Virginia."

"How did the NEA and the Children's Defense Fund come to be the plaintiffs?"

"I asked them to do it."

"Did you get clearance from anyone from the administration before you did that?"

"Yes, I was told by the president's chief of staff that the president concurred in the decision."

"Were you asked to clear this course of action with anyone else before the case was filed?"

"Yes, Senator, the chief of staff told me to talk to the key supporters of the UN Convention in the Senate."

"Did you do that?"

"Yes."

"How many senators did you talk to?"

"Seven."

"How many are present in this room?"

"Three."

"Who are they?"

"Senator Selden, Senator Bagwell, and Senator Rose."

A collective gasp followed by a murmur went through the room.

"You personally talked with Senator Rose about the issues in this case?"

"Yes."

"Did you discuss the legal issues or the political issues?"

"As I spoke with Senator Rose, we primarily discussed the legal issues. She was especially concerned with the issue of standing, and she asked a good many questions about the religious freedom questions."

"What did she tell you at the conclusion of the discussion?"

"That she fully supported the decision to have the outside groups file the case. She was doubtful that we could win all of the issues in the case but expressed her personal opinion that someday we would win, once President Rodman had a chance to push through enough appointments to the High Court."

"I have no more questions," Marshall said, leaning back with a huge grin on his face.

Half of the media got up out of their seats and raced for the door, wanting to be the first to get on the air or in print with their commentary. "Thorn in Rose's Hearing" was the banner on CNN News only five minutes later.

The eruption, as well as the personal embarrassment of his participation in the discussions, caused Selden to call for a recess. A brief caucus was held in a back room between the Democratic committee members and the White House liaison. "Get that woman off the stand and away from the camera," appeared to be the conclusion. They sent word to the chamber that the break would continue through the lunch hour, and that the second panel of witnesses would begin at 1:30.

After four days of public outcry, led by many of the nation's pastors who had finally realized that their basic freedoms were truly at stake, the Rose nomination was withdrawn at the request of the White House. The president had no desire to take the heat for Rose. She planned to send Congressman Farenholt's name forward in about ten days. He had been her first choice anyway.

CHAPTER

35

WASHINGTON, D.C.
November 3, 2005.

Every seat in the historic marble chamber was filled. Suskins, VanLandingham, and an additional associate who had clerked for Justice Wilson during the 2000-2001 term sat in the three spots allocated on the left side of the courtroom for the petitioners. Cooper, dressed in a new black suit that Laura's father had bought him for the occasion, was joined by Scott Gordon and Marian Nellis.

The clerk of the court, dressed in the traditional formal morning coat, took his place on the platform perched a few feet above the lawyers, but a couple of feet below the places where the justices would soon be seated.

"Oyez! Oyez! Oyez! The Supreme Court of the United States is now in session. All those having business before the Supreme Court of the United States draw near. God save the United States and this honorable court."

Eight justices, two women and six men, filed in and stood behind their respective chairs as the clerk completed the call to order. Cooper sat nervously at the table reading over his notes again and again, while Chief Justice Thompson, in a friendly but mechanical fashion, went through the process of admitting another twenty-six lawyers to become members of the Bar of the Supreme Court of the United States.

Finally, the chief said, "National Education Association and others against Richard Thomas and others. Mr. Suskins, for the petitioners."

"Mr. Chief Justice, and may it please the Court," Suskins began. It was his tenth oral argument before the Court. During his tenure as White House counsel, he had been to numerous social functions with members of the Court.

"The question before the Court today is whether the Supremacy Clause of the Constitution will be given the full dignity that its language demands. Treaties ratified by the Constitution are to be a part of the supreme law of the land," he began.

His hand wanted to flip his hair out of his eyes, but VanLandingham had gone to the other two name partners in the firm and gotten them to force Suskins to use some hairspray. He gripped the sides of the lectern as he continued. "However, the court below determined that mere rules of standing override that which the Constitution declares to be the Supreme Law."

"But, Counsel," Justice Hurter began, "don't we derive the rules of standing from the cases and controversies language in Article III of the Constitution? Aren't you arguing that a treaty overrides a constitutional rule? How can that be?"

"Obviously, Your Honor, a treaty can't override the specific language of the Constitution. However, this Court has permitted many instances in which private persons can file lawsuits that have traditionally been brought only by the government. For example, in consumer litigation, there is the concept of the private attorney general, which allows a private lawyer to represent the public interest as if he were the attorney general of a state. In environmental litigation, the Sierra Club and others have been allowed to represent trees and rivers and lakes. In tax policy, groups like Americans for Separation of Church and State have been allowed to sue to revoke the tax-exempt status of nonprofit organizations. If these rules of standing can be imposed by statute, then groups like the National Education Association and the Children's Defense Fund can also be given standing to protect the interests of children."

"Counsel, I want to ask you about a separate issue," the chief justice said, "about the substance of your case. Doesn't your theory of parental rights fly in the face of this Court's decisions in *Wisconsin v. Yoder* where we upheld the rights of the Amish to withdraw their children from high school? How can any component of your case survive unless we reverse *Yoder?*"

"There are three components of our case, and each will survive and should prevail even if *Yoder* is retained as the prevailing law. First, nothing in *Yoder* speaks to a parents' ability to beat their child. And this Court has never upheld parental so-called spanking—"

"Counsel," Justice Kurlowich interrupted, "you say 'so-called spanking.' Did you ever get a spanking when you were a child?"

"Yes, Your Honor, I did. But those were different times."

"Perhaps they were different times, but I am wondering if your family spoke a different language. When your father spanked you, did he call it a 'spanking'?"

"Yes, he did, Your Honor. But I fail to see the point," Suskins replied with a furrowed brow.

"The point is, Mr. Suskins, that you are trying to persuade us to your position by verbal tricks. Spanking is either constitutionally protected or it is not. Using the term 'so-called spanking' adds nothing to the strength of your argument, and in fact, your confession that your own parents spanked you highlights the long-standing nature of this parental tradition, which has been protected in law for more than four hundred years of Anglo-American jurisprudence."

Justice McNeil had had enough. It was time to come to Suskins' rescue. "Mr. Suskins, is it your contention that corporal discipline—by whatever label we call it—is nothing more than a right under state common law. And under the Supremacy Clause, any state's common law right or practice must simply yield. Isn't that your argument?"

"Yes, Justice McNeil, that is one of our positions on the point. Additionally, we contend that the Constitution is a living document, and if long experience shows that child discipline practices become inextricably intertwined with child abuse and neglect, it is within the province of the United States Senate, by treaty, to ban abusive practices."

"But what about the ability to ban certain religious doctrines?" Justice Hurter asked. "Aren't you asking this Court to say that one house of Congress—the Senate—can do what the First Amendment expressly bans. It says that Congress shall make no law denying the free exercise of religion. How can these families exercise their faith if they are banned from teaching their own children certain elements of their doctrine?"

"Your Honor, we wish to make three important points on this subject. First, religious doctrine itself is not being banned. Adults can teach and learn anything that they desire. In other First Amendment arenas, such as freedom of the press, this Court has accepted a long-standing difference between children and adults in the area of sexually explicit literature and film, for example. Second, in terms of religion itself, in *Prince v. Massachusetts,* more than fifty years ago, this Court said that while adult Jehovah's Witnesses could solicit funds while passing out religious literature, it was within the power of the government to ban Jehovah's Witness children from asking for a nickel when they handed out the *Watchtower* magazine. And third, we do not contend that the Thomas and Garvis families cannot teach what they would like to their children about their own faith. We simply ask them to teach in a way that does not force their children to follow a path of bigotry by their negative attacks that are made on the validity of other faiths."

"Counsel," Justice McNeil interjected, "isn't it a fact that the vast majority of religious groups who have filed amicus briefs in this matter supported your position?"

"Yes, Your Honor, the brief of the National Council of Churches argues strongly for the position we have articulated. They agree that this Court should adopt an independent understanding of religious freedom for the child. Our position is not opposed to religious freedom at all. We simply want to preserve the child's opportunity to freely choose his or her own religion. But this is not merely our opinion or desire; it is a treaty ratified by the full authority of the Constitution once it was signed by the president and ratified by two-thirds of the Senate."

Suskins sparred effectively with the conservatives on the Court and skillfully employed the friendly questions from the liberals to advance his argument for the remainder of his thirty minutes.

Chief Justice Thompson nodded as Suskins completed and sat back down. "Mr. Stone, we'll hear from you now."

Cooper walked two steps to his left and hung onto the lectern so tightly that his knuckles were drained of any color. "Mr. Chief Justice and may it please the Court, it is the position of the respondents, the Thomas and Garvis families, that this Court should rule for my clients if you adopt any one of our three main contentions. Our first point is, that the Supreme Court of Virginia should be affirmed. Second, that this Court hold that all three requests in this case—to ban spanking, to regulate education, and to interfere with Sunday school—are inconsistent with this Court's view of the constitutional rights of parents. Third, and this would be the ultimate disposition we desire, to rule that the original intent of the framers of the Constitution forbids the use of international treaties to govern America's domestic policy. This use of the treaty power effectively trumps the principle of self-government. If unelected officials in Geneva are afforded the ability to control America's domestic policy, constitutional government has been bargained away. If any principle can join life, liberty, and the pursuit of happiness as a self-evident truth, the principle of self-government should be the one."

"Counsel, do we have to go as far as your third theory for you to prevail?" the chief justice asked.

"No, Your Honor. You do not. If we prevail on any of these arguments, we should win. A simple affirmation of the ruling on standing results in a victory for these two families. But, if the Court does that and no more, a week later or a month later, the same forces that brought this lawsuit will reorganize under the banner of some government agency and start it all over again. A new suit will be filed against these families or, more likely, other victims. We ask for a decision on one of our theories that brings lasting victory."

Justice VonDuyke, one of the dedicated liberals, spoke quickly. "Isn't it true that this Court has never embraced anything that even comes close to your third theory? We have never said that treaties cannot be used to control domestic policy, have we, Counsel?"

"That is true, Your Honor. But the reason is clear. Our government has never before given away this much control over our internal affairs. It is this UN treaty and not our arguments that are unprecedented."

"But, Counsel, the same things could be said about international agreements like NAFTA and GATT, couldn't they? We turned decision making about economic issues over to international bodies in those agreements, did we not?" VonDuyke continued.

"Yes, Your Honor. But NAFTA and GATT were not treaties, but ordinary legislation passed by simple majorities in both houses of Congress."

"What difference is there between treaties and ordinary legislation? Both give away our sovereignty to a degree, don't they?" Justice McKenna asked.

"In terms of the principles of self-government you have a point, Justice McKenna. But, just because Congress has violated the principle of self-government on a relatively small scale, it does not excuse a massive violation of that principle in this treaty." Cooper quickly sipped from the water glass on his left side.

Justice McNeil took advantage of the moment. "But it does establish that you are wrong when you say that the idea of giving away the principle of self-government—if you wish to call it that—is unprecedented. There are plenty of precedents, as you are forced to concede. Maybe they do not seem so massive or so dramatic to you, but the principle is well-established. We have thousands of treaties and executive international agreements in force. We have bound ourselves to follow international law on countless occasions," he lectured.

"Maybe the time to stop the erosion of the principle of self-government is on this occasion, Your Honor."

"An argument worthy of the Senate, Counsel. But you are across the street in the Supreme Court of the United States. Tell us which precedent and which language of the Constitution requires the result you urge."

"Your Honor, the whole theory of the separation of powers is derived from the clear language of the Constitution. It is a cousin of the principle of federalism. Taken as a whole, it leads to the well-established rule that the federal government and each branch of government cannot invade the authority of another branch or the authority of the states. This treaty doesn't violate just one part of the Constitution; it violates the entire structure of the Constitution by allowing ten people in Geneva to decide that all the votes of all the voters in the United States do not matter, whether the ballots are cast for state or federal office holders."

During the entire procedure, neither Justice Lorence nor Justice Freed asked any questions of attorneys for either petitioners or the respondents. Cooper fended off another half-dozen similar questions from McNeil for what seemed to be hours, but it was actually about ten minutes. McNeil's commitment to internationalism was clearly evident to all in the chamber.

"Counsel, your time is up," the chief justice announced. "The Court will be in recess."

That afternoon the eight members of the Court met in the Justice's Conference room, as is their tradition after an oral argument. They shook hands all around for the second time that day and assumed their assigned seats around the massive table.

"Any discussion before we vote?" the chief justice asked.

"Suskins was his normal self, except did anyone notice he didn't flip his hair at all today? What was up with that?" Hurter asked.

"I have to say that you had a feisty young man on your side of the case," VonDuyke said with a grin. "Seemed more like a tryout for a Senate role than an oral argument though."

"I thought it was a bit reminiscent of the argument that Daniel Webster might have made," Hurter replied.

"OK, OK," the chief said. "If we aren't going to discuss the merits, then I will just take the vote. Justice VonDuyke, you can begin," he said to the justice sitting on his right."

VonDuyke looked up from his notes without hesitation. "I vote to reverse. There is little doubt in my mind that the Supreme Court of Virginia got it wrong on the standing issue. Suskins is absolutely right about the examples from environmental law and consumer law. We allow the Sierra Club to sue to protect tress; there is no reason we should reach a different conclusion when the National Education Association wants to sue to protect children. And, it should be self-evident that I am not buying any of Mr. Stone's other unprecedented theories. I'm for reversal."

Justice Hurter, sitting in order of appointment to the bench, was next. "I want to affirm the lower court. But, I am willing to sign an opinion that goes beyond the mere issue of standing. I think that Stone was right and his brief and the amicus briefs were convincing concerning the views of the Founders. There is no way those who started this nation believed that the treaty power would be used to hand over the domestic law-making authority of this nation to an international group. I agree with each of Stone's three contentions."

"I'm for affirmance," said Justice Kurlowich, leaning back in the leather conference room chair. "But, while I am intrigued with Mr. Stone's arguments on the merits, I am unwilling to go there at this time. He wins on the standing issue—that's enough for now."

MacNeil just shook his head. "Of course I am voting for reversal. I agree with what Justice VonDuyke said a moment ago."

"That's my vote as well," McKenna said quickly as the vote moved around the table.

Freed shifted in his chair. He picked up his pen. He leaned back. He placed his pen on the table. He leaned back again. McKenna and VonDuyke gave each other knowing, exasperated glances. Freed simply couldn't bring himself to make a decision, as usual.

"Well," Freed began with a sigh, "I guess I am for reversal. I think Justice VonDuyke has a good point about the Sierra Club, and I like to follow precedent. So, I guess you can put me down for reversal."

Lorence spoke quickly. "Affirmance. Our courts will simply be overrun with all manner of interlopers if we expand our rules of standing in this area. I'm not interested in any of Mr. Stone's other theories though. Let's diffuse this case with the simple answer."

"We can diffuse it for today," Chief Justice began, "but some form of it will be back shortly, and we *will* have to deal with the merits of this treaty if the government files the lawsuit. But since the votes have split the way they have, the only thing for me to do presently is to affirm on the issue of standing.

He looked at his notes to make sure. "So the vote is 4-4. Justice Hurter, you can write the plurality opinion if you like, and Justice McKenna, why don't you write the dissent?"

"Can't we wait for Congressman Farenholt to be confirmed and then reschedule oral argument?" McNeil asked.

"No, Justice McNeil. We will not. We have heard oral argument. We are an evenly divided court, and the decision of the Supreme Court of Virginia will be affirmed without an opinion of the Court."

"It will take me at least a month to prepare my dissent, and that will take me until Farenholt is confirmed. Then we'll have his potential vote and we will have to do it again. So what's the difference?" McNeil contended.

"The difference is that I am the chief justice of the United States, and I control the docket of the Court unless there are five votes to overturn me. You have forty-eight hours to prepare your dissent. I will prepare the per curium decision that simply announces that we affirm without opinion. Nothing concerning this case will remain on our docket when Farenholt is confirmed. See you tomorrow at 9:30. Good day."

PURCELLVILLE, VIRGINIA.
November 7, 2005.

Deanna called it an early Thanksgiving dinner. She and her children were free, at least for now, from any legal attack. She wanted to celebrate with about forty of her closest friends. Jeanne Garvis coordinated with all the guests to make the evening also a surprise wedding shower for Cooper and Laura. The couple got more serving dishes than they would ever need and not nearly enough wrenches and pliers, Cooper observed quietly to Rick when the women weren't listening.

About fifteen of the group stayed up late to watch Jody Easler on *Politics & Hollywood.* She was growing more and more skilled on the show, and her worldview was steadily changing. Cooper found a church for her in the Los Angeles area with a dynamic pastor and a strong home Bible study program.

Just after the show, Jody called Deanna's home as planned. Deanna and Jeanne both got on the phone to personally thank her for sacrificing her career for the good of their children and the good of America.

Laura asked for the phone next. "Hey, Jody, you were hilarious tonight. We all loved it."

"Thanks, Laura. Sometimes I wish the program were based in Washington, but this is a good breather for me from all my old acquaintances. But I wanted to call and give my congratulations to Cooper for winning the case and best wishes to both of you for your upcoming wedding."

"Actually, Jody, I wanted to talk to you about the wedding. Do you think there is any chance you can come a day early? Cooper and I have talked it over, and we would both love for you to be a bridesmaid."

"I'm there. You can count on it."

"God bless you, Jody."

"He has," she replied.

GENEVA, SWITZERLAND. *November 8, 2005.*

"So, Ambassador Stoddard, your administration is ready to bring the first of the new lawsuits on behalf of the National Commission on Children?" Erzabet Kadar asked.

"Yes, Farenholt was just confirmed on the Supreme Court. So we are ready to pursue the spanking case, and we have picked Madison, Wisconsin, as the venue," Nora Stoddard replied.

"Where are the next cases?"

"We will go after home schooling in California, the withdrawal of children from public school sex education in South Carolina, the incarceration of juvenile offenders in Florida, and the failure to spend enough on children's health issues in Massachusetts. We believe we can have them all wrapped up well before the 2006 election cycle," Stoddard said, looking at a list in front of her.

"Why is that important?" Hua Zhuan, the committee member from China, asked.

"Because the election can change the balance of power in the Senate, and the House could refuse to fund our department. If we lose our pro-treaty majority, we are dead in the water. We need to work fast so that the culture gets used to the idea of accepting UN leadership, and so families simply recognize that they must comply with our standards."

"One election can change all that?" Hua Zhuan continued.

"In the United States, one election can change everything."

Convention on the Rights of the Child

U.N. General Assembly
Document A/RES/44/25 (12 December 1989)
with Annex

The General Assembly,

Recalling its previous resolutions, especially resolutions 33/166 of 20 December 1978 and 43/112 of 8 December 1988, and those of the Commission on Human Rights and the Economic and Social Council related to the question of a convention on the rights of the child,

Taking note, in particular, of Commission on Human Rights resolution 1989/57 of 8 March 1989, by which the Commission decided to transmit the draft convention on the rights of the child, through the Economic and Social Council, to the General Assembly, and Economic and Social Council resolution 1989/79 of 24 May 1989,

Reaffirming that children's rights require special protection and call for continuous improvement of the situation of children all over the world, as well as for their development and education in conditions of peace and security,

Profoundly concerned that the situation of children in many parts of the world remains critical as a result of inadequate social conditions, natural disasters, armed conflicts, exploitation, illiteracy, hunger and disability, and convinced that urgent and effective national and international action is called for,

Mindful of the important role of the United Nations Children's Fund and of that of the United Nations in promoting the well-being of children and their development,

Convinced that an international convention on the rights of the child, as a standard-setting accomplishment of the United Nations in the field of human rights, would make a positive contribution to protecting children's rights and ensuring their well-being,

Bearing in mind that 1989 marks the thirtieth anniversary of the Declaration of the Rights of the Child and the tenth anniversary of the International Year of the Child,

1. Expresses its appreciation to the Commission on Human Rights for having concluded the elaboration of the draft convention on the rights of the child;

2. Adopts and opens for signature, ratification and accession the Convention on the Rights of the Child contained in the annex to the present resolution;

3. Calls upon all Member States to consider signing and ratifying or acceding to the Convention as a matter of priority and expresses the hope that it will come into force at an early date;

4. Requests the Secretary-General to provide all the facilities and assistance necessary for dissemination of information on the Convention;

5. Invites United Nations agencies and organizations, as well as intergovernmental and non-governmental organizations, to intensify their efforts with a view to disseminating information on the Convention and to promoting its understanding;

6. Requests the Secretary-General to submit to the General Assembly at its forty-fifth session a report on the status of the Convention on the Rights of the Child;

7. Decides to consider the report of the Secretary-General at its forty-fifth session under an item entitled "Implementation of the Convention on the Rights of the Child".

61st plenary meeting
20 November 1989

ANNEX
Convention on the Rights of the Child
PREAMBLE

The States Parties to the present Convention,

Considering that, in accordance with the principles proclaimed in the Charter of the United Nations, recognition of the inherent dignity and of the equal and inalienable rights of all members of the human family is the foundation of freedom, justice and peace in the world,

Bearing in mind that the peoples of the United Nations have, in the Charter, reaffirmed their faith in fundamental human rights and in the dignity and worth of the human person, and have determined to promote social progress and better standards of life in larger freedom,

Recognizing that the United Nations has, in the Universal Declaration of Human Rights and in the International Covenants on Human Rights, proclaimed and agreed that everyone is entitled to all the rights and freedoms set forth therein, without distinction of any kind, such as race, colour, sex, language, religion, political or other opinion, national or social origin, property, birth or other status,

Recalling that, in the Universal Declaration of Human Rights, the United Nations has proclaimed that childhood is entitled to special care and assistance,

Convinced that the family, as the fundamental group of society and the natural environment for the growth and well-being of all its members and particularly children, should be afforded the necessary protection and assistance so that it can fully assume its responsibilities within the community,

Recognizing that the child, for the full and harmonious development of his or her personality, should grow up in a family environment, in an atmosphere of happiness, love and understanding,

Considering that the child should be fully prepared to live an individual life in society, and brought up in the spirit of the ideals proclaimed in the Charter of the United Nations, and in particular in the spirit of peace, dignity, tolerance, freedom, equality and solidarity,

Bearing in mind that the need to extend particular care to the child has been stated in the Geneva Declaration of the Rights of the Child of 1924 and in the Declaration of the Rights of the Child adopted by the General Assembly on 20 November 1959 and recognized in the Universal Declaration of Human Rights, in the International Covenant on Civil and Political Rights (in particular in articles 23 and 24), in the International Covenant on Economic, Social and Cultural Rights (in particular in article 10) and in the statutes and relevant instruments of specialized agencies and international organizations concerned with the welfare of children,

Bearing in mind that, as indicated in the Declaration of the Rights of the Child, "the child, by reason of his physical and mental immaturity, needs special safeguards and care, including appropriate legal protection, before as well as after birth",

Recalling the provisions of the Declaration on Social and Legal Principles relating to the Protection and Welfare of Children, with Special Reference to Foster Placement and Adoption Nationally and Internationally; the United Nations Standard Minimum Rules for the Administration of Juvenile justice (The Beijing Rules); and the Declaration on the Protection of Women and Children in Emergency and Armed Conflict,

Recognizing that, in all countries in the world, there are children living in exceptionally difficult conditions, and that such children need special consideration,

Taking due account of the importance of the traditions and cultural values of each people for the protection and harmonious development of the child,

Recognizing the importance of international co-operation for improving the living conditions of children in every country, in particular in the developing countries,

Have agreed as follows:

PART I

Article 1

For the purposes of the present Convention, a child means every human being below the age of eighteen years unless, under the law applicable to the child, majority is attained earlier.

Article 2

1. States Parties shall respect and ensure the rights set forth in the present Convention to each child within their jurisdiction without discrimination of any kind, irrespective of the child's or his or her parent's or legal guardian's race, colour, sex, language, religion, political or other opinion, national, ethnic or social origin, property, disability, birth or other status.

2. States Parties shall take all appropriate measures to ensure that the child is protected against all forms of discrimination or punishment on the basis of the status, activities, expressed opinions, or beliefs of the child's parents, legal guardians, or family members.

Article 3

1. In all actions concerning children, whether undertaken by public or private social welfare institutions, courts of law, administrative authorities or legislative bodies, the best interests of the child shall be a primary consideration.

2. States Parties undertake to ensure the child such protection and care as is necessary for his or her well-being, taking into account the rights and duties of his or her parents, legal guardians, or other individuals legally responsible for him or her, and, to this end, shall take all appropriate legislative and administrative measures.

3. States Parties shall ensure that the institutions, services and facilities responsible for the care or protection of children shall conform with the standards established by competent authorities, particularly in the areas of safety, health, in the number and suitability of their staff, as well as competent supervision.

Article 4

States Parties shall undertake all appropriate legislative, administrative, and other measures for the implementation of the rights recognized in the present Convention. With regard to economic, social and cultural rights, States Parties shall undertake such measures to the maximum extent of their available resources and, where needed, within the framework of international co-operation.

Article 5

States Parties shall respect the responsibilities, rights and duties of parents or, where applicable, the members of the extended family or community as provided for by local custom, legal guardians or other persons legally responsible for the child, to provide, in a manner consistent with the evolving capacities of the child, appropriate direction and guidance in the exercise by the child of the rights recognized in the present Convention.

Article 6

1. States Parties recognize that every child has the inherent right to life.

2. States Parties shall ensure to the maximum extent possible the survival and development of the child.

Article 7

1. The child shall be registered immediately after birth and shall have the right from birth to a name, the right to acquire a nationality and, as far as possible, the right to know and be cared for by his or her parents.

2. States Parties shall ensure the implementation of these rights in accordance with their national law and their obligations under the relevant international instruments in this field, in particular where the child would otherwise be stateless.

Article 8

1. States Parties undertake to respect the right of the child to preserve his or her identity, including nationality, name and family relations as recognized by law without unlawful interference.

2. Where a child is illegally deprived of some or all of the elements of his or her identity, States Parties shall provide appropriate assistance and protection, with a view to speedily re-establishing his or her identity.

Article 9

1. States Parties shall ensure that a child shall not be separated from his or her parents against their will, except when competent authorities subject to

judicial review determine, in accordance with applicable law and procedures, that such separation is necessary for the best interests of the child. Such determination may be necessary in a particular case such as one involving abuse or neglect of the child by the parents, or one where the parents are living separately and a decision must be made as to the child's place of residence.

2. In any proceedings pursuant to paragraph 1 of the present article, all interested parties shall be given an opportunity to participate in the proceedings and make their views known.

3. States Parties shall respect the right of the child who is separated from one or both parents to maintain personal relations and direct contact with both parents on a regular basis, except if it is contrary to the child's best interests.

4. Where such separation results from any action initiated by a State Party, such as the detention, imprisonment, exile, deportation or death (including death arising from any cause while the person is in the custody of the State) of one or both parents or of the child, that State Party shall, upon request, provide the parents, the child or, if appropriate, another member of the family with the essential information concerning the whereabouts of the absent member(s) of the family unless the provision of the information would be detrimental to the well-being of the child. States Parties shall further ensure that the submission of such a request shall of itself entail no adverse consequences for the person(s) concerned.

Article 10

1. In accordance with the obligation of States Parties under article 9, paragraph 1, applications by a child or his or her parents to enter or leave a State Party for the purpose of family reunification shall be dealt with by States Parties in a positive, humane and expeditious manner. States Parties shall further ensure that the submission of such a request shall entail no adverse consequences for the applicants and for the members of their family.

2. A child whose parents reside in different States shall have the right to maintain on a regular basis, save in exceptional circumstances personal relations and direct contacts with both parents. Towards that end and in accordance with the obligation of States Parties under article 9, paragraph 2, States Parties shall respect the right of the child and his or her parents to leave any country, including their own, and to enter their own country. The right to leave any country shall be subject only to such restrictions as are prescribed by law and which are necessary to protect the national security, public order (order public), public health or morals or the rights and freedoms of others and are consistent with the other rights recognized in the present Convention.

Article 11

1. States Parties shall take measures to combat the illicit transfer and non-return of children abroad.

2. To this end, States Parties shall promote the conclusion of bilateral or multilateral agreements or accession to existing agreements.

Article 12

1. States Parties shall assure to the child who is capable of forming his or her own views the right to express those views freely in all matters affecting the child, the views of the child being given due weight in accordance with the age and maturity of the child.

2. For this purpose, the child shall in particular be provided the opportunity to be heard in any judicial and administrative proceedings affecting the child, either directly, or through a representative or an appropriate body, in a manner consistent with the procedural rules of national law.

Article 13

1. The child shall have the right to freedom of expression; this right shall include freedom to seek, receive and impart information and ideas of all kinds, regardless of frontiers, either orally, in writing or in print, in the form of art, or through any other media of the child's choice.

2. The exercise of this right may be subject to certain restrictions, but these shall only be such as are provided by law and are necessary:

(a) For respect of the rights or reputations of others; or

(b) For the protection of national security or of public order (order public), or of public health or morals.

Article 14

1. States Parties shall respect the right of the child to freedom of thought, conscience and religion.

2. States Parties shall respect the rights and duties of the parents and, when applicable, legal guardians, to provide direction to the child in the exercise of his or her right in a manner consistent with the evolving capacities of the child.

3. Freedom to manifest one's religion or beliefs may be subject only to such limitations as are prescribed by law and are necessary to protect public safety, order, health or morals, or the fundamental rights and freedoms of others.

Article 15

1. States Parties recognize the rights of the child to freedom of association and to freedom of peaceful assembly.

2. No restrictions may be placed on the exercise of these rights other than those imposed in conformity with the law and which are necessary in a democratic society in the interests of national security or public safety, public order (order public), the protection of public health or morals or the protection of the rights and freedoms of others.

Article 16

1. No child shall be subjected to arbitrary or unlawful interference with his or her privacy, family, home or correspondence, nor to unlawful attacks on his or her honor and reputation.

2. The child has the right to the protection of the law against such interference or attacks.

Article 17

States Parties recognize the important function performed by the mass media and shall ensure that the child has access to information and material from a diversity of national and international sources, especially those aimed at the promotion of his or her social, spiritual and moral well-being and physical and mental health. To this end, States Parties shall:

(a) Encourage the mass media to disseminate information and material of social and cultural benefit to the child and in accordance with the spirit of article 29;

(b) Encourage international co-operation in the production, exchange and dissemination of such information and material from a diversity of cultural, national and international sources;

(c) Encourage the production and dissemination of children's books;

(d) Encourage the mass media to have particular regard to the linguistic needs of the child who belongs to a minority group or who is indigenous;

(e) Encourage the development of appropriate guidelines for the protection of the child from information and material injurious to his or her well-being, bearing in mind the provisions of articles 13 and 18.

Article 18

1. States Parties shall use their best efforts to ensure recognition of the principle that both parents have common responsibilities for the upbringing and development of the child. Parents or, as the case may be, legal guardians, have the primary responsibility for the upbringing and development of the child. The best interests of the child will be their basic concern.

2. For the purpose of guaranteeing and promoting the rights set forth in the present Convention, States Parties shall render appropriate assistance to parents and legal guardians in the performance of their child-rearing responsibilities and shall ensure the development of institutions, facilities and services for the care of children.

3. States Parties shall take all appropriate measures to ensure that children of working parents have the right to benefit from child-care services and facilities for which they are eligible.

Article 19

1. States Parties shall take all appropriate legislative, administrative, social and educational measures to protect the child from all forms of physical or mental violence, injury or abuse, neglect or negligent treatment, maltreatment or exploitation, including sexual abuse, while in the care of parent(s), legal guardian(s) or any other person who has the care of the child.

2. Such protective measures should, as appropriate, include effective procedures for the establishment of social programs to provide necessary support for the child and for those who have the care of the child, as well as for other forms of prevention and for identification, reporting, referral, investigation, treatment and follow-up of instances of child maltreatment described heretofore, and, as appropriate, for judicial involvement.

Article 20

1. A child temporarily or permanently deprived of his or her family environment, or in whose own best interests cannot be allowed to remain in that environment, shall be entitled to special protection and assistance provided by the State.

2. States Parties shall in accordance with their national laws ensure alternative care for such a child.

3. Such care could include, inter alia, foster placement, kafalah of Islamic law, adoption or if necessary placement in suitable institutions for the care of children. When considering solutions, due regard shall be paid to the desirability of continuity in a child's upbringing and to the child's ethnic, religious, cultural and linguistic background.

Article 21

States Parties that recognize and/or permit the system of adoption shall ensure that the best interests of the child shall be the paramount consideration and they shall:

(a) Ensure that the adoption of a child is authorized only by competent authorities who determine, in accordance with applicable law and procedures and on the basis of all pertinent and reliable information, that the adoption is permissible in view of the child's status concerning parents, relatives and legal guardians and that, if required, the persons concerned have given their informed consent to the adoption on the basis of such counselling as may be necessary;

(b) Recognize that inter-country adoption may be considered as an alternative means of child's care, if the child cannot be placed in a foster or an adoptive family or cannot in any suitable manner be cared for in the child's country of origin;

(c) Ensure that the child concerned by inter-country adoption enjoys safeguards and standards equivalent to those existing in the case of national adoption;

(d) Take all appropriate measures to ensure that, in inter-country adoption, the placement does not result in improper financial gain for those involved in it;

(e) Promote, where appropriate, the objectives of the present article by concluding bilateral or multilateral arrangements or agreements, and endeavor, within this framework, to ensure that the placement of the child in another country is carried out by competent authorities or organs.

Article 22

1. States Parties shall take appropriate measures to ensure that a child who is seeking refugee status or who is considered a refugee in accordance with applicable international or domestic law and procedures shall, whether unaccompanied or accompanied by his or her parents or by any other person, receive appropriate protection and humanitarian assistance in the enjoyment of applicable rights set forth in the present Convention and in other international human rights or humanitarian instruments to which the said States are Parties.

2. For this purpose, States Parties shall provide, as they consider appropriate, co-operation in any efforts by the United Nations and other competent intergovernmental organizations or non-governmental organizations co-operating with the United Nations to protect and assist such a child and to trace the parents or other members of the family of any refugee child in order to obtain information necessary for reunification with his or her family In cases where no parents or other members of the family can be found, the child shall be accorded the same protection as any other child permanently or temporarily deprived of his or her family environment for any reason, as set forth in the present Convention.

Article 23

1. States Parties recognize that a mentally or physically disabled child should enjoy a full and decent life, in conditions which ensure dignity, promote self-reliance and facilitate the child's active participation in the community.

2. States Parties recognize the right of the disabled child to special care and shall encourage and ensure the extension, subject to available resources, to the eligible child and those responsible for his or her care, of assistance for which application is made and which is appropriate to the child's condition and to the circumstances of the parents or others caring for the child.

3. Recognizing the special needs of a disabled child, assistance extended in accordance with paragraph 2 of the present article shall be provided free of charge, whenever possible, taking into account the financial resources of the parents or others caring for the child, and shall be designed to ensure that the disabled child has effective access to and receives education, training, health

care services, rehabilitation services, preparation for employment and recreation opportunities in a manner conducive to the child's achieving the fullest possible social integration and individual development, including his or her cultural and spiritual development.

4. States Parties shall promote, in the spirit of international co-operation, the exchange of appropriate information in the field of preventive health care and of medical, psychological and functional treatment of disabled children, including dissemination of and access to information concerning methods of rehabilitation, education and vocational services, with the aim of enabling States Parties to improve their capabilities and skills and to widen their experience in these areas. In this regard, particular account shall be taken of the needs of developing countries.

Article 24

1. States Parties recognize the right of the child to the enjoyment of the highest attainable standard of health and to facilities for the treatment of illness and rehabilitation of health. States Parties shall strive to ensure that no child is deprived of his or her right of access to such health care services forth in the present Convention and in other international human rights or humanitarian instruments to which the said States are Parties.

2. For this purpose, States Parties shall provide, as they consider appropriate, co-operation in any efforts by the United Nations and other competent intergovernmental organizations or non-governmental organizations cooperating with the United Nations to protect and assist such a child and to trace the parents or other members of the family of any refugee child in order to obtain information necessary for reunification with his or her family. In cases where no parents or other members of the family can be found, the child shall be accorded the same protection as any other child permanently or temporarily deprived of his or her family environment for any reason, as set forth in the present Convention.

States Parties shall pursue full implementation of this right and, in particular, shall take appropriate measures:

(a) To diminish infant and child mortality;

(b) To ensure the provision of necessary medical assistance and health care to all children with emphasis on the development of primary health care;

(c) To combat disease and malnutrition, including within the framework of primary health care, through, iner alia, the application of readily available technology and through the provision of adequate nutritious foods and clean drinking-water, taking into consideration the dangers and risks of environmental pollution;

(d) To ensure appropriate pre-natal and post-natal health care for mothers;

(e) To ensure that all segments of society, in particular parents and children, are informed, have access to education and are supported in the use of basic knowledge of child health and nutrition, the advantages of breast-feeding, hygiene and environmental sanitation and the prevention of accidents;

(f) To develop preventive health care, guidance for parents and family planning education and services.

3. States Parties shall take all effective and appropriate measures with a view to abolishing traditional practices prejudicial to the health of children.

4. States Parties undertake to promote and encourage international co-operation with a view to achieving progressively the full realization of the right recognized in the present article. In this regard, particular account shall be taken of the needs of developing countries.

Article 25

States Parties recognize the right of a child who has been placed by the competent authorities for the purposes of care, protection or treatment of his or her physical or mental health, to a periodic review of the treatment provided to the child and all other circumstances relevant to his or her placement.

Article 26

1. States Parties shall recognize for every child the right to benefit from social security, including social insurance, and shall take the necessary measures to achieve the full realization of this right in accordance with their national law.

2. The benefits should, where appropriate, be granted, taking into account the resources and the circumstances of the child and persons having responsibility for the maintenance of the child, as well as any other consideration relevant to an application for benefits made by or on behalf of the child.

Article 27

1. States Parties recognize the right of every child to a standard of living adequate for the child's physical, mental, spiritual, moral and social development.

2. The parent(s) or others responsible for the child have the primary responsibility to secure, within their abilities and financial capacities, the conditions of living necessary for the child's development.

3. States Parties, in accordance with national conditions and within their means, shall take appropriate measures to assist parents and others responsible for the child to implement this right and shall in case of need provide material assistance and support programs, particularly with regard to nutrition, clothing and housing.

4. States Parties shall take all appropriate measures to secure the recovery of maintenance for the child from the parents or other persons having financial

responsibility for the child, both within the State Party and from abroad. In particular, where the person having financial responsibility for the child lives in a State different from that of the child, States Parties shall promote the accession to international agreements or the conclusion of such agreements, as well as the making of other appropriate arrangements.

Article 28

1. States Parties recognize the right of the child to education, and with a view to achieving this right progressively and on the basis of equal opportunity, they shall, in particular:

(a) Make primary education compulsory and available free to all;

(b) Encourage the development of different forms of secondary education, including general and vocational education, make them available and accessible to every child, and take appropriate measures such as the introduction of free education and offering financial assistance in case of need;

(c) Make higher education accessible to all on the basis of capacity by every appropriate means;

(d) Make educational and vocational information and guidance available and accessible to all children;

(e) Take measures to encourage regular attendance at schools and the reduction of drop-out rates.

2. States Parties shall take all appropriate measures to ensure that school discipline is administered in a manner consistent with the child's human dignity and in conformity with the present Convention.

3. States Parties shall promote and encourage international co-operation in matters relating to education, in particular with a view to contributing to the elimination of ignorance and illiteracy throughout the world and facilitating access to scientific and technical knowledge and modern teaching methods. In this regard, particular account shall be taken of the needs of developing countries.

Article 29

States Parties agree that the education of the child shall be directed to:

(a) The development of the child's personality, talents and mental and physical abilities to their fullest potential;

(b) The development of respect for human rights and fundamental freedoms, and for the principles enshrined in the Charter of the United Nations;

(c) The development of respect for the child's parents, his or her own cultural identity, language and values, for the national values of the country in which the child is living; the country from which he or she may originate, and for civilizations different from his or her own;

(d) The preparation of the child for responsible life in a free society, in the spirit of understanding, peace, tolerance, equality of sexes, and friendship among all peoples, ethnic, national and religious groups and persons of indigenous origin;

(e) The development of respect for the natural environment.

2. No part of the present article or article 28 shall be construed so as to interfere with the liberty of individuals and bodies to establish and direct educational institutions, subject always to the observance of the principles set forth in paragraph 1 of the present article and to the requirements that the education given in such institutions shall conform to such minimum standards as may be laid down by the State.

Article 30

In those States in which ethnic, religious or linguistic minorities or persons of indigenous origin exist, a child belonging to such a minority or who is indigenous shall not be denied the right, in community with other members of his or her group, to enjoy his or her own culture, to profess and practice his or her own religion, or to use his or her own language.

Article 31

1. States Parties recognize the right of the child to rest and leisure, to engage in play and recreational activities appropriate to the age of the child and to participate freely in cultural life and the arts.

2. States Parties shall respect and promote the right of the child to participate fully in cultural and artistic life and shall encourage the provision of appropriate and equal opportunities for cultural, artistic, recreational and leisure activity.

Article 32

1. States Parties recognize the right of the child to be protected from economic exploitation and from performing any work that is likely to be hazardous or to interfere with the child's education, or to be harmful to the child's health or physical, mental, spiritual, moral or social development.

2. States Parties shall take legislative, administrative, social and educational measures to ensure the implementation of the present article. To this end, and having regard to the relevant provisions of other international instruments, States Parties shall in particular:

(a) Provide for a minimum age or minimum ages for admission to employment;

(b) Provide for appropriate regulation of the hours and conditions of employment;

(c) Provide for appropriate penalties or other sanctions to ensure the, effective enforcement of the present article.

Article 33

States Parties shall take all appropriate measures, including legislative, administrative, social and educational measures, to protect children from the illicit use of narcotic drugs and psychotropic substances as defined in the relevant international treaties, and to prevent the use of children in the illicit production and trafficking of such substances.

Article 34

States Parties undertake to protect the child from all forms of sexual exploitation and sexual abuse. For these purposes, States Parties shall in particular take all appropriate national, bilateral and multilateral measures to prevent:

(a) The inducement or coercion of a child to engage in any unlawful sexual activity;

(b) The exploitative use of children in prostitution or other unlawful sexual practices;

(c)The exploitative use of children in pornographic performances and materials.

Article 35

States Parties shall take all appropriate national, bilateral and multilateral measures to prevent the abduction of, the sale of or traffic in children for any purpose or in any form.

Article 36

States Parties shall protect the child against all other forms of exploitation prejudicial to any aspects of the child's welfare.

Article 37

States Parties shall ensure that:

(a) No child shall be subjected to torture or other cruel, inhuman or degrading treatment or punishment. Neither capital punishment nor life imprisonment without possibility of release shall be imposed for offenses committed by persons below eighteen years of age;

(b) No child shall be deprived of his or her liberty unlawfully or arbitrarily. The arrest, detention or imprisonment of a child shall be in conformity with the law and shall be used only as a measure of last resort and for the shortest appropriate period of time;

(c) Every child deprived of liberty shall be treated with humanity and respect for the inherent dignity of the human person, and in a manner which takes into account the needs of persons of his or her age. In particular, every child deprived of liberty shall be separated from adults unless it is considered in the child's best interest not to do so and shall have the right to maintain contact with his or her family through correspondence and visits, save in exceptional circumstances;

(d) Every child deprived of his or her liberty shall have the right to prompt access to legal and other appropriate assistance, as well as the right to challenge the legality of the deprivation of his or her liberty before a court or other competent, independent and impartial authority, and to a prompt decision on any such action.

Article 38

1. States Parties undertake to respect and to ensure respect for rules of international humanitarian law applicable to them in armed conflicts which are relevant to the child.

2. States Parties shall take all feasible measures to ensure that persons who have not attained the age of fifteen years do not take a direct part in hostilities.

3. States Parties shall refrain from recruiting any person who has not attained the age of fifteen years into their armed forces. In recruiting among those persons who have attained the age of fifteen years but who have not attained the age of eighteen years, States Parties shall endeavor to give priority to those who are oldest.

4. In accordance with their obligations under international humanitarian law to protect the civilian population in armed conflicts, States Parties shall take all feasible measures to ensure protection and care of children who are affected by an armed conflict.

Article 39

States Parties shall take all appropriate measures to promote physical and psychological recovery and social reintegration of a child victim of: any form of neglect, exploitation, or abuse; torture or any other form of cruel, inhuman or degrading treatment or punishment; or armed conflicts. Such recovery and reintegration shall take place in an environment which fosters the health, self-respect and dignity of the child.

Article 40

1. States Parties recognize the right of every child alleged as, accused of, or recognized as having infringed the penal law to be treated in a manner consistent with the promotion of the child's sense of dignity and worth, which reinforces the child's respect for the human rights and fundamental freedoms of others and which takes into account the child's age and the desirability of promoting the child's reintegration and the child's assuming a constructive role in society.

2. To this end, and having regard to the relevant provisions of international instruments, States Parties shall, in particular, ensure that:

(a) No child shall be alleged as, be accused of, or recognized as having infringed the penal law by reason of acts or omissions tɪ t were not prohibited by national or international law at the time they were cᴄ ᴨmitted; (b) Every child alleged as or accused of having infringed the penal law ɪ.as at least the following guarantees:

(i) To be presumed innocent until proven guilty according to law;

(ii) To be informed promptly and directly of the charges against him or her, and, if appropriate, through his or her parents or legal guardians, and to have legal or other appropriate assistance in the preparation and presentation of his or her defense;

(iii) To have the matter determined without delay by a competent, independent and impartial authority or judicial body in a fair hearing according to law, in the presence of legal or other appropriate assistance and, unless it is considered not to be in the best interest of the child, in particular, taking into account his or her age or situation, his or her parents or legal guardians;

(iv) Not to be compelled to give testimony or to confess quilt; to examine or have examined adverse witnesses and to obtain the participation and examination of witnesses on his or her behalf under conditions of equality;

(v) If considered to have infringed the penal law, to have this decision and any measures imposed in consequence thereof reviewed by a higher competent, independent and impartial authority or judicial body according to law;

(vi) To have the free assistance of an interpreter if the child cannot understand or speak the language used;

(vii) To have his or her privacy fully respected at all stages of the proceedings.

3. States Parties shall seek to promote the establishment of laws, procedures, authorities and institutions specifically applicable to children alleged as, accused of, or recognized as having infringed the penal law, and, in particular:

(a) The establishment of a minimum age below which children shall be presumed not to have the capacity to infringe the penal law;

(b) Whenever appropriate and desirable, measures for dealing with such children without resorting to judicial proceedings, providing that human rights and legal safeguards are fully respected.

4. A variety of dispositions, such as care, guidance and supervision orders; counselling; probation; foster care; education and vocational training programs and other alternatives to institutional care shall be available to ensure that children are dealt with in a manner appropriate to their well-being and proportionate both to their circumstances and the offense.

Article 41

Nothing in the present Convention shall affect any provisions which are more conducive to the realization of the rights of the child and which may be contained in:

(a) The law of a State Party; or

(b) International law in force for that State.

PART II

Article 42

States Parties undertake to make the principles and provisions of the Convention widely known, by appropriate and active means, to adults and children alike.

Article 43

1. For the purpose of examining the progress made by States Parties in achieving the realization of the obligations undertaken in the present Convention, there shall be established a Committee on the Rights of the Child, which shall carry out the functions hereinafter provided.

2. The Committee shall consist of ten experts of high moral standing and recognized competent in the field covered by this Convention. The members of the Committee shall be elected by States Parties from among their nationals and shall serve in their personal capacity, consideration being given to equitable geographical distribution, as well as to the principal legal systems.

3. The members of the Committee shall be elected by secret ballot from a list of persons nominated by States Parties. Each State Party may nominate one person from among its own nationals.

4. The initial election to the Committee shall be held no later than six months after the date of the entry into force of the present Convention and thereafter every second year. At least four months before the date of each election, the Secretary-General of the United Nations shall address a letter to States Parties inviting them to submit their nominations within two months. The Secretary-General shall subsequently prepare a list in alphabetical order of all persons thus nominated, indicating States Parties which have nominated them, and shall submit it to the States Parties to the present Convention.

5. The elections shall be held at meetings of States Parties convened by the Secretary-General at United Nations Headquarters. At those meetings, for which two thirds of States Parties shall constitute a quorum, the persons elected to the Committee shall be those who obtain the largest number of votes and an absolute majority of the votes of the representatives of States Parties present and voting.

6. The members of the Committee shall be elected for a term of four years They shall be eligible for re-election if renominated. The term of five of the members elected at the first election shall expire at the end of two years; immediately after the first election, the names of these five members shall be chosen by lot by the Chairman of the meeting.

7. If a member of the Committee dies or resigns or declares that for any other cause he or she can no longer perform the duties of the Committee, the State Party which nominated the member shall appoint another expert from among its nationals to serve for the remainder of the term, subject to the approval of the Committee.

8. The Committee shall establish its own rules of procedure.

9. The Committee shall elect its officers for a period of two years.

10. The meetings of the Committee shall normally be held at United Nations Headquarters or at any other convenient place as determined by the Committee The Committee shall normally meet annually. The duration of the meetings of the Committee shall be determined, and reviewed, it necessary, by a meeting of the States Parties to the present Convention, subject to the approval of the General Assembly.

11. The Secretary-General of the United Nations shall provide the necessary staff and facilities for the effective performance of the functions of the Committee under the present Convention.

12. With the approval of the General Assembly, the members of the Committee established under the present Convention shall receive emoluments from United Nations resources on such terms and conditions as the Assembly may decide.

Article 44

1. States Parties undertake to submit to the Committee, through the Secretary-General of the United Nations, reports on the measures they have adopted which give effect to the rights recognized herein and on the progress made on the enjoyment of those rights:

(a) Within two years of the entry into force of the Convention for the State Party concerned;

(b) Thereafter every five years. 2. Reports made under the present article shall indicate factors and difficulties, if any, affecting the degree of fulfillment of the obligations under the present Convention. Reports shall also contain sufficient information to provide the Committee with a comprehensive understanding of the implementation of the Convention in the country concerned.

3. A State Party which has submitted a comprehensive initial report to the Committee need not, in its subsequent reports submitted in accordance with paragraph 1 (b) of the present article, repeat basic information previously provided.

4. The Committee may request from States Parties further information relevant to the implementation of the Convention.

5. The Committee shall submit to the General Assembly, through the Economic and Social Council, every two years, reports on its activities.

6. States Parties shall make their reports widely available to the public in their own countries.

Article 45

In order to foster the effective implementation of the Convention and to encourage international co-operation in the field covered by the Convention:

(a) The specialized agencies, the United Nations Children's Fund, and other United Nations organs shall be entitled to be represented at the consideration of the implementation of such provisions of the present Convention as fall within the scope of their mandate. The Committee may invite the specialized agencies, the United Nations Children's Fund and other competent bodies as it may consider appropriate to provide expert advice on the implementation of the Convention in areas falling within the scope of their respective mandates. The Committee may invite the specialized agencies, the United Nations Children's Fund, and other United Nations organs to submit reports on the implementation of the Convention in areas falling within the scope of their activities;

(b) The Committee shall transmit, as it may consider appropriate, to the specialized agencies, the United Nations Children's Fund and other competent bodies, any reports from States Parties that contain a request, or indicate a need, for technical advice or assistance, along with the Committee's observations and suggestions, if any, on these requests or indications;

(c) The Committee may recommend to the General Assembly to request the Secretary-General to undertake on its behalf studies on specific issues relating to the rights of the child;

(d) The Committee may make suggestions and general recommendations based on information received pursuant to articles 44 and 45 of the present Convention Such suggestions and general recommendations shall be transmitted to any State Party concerned and reported to the General Assembly, together with comments, if any, from States Parties.

PART III

Article 46

The present Convention shall be open for signature by all States.

Article 47

The present Convention is subject to ratification. Instruments of ratification shall be deposited with the Secretary-General of the United Nations.

Article 48

The present Convention shall remain open for accession by any State. The instruments of accession shall be deposited with the Secretary-General of the United Nations.

Article 49

1. The present Convention shall enter into force on the thirtieth day following the date of deposit with the Secretary-General of the United Nations of the twentieth instrument of ratification or accession.

2. For each State ratifying or acceding to the Convention after the deposit of the twentieth instrument of ratification or accession, the Convention shall enter into force on the thirtieth day after the deposit by such State of its instrument of ratification or accession.

Article 50

1. Any State Party may propose an amendment and file it with the Secretary-General of the United Nations. The Secretary-General shall thereupon communicate the proposed amendment to States Parties, with a request that they indicate whether they favor a conference of States Parties for the purpose of considering and voting upon the proposals. In the event that, within four months from the date of such communication, at least one third of the States Parties favor such a conference, the Secretary-General shall convene the conference under the auspices of the United Nations. Any amendment adopted by a majority of States Parties present and voting at the conference shall be submitted to the General Assembly for approval.

2. An amendment adopted in accordance with paragraph 1 of the present article shall enter into force when it has been approved by the General Assembly of the United Nations and accepted by a two-thirds majority of States Parties.

3. When an amendment enters into force, it shall be binding on those States Parties which have accepted it, other States Parties still being bound by the provisions of the present Convention and any earlier amendments which they have accepted.

Article 51

1. The Secretary-General of the United Nations shall receive and circulate to all States the text of reservations made by States at the time of ratification or accession.

2. A reservation incompatible with the object and purpose of the present Convention shall not be permitted.

3. Reservations may be withdrawn at any time by notification to that effect addressed to the Secretary-General of the United Nations, who shall then

inform all States. Such notification shall take effect an the date on which it is received by the Secretary-General.

Article 52

A State Party may denounce the present Convention by written notification to the Secretary-General of the United Nations. Denunciation becomes effective one year after the date of receipt of the notification by the Secretary-General.

Article 53

The Secretary-General of the United Nations is designated as the depositary of the present Convention.

Article 54

The original of the present Convention, of which the Arabic, Chinese, English, French, Russian and Spanish texts are equally authentic, shall be deposited with the Secretary-General of the United Nations. In witness thereof the undersigned plenipotentiaries, being duly authorized thereto by their respective Governments, have signed the present Convention.

Cite as:
U.N. Convention on the Rights of the Child (1989). UN General Assembly Document A/RES/44/25.

HTML by Catherine Hampton (ariel@best.com)
Parent Directory

(File revised 20 June 2001)
Return to CIRP library
http://www.cirp.org/library/ethics/UN-convention/